Revenge in Mind

Jason M Hanson

Revenge in Mind

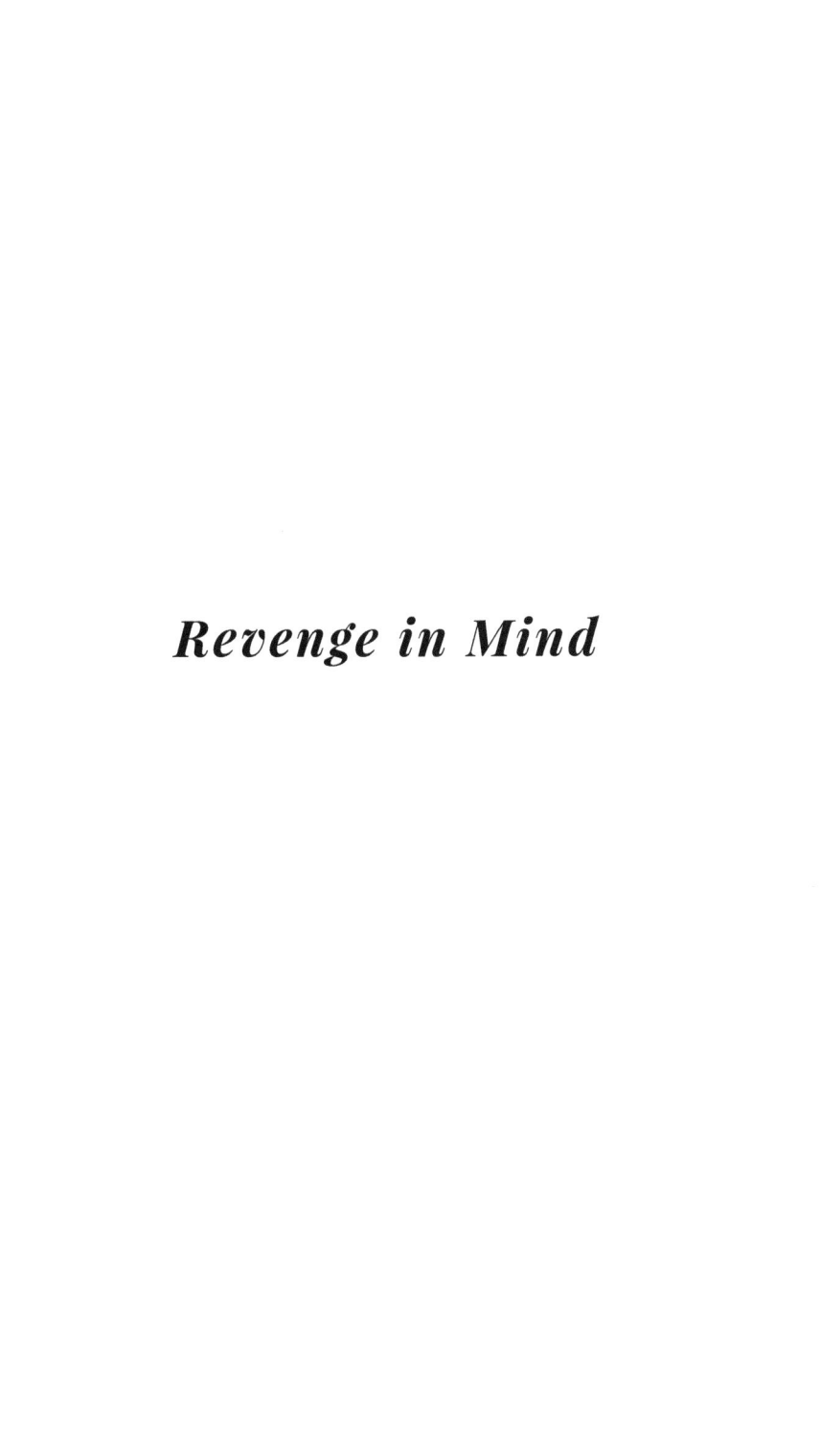

Jason Hanson Counselling

First published by Jason Hanson Counselling 2024

Printed in Great Britain
Available worldwide

Copyright © Jason Hanson Counselling, UK

All rights reserved. No part of this book may be reproduced or distributed in any form without prior written permission from the author, with the exception of non-commercial uses permitted by copyright law

All rights reserved. No portion of this book may be reproduced, copied distributed or adapted in any way, with the exception of certain activities permitted by applicable copyright laws, such as brief quotations in the context of a review or academic work. For permissions to publish, distribute or otherwise reproduce this work, please contact the author at therapy@jasonhansoncounselling.co.uk

ISBN: 978-1-7399007-3-1

Disclaimer

All characters appearing in this book are fictitious. Any resemblance to real persons living or dead is purely coincidental. No locations mentioned are based on real-life places in any way.

{ 1 }

    This wasn't how she thought her life would turn out. Being only twenty-six, she was essentially trapped within the confines of her own home. Money was something other people had, and the most basic of freedoms afforded to most was a luxury for her. Once, she'd had dreams and had and romanticised what her future would look like. This was not it. She had suffered lies, deception, and mistreatment from him. She had physical reminders of her plight, but the emotional scars would take the longest to heal. Her love for him had transformed into bitter resentment, but she shouldered the blame for her anger. She felt weak, submissive, and a pale shadow of the effervescent individual she had been previously. Once proud of her appearance, she now lacked the energy to even leave her bed. He, of course, blamed her and would use her lack of motivation as a justification for his behaviour. He'd been so convincing when they had first met, she thought. Charming, handsome and attentive. It was only a year and a half ago that they had laid eyes on one another in a crowded bar, after he had accidentally collided with her, causing her drink to spill. The subsequent apology had served as an ice-breaker, eliminating an awkwardness, not uncommon on a first date, yet this was anything but. He was witty, charismatic, and she had found herself immediately drawn to him. Despite being cautious in past relationships, she had quickly developed strong feelings for him and had no doubts about them moving in together after just six months. She believed that had been the moment when things had changed, when his mask had begun to slip, and when she saw the reality of who he was and what he represented. The promises of a wonderful life together had proven empty, the assurance he would never hurt her, a lie. She now realised he hadn't changed, he had simply changed back. He had manipulated her, shown her the person he knew she would want to see, before shattering her illusions, leaving her facing the stark reality that her relationship wasn't one of reciprocated love, but of abuse. She suddenly thought of just how subtle he had been. A gradual persuasion that her friends were unreliable and self-serving, that she deserved better. Encouragement to give up her job as he could offer financial stability for the both of them. The signs had been there all along, she just hadn't been looking. She hadn't felt the need to until now. It had been slow and clandestine, almost unnoticeable. However, the rape was anything but. This had taken her by surprise, and three months later, she was still reeling from the shock. It had happened only once, but had been brutal and humiliating. He hadn't acknowledged it, aside from *that* one comment he had made. The comment which would either convince her it hadn't happened the way she had first thought, or would confirm he was a remorseless son of a bitch. The moment she saw the gaze in his eyes and heard him mention her love for role-playing, there was little doubt in her mind what had taken place. He had been terrifying, as she had dared to reject his advances. This wasn't role-playing. It wasn't her fantasy. She wasn't consenting. It was rape. It was him taking what he wanted, in the process taking away her control, her basic right over her own body. As she stared into the mirror, she barely recognised the pale figure staring back at her. She felt powerless and questioned how she had allowed this to happen. There was no opportunity to change her past, but she could shape her future. She needed to find some strength, find herself, find a way out of her situation. Although he wasn't physically threatening, his actions over the last year had eroded her self-esteem to the point where she had felt completely dependent on him. He had stood by her in her darkest moments, her dalliance with drugs and subsequent skirmish with the law. She paused for a moment, wondering why she was defending him. Why was she excusing his behaviour? She couldn't afford to be sentimental about the first six months of their relationship because that wasn't the reality. Now she realised this. The reality was the last year, which had been a long battle with herself and her inability to see what was right in front of her. She felt conflicted because she knew there had been signs that he perhaps wasn't the person she thought he was, but it was easier to look back now and see that. She had never seen herself as a victim, but now acknowledged she had been in victim mode for a long time. *He* had done this to her, and she would never forgive him for that. She looked around the room, a place which had been familiar to her for the last year, a place which had been her refuge during her most vulnerable moments. She would miss this, but knew the unknown she was about to step into would ultimately be better than the world she was living in right now. The hardest part for her was the realisation that he wouldn't miss her. He would likely move on to his next victim without giving her a second thought. She was nothing special. He had no love for her. Despite her isolation, he never placed restrictions on her leaving the house, leading her to wonder whether it was about control or his enjoyment of having someone entirely reliant on him. As she looked at the case in the corner of the room, it reminded her of what little she had to show for the last eighteen months. She had no job, she was estranged from her family, and had few friends. She opened her purse and removed a photograph from it. A young couple very much in love stared back at her. She wiped a tear away from her cheek as she was overcome with a sense of nostalgia and sadness. She wondered what might have been had the circumstances been different. He had been her first love, her only love, and she had never completely processed the breakdown of their relationship. A mere teenager, but she'd never escaped the thought of him being the one who'd got away. Nobody since had come close in comparison. She felt like she had simply settled and questioned whether she had been holding herself back, but for what? In the hope that he may one day sweep her off her feet and rekindle their romance? The photograph had been her comfort in times of need, but deep down, she knew she had been chasing a lost dream. Gripping it tightly, she sobbed. She didn't know where she was going but knew that when she closed her eyes that night, it wouldn't be in the house she had closed them in every night for the past year. She felt a tinge of sadness, not for him, but for the fact she had wasted her time on a failed relationship. There would be no note, no explanation, and she had made sure he wouldn't be able to contact her. One day she would confront him, she was sure of that, but right now, she needed to use all the strength she had to walk out of the door. She placed the picture back in her purse, taking a deep breath to compose herself. Picking up her case, she slowly descended the staircase. The house was spacious, too big for the two of them, really. The area was tranquil and there would be some fond memories of living there. Yet as she moved through the hallway and into the lounge towards the front door, she had no regrets about leaving. He was away and wouldn't be back until tomorrow, which would give her sufficient time to get as far away from him as possible. He had left his bank card on the bedside table and she felt little guilt about knowing his PIN. The thought of him financing her escape felt like poetic justice. As she exited the house, she turned to take one last look at her past, before heading towards the bus stop, suitcase in tow. There was one person whom she could trust, one person whom she felt sure would be there for her, but it had been such a long time since they had spoken. How would she track him down, and even if she did, would he want to see her? She opened her purse once again, and clutched at the photograph, agonising over her past. As the internal conflict raged on, she returned it to its rightful position in her purse, deciding now was not the right time for that reunion. As the bus began its journey towards the train station, Georgina Sampson sat back, closed her eyes and wondered what future awaited her.

{ 2 }

'I got your message. It's been a while.'

For a moment there was a silence on the other end of the line, a silence which confused him, as it was she who had initiated the contact. But he knew she was there. After a few moments, which seemed much longer, the faint sound of sobbing interrupted the uncomfortable silence. He inhaled slowly, closing his eyes as he did so to position himself mentally. He had a strong suspicion about the type of discussion he was about to have, and it would stretch him to the boundaries of his comfort zone. His job had required him to think quickly and handle tense situations, but he acknowledged he had become emotionally numb as a result. It wasn't that he didn't care, he simply found himself unable to empathise. To him, feelings were an Achilles heel, which others could use against you. To show emotion was to show weakness, to care was to show vulnerability, and he couldn't afford to be weak or vulnerable. But there was one overarching emotion which continued to surface. One which he had battled with for several years, to no avail. One which had cost him his job, and on more than one occasion, nearly his life... anger. In the early days, it wasn't problematic; perhaps because it wasn't there, perhaps because he was just better at controlling it. However, things had reached a climax on a night out after a particularly tough day. After a few drinks, he had spotted a group of people nearby laughing and believed it to be aimed at him. There had been no prior warning for the group as he had launched an attack on one of the men. A small, lean man had been the victim, and had been critically injured. Altercations out of camp weren't unheard of, and wouldn't ordinarily have been dealt with so harshly. However, the man hadn't put up any resistance, and the attack had continued, regardless of him being knocked unconscious. This in itself was enough to seal his discharge.

Any thoughts that his behaviour would lead him down a path of guilt or remorse, with promises to be better, quickly vanished. He felt aggrieved at how they had handled him, which further fuelled the fire burning in the pit of his stomach. There was one thing he was sure of right now, however, and that was the conversation he was about to engage in would do nothing to extinguish that fire. The sobbing had now subsided and he could make out the soft sound of a sniffle.

'Are you okay?'

His voice was calm, but lacked any genuine emotion. Finally, the voice on the other end spoke.

'I'm sorry, it's just a little emotional hearing your voice after all this time.'

'How long has it been?'

'Three years, two months. I remember because it was on...'

'My birthday,' he interrupted.

'Your fortieth.'

He bowed his head for a moment. Had it really been that long? How had he allowed this to happen? They'd always been close growing up, though naturally as they had aged, their lives had taken very different paths. There had been no cross words or falling out. They had simply drifted apart.

'My fortieth,' he repeated with a hint of resignation and disappointment in his voice.

For a moment neither of them spoke, likely feeling the same regret of a close bond eroding over time, with no justifiable reason. He had been on tour and incommunicado for a while, and she had been battling mental health problems. They had lost contact, and of course, the more time that elapsed, the more difficult it became for either of them to reach out.

'What do you need from me?'

He spoke sharply, making a hasty retreat after catching himself off guard with the sudden wave of emotion. This was something he simply wasn't accustomed to. It wasn't about her. He wasn't upset or angry, it was just the way he handled things. He was fairly sure she hadn't contacted him for emotional support. He was pragmatic; he was a fixer. She had contacted him because there was something she needed doing.

'My past has just stepped into my present uninvited, and I'm not sure how to deal with it. It's stirred up a lot of unwelcome memories, memories I thought I had well and truly buried. Now, I'm afraid, but I'm also angry.' Her voice tailed off. 'I need to be freed from my past,' she added.

He remained quiet, listening intently.

'When I was twenty-six, I began seeing this guy. In the beginning, he was sincere, charismatic, and made me feel unique.

I moved in with him quickly, and that's when things changed. I saw a different side to him.'

'Different how?' he asked suspiciously.

'He began controlling me, but I didn't realise it at the time. He was very clever with the way he did it, gradually and subtly, so I wouldn't question him. I had no need to.'

'You didn't recognise the control, yet you realised things had changed. I'm confused.'

'There were other things which weren't so easy for him to hide.'

'Like what?'

For a moment, there was a pause. It was clear to him she was building up to something. Something she was struggling to verbalise. He wondered whether she was afraid of his reaction, and was considering how to soften the blow. Or perhaps his ability to take action without hesitation might have been what she was counting on.

'Like the rape.'

He had his answer. His fists clenched as a rage he hadn't encountered for quite some time overcame him. He gritted his teeth and moved his face away from the phone as he desperately tried to find the right words to respond with. Inside he was apoplectic but, on the surface, he was calm. He had to be. There would be a time when he would unleash the anger which was wreaking havoc deep within his stomach, but for now, he had to be the person he had always been for her. She needed him, and it wasn't for his sensitive nature.

'Say something,' she said, clearly aware of the uncomfortable quietness which had developed.

He had been stunned into silence. Feeling awkward in these situations, however, didn't deter him from engaging in deep and emotional conversations when necessary. Underpinning his reaction was an incandescent rage and instinctive need for retribution. His mind was now occupied contemplating the different methods he could use to retaliate.

'Why now?' he asked calmly. 'This happened over ten years ago. Why now?'

He was aware his voice was rising, but it wasn't aimed at her.

'Things have happened, and it's brought it all back again.'

'Who have you told?'

'You're the first,' she replied hesitantly.

His head dropped once again. She had lived with this for these years, kept a dark secret hidden from others. She had been alone, and suffering immensely, he assumed. Why had it taken her this long to tell him?

'I wish you'd told me sooner.'

'What could you have done?'

'Kept you safe.'

She began to speak but stopped herself. He had missed her and until now hadn't realised quite how much. As he stood deep in thought, he felt glad she had reached out to him after all this time.

'You asked me why now. I thought I'd dealt with this. I thought both he and my ordeal were in the past, but then recently something happened that I couldn't ignore.'

'Has he contacted you?'

'No, but that dark memory I buried all those years ago has made its way back to the surface. Do you remember Toby Reynolds?'

'The kid you dated in college?'

'Yeah.'

'He's not involved in this, is he?'

'No, no, of course not. Well, not how you might think.'

'What do you mean?'

'Have you seen the news recently?'

'I try to avoid it if I can. Too much shit in the world.'

'The police arrested Toby under suspicion in a high-profile attempted murder case.

He flinched in disbelief.

'Did he do it?'

'Ultimately, they charged Olivia Stanton, the wife. Toby was cleared.'

'How does this involve you?'

She paused for a moment.

'The man who was left for dead was my rapist.'

'Karma can be a bitch.'

'When I saw the news, I knew I wasn't the only victim. He must have wronged somebody else for them to want him dead. Then I wondered how many others there had been. Where does this stop? Where will he stop?'

'You think he'll strike again?'

'The fact she was willing to kill him serves up two key questions. What did he do to her? And what else did she find out about?'

As he sat there, phone pressed against his cheek, he felt a sadness at the fact this was what had brought them back together again. It had taken a suffering he could never understand. An unfamiliar wave of guilt and regret took over, and he wondered when, or indeed whether, they would have spoken again had she not been subjected to a brutal ordeal.

'I'm going to see Toby,' she said, as though just deciding at that moment.

'How long has it been?'

'I haven't seen him since our relationship ended nearly twenty years ago, but I think he can get me close to Eric. I'm going to see him today.'

'How did he react when you told him?'

'I haven't spoken to him. He doesn't know I'm going to see him. I did some digging and managed to find a contact number. He's a therapist now, or at least he was before the incident. I posed as a former client, wanting some advice. His wife refused to disclose his exact location but alluded to the fact he was at Stanford Cross. There's only one thing of any note there.'

'The prison.'

'That's where Olivia Stanton is. He's gone to see her.'

'Why would he go to see her, and why would his wife be okay with it?'

'That's the part I haven't figured out yet, but I'm almost certain that's where he's headed. I checked the prison visiting times, the timings would make sense.'

'You're just gonna walk right up to somebody you haven't seen in twenty years and say hey, remember me? That'll be some fucking reunion.'

She let out a nervous giggle, which appeared to further chip away at the tension.

'I'm not far from Stanford Cross and could likely be there in thirty minutes, but the problem isn't getting there. You're right, springing back into Toby's life after all these years won't be easy. What do I say when I come face to face with my past, my first and only genuine love? The man, who, as a boy, had been my world for over two years. I don't know what I'm expecting. He's married now and we've both grown up. Our lives have taken very different routes, and we have both experienced things we would rather forget. Maybe that's the common ground? Trauma.'

'What next?' he asked, eager to understand where precisely he fitted into all this.

'What do you mean?'

'Let's say you manage to track down Toby and he gets you close to this guy, Eric. Then what?'

He heard her draw in a deep breath.

'You know, this hotel room is tragically symbolic of another failed relationship. He wasn't abusive, thankfully. Hell, what's it come to when that's something I'm grateful for?'

'What happened?'

'He was offered a job overseas and believed it was an opportunity he shouldn't miss. He asked me to go with him, but it wasn't for me. Ultimately, he chose the job, and I was left yet again feeling abandoned. I don't hold it against him, but that doesn't mean it hurt any less. The flat we were living in though belonged to him, and with no interest in becoming a landlord, he opted to sell it. I spent a few days on the sofa at a friend's house, but felt like I was intruding. I needed my space.'

'So, you moved into a hotel room?'

'This is just a temporary measure. It's not ideal, but I have my privacy.'

'I'm sorry.'

He didn't know what else to say.

'I never questioned Eric. I questioned myself, but never him. Even after the rape, after that bastard took what he wanted from me without my consent, I still questioned myself, my grasp on reality. It took me a while to realise what was happening, to gather the courage to leave him, but I finally managed it. But do you know what? He got away with it. I left him unscathed. I never confronted him. I didn't have the strength.'

He sensed she was getting angry, and strangely revelling in it, too. He smiled. She was more like him than she realised.

'But now, now I do. You asked me what's next, well here it is. I want to look that son of a bitch in the eye and confront him about what he's done, not just to me, but to the others. I want to see the look on his face. I want to see the bastard squirm as he comes face to face with his demons. I want him to know that whilst he may have got away with what he did to Olivia Stanton, I'm still here, and I know the evil that lies beneath his charming façade.'

'You want revenge?'

'I want more than revenge,' she responded sharply, now in a tone he didn't recognise.

'I want him to feel what it's like to have something sacred taken away. I want him to feel the pain, the anguish not just in the moment, but for years afterwards, just like I have. I want him to look up at me, knowing he didn't beat me, he just strengthened me. I want him to suffer for every person he has wronged, every vile act he has committed, and every repulsive thought he has ever had. I can't make him feel remorse, but I can make sure that son of a bitch thinks twice about ever subjecting anybody else to such a sick and twisted attack.'

She paused and drew breath. This had been an emotional outburst, something which had clearly been lying dormant for some time. He'd never heard her speak like this before, but her purpose was very clear. There followed a brief silence as he contemplated what he'd just heard. He became aware of a smouldering anger. He had a temper and now knew she was counting on it. Though they had not spoken for a while, he had remained protective of his sister. She allowed him the time to process, remaining silent on the other end of the line. Finally, he spoke. It was calm and measured, devoid of any emotion.

'You're still not telling me where I fit into this.'

Georgina Sampson sighed, moving the phone away from her face. She knew precisely why she had called him. The conversation was always going to lead up to this point, the crescendo. She'd intended to be guarded in her approach, giving him enough to elicit the desired response, but not so much as to send him off in a fit of rage where he would be unpredictable. She wondered whether she had succeeded. She felt like her emotion had got the better of her and she had told him more than she had originally planned to. Ordinarily, she was placid and agreeable, and had spent a long time wrestling with her own self-loathing, but that was when she believed she was the only victim. Now there were others, and that changed things. The very thought of him manipulating his way into the lives of other women, leaving a trail of devastation in his wake, was unbearable for her. He had been consigned to her past. That was, until now. She tried to convince herself that she had intended to forget about him, but in truth, there had always been an inevitability about the way things would turn out. When she had walked out on him thirteen years ago, their story hadn't ended. It had just been paused. He needed to be stopped. She slowly returned the phone to where it had been positioned, cradled between her chin and shoulder. She was staring at the wall in front of her, eyes as wild as a winter's night. With a slow, yet definitive whisper, she finally answered his question. They were the last words exchanged between the two as the call ended. In one hotel room, a scorned woman refusing to be a victim any longer. In another, a dangerous man who had just found his reason to release the pent-up anger which had been an unwelcome guest since his discharge.

{ 3 }

The prison had now faded into the background, and with it, Olivia Stanton. The last few months had been torturous for Toby, and it was far from over for him. He could begin the process of putting Olivia into the past, but as he glanced over to the passenger seat, he saw another past, one which had somehow made its way into his present. They had been driving a short while, yet Toby was no closer to understanding what Georgina Sampson was doing here, how she had found him, and what sort of trouble she was in. The conversation so far had been a simple exchange of pleasantries, though there was an inevitability that it would move from its current superficial level to something much more profound.

'You look well.'

'Thank you', she said tentatively, seemingly uncomfortable with the compliment. Toby noted this but didn't want to risk making her feel more awkward, so didn't offer a reply.

'I have often thought about you, about contacting you, but the more time passed by, the harder it became. You know how it is.'

Now it was Toby's turn to feel awkward. His awkwardness, however, wasn't directly from her words, but from their impact.

As he looked across at her, he was taken back twenty years to a time when he first experienced love. Suddenly, he was once again sitting with her in class; he was tightly embracing her as they lay together on the sofa; he was outside her house, hoping to catch a glimpse of her. The memories were vivid and, for a moment, Toby felt overcome with nostalgia. He remembered just how deep his feelings for her had run and wondered whether they had ever really disappeared or simply been lying dormant.

'Seeing you now...'

'Transports you back about twenty years?' George interrupted.

Toby smiled, mouth slightly ajar. She was right. It felt like nothing had changed, aside from the fact they both looked a little older. George, he thought, had aged well, better than he, but then the last year had taken its toll on him. He felt like the trauma had aged him, more physically than anything else. Though mostly recovered from his injuries, his once regular personal training sessions with Dan had become a thing of the past. He was engaged in a battle with motivation, a battle he was not winning. Every week that passed served up a different reason he couldn't attend, but deep down, he knew the truth. Once his respite and safe place, the gym now contained unwanted memories of Olivia Stanton. After discovering that their apparent chance meeting was not a coincidence, Toby now found the place tainted. For the past few weeks, he'd been trying to remove any memories of her from his life. He smiled to himself at the irony of orchestrating a meeting with the very person who he was trying to remove all traces of. However, this had been a necessary step, and though Toby had left feeling emotionally bruised. He'd received some of the answers he had been seeking, though not all. Confident he could consign Olivia Stanton to the past over time, his attentions had now turned to her estranged husband.

Olivia's words of warning were playing on repeat in his mind.

If he thinks you're suspicious of him, you're not safe. Don't be fooled by him, Toby.

Her final words to him as he left the prison.

Upon noticing Toby's distraction, George placed her hand on his arm.

'Of all the places I envisaged our paths crossing again, prison wasn't one of them.'

'Of all the people I envisaged I may bump into today, you weren't one of them.'

George smiled, but Toby sensed there was something hidden behind it, though he couldn't figure out what. This wasn't a chance meeting. She had managed to track him down, but how? How did she know he would be here when he hadn't told anybody? Only Beth knew. The intrigue he had felt when first meeting her had now turned to suspicion. He wondered whether Olivia Stanton had impacted his ability to trust more than he had first thought. He felt pained that since the extent of her deception had been exposed, his automatic response to others was suspicion and doubt. He'd found himself analysing people and conversations so much that he had actively removed himself from many of his social circles. He had questions for George but doubted she would be forthcoming with her answers. More importantly, would he believe those answers?

'You must be wondering why I'm here?' George said with a shyness not familiar to Toby.

Toby nodded his head slowly, unsure how to respond. He had a burning desire to understand why his college sweetheart, his first love, the girl who had taken his virginity, was suddenly sitting in his passenger seat some twenty years after they had last spoken. He wanted to know precisely how she had managed to locate him when only his wife knew of his whereabouts. Most importantly, he wanted to know why. Why now? After everything he had been through, why had she tracked him down at this moment, when he felt at his most vulnerable and was desperately searching for something resembling normality? He was keen to learn what she was hiding, what her secret was, and what sort of trouble she was in. Yet also, he wasn't. Trepidation outweighed intrigue. When he thought about her sudden reappearance in his life, he knew as he closed the door on one battle, he was inevitably about to open the door to another. Georgina Sampson hadn't gone to the effort of tracking him down, simply to reminisce. She was here for a reason, and whatever she was about to involve him in would undoubtedly have consequences. He didn't answer her question. He simply offered her a smile, which looked forced. He wondered if she had noticed.

'Do you ever wonder what might have been, Toby?'

'George...'

'I'm sorry. I didn't mean to make you feel uncomfortable.' She replied quickly, cutting him off.

She let out an exasperated sigh. She appeared frustrated with herself for creating tension. There was an uncomfortable silence between the two, which lasted only a few moments but felt to Toby like hours. He slowed the car down, pulled over, and turned to face her.

'You haven't tracked me down after twenty years to take a trip down memory lane,' he said, taking himself by surprise at the sternness of his voice.

'You're right, I haven't.'

'What are you doing here?'

'All in good time.'

Toby noticed the change. A few minutes ago, she had broached the subject of why she was here. Suddenly, when he had probed, she had retreated. She no longer felt comfortable having this conversation with him, at least not now. This did nothing to quash his suspicion. Their brief interaction made him certain that the uncomfortable conversation he had feared was on the horizon.

'I never stopped thinking about you, Toby.'

'George...'

'You need to hear this,' she replied, holding her hand up to him.

Toby inhaled slowly. Regardless of the difficulty he faced, he recognised it must be even more challenging for her, having waited approximately twenty years to reveal something she had deliberately kept secret. He gestured for her to continue.

'To this day, losing you, losing your love, is one of the hardest things I have ever had to deal with. I spent weeks crying, months in depression, and years in regret.'

'Regret?' Toby asked softly.

'The way things ended between us.'

'We grew apart, George. Our lives were taking a different path. We had to grow up,' he said, taking her by the hand and offering her a smile, a smile which now seemed warmer and less anxious.

'Is that how you remember it?'

Toby looked puzzled and wondered where George was going with this. Whilst it was twenty years ago, this had been a significant part of his life. His first real heartbreak. He remembered it well, or at least he thought he did. What was he missing?

'I remember the distance between us while I was at university became too much.'

'It was never about the distance.'

Toby jerked his hand back as he recognised the change in her tone. Her facial expression was no longer warm and welcoming. He was certain he was about to hear something he wouldn't like, and wondered whether after the recent trauma, and being less than an hour removed from a gruelling encounter with Olivia Stanton, he had the emotional capacity to deal with it. He stared at George, open-mouthed, and found his eyes drawn to just how beautiful she looked. The casual look was something she pulled off remarkably well. Her makeup looked freshly applied, and her shoulder-length blonde hair flowed freely, yet without a hair out of place. She wore a pair of diamond stud earrings, white gold, Toby thought, which completed the look.

He felt mesmerised. Not sexually, but more an admiration for how well she carried herself.

'I'm not sure what you mean,' he said hesitantly, feeling confused.

George took a deep breath, reached out for his hand, and looked him directly in the eye. Toby felt his heart skip a beat, but couldn't determine whether this was because of her taking his hand, or in anticipation of what she was about to reveal.

'When I said I'd been living with regret for years, I didn't mean specifically about us breaking up.'

'Then what did you mean?' he asked.

His subconscious screamed at him not to listen to the answer.

George looked troubled. Toby realised just ahead lay a revelation, which would no doubt change things. Yet he had no inclination as to what would come next. Suddenly, he didn't want to hear whatever it was she was about to say and tried desperately to retreat.

'Perhaps it's best we don't tread this path,' he said, trying to manoeuvre her away from her thought process.

Toby started the car and moved to shift the paddle into drive. George grabbed his hand.

'I was pregnant.'

There it was. It hit him like a sledgehammer. No, it was more of a blow to the stomach. For a moment he couldn't breathe, it had taken his breath away. George sat expressionless, waiting for Toby to absorb what she had just told him. When he eventually regained some semblance of composure, he switched off the engine and slowly turned towards her, the colour having now drained from his face.

He tried in vain to speak, but shock had taken a tight hold of him and wasn't letting go. This changed nothing, yet it changed everything. Having children had never really been something he or Beth had given serious consideration to, but at least that had been a discussion he had been involved in. He wouldn't have been ready to be a parent back then, neither of them would, but shouldn't this have been a discussion? The shock quickly dissipated. He felt angry.

'Why didn't you tell me?'

'Neither of us were ready to have a child, Toby.'

'So, you terminated the pregnancy?'

'We were drifting apart. I worried we would either stay together just for the sake of the baby, or I would end up a single mum. I didn't relish either of those options.'

'All this time you've carried this secret. Why are you telling me now?'

'You have a right to know.'

'I had a right to know twenty years ago when you aborted my child,' he snapped angrily.

George recoiled and sat quietly, pondering. The shock on her face highlighted the fact not only had she misread the situation and not expected Toby's reaction, but also that she had likely never seen this side of him. Sat just inches apart, it felt like a standoff. Neither wanting to flinch first or give any sign of what they were thinking. Once lovers, they were now strangers, but Toby questioned whether strangers would react to one another in this way. Though reluctant to admit it to himself, he knew the moment he had laid eyes on George in the prison car park, something had been ignited deep inside of him. He realised he wasn't angry with the woman seated next to him. He was angry at the nineteen-year-old girl who had made that decision. Toby bowed his head and closed his eyes. George reached over and tentatively placed her hand on his shoulder, stroking it like she used to do. He turned to look at her.

'You couldn't face me, could you?'

'I'm sorry?'

'You said earlier it wasn't about the distance, but it was, just not in the physical sense. You withdrew from me, from us.'

George screwed her eyes up tight, as if carefully considering how to respond in a way that wouldn't further inflame an already volatile situation.

'The thought of hurting you broke my heart, but I panicked. I was pregnant, and we were young. There was uncertainty around the relationship, around our future. I was completely alone.'

'Your parents?'

'They never knew. Nobody did. It's a secret I began keeping twenty years ago, and it's held me prisoner ever since.'

Her voice broke, and Toby noticed her lips were quivering. He felt conflicted. He wanted to reach out, take her hand, and tell her everything would be okay, but the anger which had been bubbling away under the surface since her revelation had intensified, and was showing no signs of easing. He sat gazing into the eyes of his first love. He had once held such potent feelings towards her, but right now was struggling to feel any empathy. He watched her relive a trauma likely suppressed for many years, and felt nothing, only resentment. He wondered whether this was a product of the anger, or of the bruising emotional encounter with Olivia, which had left him questioning so many things about himself. He deliberated whether this was resilience or numbness, a temporary response to his own trauma, or a permanent transformation.

'I know you're angry with me.'

'Don't tell me how I feel,' Toby said sternly.

George jumped back at the harshness of his tone. She looked at him with tears flowing. A sudden thought hit Toby. This wasn't the reason George was here. She hadn't tracked him down after twenty years to casually tell him she had aborted their child as a nineteen-year-old girl. He wondered whether she had ever intended to tell him, or whether this was unplanned. Was this meant to distract him from her real motive for tracking him down? In practice he would have drawn the positive elements from this, recognising it as somebody feeling comfortable enough to show their vulnerability. But this wasn't therapy, and he couldn't detach. He was emotionally invested in this, and he realised part of his anger was about him not wishing to know. Why would she choose to tell him now when he had been happily married for over ten years? He was only weeks removed from being cleared of attempted murder, just hours removed from a brutal conversation with a highly manipulative woman who had used him as an alibi. His confidence, his self-esteem, and his trust had evaporated in an instant. He had no emotional capacity to deal with this, and that realisation gave him his answer. He had nothing left. He was numb, almost impervious. The anger had been transient. And now, nothing.

'You left me, Toby. It was your decision. I should be the one who's angry,' George said defensively.

'That's not how it was...'

'Don't sit there and pretend I had any say in our break-up. I didn't want to lose you, and have spent every day since then thinking, no, knowing, that you were the one that got away,' she interrupted, now visibly frustrated.

Toby felt cornered, and not for the first time that day. He didn't know how to respond, and even if he did, he didn't have the energy to face another battle right now. George had been carrying this for a long time, and out of respect for what she had once meant to him, he needed to let her have this moment.

'I know we agreed it was best Toby, but I did that to protect myself. I knew you were pulling away from me, and towards your university life. At least this way I could try to convince myself it was mutual. But I knew Toby, and now you need to know. I felt devastated, and would have sacrificed anything to avoid losing you.'

She was now much calmer, her voice softer. She wasn't trying to attack him; she was simply trying to protect herself. Now he understood. After all these years, still, she valued his opinion of her. It would shatter her if she thought he held any ill feelings toward her. Even now, it was his opinion, and only his, that mattered to her. Yet her disclosure had challenged this to the very core. She had taken a risk here. He would never have found out about the pregnancy otherwise. What did she have to gain?

Distraction.

Toby looked down at his watch. They had been stationary for around twenty minutes now. He hadn't spoken to Beth since that morning, and felt uneasy at the prospect of having to explain why his childhood sweetheart had suddenly reappeared. He shivered as he realised he didn't know what George wanted from him, why she was here, and more importantly, where he was taking her.

'George, up ahead is a crossroads. One way leads directly to my village, the other two out of town. I need to know which way I am turning.'

Whilst not intended in this way, he realised the symbolism of his words. It wasn't solely the physical direction he was seeking. The last few weeks had been turbulent, pushing him to the limit both physically and mentally. More than anything now, he needed clarity, he needed serenity. What he didn't need was any more drama, yet as he sat staring at George, watching her struggling to hold eye contact as she considered his question, he felt an inevitability about what was around the corner. She was here for a reason. It wasn't what she had said, but more what she had not said, that saw suspicion arise in him. George was now holding her head in her hands. Toby felt himself tense up. His heart beat quicker, and he found his breathing intensifying. He was having a panic attack. George, alerted to this, quickly sat upright and leaned towards him, placing her hand on his shoulder.

'Toby?' she asked with a panic in her own voice.

Toby tried to reply, but a sudden aphasia overcame him. This felt like one of those dreams where you were desperately trying to run away, but in a battle with paralysis, were on the losing side. He tried to compose himself, but to no avail. He quickly unfastened his seatbelt and got out of the car, running towards the field situated to the side of the lay-by. As he approached the hedge, he leaned over and vomited. George got out of the car and ran towards him.

'Toby, are you okay? Shit, what's happening?'

Toby, now stood upright wiping his mouth, saw the panic on George's face, heard it in her voice. As he noticed the irony of her panic over his panic attack, he smiled up at her.

'Toby, what's going on?'

'I'm not sure.'

George looked at him, perplexed, but Toby could do nothing to allay her confusion. He had no rational explanation for the sudden panic. Anxiety had been nothing more than a very casual acquaintance of his over the years. He'd occasionally been nervous but had only experienced raw panic recently with the unpleasant situation involving Olivia Stanton. Then it hit him with force. Olivia. It was still about Olivia. Even from her prison cell, still, she was able to impact his life. How could he ever commit her to his past, when she was still very much part of his present? He slowly looked up at George, taking in a deep breath. Now he was at his own crossroads. Did he open up to George about everything that had happened to him over the past few months, or did he keep her at arm's length to protect her? But as he stared into her eyes, he wondered how much she already knew. A prison car park wasn't somewhere you would expect to experience a chance meeting with an old flame. Besides, she had already disclosed she was in trouble and needed his help. In order to find him, she must have had some awareness of what had been happening lately. The question was, how much?

'How did you know where I would be?' Toby asked in a manner which conveyed intrigue, yet also suspicion.

George looked at him wide-eyed, as though she had just been discovered smoking in the school toilets. She didn't get the chance to answer.

'You said you needed my help. That means this wasn't a co-incidence. The question is, how did you know where I would be?'

George looked down at her feet, desperately trying to avoid eye contact. Without looking up, she replied.

'Toby, you've been all over the news. When I saw your name, I knew it was time to reach out. After a lot of digging, I was able to get your wife's contact details. Don't worry, I didn't tell her who I was. I posed as a past client, looking to obtain my case notes for legal purposes. She said you were at Stanford Cross, and after piecing things together, I realised there was only one reason you would be there.'

'How did you know I'd be there at that precise moment?'

'I called the prison and asked what time visiting hours were.'

Toby couldn't help but feel impressed with the level of detail involved. In another scenario, he would commend her for her research and deduction...in another scenario. Yet, as he listened, he couldn't ignore the similarities between her and Olivia. Now he had his reason for experiencing a panic attack. The lowering of the head to mask the emotional outpouring was something Olivia had perfected in therapy. Now George was displaying a meticulous and disingenuous nature, which he had never seen in her before. He felt his heart pound at the walls of his chest as he realised George reminded him of Olivia. He could see the similarities between a girl who had loved him unconditionally and a woman who had manipulated him. But this wasn't a conversation he wanted to get into. His primary concern right now was understanding what George was doing here. What kind of trouble was she in? Why had she actively sought him out? Without saying a word, Toby smiled and walked past her back towards the car. Noticing George had not followed, Toby signalled for her to join him. As the two got back into the car, he started the engine and looked across at her.

'So where are we heading?'

George replied in a whisper, but it was loud enough for him to hear. He stared at her for a moment before shifting the car into drive and re-joining the road. As he did so, he looked in the rear-view mirror at what was behind him, before switching his focus to the road ahead, the symbolism not lost on him.

{ 4 }

Dylan Sampson strolled casually through the door, stopping briefly to study the surroundings. The bar was in the middle of town and came with a reputation. He, of course, knew all about this. In fact, it was part of what had lured him to this establishment. Nobody knew him here, and that suited him just fine. Soon enough, he would be known, but right now, that wasn't a priority. It had been two days since his conversation with George. He'd made his way to town and was staying at a local budget hotel. He didn't know how long he'd be here, but the duration of his stay wasn't at the forefront of his mind as he walked up to the bar to order a drink. The bartender cast a suspicious eye over him as he noticed the scar on his face. Staring back at him was a six-foot plus, muscular individual who was clearly no stranger to the gym.

'Shrapnel wound from my last tour,' he said sharply.

'I'm sorry?' the bartender asked, taken aback.

'The scar on my face you're trying desperately not to look at,' he responded without taking his eyes off the man.

'You're in the forces?'

'Was.'

Revenge in Mind

'I see,' the bartender said, a little coyly, perhaps recognising any conversation here was going to be succinct.

'Whiskey and Coke.'

The bartender smiled politely as he turned to pour the drink, his acknowledgement of the hostile attitude apparent. Working in a bar like this, he was likely no stranger to antagonism. His demeanour, however, suggested he had no intention of challenging it here. Dylan Sampson, having paid for his drink, headed away from the bar. He found a table towards the back of the room and took a seat. This wasn't his first drink of the day, nor did he qualify for anything resembling inebriated. His time in the armed forces had seen him have more than a passing relationship with drinking, excessively on occasion, and this only exacerbated an anger which had been slowly building over time. He rarely found trouble, but there had been exceptions. He had been trained to talk his way out of almost any situation, but anybody who mistook this for weakness in the past had done so to their detriment. If trouble found him, there was no mistaking, he was more than equipped to handle himself. This, however, was very different. He was now a civilian, an angry one, and was in town for a reason. He no longer operated by the same code he had done for over twenty years. Even though his discharge took place almost a year ago, he had been living in France during that time until recently when he had returned home. Adapting to civilian life had proved challenging for him, making him question whether he'd changed or simply returned to his former self. Whilst he wouldn't consider himself to be suspicious by nature, he was certainly astute, hyper-vigilant, some might argue. As he sat deep in thought, a commotion in the corner of the room caught his attention. An argument had broken out between a group of people, he estimated were probably in their early twenties. Typically, his instinct would have been to make his way over and defuse the situation, but he simply picked up his drink and took another sip, watching with intrigue rather than trepidation. As he did so, he caught the eye of one individuals involved in the fracas. The man glared at him before tapping the shoulder of another man in the group and gesticulating. Dylan Sampson took a deep breath and smiled inwardly. He knew what was coming. Bar fights were a common occurrence here, and he had known from the moment he set foot through the door, if he stayed long enough, trouble would be an inevitability, should he look in the right direction. He had business back in town, and this was the first step. Letting out some of the aggression which had been building up since he'd received the phone call from George was simply an added attraction for him. As the two individuals walked over towards him shouting expletives, Dylan Sampson rose out of his chair, took another sip of his drink, and slammed the glass down on the table, hard. Trouble had found him, and he was in no mood for a discussion. As the two men drew closer, one of them came within earshot.

'What the fuck are you looking at?'

Dylan Sampson casually rolled up his shirt sleeves and stood facing the individuals, who were now just inches away from him. He considered his response for a moment as a smile spread across his face.

'Believe me when I tell you that you don't want this,' he said calmly, not taking his eyes off either of the men.

Revenge in Mind

'You think you're some sort of tough guy?'

The man, now appearing more aggressive, was a tall, slender individual with cropped hair. He was dressed casually in jeans and a T-shirt. Whilst he'd likely had a few drinks, he didn't portray a drunk.

'Listen gents,' Dylan Sampson replied in a condescending manner he had no intention of hiding. 'What you find yourself in here is what we call a predicament. If you turn and walk away, you're gonna look weak in front of your friends over there,' he said, pointing towards the corner of the room with a smile on his face. He picked up his glass, took another drink, and continued.

'But stay here and try to play the big men, and it won't end well for you. Either way, your decision to walk over here and start something isn't looking like a good one right now.'

His smile had quickly disappeared, and it was clear the two men had no idea whether or not he was bluffing. They pondered for a moment, looking to each other for guidance, but neither seemed sure. Dylan Sampson had taken a step back but hadn't dropped eye contact with the men in front of him. Though he was ready, he was still wary of leaving himself susceptible to any kind of surprise attack. His record in the armed forces wasn't unblemished, some of which he disputed, but he was quick to credit them with an excellent training regime, which had fully prepared soldiers in the face of combat. Those early training drills on cold winter mornings had been gruelling, and he'd invested in them only begrudgingly, but on more than one occasion, he'd been grateful for their teachings. He'd seen some haunting images which would stay with him for the rest of his life. He'd survived seemingly hopeless situations he had no right to. By all accounts, Dylan Sampson should be dead right now. But he wasn't. Most of the time, he was grateful for this, but sometimes, on his darkest days when the intrusive images and thoughts surfaced, he wished he had been taken. Instead, he carried survivor's guilt at the thought of those he had fought alongside and lost. They weren't just fellow soldiers; they were friends. He had long lived by the mantra that when you're in that situation, you develop that bond. You have to trust those around you. They're all you have, and you're all they have.

Just then, a doorman approached.

'I'm not going to have any trouble out of you boys, am I?' he said in a controlled, yet authoritative manner. Dylan Sampson turned to him, noticing how large the man was. He looked well over six feet and perhaps as wide. He wondered whether the man knew how to fight, or was simply relying on his size to act as a deterrent.

'I think these gentlemen were just heading back over there to continue their evening,' he replied, picking up eye contact with the two men once again. At this, they turned around and sauntered away. One of them mumbled something quietly, the details of which were unknown to Dylan Sampson, but he knew it was likely less than complimentary. He stood smiling for a moment as the two men re-joined their friends, their earlier altercation now apparently forgotten.

'They have a reputation those boys. Watch yourself,' the doorman said, turning his way.

'I've seen many like them before. They're tough in groups but isolate them and they're nothing.'

Revenge in Mind

'There are six or seven of them, and I've seen what happens when they take a disliking to somebody. I can protect you in here, but watch your back when you leave.'

'I appreciate you looking out for me, but it won't be me that needs your protection,' Dylan Sampson replied nonchalantly.

'Don't say I didn't warn you.'

At this, the doorman turned and walked back to join his colleague at the entrance. The two exchanged words, and looked over towards the group of men, before turning towards Dylan, but his interests didn't sit with them. He knew he would not escape the evening without conflict. In fact, he was counting on it. He just needed to figure out where the attack was going to come from. He hadn't lied to the doorman. He'd encountered groups like this before. They created a tough persona, but that persona was linked to being part of a wider group. When you fought these people, you didn't just fight one, you fought them all, and he knew this would be no different. When he exited the bar later, he would do so with a target on his back. He strolled casually towards the barman and ordered another drink, but this time something a little less potent. He needed to have his faculties about him, as the inevitability of trouble finding him at some point this evening settled. The rest of his time in the bar was spent oscillating between quiet contemplation and vigilance. The group of men in the corner had continued to drink, which had led to them becoming more lairy as the night progressed. But this would be their downfall, he felt. They were intoxicated and fuelled by frustration. He was calm and sober, but more importantly, he knew how to handle himself. He looked at his watch. It was just after nine, and outside the clear skies and stars had replaced the sunshine. There was an exit towards the back of the pub, which didn't appear to have any doormen occupying it.

'Perfect', he said to himself quietly. He placed his glass down slowly on the table and stood up from his seat. The men he had clashed with earlier were now assembled near the exit he was making his way towards. As he approached, smiling, the raucous group fell silent. The smile, however, was anything but friendly. Behind this and the ostensive calm exterior boiled a rage, which was rapping at the door relentlessly to come out. All in good time, he thought. He had known an attack was coming, but this way he could control when it happened, removing the element of surprise. He would take a blow or two, but that was fine. He had two purposes here. Primarily, this was about finding a way to release the built-up aggression from the phone call. Then it was about locating Eric Stanton.

The first blow hurt, it appeared to be with a blunt object. This he hadn't expected. Suddenly he felt the weight of more than one person on him, punches being thrown from several directions, but few landing, perhaps because of the drunken state of his aggressors. Regardless, he was able to swing around and strike one of them on the bridge of the nose. He heard a crack, which, with the accompanying cry, told him he had broken it. The man cupped his nose, now haemorrhaging blood at an alarming rate, and ran screaming down the street. As Dylan Sampson looked up, he saw there were three more now stood around looking at him. The sight of the blood and the sound of the pained shrieking had been enough to stop them in their tracks. They now stood facing each other, in what would appear to an observer as a standoff. He couldn't tell whether they were planning to retreat through fear or gain retribution for the damage he had inflicted upon their friend. It didn't matter. He had no interest in allowing them to make that decision themselves. Stepping forward, he grabbed one of the individuals by the neck and lifted him several inches off the ground, pushing him against the wall in the process. The other two men stood frozen to the spot, staring in disbelief and unsure of how to react.

'When you run your mouth off, you need to make sure you can back it up with your fists,' he said calmly, which seemed out of place considering the preceding chaos.

He had their attention. He'd taken down one of them, and currently held another, who was scrambling desperately, yet unsuccessfully, to free himself of his grasp. If they hadn't done so before now, this would be the point they realised they had picked on the wrong person. He imagined there had been many poor, unsuspecting victims who had been on the receiving end of their pent-up aggression and penchant for exerting dominance. His name would not be appearing on that list.

'There are two ways this can go down.'

The two men looked at one another, with the third still frantically trying to squirm his way out of Dylan Sampson's grip.

'If you want to continue this, I'll go through every fucking one of you, and I promise I will hurt you...badly. However, if you give me the information I need, I'll let you all walk away from here under your own free will. You could be sitting with your friend in the hospital by ten.'

He said this with a wry smile with the sole intention of further tormenting the men. He took pleasure in this in a way that could only be described as sadistic. There was no denying the rush of adrenaline he was feeling right now.

'Information?'

'I'm looking for Eric Stanton. Know him?'

'Isn't he the guy who was stabbed by that crazy bitch? I heard about that.'

'Do you know where I might find him?'

'What do you want with him?' asked the younger of the three men.

Dylan Sampson spun quickly, in the process relinquishing his grip on the attacker who was now desperately gasping for breath after being choked. The young man looked nervous, having more than likely realised it would serve him best to answer the questions, rather than ask his own. He wore dark jeans and a navy-blue jumper. He didn't look like a fighter; he looked like a follower. He looked like somebody who had found himself on the periphery of society and had sought acceptance and validation by any means necessary. He didn't fit in here. There was something distinctive about him, which seemed to suggest with a little guidance and an opportunity his life could take a very different path. Dylan Sampson recognised this, but he wasn't a social worker. Compassion could be misconstrued as weakness, and he knew the importance of maintaining the upper hand. He wasn't a bully, and wouldn't fight people who wouldn't or couldn't fight back. This had made the vicious attack responsible for his discharge even more unfathomable.

Regardless, he had experienced a life-or-death environment for many years. His reply was sharp and concise.

'That's my business.'

The young man retreated, with his facial expression changing to something resembling apologetic. The three men now stood together facing Dylan Sampson, but they knew an attack in any form would be fruitless.

'He lives in a village a few miles out of town. There are some nice places out that way. Not like this shithole.'

The voice came from the man who had moments ago become acquainted with the grip of the giant man, now standing opposite him. He was a slender man, with facial hair that appeared to compensate for his shaved head. He had a face that could tell a thousand stories and looked older than his years.

'You know him?'

'I used to. Haven't seen him for a while.'

'You were friends with this guy?'

'I wouldn't say friends. We had a mutual acquaintance, if you get what I mean.'

'I'm not sure I do.'

'A dealer,' the man replied coyly.

'Listen, I don't give a fucking damn about your drug habit, or his, for that matter. I just wanna know where I can find him. Understand?'

'If you really want to find him, just follow the women,' the young man said, grinning.

Dylan's face dropped as he lurched forward, grabbing the man by the throat and lifting him off the floor in one motion.

'What the fuck is that supposed to mean?' he asked with ferocity.

'You're choking him.'

He was oblivious. An incandescent rage flowed through him, so aggressively that he lost all concept of reality for a moment. Suddenly, he heard nothing. Panic surrounded him, but for him, simply an internal stillness. The next time he was conscious in the moment, the two men were frantically pulling at his arm to release his grip. He shook his head and let go. It was as if he had momentarily blacked out, yet he had remained conscious throughout. The young man moved back, gasping for breath, kneeling because he couldn't maintain his balance. He was badly shaken, but there was no remorse coming his way. For a moment, there was silence as all four men attempted to gather their thoughts. Finally, Dylan Sampson spoke.

'What do you know about Eric Stanton?'

'You're asking the wrong people. We only know of him.'

'Follow the women. What was that supposed to mean?'

'Only what I heard.'

'And what have you heard?'

If patience was on a timer, his was about to expire.

'Rumour has it, he likes his women and doesn't enjoy taking no for an answer if you get me?'

'I see.'

He didn't want the men to know just how much that resonated with him. He was also wary that they could be friends or associates of Eric Stanton, and couldn't risk him being warned.

'You'd be better off speaking with Toby Reynolds.'

'Toby Reynolds?' he asked, not letting on that he knew of him.

'Yeah, he was the guy arrested for attempted murder. He was at the house with her. They let him go, but it was all very suspicious if you ask me. You don't end up at a scene like that by accident.'

'Are you speaking from experience?'

He was unable to resist the temptation to rile his antagonist. The man just shook his head without replying.

'Where might I find this Toby Reynolds?'

'He was her therapist, had his own business. It's about twenty minutes from here. It's off Copper Road, I believe. You should start by reading the online articles about him. He wouldn't be hard to find.'

He had what he needed, for now anyway. He was still angry from the attack and was desperate to teach the remaining men a lesson, but he knew he could cause some damage and had little to gain now.

'Okay, I suggest you get out of here before my goodwill expires. I'd suggest you think twice before pulling this shit again. Next time, you may come across somebody less accommodating than me.'

At this, the group of men turned and walked away briskly. They wouldn't heed his warning, but that wasn't his problem. He surveyed his surroundings before deciding his next move. The night was crisp, yet clear. He pulled his phone from his pocket and stared at it intently for a moment before dialling. Several rings, and still no answer. He waited impatiently and was about to hang up when he heard a voice on the other end. He was in no mood for any sort of conversation now; the exchange would be concise and swift. He swallowed, looked up into the clear night sky, and spoke slowly and deliberately.

'I think we need to have a little talk.'

{ 5 }

Dressed in an old t-shirt and a pair of shorts which were threadbare in places, Georgina Sampson sat at the breakfast bar, head in hands, waiting anxiously for the coffee machine to provide her with the now obligatory morning kick-start. She had been a guest at the Reynolds household for a little over a week, and though she had been made to feel welcome, she felt like an outsider, a stranger no less. She was clear in her own mind why she was here, though the necessary finer details were lacking. In that respect, she had been hasty, careless to a point. She knew Toby had a role to play, a significant one, but right now, she was guarded. She had told him her relationship had broken down, and that this coupled with seeing him in the news had felt like a sign that she should reach out to him. She had admitted to feeling regret about the unresolved nature of their past relationship and expressed a wish to have transparency. Recognising the irony, George smiled at the contrast between her openness about the past and her reluctance to be open about the present. Beth had been kind to her. George admired her, but got the feeling whilst she was a compassionate woman, Beth Reynolds was somebody whom you would underestimate to your detriment. George struggled to read her.

A passive nature with a quiet assertiveness perhaps? But how could that be? Either way, she had ensured she would tread with caution and would be selective about her disclosure. She wasn't mistrusting of Beth specifically, more people in general. George had been let down, meaning people would have to work hard to gain her trust. Right now, there were only two people she trusted. One of them was her brother, the other was Toby Reynolds. This in itself presented a dilemma for her. Toby and Dylan were very different in nature. In a short space of time, she had already recognised how laid-back Toby's demeanour was. He was balanced and used reason, not impulse. She imagined these traits would have served him well in his profession. He was different now from when he was younger, but so was she. Dylan, by contrast, was reactive and, at times, could be described as nothing less than volatile. Growing up, she had likened him to a coiled spring, ready to explode at a moment's notice. Though she had once feared his anger, now she was relying on it. She paused for a moment and thought about how her plan would play out. A feeling of guilt overcame her as she considered whether she was using the two people she loved the most to get what she wanted. She knew her brother could be easily manipulated, and had carefully thought out exactly what to say to him. She hadn't lied but had been very clever with how she had portrayed her ordeal to him. She had known what his reaction would be, and that was precisely what she wanted. Toby, by comparison, was different. He wasn't reactive. She imagined in times of adversity he used his intellect, not his fists. But wasn't that what she was looking for? She didn't need muscle, she already had that in Dylan. What she needed now was a way in, and she knew whilst Dylan was likely lurching from one brawl to another in a fit of rage, Toby could get her close to her rapist. The town was relatively small and people talked. If Eric Stanton didn't already know about Dylan Sampson, he soon would. This would serve as the perfect distraction for her to gain access to him while he was focused elsewhere. He would never suspect her. She doubted he would make the link to her, even if he discovered Dylan's surname. There were still things to consider, but Georgina Sampson felt confident things would fall into place. The guilt had now disappeared, replaced with a remorseless appetite for revenge.

The coffee machine buzzed, alerting George to the fact it had completed its task. As she gripped the plain white cup, she looked around the kitchen with slight sadness. In every corner were reminders of the things she no longer had. It wasn't about the extravagant coffee machine, the triple oven, or even the ostentatious sound system she was yet to experience. It was about what they symbolised. They denoted a complete household, clearly meticulously thought out. She imagined the fun they must have had creating their dream home with sporadic luxuries. She lowered her head and felt a tear roll down her face. It had been a while since she had shown emotion like this, having felt nothing but numbness since her most recent breakup. She associated love with deceit and abandonment, and had no interest in putting herself through that pain again, but that didn't stop her from yearning. All she had wanted growing up was to have somebody to love, to experience a loving and stable household. For a long time she had believed this would be with Toby. Even after they had gone their separate ways, she had still hoped their paths would cross again, that their love would prosper. She still loved him, she always had, but romance wasn't on her mind, not right now anyway. George had taken a tissue and was wiping the tears from her cheek when Beth Reynolds entered the kitchen. She hesitated for a moment as she noticed George crying.

'Toby's coffee has that effect on me too,' she said with a smile, clearly uncomfortable. George giggled, and noting Beth's awkwardness, attempted to compose herself hastily. Of course, it was more than that. She felt embarrassed, displaying an outpouring of emotion in front of a stranger. So far, the two hadn't really spoken at any great length. She got the impression Beth was feeling her out and wondered whether she saw her as a threat. Part of her took this to be a compliment, but she had been clear in her own mind that this wasn't about romance, it was about revenge. This wasn't about Beth, it was about Eric Stanton. Her story wasn't about getting Toby, it was about getting even.

'I'm sorry. I didn't mean for you to see me like this,' she finally replied.

'It's quite okay, believe it or not, you're not the first person I've seen upset.'

At this, George raised a smile. She was still getting to know Beth and whilst George still felt sure there was more to her than met the eye, she couldn't help but feel the warmth emanating from her. She had a radiant smile and a face that George imagined could reassure you, even in the darkest and most desperate of moments. As she stared at Beth, she suddenly realised why Toby had fallen in love with her. The effervescent nature, the sense of humour, the warmth. These were all things that George recognised were part of her younger self. Toby loved the same things in Beth now, that he'd loved in George over twenty years ago. Unsure of how to react to this realisation, she made sure to hide her thoughts from Beth.

'I really appreciate you taking me in.'

'I trust Toby,' Beth smiled.

George wondered what this meant, but didn't let the passing thought overstay its welcome. She felt a moment of sadness as she slowly realised just how emotionally damaged she was. She had become highly suspicious of people, her natural position now being one of distrust. She was wary of strangers, but perhaps more wary of the people she knew. She had been hurt, let down, abandoned, all by people she had loved. Georgina Sampson now associated trust with vulnerability, love with abandonment. Gaining her trust, once automatic, was now something which was hard-earned. She felt sad at what she had become and questioned whether she would ever return to the fun-loving person she had been in her younger years. She smiled inwardly upon recognising the person best equipped to help her find herself was the person she was trying to hide part of herself from. Beth had now pulled up a chair at the breakfast bar and was sitting, coffee in hand, staring out of the bi-fold doors. The weather was pleasant, with clouds sporadically scattered, signifying it would remain that way. A group of birds gathered in the trees, and the pond produced a calmness which wasn't reflected in the kitchen right now. George wondered whether Beth would want to engage in an in-depth conversation. This was the first time they had been in the house alone without

Toby present, and George felt Beth had been waiting for an opportunity to feel her new guest out, to gauge her and her motives. She couldn't tell whether this was her suspicious nature or whether she was projecting on Beth precisely what she would do were the situation reversed. George took a drink of her coffee and cleared her throat.

'I love your garden.'

'Thank you. Toby and I both like being outdoors, so having an inviting space outside was important to us.'

'It looks like you put a lot of effort into it.'

'The landscape gardeners did,' Beth replied, smiling as both women laughed.

'Well then, it looks like you put a lot of thought into it,' George said with a grin.

'Now that I will accept.'

With this, George relaxed a little, and questioned whether the niggling suspicion of Beth she had been carrying since meeting her was, in fact, misplaced. She thought about how difficult this must be for Beth. Her husband had walked away from his career, had to fight his innocence in an attempted murder case, and had now brought his childhood sweetheart into their marital home with little to no warning. She wondered how she might feel faced with the same situation. Suddenly, she felt the beginnings of an internal conflict. What she was feeling was empathy. What her mind was screaming at her was weakness. As the inner debate raged on, she exercised considerable restraint in not allowing it to show.

'It took them nearly two weeks to complete. It looked more like a quarry than a garden.'

'I'm not so sure I could have coped with that,' George said earnestly.

'We've survived bigger challenges.'

George sat silently for a moment, unsure of whether or not to probe. She looked at Beth in awe of how well she carried herself. There was a radiance which emanated from her, but it was more than just aesthetics. She appeared to take things in her stride, exhibiting a composure which really had no place in the preceding chaos she had found herself enveloped in. George knew enough about Toby to know he was methodical and intelligent, but there was little doubt in her mind that within the relationship, Beth was the driving force. She was the constant and the voice of reason.

'I can imagine,' George offered.

Beth placed her hand on George's knee.

'Listen, I know all about your history with Toby. In fact, I think he told me all about you on our second date,' she added with a facial expression which, if it was designed to break any tension, did so. Beth continued. 'I can imagine it must feel strange for you to be here after all this time, but I want you to know you are welcome. Toby and I trust each other implicitly. Besides, he is mostly a good judge of character.'

'Mostly?'

'How much do you know about Olivia Stanton?'

'I only know what I saw in the news, really.'

She had lied. Whilst she didn't know the specifics of the case, she had met Olivia Stanton previously, but this wasn't a conversation for now, if at all. Despite their brief acquaintance, she was certain that Beth wouldn't invite someone into her home connected to the person who had drastically altered their lives, no matter how tenuous that connection may be.

'Toby is experienced at what he does.' Beth paused. 'Did,' she corrected. Her head dropped, and for a moment, George glimpsed the pain in her eyes. This was the first time she had seen her show any vulnerability. Beth drew a deep breath and continued.

'Toby's biggest asset is that he loves helping people. It's why I fell in love with him. But his biggest asset is also his biggest weakness, if you understand what I mean?'

'I'm not sure I do.'

'He dedicates all aspects of his life to helping others. It's in his nature. It's an endearing quality, and he rarely gets his judgement wrong. But something happened to him with Olivia Stanton. She impacted him in a way I've never seen before. I didn't realise the full extent of the damage at the time, but now I do, and it frightens me.'

'Is she not in prison serving a long sentence?'

'It's not her I fear. It's what she did to my husband.'

This was the first time George had heard Beth refer to Toby in this way. Was she trying to emphasise a point? Beth took a long drink out of her coffee cup before continuing.

'Toby had his suspicions from the beginning. Of course, professional ethics meant he couldn't discuss the case with me, but there was enough there to sound the alarm bells.'

'What was he able to share with you?'

'It wasn't about what he said, but I always knew when he'd seen her. Sometimes he would be physically present, but his mind elsewhere. Other times he would be late home, having stayed in the office to process his sessions with her. I've never seen him do that with any other client in his years of practising. Then there was the accident...'

'Accident?' George asked hastily, cutting Beth off.

'You didn't know? Of course you didn't. Why would you? Before everything came to a head, Toby went away for the weekend to take some time out. You know, clear his mind. I didn't want him to go. The forecast was awful, but he was insistent he needed time away.'

'Was it a car crash?' George asked inquisitively, before questioning whether she had come across insensitively.

Beth didn't seem to notice and didn't answer the question directly.

'It nearly killed him. He was in hospital for a while and had a long period of rehabilitation. I blame her for that. Had she not walked into his life, our lives, Toby wouldn't have had to endure so much physical and emotional torture.'

'Why her?' George asked.

Beth, who had looked in a trancelike state, turned towards George.

'I'm sorry?'

'What was it about Olivia Stanton specifically, do you think? Toby must have worked with many clients over the years. What made her different?'

'That's a question I've never been able to answer. Toby, to this day, doesn't talk about her. I'm not even sure *he* knows what happened.'

She paused for a moment.

'I suppose Richard may have some insight.'

'Richard?' George asked curiously.

'Toby's clinical supervisor.'

She bowed her head for a moment and closed her eyes before correcting herself for the second time during their conversation.

'Former clinical supervisor, I mean.'

George could see this had taken its toll on her. He had lost his career and nearly his freedom. Beth had come close to losing her husband. She also wondered what the financial impact of Toby losing his practice would be. This was a big house, and he drove an expensive-looking car. As she sat there, Georgina Sampson felt a deep sympathy for the woman sitting opposite her.

'This entire ordeal must have been awful for you,' she said, placing her hand on Beth's knee.

'Toby's a strong character. He'll get through it in his own time.'

'I wasn't talking about Toby.'

Beth smiled and looked up. George sensed any trepidation Beth may have had towards her was disappearing. Perhaps she was even warming to her.

'Everybody has their own battles, George.'

'Some are more difficult than others.'

'Many have it worse than me.'

'I wonder how many have it better, though?'

George relaxed. The topic of conversation moving away from herself felt good. As Georgina Sampson and Beth Reynolds sat talking, it would have been easy to mistake their conversation for a catch-up between two close friends, rather than the complex and tentative situation it actually was. The reality was Beth still had very little insight into the reasoning behind

Revenge in Mind

George's presence in her house, but that wasn't the origin of her guilt. Her guilt was driven by the fact that neither did Toby.

'When I was a young girl, I lost my parents in a car accident. I went from having fun at a party to being orphaned in a matter of hours.'

'I'm so sorry. I don't know what to say,' George said sympathetically.

'Thank you, but I'm not telling you for sympathy. The distance, the emotional investment in her, even his decision to drive to a client's house, all that I could deal with. But that car crash, that fucking crash, that was the one thing which could penetrate these walls I have spent years building. I blame her for that, but I also blame him. *He* made that decision to get into the car. *He* made the decision to leave that weekend. *He* allowed his mind to become preoccupied with Olivia Stanton, resulting in a near-fatal crash.'

Beth was becoming animated, and George sensed she was getting angry. This made her feel uncomfortable, as she was simply a guest in their home. They weren't friends, past or present, and were only linked through Toby. She recognised a certain irony in Beth opening up to her freely, whilst she remained guarded about what she did and didn't disclose in return. She knew this was how it had to be but still felt bad that there appeared to be an imbalance in the relationship developing with Beth. She wasn't a bad person, she'd just been hurt too many times and the pain arising from this sparked her anger. Before she could get too immersed in her own thoughts, Beth got up out of her seat and poured them both another coffee. The kitchen, which looked and felt incredibly spacious, had a red and black colour scheme, which likely reflected the owners' colourful nature. The coffee machine in the corner was grand. George wondered how much something like that would cost. Beth placed a freshly brewed cup of coffee on the table in front of them and took her seat.

'You must think I'm an awful person.'

'Why would I think that?' George replied softly.

'Because I'm not the one who nearly lost my freedom. I'm...'

She broke off and looked up at the ceiling as if searching for the right words. She closed her eyes and drew a small, yet pronounced breath before continuing, her voice now a little quieter.

'I'm not the one who nearly lost my life.'

For a moment, George didn't know how to react. She was uncertain of what to say, or if indeed she should say anything at all. She once again felt the unease making its way to the surface from deep within the confines of her stomach. All she could offer was a sympathetic smile. Beth, noticing her guest's awkwardness, returned the smile and placed her hand on George's.

'I'm sorry, you're a guest, not a therapist.'

They both giggled, but George felt Beth's smile was masking a deep pain. On the surface, she presented as a strong woman, but there was a vulnerability there, and it hadn't gone unnoticed. George studied Beth for a moment.

'Did you ever meet her?'

'Who, Olivia Stanton?'

'Yes.'

Revenge in Mind

Beth's expression suddenly changed from one of anguish to something George was struggling to place. Her face had answered the question, piquing George's intrigue. She waited patiently for Beth to continue.

'I was present at the remand hearing. I had to see her in the flesh, the person who nearly took everything from Toby, from us both. I had to see whether there was any remorse, any humane part of her. Toby doesn't know.'

'What did you see?'

'Nothing. I saw absolutely nothing. Her expression never changed. I've never come across anybody who looked so cold, so devoid of emotion.'

'How did you feel?'

'You sound like Toby.'

George let out a sharp laugh, before quickly putting her hand to her mouth as she realised Beth hadn't intended it as a joke.

'I'm sorry,' she said, genuinely apologetic.

'Do you know what really struck me about her?'

Knowing the question was rhetorical, George simply shook her head without taking her gaze away from Beth's.

'How easily she manipulated my husband. Of all the therapists within her vicinity, she specifically targeted Toby. How long did she study him? Why did she feel he would be so easy to control?'

'Are you angry at Toby?'

'I guess I am, but I know everything he did was for the right reasons. Toby and I have always trusted each other wholeheartedly. We have no secrets, and that trust has never been betrayed. But I've always known that the thing that makes him so wonderful also makes him vulnerable.'

'You feared something like this would happen?'

'In the depth of my darkest nightmares, I couldn't have created this scenario, but yes, I feared something or someone would penetrate his professional walls and reach him as a person.'

'I'm not sure I understand.'

'Toby cares, I mean genuinely cares. In most situations, that's a wonderfully endearing quality, but to the wrong person...'

'It's a weakness that can be exploited,' George interrupted.

'Right,' Beth replied, nodding slowly in agreement.

'She was a dangerous individual for him, but he was the perfect target for her,' she continued.

Beth sat back and adjusted her chair. After glancing outside and grasping her mug with both hands, she settled her eyes on her house guest.

'Why are you here, George?'

She hadn't expected this and the question, not just the question, but the manner in which it had been asked, visibly surprised her. It was succinct and sharp.

'The honest answer is, I don't know. I've found myself at a crossroads recently and after seeing Toby on the news, decided to reach out. It was an opportunity to catch up with an old friend with the hidden bonus of getting a little perspective.'

Without breaking eye contact, Beth sat back in her chair.

'That's the second time you've lied to me during this conversation.'

George recoiled, unable to hide her shock. She tried in vain to compose herself to respond, but she couldn't find the words.

Revenge in Mind

'Being the wife of a psychotherapist has its perks. You see, when people lie, most often there are subtle giveaways. Most commonly, this will be something in the body language. Olivia Stanton blindsided Toby because she knew how to, but most people will trip themselves up,' Beth smiled.

'Beth, I assure you I'm not lying to you.'

In this moment, George sounded panicked and wanted to be anywhere other than facing an interrogation from Beth Reynolds.

'Your hair,' Beth replied, as if not hearing her.

'My hair?'

'You curl your hair around your finger. You've done it twice. Just now, and...'

She paused.

'...And when you told me you only knew of Olivia Stanton through the news.'

George was left speechless and under no illusion as to just how important her next words were. She felt desperately uncomfortable, not because of Beth's antipathy towards her, but because she was right. She had lied, and her entire plan now rested on how she responded here. It wasn't that she needed Beth on side, more she didn't need her as an adversary. Beth was protective of Toby, especially when it came to Olivia Stanton. Telling her the whole truth, at this point anyway, wasn't an option. But she had misjudged just how astute Beth Reynolds was, so lying would serve no purpose other than to antagonise her further.

'You're right, I'm not here simply to catch up with Toby, and I have met Olivia Stanton previously.'

George paused, knowing she needed to tread carefully.

'I don't have any kind of relationship with Olivia Stanton, past or present, but we are linked, but not in a positive way.'

Beth gazed at her with intrigue, but remained silent.

'Right now, I can't go into it, but let's just say we have a mutual friend.'

'A friend?'

George didn't answer the question.

'She tracked me down a few years ago, and that's the only time I have ever met the woman. I didn't care for her then and I certainly don't care for her now.'

'Where does Toby fit into all this?' Beth asked sternly.

'I've been carrying trauma for a long time and had hit crisis point. I needed somebody who could help me work through things, but it also had to be somebody I could trust. I've placed my trust in the wrong people before and paid the price. I couldn't risk it happening again. I haven't seen Toby for a number of years, but when I saw him on the news, I realised looking back, he was the one person whom I felt safe with. He never lied to me.'

She had Beth's attention but braced herself for what she felt would be the inevitable interrogation. She hadn't lied; she had simply left out a lot of detail. The expected interrogation didn't come.

'George, I have no idea what you've been through, but Toby is still recovering emotionally from the Olivia Stanton ordeal. You understand I can't have anybody jeopardise that, right?'

'He's lucky to have you.'

Revenge in Mind

'I nearly didn't have *him*. That's why I need to protect him. He isn't a therapist anymore and the last thing he needs is the wounds left by Olivia Stanton reopening.'

'I would never hurt Toby.'

'You're not gonna get the chance to. I sympathise with your situation, but Toby has nothing to do with it.'

The room was now filled with palpable tension. The two women sat in silence, neither of them taking their eyes off the other. Beth had her legs crossed and was sitting upright. George was now slumped back in her chair. If this had been a fight, the contrast in body language would have given a clear indication of the outcome. George sat contemplating looking down at her feet, Beth now looking out of the window. The conversation had ended abruptly, and the atmosphere was getting more tense with every moment that passed. It was only disrupted by heavy footsteps in the hallway. Out of the shadows, a familiar figure appeared at the kitchen door, greeting both women with a smile. Returning the smile, George got up out of her seat and excused herself. Beth grabbed the pair of hands, now rubbing her shoulder, and pulled them down, holding them tight. Moving her head close to his, she whispered quietly in his ear.

'We need to talk about George.'

{ 6 }

Driven by rage, Dylan Sampson stomped through the scarcely lit streets into the cool night air. The adrenaline had now subsided, and he was feeling the pain in the back of his head; the result of the blow suffered at the hands of an intoxicated man who would now be regretting that decision. To him though, it served as little more than a physical reminder of the altercation earlier in the night. It was now after midnight. The bars had long since emptied, and the streets were quiet. He paused for a moment to take in his surroundings. The sky was clear, the lack of cloud cover producing a crisp temperature, though he noticed there were some clouds approaching from the distance. Leaving the hotel room in a black tee shirt and khaki-coloured shorts had seemed a good idea earlier in the day with the enthusiastic sunshine, but it was a decision he was regretting now, as the cold air bit. As he stood, he thought about the last year of his life. He thought about his discharge from the army. He thought about the relationships which had fallen victim to his lifestyle. He thought about his sister and everything she had endured. He thought about Eric Stanton...he settled on Eric Stanton. His journey to find him had only just begun, yet he had to battle an intense level of impetuosity. In his job, patience had been vital.

Revenge in Mind

He had needed to be methodical and composed. His life had depended on it. Yet here he was fighting an impulsiveness which could ultimately have catastrophic consequences. She had been very clear with her intentions, and what role she needed him to play. He was still unsure whether he had obliged through a thirst for retribution or a sense of guilt. Either way, here he was trudging through the streets searching for a man who wouldn't even see him coming. Tonight had simply been about dusting off some cobwebs. Interrogating the group had been opportunistic, not planned. As he stood reflecting, he wondered whether this had been an error on his part. If they were associated with Eric Stanton, they would almost certainly forewarn him. Whilst this wouldn't be too problematic, it would certainly be an obstacle he would rather avoid. He had hoped for stealth, but questioned whether this was still an option. Then he smiled to himself at the thought of Eric Stanton fearing an inevitable confrontation, but having no concept of when it was going to happen and what it was going to entail. There was a sadistic, twisted feeling as this thought developed. Suddenly, he was filled with a temptation to draw out this process and watch his adversary suffer from a distance. His tours had not instilled this hunger for revenge into him. The enemy had simply been doing the same job he had, just on a different side. War had never been personal, but this was. Eric Stanton had deliberately targeted and hurt somebody he loved. That wasn't a job, it was a conscious decision to exercise control. He grimaced as the internal conflict became overwhelming. All of his training had guided him to be meticulous and without emotion, even in the most challenging of situations. Yet here he was, feeling like a passenger in an out-of-control car, with emotion behind the wheel. As the palpitations exerted their dominance, and a cold sweat poured down his face, it was the thought of George, which pulled him back into the moment again. This wasn't about him, it was about her. Whilst it was clear he would play a pivotal role in this battle, the battle wasn't his. He was merely a guest. He needed to remove the emotion and use the skills he had perfected over the last twenty years. Though he was no longer a soldier in title, the attributes that had allowed him to escape many volatile situations remained. A drop of rain fell onto his forehead and rolled down his face. Noticing the skies had become overcast with the sudden appearance of clouds, he picked up the pace and wondered how long he had been quietly contemplating. He had spent years in warm climates when on tour, and even living in the South of France, he had enjoyed pleasant weather. He had spent little time in England over the years and was, as a result, still acclimatising to its cooler weather. The nights were sharp, the cold now beginning to exert its authority, regardless of entering springtime. As he walked, he noticed the trees shaking more and wondered whether inclement weather was approaching. Aside from the occasional taxi, the roads were now almost deserted, and he hadn't seen another person in quite some time. Making his way out of town on what would turn into a country road, he removed his phone from his pocket. There was a message from George.

'I'm safe at Toby's house. I'll contact you when I can speak freely. Don't do anything that might draw attention to yourself.'

Revenge in Mind

 He smiled as he considered whether hospitalising a man, and roughing up three others, would qualify as drawing attention to himself. Nothing he had done that evening had been done so in a clandestine manner. He knew there was every chance his description would now be out there among the wrong people. His size made it difficult to remain inconspicuous. His fear wasn't surrounding his own personal safety; he could handle himself. His fear was around the impact his actions could have on George and her quest to hold her rapist accountable. He scolded himself at the prospect of removing the element of surprise, or worse still, word reaching Eric Stanton prompting him to abscond. He felt a frustration at allowing his anger to take control. But this was his sister, the person he cared for above all others. This was no time for self-reproach. He couldn't control what had happened, simply what would happen from here. He studied his phone for a moment but opted against replying to George's message. Placing it back into his pocket, he continued his walk back to the hotel, where he would await further instruction. Eric Stanton now had his attention. The question was whether soon enough he would have Eric Stanton's.

{ 7 }

'I have to be honest, you're the last person I expected to see here.'

'I'm surprised you agreed to see me.'

'My first thought was to tell you to go fuck yourself. Then I became intrigued, you could say.'

'Your suspicion and overactive imagination are going to be your downfall. Oh, wait.'

He had shown his hand early and struck the first blow. This wouldn't be a trip down memory lane, and there certainly wouldn't be any pleasantries. Once exchanging looks of adoration, they now sat gazing at one another with nothing more than hatred and suspicion. Any smiles would be insincere, masking a deep resentment both of them undoubtedly possessed. There had been a time when they had enjoyed each other's company. Now it would take a concerted effort from her to merely get through the next hour in his presence.

Olivia Stanton sat back in her chair. Her hair was short, and darker than he would remember. She looked older than her thirty-four years. Ordinarily, she still liked to make the effort, well as much of an effort as she could make in a place like this. Today, however, she had no interest in showing him what he was missing. Appearance wasn't at the forefront of her mind right now as she sat face-to-face with the man whom she had hoped she would never see alive again. She remembered Toby asking her if she was able to separate Eric Stanton the husband and Eric Stanton the father. She had thought about this, but as time had gone on and the resentment had built, she had become more and more convinced her son would have a better future without his father in it. The dream had been for her and Tyler to have a life together without Eric. The reality was that she was enduring an extended stay in a shared room, her every move scrutinised. The little things she had once taken for granted now seen as luxurious, a privilege no less. As she gazed at the man sitting opposite her, she didn't see a rapist, an abusive husband, or even a manipulative, deeply flawed individual. What she saw was the person responsible for her being separated from her son. Of course, he had refused to bring Tyler, not because he believed this wasn't a place for a young boy, she thought, but because he was twisting the knife, striking a blow in a place he knew would have the greatest impact. Whatever she was, whatever she had been reduced to, there was one thing about her which had never changed…her love for her son. Tyler had been her everything from the moment she had introduced him to the world. They had enjoyed a close bond, something she had always believed Eric was jealous of. Being incarcerated had so many implications, but for her, there was only one that mattered, and that was no longer having unrestricted access to her son. She would miss so many key moments of his growing up. More importantly for her, the bond they had shared for so long would be slowly and cruelly ripped apart. Eric was now his sole caregiver. He had complete control, and the narrative was his to create. The police and the media already saw him as the victim, and she as the perpetrator. They hadn't portrayed her as a woman who had been subjected to heinous abuse and who had fought back. They had simply seen her as a bitter, cold-blooded killer who had premeditated the murder of her husband. If it hadn't already happened, it wouldn't be long before Tyler thought the same.

'You look different.'

'Prison does that to you,' she replied sharply.

'How did we get here?'

'I'm assuming you didn't come here to analyse our marriage.'

'You're right, I didn't. But that doesn't stop me from wondering how it all came to this.'

'It came to this because you couldn't keep your fucking hands off other women. It came to this because you have the inability to comprehend what the word no means. It came to this because you're a self-centred and self-absorbed prick who believes he has a right to take whatever he wants. And it came to this because I wasn't prepared to take your shit any longer.'

She had been holding this in for a long time. The release felt good.

Eric Stanton sat back in his chair, with a warped grin slowly spreading across his face. The fact he hadn't even feigned being offended angered her further. She despised him, more than Toby Reynolds, whose actions had brought her plan crashing down and had resulted in her arrest. Toby had acted in a way he thought was protecting her. Eric had done anything but. Whilst she was still angry with Toby's role in this, she had sympathy for him, unwittingly becoming an alibi for her. When she looked at Eric, she felt nothing but disdain.

'We had it all Liv...'

'Don't call me that,' she snapped, not allowing him to finish.

'You never had a problem with that in the past,' he replied, grinning.

'And you never had a problem violating me without consent,' she snapped back.

She said this with calmness, but internally she was wild with anger. She suddenly thought how good it would feel to reach over the desk, grab the cord attached to his hoodie, and pull it tightly around his neck, watching the life seep out of him until he expelled his final breath. This man had taken everything from her. She now knew their entire relationship had been a lie. There had been others. They hadn't been isolated incidents fuelled by alcohol as she had first thought. They had been a method for him to exert control over her. He hadn't suddenly changed as a person; this had always been inside him. It had taken her a while, but now she finally acknowledged that she had married a rapist. That realisation had hit her hard, not just because of the impact it had on her, but also the effect it would have on their son. Aside from his father being a sexual predator, she had grown increasingly concerned about Eric's influence on Tyler. It was that concern which had ultimately led to the plotting of her husband's murder. The damage done to her was one thing, but she couldn't risk her son becoming a victim. She couldn't risk him growing up to be like his father. Olivia Stanton had become adept at showing emotion to manipulate her way through situations, but when it came to her son, that emotion was genuine. Eric had leaned forward so his head was much closer to hers.

'As far as I can see, there's only one of us behind bars here,' he whispered.

'Give it time,' she replied, smiling confidently.

Eric shuffled back into his chair. His smile had waned a little, though hadn't disappeared completely. She had his attention.

'Some thug has been asking around after me. Now what possible reason is there for somebody to do that?'

'Perhaps your past has finally caught up with you? I'm not the only person out there you've wronged. I believe this is what they refer to as karma,' she said with a grin she couldn't hide.

'I know you're behind this.'

'I'm the one behind bars, remember?'

'That doesn't stop you from spreading your poison to any unsuspecting fool who'll listen.'

As she crossed her legs, she realised how much she was enjoying hearing the veiled desperation in his tone. The confidence he had been exuding to this point, she now realised, had been a mask. For all the gloating and swagger, he was worried.

'Are you sleeping with one eye open?' she enthused.

He let out a small sigh, as though to let her know he was becoming bored with her tedious quips. She could see the dynamics were changing. He needed something from her, either answers or peace of mind. She would give him neither.

'Whatever you've done, just remember it's me who controls whether you see your son.'

'You son of a bitch,' she snapped angrily, banging her hands on the table, which made him jump back. A prison officer walked over to the table to see what the sudden tumult was about.

'It's fine, she's just received some bad news, that's all,' Eric Stanton said, waving his hands. Seeing the officer move away, he leaned into Olivia and spoke in a quiet yet assertive voice.

'All I want are answers, nothing more.'

'What makes you think I have them?'

'You tried to kill me, and right now, I'm the one standing between you and your son. A week after I deny your request to have Tyler visit, some unsavoury character suddenly shows up in town asking about my location. Surely, it's not that difficult to see why I'm here.'

'The fact you're referring to somebody as unsavoury amuses me.'

Eric ignored the jibe.

'He beat up somebody I know, hospitalised another. He was very specific in asking for me by name. Who's out there looking for me?' he said now with a hint of panic in his tone. She, of course, picked up on this and couldn't help but feel smug. She was aware that no amount of pacifying Eric would alter his decision to prevent Tyler from seeing her. That was the harsh reality. She had nothing to lose. If he genuinely believed she had put a target on him, he needed her more than she needed him. She had the advantage.

'Sounds like you're finally about to get your comeuppance,' she said, closing her eyes and exhaling slowly through her nose as she smirked. She was sending a clear message to him that she was enjoying the balance of power tipping in her direction.

Until this point, he had maintained his composure, but it wasn't difficult to see he was rattled.

'Olivia, who is this guy, and what does he want with me?'

'Perhaps you fucked with the wrong person?'

She laughed as she recognised the unintended pun but immediately reproached herself.

'Olivia, I regret what happened in our marriage...'

'You regret the fact I found out about the others,' she interrupted loudly, pointing her finger aggressively at him.

'Look, I admit I had a string of affairs, but that's no reason to want me dead.'

'Affairs? Is that what you call them?'

She was visibly shaking. Still, he was trying to gaslight her. He may be regretful, but he certainly wasn't remorseful. Her anger was increasing with every moment she spent in his presence. She gripped the table tightly, trying to suppress the rage inside her. Sat in front of her was a rapist, her rapist, attempting to trivialise his heinous crimes by passing them off as something consensual. She felt sick, and not for the first time that day. He sat quietly, contemplating. She wondered whether he was intentionally lying, or whether he had convinced himself of an alternative narrative. Hadn't Toby once said that people can suppress memories for self-preservation, that absolving themselves of blame protects them from guilt and self-reproach? Perhaps he had convinced himself that it was consensual. She couldn't speak for the others, but with her, he had done a very convincing job of carrying on as normal, which had made her question whether it really happened as she remembered it.

Revenge in Mind

'This isn't the first time you've antagonised somebody, yet I've never seen you this uptight before. What's different?'

Then it hit her. She didn't need him to answer. The reason he was now so anxious was because he had already had an attempt on his life. She hadn't succeeded that time, but that wouldn't give him closure, or even relief. He would now always be looking over his shoulder, waiting for the next attempt. It must be like being on death row, she thought, and smiled outwardly as she realised she was the one who had done this to him. She was in prison, yet he was also living as a prisoner, just in a different form.

'If I went to the police with this, it would bring unwelcome attention to you. I'm sure that's the last thing you need with your sentencing around the corner.'

'Thankfully, the police work with evidence, not fantasy,' she replied smugly.

There was a standoff for a moment, with both of them silent, appearing deep in thought. He was difficult to gauge. Oscillating between confident and wary, she was still unsure whether he was bluffing. It felt like a game to her and it was now just a case of seeing who blinked first. She had nothing to lose, but could certainly gain from the deep satisfaction of watching him squirm.

'I see Toby Reynolds came to see you. Now why would you agree to see the person who foiled your plan and put you in here?' he asked curiously.

'Perhaps the same reason I agreed to see the man who raped me, and several other women.'

His smile disappeared. He clearly didn't like being called a rapist, but she couldn't figure out whether this was because of him protecting his reputation, or whether it was indeed self-preservation and he was in denial.

'Don't call me that,' he snapped angrily.

'Truth hurts?'

'Listen, I know I made mistakes, but I didn't rape you or anybody else, you poisonous little bitch.'

If he wasn't rattled before, he certainly was now. She'd found his pressure point and had every intention of pushing down on it as hard as she could. This had been the real reason for her agreeing to see him. She wanted to punish him. She wanted to show him the pure contempt with which she now viewed him. More than anything, she wanted to show him that regardless of what he did to her, regardless of where she was, he had not beaten her. She had not allowed herself to be broken and she could still come out swinging. He couldn't control her or keep her down. She needed him to see this. In fact, she had needed him to see this for years, she just hadn't realised it until now. She looked him straight in the eye as her smile slowly disappeared.

'I spent a long time trying to come to terms with what you did to me. The self-loathing was unbearable, as I agonised over whether I deserved it. You left me feeling powerless. When you took my body, you also took my self-respect, my dignity. But more than that, you took my basic right to be able to live my life without fear. Every time you had a drink, I slept with one eye open. Now you're gonna know exactly what it feels like to be looking over your shoulder, wondering when somebody is going to strike.'

Eric Stanton's face dropped. His wife's bitter words had clearly taken aim and not missed.

'Olivia, what did you tell Toby? Is he behind this?'

'I didn't need to tell him much. He's an intelligent guy and saw right through you when he visited you in the hospital.'

He recoiled in surprise as she grinned at him triumphantly.

'You thought I didn't know? Oh, Toby was very open with his thoughts on you. Sure, I gave him a little nudge, an insight into the evil that lurked behind that charming smile, but as I said, it didn't take much.'

'Toby Reynolds is a disgraced former therapist who was arrested on an attempted murder charge. I'm not so sure his opinion of me is going to hold much water.'

'The fact your smile vanished when his name was mentioned would suggest differently, don't you think?'

Eric didn't answer. He glared at her with an intensity she couldn't put into words, eyes wild with fire. Whatever her feelings were towards him, they were reciprocated. He leaned over the desk and spoke quietly, yet with purpose.

'Listen here you bitch, be careful who you're messing with. If you and that shrink friend of yours are right about me, you should be very afraid of what I am capable of. Not only will you never see your son again, but I will make life so difficult for you that when you are eventually released, you will beg to be put back in here. Do you understand me?'

As he moved back slowly to his chair, she grabbed his head and whispered into his ear.

'You have a target on your back, sweetheart, and it won't be long before somebody takes aim. Perhaps they'll succeed where

I failed. Your past is catching up with you, but here's the thing. As much as I would love to take credit for this, it has nothing to do with me. So that begs the question, who else have you upset?'

He snatched back from her, sinking into his chair. He looked shocked, and for the first time, she thought, frightened as well. She had no sympathy, however, and no desire to relent. She had her foot on his jugular and wasn't about to release it.

'Toby is on to you, you know. He knows all about your past, your victims. And if there's one thing Toby loves, it's rescuing a victim. He won't stop looking into you until he finds what he needs. Maybe he already has, and that's why you're sleeping with the light on.'

She grinned at him, savouring the moment, basking in his fear. She firmly believed he was here for answers, but also felt there was a hidden agenda of trying to intimidate her. This was about control. It was about him showing he could still get what he wanted from her. It was about him exerting his authority, his dominance, just like he had over her in the past. Not just her, but the others as well. But he had underestimated her, and if his plan had been to charm his way into getting what he wanted, he had failed. If he had planned to use intimidation, he had failed. He would leave here with more questions than answers. Any fear he had coming in would almost certainly have amplified when he made his way out. He would be looking over his shoulder from now on, never sure where the inevitable attack would come from. She was interrupted by the ringing of the bell, which signalled the end of visiting. As he slowly rose out of his seat and turned to walk away, Olivia grabbed her husband by the arm.

Revenge in Mind

'A word of warning. Toby Reynolds isn't the person you think he is. He's more than capable of orchestrating this, and he has a grudge.'

At this, Eric removed his arm from her grasp and made his way out of the visiting area. She watched as he left, her confident demeanour diminishing as she began to shake and the smile disappeared from her face. As she walked back to her cell, she wondered whether she would see her husband alive again. Was this somebody who simply wanted him roughed up, or did they want him dead? Was it somebody he had upset in the present, or a ghost from his past? Then she paused and stared up at the ceiling. Could Toby really be behind this? He was certainly clever enough, but surely revenge went against everything he had been as a professional, and still was as a person. Yet still, there was this niggling doubt. That doubt hadn't left her as she settled down to sleep later that evening, a conflict erupting in her head. Her last words to Toby had been to warn him that Eric may come after him or his family. He had already risked his freedom and career for a client he had no emotional ties to. She wondered just how far he would go to protect those he loved.

{ 8 }

As he made his way out of the prison gates, Eric Stanton cut a nervous figure. Though he and Toby Reynolds were adversaries, they had much in common when it came to his estranged wife. Both had piqued her intrigue with an impromptu visit. Both had sought answers, though for different reasons, and both had been subjected to her acidic tongue. Ultimately, they had each left unsatisfied, with more questions than answers. She had blamed Toby for unravelling her plans, but she also had sympathy for his naïve innocence. What she felt for her husband was nothing short of unfiltered hatred, the depths of which he couldn't possibly have imagined until recently. Walking slowly back to his car, he paused to take in the view. If the sole purpose of the prison was geographic isolation, it had achieved this. It sat on its own grounds, with a structure you couldn't help but admire. There was one road in and one road out. The nearest town was located over a mile away. In contrast to the modern building and its large grounds was the small, forlorn figure of the last visitor to exit the prison. Deep in thought, he was likely considering his next move. His plans to manipulate his wife into getting what he wanted had failed. The palpable confidence he had walked in with had disappeared somewhere between the visiting room and the gates. The last hour hadn't turned out how he would have wanted or expected it to. Instead of leaving with relief, he now looked like a man who carried a heavy burden. He was troubled, and for somebody with his background and reputation, that wasn't something you could say often. It would have been easier for him to know Olivia was behind this, as there would only be one variable to control and he had leverage...Tyler. Now, he faced the prospect of there being another person somewhere whom he had antagonised enough for them to want to exact revenge on him. He had no foresight into what that would look like, when it was coming, nor who would be the perpetrator. All he knew was somebody had been asking about him and had beaten up some of his associates in the process. The description of the man had been hazy, likely down to the volume of alcohol consumed prior to the altercation, but regardless, Eric would not see it coming. It was that uncertainty that perhaps explained the ponderous look on his face. He was somebody who was used to being in control and having things his own way, though climbing into his car he looked like somebody who wasn't in control at all. There would be a certain irony if Toby Reynolds was indeed behind this. It wasn't beyond the realm of possibility that the very person who had once saved his life was now looking to endanger it.

Though she had denied it vehemently, there was a chance Olivia may have been lying about her involvement. She would have likely derived a perverse pleasure from watching him work tirelessly and in vain, trying to piece together the identity of his would-be assailant. She had taken great pleasure in showing him she was in control, even though she was in a place where she had very little. She had taken it back from the very man who took it from her in the first place, reducing her to a bitter and manipulative individual. She was vengeful, and she was calculating. She had the persistence and the anger to succeed where she had failed last time. However, she was also the type of person who would enjoy watching him squirm, consumed by an anxiety he was simply not acquainted with. This would be Eric's dilemma. It was conceivable she was behind this, but it was equally possible she wasn't. Either way, she could use it to her advantage and as he sat in his car, engine idling, he would likely realise he had just handed the control over to her. He had shown his hand, given her a glimpse of his vulnerability, and she had made no mistake in identifying it and twisting the knife. However, he had committed his real mistake before that. His very decision to visit her in the first place had been a bad one. He had been guilty of either overestimating the hold he had on her, or underestimating the contempt she had for him. Either way, attempts to persuade or threaten her had fallen short. There was one thing he had succeeded in, however, and that was further antagonising his wife. She was behind bars, but she was still a dangerous and vindictive woman, and being subjected to threats and taunts would have done nothing to mellow her. He would now realise that whilst he had something to gain from his visit, there was always the chance he had more to lose. He perhaps regretted that decision now as he slowly pulled out of the prison car park. The comment she had gleefully made about him sleeping with one eye open was vitriolic, but also accurate. The man driving down the road hastily now had always considered himself untouchable, but had displayed this in a charming rather than arrogant way. Most people would know him as a polite individual. Few would see the other side of him, but this didn't matter. There was someone, and clearly that someone had a vendetta big enough to want revenge. The options for Eric Stanton were simple. Either he could leave town and head somewhere nobody would find him, or he could try to figure out who was behind this and strike first. Arrogance or defiance, he wasn't accustomed to running away and had built a comfortable life for himself here. His visit to Olivia had given him one answer, though. It wasn't safe to return home at the moment. He would lie low for a while. Tyler was on holiday with his grandparents, an attempt to try and take his mind off his mother's absence. He was afforded the option of staying in a hotel for a few nights whilst he figured out what to do next. Tomorrow would be a big day for him. Olivia had served up Toby Reynolds, and though Eric hadn't appeared convinced, he wouldn't take any chances. He had met Toby twice before, both in very different circumstances. This wouldn't be the same. Whilst he didn't know exactly what Olivia had told Toby about him, he knew it would be enough to sow the seeds of doubt and arouse his suspicion. The question was, would it be enough for him to seek retribution of some sort? But he hadn't wronged Toby, had he? Wouldn't he direct his animosity toward Olivia? It was she who had manipulated him, used him, cost him his career. It had been she who had played a role in his arrest for attempted murder. Why would Toby be interested in him? As he approached a set of crossroads, he paused briefly before turning to head out of town towards a countryside hotel. Once there, he would need to give some serious consideration to how he planned to approach Toby Reynolds. He was clever, and if he was the one who had instigated this, he shouldn't be underestimated. Eric would need to tread carefully, but firstly he would have to find the opportunity to orchestrate a chance meeting. It was that thought Eric Stanton went to bed with that night and woke up with the following morning. As he sat on his bed, quietly contemplating, the answer came to him. With a smirk on his face, he placed his cup on the desk, grabbed his bag, and exited his room.

{ 9 }

Toby inhaled slowly, smiling at the sweet aroma of coffee beans emanating from behind the counter. It was just after nine-thirty and he was in his favourite place, the coffeehouse. This had become his new sanctuary. As much as he loved time with Beth, he also enjoyed his moments of solitude. Combining those with his love of coffee seemed like the perfect replacement for the gym. Physically, he was still feeling the effects of the crash, which affected his ability to work out, but if he was honest, the reasons behind his sessions with Dan ending weren't physical. The gym had been the one thing that was about him, a place where he could enjoy being the client. It had served as an emotional break from psychotherapy. Olivia Stanton had changed this. Encountering a client wouldn't have altered his gym passion, but that encounter wasn't accidental. The gym was now a harsh reminder of how he had been manipulated, and how his inability to maintain boundaries and read his clients had cost him his career. It was more than simply his career, though. It had put a strain on his marriage, almost cost him his freedom, and nearly claimed his life. In his darkest moments, Beth had stayed by his side, but part of him knew he had prioritised Olivia over her, over everything. The daily guilt had provided a constant reminder of this and was part of the reason his emotional recovery from the ordeal had been much longer than his physical recovery from the accident. He had let Beth down, and he knew it. Losing his practice naturally had financial implications, something else he carried guilt for. As he neared the front of the queue, he lamented how his simple and comfortable life had become an unrecognisable speck in the rear-view mirror. A year ago, his marriage was strong, his career was thriving, and he had never heard of Olivia Stanton. Now, his career was gone and his marriage had been pushed to its limits. He still hadn't figured out what he wanted to do with his life. His plan had been to take some time out to recover emotionally and then assess his situation. Though they had been impacted financially, they weren't destitute. They had been cautious with money and invested wisely whilst Toby's practice had been busy. Although he could never have envisaged what would transpire, he now felt grateful for the decisions they had made. The financial impact didn't directly affect their daily living, but it required them to make some sacrifices on the luxuries they had become accustomed to. Toby ordered his drink and stood at the counter, watching the barista perform her artistry. He admired just how efficient she was and wondered what it would be like to work in a place like this. After preparing his drink with precision, she handed it to him politely. He had become a familiar face over the last few weeks and was now met with a smile by the staff who recognised him. Of course, there was every chance they recognised him from the news as opposed to his regular visits. This upset him, and had resulted in him becoming obsessed with the body language of those he came into contact with. The vulnerable side of him desperately sought sincerity. Being recognised for the right reasons was important to him. He wanted to be known as a regular patron with a smile on his face, not the guy in the news who got caught up in an attempted murder charge. He took his drink, thanked the girl, and walked over to take a seat near the window. Though no longer a therapist, Toby still had an interest in human behaviour and possessed an ability to lose himself simply by watching passers-by. He would study the interactions between people, look at their non-verbal cues, and imagine what their lives might look like. The sound of a chair being pulled out abruptly ended Toby's daydream as an unfamiliar figure took a seat opposite him. It took him a moment, perhaps because of the initial surprise, but suddenly the realisation of who was sitting staring at him set in. The man was quite tall and dressed smartly. Toby's first observation was that his grooming didn't complement his attire. He was unshaven, and his hair looked like it hadn't seen a brush in quite some time. He looked troubled, Toby thought, and ordinarily, this would gain his sympathy, but this wasn't a family member, a client or a loved one. The person who had encroached on his personal space and disrupted his quiet reflection was Eric Stanton. At first, there was an awkward silence, but Toby wondered whether this was simply the calm before the storm and took a long, drawn-out breath as he braced himself for what was about to follow. Toby was responsible for Eric still being alive, but the last time he had been in his company, he had felt a sense of unease right before he left. It wasn't this which made him wary, however; it was the last words Olivia had shouted at him as he had left the prison. She had told him that if

Eric believed Toby suspected him in any way, he wasn't safe. Toby had left questioning whether he had inadvertently put a target on his own back. But surely Eric hadn't picked up on his suspicion, had he? He hadn't verbalised anything, but had Eric sensed a change in his demeanour, perhaps? Had his body language given him away? His tone of voice? The sound of Eric Stanton's voice brought him back to the moment.

'Hello again Toby.'

There was a smile, but Toby doubted its sincerity.

'It's nice to see you out of the hospital bed. How are you feeling?'

A quick exchange of pleasantries, but a more polite courtesy than anything containing any genuine feeling, Toby thought.

'Recovery has been slow, but I guess I should be grateful I'm still alive.'

Toby wasn't sure how to respond to this. An awkward moment of silence ensued before Eric continued.

'It's nice here,' he said, looking around his surroundings.

'I like it,' Toby replied succinctly.

'Is this a regular thing for you?'

'I try to get here a couple of times during the week if I can. I find it quite cathartic, really.'

'Kind of like cleansing the soul?'

'Something like that.'

Eric looked like he was about to speak, but was interrupted by the Barista placing his drink on the table. Toby realised this was now going to be more than a quick and superficially affable exchange. He had spent years in somewhat uncomfortable situations, but that had been in a professional setting with scheduled appointments. This was different. This wasn't a professional setting. The meeting hadn't been prearranged, and Toby had an inkling he wouldn't be in control of the conversation. Though he felt at ease here, it could never provide him with the same feeling of security that his practice had. He missed that. He missed having his own space to sit and reflect, a safe place where he could feel vulnerable and just be himself in between clients. Whilst Toby was no longer in psychotherapy, the psychotherapist in him would remain, a feeling which grew as he sat studying Eric's body language. Eric thanked the young girl and turned towards Toby whilst taking a tentative sip out of his cup, which was emitting steam.

'You and I have a lot in common Toby,' he said with a grin which almost passed as a smile.

'Oh?'

'Both of us have had near-death experiences, both of us have been left with physical and emotional scars, and both of us have been fucked over by my wife.'

'I'm not so sure a car crash is comparable to attempted murder.'

'Perhaps not, but it nearly cost you your life all the same.'

'Your ordeal is still raw and possesses complexities many would not understand. It must have been incredibly difficult for you to process.'

'I don't frighten easily, Toby. As I said to you in the hospital, the hardest part was knowing my wife to whom I have given everything could hate me enough to want me dead.'

'I can't imagine how that must feel for you.'

On the surface Toby was empathic, but underneath, scepticism consumed him. He wanted to believe this was a chance meeting, but he'd been burned with Olivia in a similar fashion, and remained suspicious. There was no doubting Eric had been a victim. Perhaps he still was, but Toby believed he was also a perpetrator. What he didn't know, however, was the extent of this. Olivia, with seemingly nothing to gain, had warned Toby about her husband. Eric, with perhaps a lot to lose, had been very vociferous about Olivia's failings, her vindictiveness and her thirst for revenge. There was no getting away from the fact Olivia had lied. She was caught out, and Toby was taken aback when she happily taunted him with those lies, contrary to his expectations of a denial of some sort. But Olivia was in prison and Eric was a free man on his way to recovery. What could he possibly want with Toby? Perhaps this was simply a coincidence. Their houses were a little over ten minutes apart. It wasn't inconceivable that they could be in the same place at the same time. Still, something troubled Toby, and though he hadn't picked up on the signs with Olivia, when he had a hunch, he wasn't often wrong.

'I'm not gonna lie. It's been tough, but I'm trying to put the focus on Tyler. It distracts me from the reality of the situation. The emotional scars will take the longest to heal.'

Toby thought for a moment about how perfectly Eric was delivering this. He was saying all the right things, and that aroused his suspicion further. This all felt a little too contrived. Whatever Toby was thinking, he made a conscious effort not to show his hand to Eric. If Olivia had been truthful with him, he needed to exercise caution.

Revenge in Mind

'If you don't sample the latte here, you're missing out,' Toby said, changing direction.

'You got me. I'm a tea drinker,' Eric replied playfully, holding his hands up as if submitting.

Toby let out a muffled laugh.

'I could spend hours in here if I allowed myself to,' he replied.

'I wish I had the time to do the same. I'm just passing by on my way to a meeting in Springdale. I'm up there quite often,' Eric responded.

Toby felt a shiver inside. Eric had lied. Whilst you could get to Springdale this way, it wouldn't be the route you would take from Eric's house. More importantly, the main road you would use to get there was under construction. Anybody who knew the area or travelled that way regularly would know this and avoid it at all costs. Eric had slipped up, which confirmed Toby's suspicions. This wasn't a chance meeting. He had somehow known Toby would be here, or worse still, he had followed him. This stark realisation served up a bigger question. Why? What did Eric Stanton want with him? What made Toby so important to him that he felt the need to orchestrate a meeting and disguise it as coincidence? Toby felt cold as he relived the gym scene with Olivia, which he had discovered had also been staged. The difference was, with Olivia, he was oblivious and therefore able to act naturally without fear or trepidation. Here, he was acutely aware something was wrong and wasn't afforded that luxury. For self-preservation, his thoughts and his reactions needed to remain strangers to one another. He couldn't allow Eric to discover his doubt.

'It can't have been easy going back to work so soon after...'

Toby hesitated.

'It's okay, you can say it. The attack.'

'I'm sorry.'

'For what? You were the one who saved me, remember?'

Toby smiled. And this was genuine. He knew there was something deeply troubling about the man sitting opposite. Nevertheless, there were glimpses of sincerity and a pleasant manner you couldn't help but warm to. But Olivia had warned him about Eric's tendency to create a charming persona to draw people in. Toby imagined this would fool many people, but he was more experienced. He knew there was an ulterior motive for Eric being here. He just needed to establish what that was without jeopardising his safety. Right now, he didn't know what this man was capable of, and he had no intention of finding out either. Toby saw himself as a healer, not a fighter. If Eric became violent, there would only be one winner. Toby's most potent weapon was his mind. He was intelligent and had the ability to display calmness when feeling panic. His only aim now was to establish Eric Stanton's motives without putting himself at risk.

'I did whatever anybody else would have done in that situation.'

'Most people would have called the police.'

'I think unless you're faced with a situation like that, it is difficult to really say how you would react.'

'I admire your modesty. You risked everything to save a client. It cost you your career and nearly your freedom. Yet here you are still downplaying your bravery.'

'I think it was perhaps more instinctive than brave.'

Revenge in Mind

Eric Stanton stared at Toby for a moment, saying nothing. Toby wondered what he was thinking. He had tried desperately to get the balance between not being overly engaging, yet not appearing dismissive. Moving too far either way could be problematic. He didn't want to antagonise Eric, but he was also aware the more he talked, the more likely it would be he would say something which may put him in danger. Eric gave him a wry smile as he looked down into his cup, before lifting his head and glancing around the room.

'I like it here. The last time I was here was just before last Christmas. I had three of those berry coolers. Have you ever had one?'

Lie number two

Berry coolers were a seasonal drink, served throughout the spring and summer. They also happened to be Toby's drink of choice in the warmer climate. He expressed his disappointment when they were unexpectedly removed from the menu at the turn of autumn. Soon, they would be making their way back onto the menu, but at Christmas time, they would be a distant memory of the summer. If this had been planned meticulously by Eric, his research had been poor. It felt rushed. It wouldn't have taken much to cover his tracks, but he had now slipped up twice. Toby's heart was pounding as he now realised beyond doubt the person opposite was lying to his face. What added to his anxiety was he now knew Eric wanted something from him, and though he was unsure presently what that was, it was inevitable he was going to find out before he left his seat. Whatever

Toby was thinking, he didn't allow it to show. Instead, he told his own lie.

'I've never had that pleasure,' he said warmly, not wishing to alert Eric to his suspicion.

Eric reached over and placed his hands on Toby's arm in a friendly manner.

'You're missing out, old boy.'

Small talk. Toby had spent years with clients skirting around the actual issues, the reasons they were in therapy. Now Eric Stanton was doing the same thing. He had something to say; he was just building up to it. In another situation, Toby would have probed and asked the right questions. He had no interest in doing this here, mainly because part of him really didn't want to know Eric's agenda. He wondered whether Olivia had anything to do with this. He looked down at his watch, then his cup, which was now almost empty. He decided to force Eric's hand.

'I should be going. Nice to see you looking well,' Toby said, getting up to leave the table.

Eric grabbed his wrist and glared at him. He looked down at Eric's hand and then back into his eyes.

'I know you went to see Olivia.'

Toby had succeeded in pushing him into making his move. Eric had already lost his composure because this was no longer on his terms. Toby was in control, but that didn't make Eric any less dangerous, and what Toby was presenting on the surface was a far cry from what he was actually feeling. He sat back down in his chair as Eric relinquished the grip on his wrist. Toby remained silent. Allowing Eric to do the talking would provide him with time to contemplate his response and formulate a plan to remove himself from this situation.

'I went to see her. She told me all about your visit.'

'I had some questions for her,' Toby replied calmly.

'I know there was more to it than that.'

'Like what?'

'She said you talked about me.'

'Olivia mentioned you. I simply listened.'

'And what did she tell you?'

If he thinks you're suspicious of him, you're not safe. Don't be fooled by him, Toby.

Olivia's final words to Toby as he left the prison visiting area were playing on repeat in his head. Was this the Eric she had warned him about? Toby had glimpsed something he was unsure of when he had visited Eric in the hospital, but it was Olivia's words that had confirmed his unease. Suddenly the place felt warm and Toby was perspiring. Of course, this was nothing to do with the heat. His heart beat faster. Now overcome with panic, he was reminded of the last time he had felt this way. It had been in Eric's house. *That* night.

'Whatever's between you and Olivia has nothing to do with me.'

'I wish that were the case, but I know she has been filling your head with things about me. She took great delight in taunting me.'

For a moment, Toby sat quietly. Going toe to toe with Eric would not end well for him. Allowing himself to be drawn into an argument wasn't the way forward. He needed to outwit him. The way to do this was to deflect the attention away from himself and onto Olivia. He had no loyalty to her. He just needed to convince Eric they had a common enemy.

'Do you think Olivia got what she needed from you?'

'What do you mean?' Eric said, face screwed up in a manner that suggested he was becoming impatient.

'If, as you say, she took great pleasure in taunting you, could it be that she told you what she knew would elicit the very response she craved?'

'You mean she lied to me for some sick and perverse pleasure?'

'Perhaps.'

Eric studied him for a moment. Toby could see he had planted a seed of doubt, but he needed to remain cautious. There was no mistaking Eric had the potential to be dangerous. If there had been any doubt remaining as to the type of person Eric Stanton was, his lies had settled that doubt. He could forgive an unintentional oversight, he could forgive a memory lapse, but neither of these would serve as accurate descriptions. These were lies, lies told with intent and agenda. The part Toby hadn't yet figured out was what that agenda was.

'There's one question I've wanted to ask you since you came to visit me. Your reputation precedes you, and clearly, you're smart. How did you get taken in by her deception?' Eric asked, now relaxing back into his chair with a smile.

'We believe our clients. Our job isn't to speculate on what they're not telling us, it's to explore what they are.'

'How could you not have noticed?'

Revenge in Mind

'Perhaps the same way you didn't notice her resentment building towards the crescendo of an attempt on your life. I wasn't looking in that direction.'

Toby had landed a direct hit. He hadn't intended it in that way, but his reply had clearly rocked Eric. He scratched his forehead slowly, eyes squinted deep in thought.

'I guess we both got taken in, didn't we?'

'Things become much more obvious with hindsight,' Toby replied quietly.

'Why did you go to see her? After what she put you through, why would you go to see her?' Eric repeated.

'Maybe the same reason you went to see her,' Toby said hesitantly.

'Oh?'

'I'm assuming you were searching for answers?'

Eric smiled, more of a grin, really.

'Something like that.'

Toby sensed he was hiding something, but didn't want to push. The last thing he wanted to do was poke the bear or even rattle its cage. Whatever Eric wanted from him, it wasn't anything good. This had become clear the second Eric lied to him. He sat for a moment and wondered whether the man sitting opposite him was a psychopath. He certainly had the superficial charm, but Toby felt this masked a deeply manipulative individual. From his short time in the presence of Eric, coupled with what he had learned from Olivia, he seemed like he wanted to be in control, and Toby questioned whether he had any concern for others. What about Tyler, though? Was his son really his world, or simply a weapon to be used in his quest for revenge on his wife? He realised he didn't know enough about Eric to make a diagnosis like that and put the thought out of his mind...for now.

'Did you find them?'

'Did I find what?'

'The answers you were looking for from my darling wife.'

Toby smiled, but it felt forced. He wasn't sure where this line of questioning was leading and opted to stall for time whilst he carefully considered his answer.

'Did you?'

He had deflected the question. This was a technique he had often used in practice when his clients would ask him a question.

'Olivia is a complex and deeply flawed individual. It may be difficult to believe, but there were some memorable occasions. When things were good, they were great. Of course, that all changed the moment she plunged a knife into me, but I really loved her regardless of her demons. When I went to see her, I just wanted to look her in the eye and ask her why. I wanted to understand how she could want me dead after everything we had been through. Her husband, the father of her child. But no, I didn't get the answer I was looking for.'

Eric bowed his head, but Toby couldn't feel any sympathy. He had been asked a closed question and had elaborated before he answered. This symbolised deception. Upon bowing his head, he had looked down to the right, which Toby knew was a search for emotion. This didn't come naturally to him; it was all too forced, but Toby would play the game.

Revenge in Mind

'When I came to visit you in the hospital, you asked me if I thought Olivia was capable of doing what she did, but you never told me whether you did.'

'Whether I thought she was capable of murder? No,' he laughed dismissively.

'You said she had a temper. Did you fear her?'

'Is this therapy or an interrogation?' Eric replied, grinning.

Toby smiled.

'Neither. I apologise if I've made you feel uncomfortable.'

Eric looked up at Toby, picked up his cup to take a drink and then thought better of it, placing it back down on the table.

'Olivia had a temper, but never for a moment did I fear for my physical wellbeing. I was more concerned with her acidic tongue damaging my reputation.'

Lie number 3

When Toby had been to see him in the hospital, Eric had described locking himself in the bathroom to escape Olivia's anger. He had been very specific about calling the police at that moment. Mike Thomas had verified this. Was this simply a case of being careless, or had he underestimated Toby? What compounded the lie was the subtle chin thrust, perhaps involuntarily. Toby had spent years studying body language and knew this to be a sign of pride or strength. Eric was presenting an alpha male persona, which was confusing, as he had shown glimpses of vulnerability when the two had last met. Toby was almost certain the pretence masked an insecurity, a fear of some sort, but was still trying to ascertain what that fear was.

He didn't believe it to be wholly about reputation, but Eric was protecting something.

'Olivia's decision to come and see you has always puzzled me. She never struck me as someone who needed therapy because she was never depressed. She had everything.'

'There are many reasons people attend therapy. Depression is just one of them.'

'It was never about that though, was it?'

'About what?' Toby replied inquisitively.

'Therapy. She didn't need a therapist. She needed an alibi. She used you. That must hurt.'

Toby couldn't determine whether Eric was gloating or trying to get him on side by creating a common enemy. If Eric vilified Olivia, if he got Toby looking in her direction, then he took the attention away from himself. Eric's intention was becoming clearer. He was trying to build a rapport with Toby to quash any suspicions he may have of him. This may have been more successful had he not lied several times during the short time they had spent together in the coffeehouse. Any suspicions Toby had had only grown, but he had one advantage…Eric didn't know his lies had been noticed.

'If clients come to therapy to lie, that's their thing. It doesn't affect me.'

'Did being arrested for attempted murder and losing your career affect you?'

Eric had struck a low blow. Toby, however, didn't see this as a personal attack. He was simply trying to discredit Olivia. Intensifying Toby's feelings of anger and resentment towards her would mean he was less likely to have any dealings with her and more likely to doubt any disparaging comments she had made about her husband. Strangely, he found himself feeling impressed with Eric's efforts, but Toby was one step ahead of him. Even before he had grabbed his wrist, Eric had already given away his intentions. He just hadn't realised it.

'It was a tough time for me, but the arrest didn't end my career.'

'Oh?' Eric said, somewhat intrigued.

'Clients can choose to lie and that's on them, but how I respond is on me. I crossed lines in that profession that should never be crossed, regardless of my intent or the outcome.'

'Crossing those boundaries saved my life.'

Toby smiled.

'I often wonder whether part of me consciously knew I was choosing between my career and saving a life.'

'You sacrificed your career for a stranger, yet there are some who know me who would gladly have let me die.'

Toby wasn't sure where this was going, but he suspected Eric was now manoeuvring towards the real reason he was here. He wasn't simply in the mood for sharing; there was a motive hidden away. Toby was in complete control of the conversation now, yet Eric remained oblivious to this. He knew Eric would no doubt have enemies, but twisting the knife and antagonising him would serve no purpose.

'Olivia?'

Eric smiled and lowered his head for a moment. He tapped his fingers on the table. Toby could see he was frustrated, searching desperately for a way to contain it.

'When I went to see Olivia, she told me you were on to me. She took great pleasure in detailing all the negative things she had told you about me. She smiled sadistically as she told me you now knew I was a dangerous man.'

He paused, grinning, as though waiting for a response. Toby felt an icy shiver at the base of his spine and fought to keep his composure. Whatever he was feeling, he couldn't let it show.

'Olivia spent several months creating a false narrative, manipulating me. What makes you think anything she told me was met with anything other than scepticism?'

'Then why visit her?'

He was baiting Toby, waiting for him to slip up.

'I went to prove something to myself. The experience with Olivia made me question my practice, my attention to detail, my ability to recognise verbal and non-verbal inconsistencies. It wasn't about you; it wasn't even about Olivia…it was about me.'

Eric's expression left Toby uncertain if he was sceptical or deep in thought, crafting his own reply.

'A few nights back, somebody was asking after me. An unsavoury character, I hear. He beat a few lads up I know. Hospitalised one of them.'

He noticed something in Eric he hadn't done so previously. He was scared. Looking closely at him now, it was clear he hadn't been sleeping. But what did any of this have to do with Toby?

'Were you behind it?' Eric asked abruptly.

Toby was unable to hide the surprise. He had spent years dedicating his life to helping others. He had risked his career to save Eric's life. Toby's weapon of choice was his intellect, nothing more.

'I'm not sure how to even answer. Why would you think I would be behind something like that? What makes you think I'm even capable of something like that?'

He was mindful not to sound too defensive. He really didn't want to anger Eric, but clearly, Eric had angered somebody.

'The obvious choice was Olivia, but when I looked her in the eye and asked her, she had a genuine look of surprise on her face. That bitch was actually telling the truth for once. Then she pointed me in your direction.'

Toby shrugged his shoulders, unable to manage a reply. Eric grabbed his hand, pulled him closer, and squeezed tightly.

'Listen here you failed shrink. Be very careful about digging into the past. You might find something you really wish you hadn't.'

Toby grimaced, but this only motivated Eric to squeeze harder. As he let go, he stood up from his seat, finished his drink and walked around the table to Toby, placing his hand firmly on his shoulder.

'Take this as a warning. Call off your goons and stop digging.'

At that, Eric Stanton was gone. Toby exhaled a long, drawn-out breath. He was visibly shaken but no longer needed to disguise it. Olivia had been right. Toby had put a target on his own back, but he wasn't sure how. What made Eric think Toby was looking into him? Why would Toby want to look into him? They had no relationship and no link other than Olivia. They had met by chance and had been nothing more than passing acquaintances. That had now changed. Eric had changed it the second he tracked him down for a confrontation. Until that moment, Toby had shown no interest in him, but whatever was happening with Eric, he had now involved Toby. As he rose slowly from his seat, intrusive thoughts overwhelmed him, but once they had dissipated, one thought, one sentence remained.

Be very careful about digging into the past. You might find something you really wish you hadn't.

What had Eric meant? The words echoed in his head for the rest of the evening. Regardless of the clement weather, Toby went to sleep feeling cold that night. He was troubled and wondered what he had got himself into. He thought his ordeal with the Stanton's was over, but as he turned over next to a sleeping Beth and closed his eyes, he questioned whether what had started with Olivia would ultimately end with Eric.

{ 10 }

It had been a few weeks since Georgina Sampson had arrived at the Reynolds' residence. She felt Beth had thawed a little, but still remained cautious of her. George had been mindful of encroaching on their space, so had spent a good part of her time in her own room, in her own company. This had provided her with a little more thinking time than she would have liked. They had spoken about her situation, but she had only told them what she wanted them to know. It was best that way. As far as they knew, she had fallen on hard times after her relationship had ended, and as a result, been made homeless. After seeing Toby in the news, she had reached out to him. Toby had sensed there was something more to her story. He was a very astute individual, and whilst in time she knew she would have to answer his questions, for now, she felt sure she had thrown him off the scent. Beth, she couldn't read. Toby was smart, but she got the impression he would be easier to win over than Beth. She came across as a strong and confident woman who knew what she wanted. She had a kind and caring nature, but George had already deduced that if you hurt those close to her, Beth Reynolds could make a powerful enemy. George needed allies, not enemies. Besides, she had no reason to put Beth's temperament to the test. They had been kind to her and taken her in whilst she found her feet again. George had been carrying a deep-seated anger for some time, but none of this was directed at Toby or Beth. She was very clear about what she needed to do, and it didn't involve them, not directly anyway.

As she strolled through the quiet town, George noticed the sudden change in temperature, which felt disappointing for this time of year. It felt more like autumn than spring. She was suddenly reminded of Halloween. She enjoyed Halloween. In the past, the visitors who had been committed enough to walk the somewhat daunting length of the drive to chance the reward at the end had brought a smile to her face. A smile which was otherwise absent. *He* had always put on a show with jokes and excessive amounts of sweets. He could do that. She, of course, had been only too aware of the real person lurking underneath the charm and charisma. But for that one evening, she could pretend her life was normal. Though Halloween was several months and two seasons away, the very thought of it made her smile. She stopped briefly to absorb her surroundings. It was a beautiful town. She could see the appeal and now understood why Beth and Toby chose to settle close by. It was a quaint and kind of sleepy town, far removed from the hustle and bustle you would experience in the city. She looked down at her watch. Just after two o'clock, but it felt a lot later. The wind was now beginning to pick up and the cool snap made it feel more like October than March. As she walked past the tall monument in the middle of the square, which had a handful of quirky shops surrounding it, a young couple passed her, holding hands. The smiles on their faces and the way she giggled as he pulled her in for a kiss highlighted their love for one another. This wasn't a show, it was genuine, and George couldn't help but feel a deep sadness. She hadn't experienced that kind of affection in many years. There had been only one person she had shared such moments with and who had made her feel so special, and that was Toby. As she walked by a shop window, she caught a glimpse of her reflection. For a moment, she saw an effervescent and carefree teenager staring back at her, but something was missing. The smile had gone and George couldn't figure out whether she looked hurt or angry. In a fleeting moment, she noticed her reflection shaking its head in disbelief, wondering how she had lost her spark and transformed into a faded version of her teenage self. George felt a tear roll down her cheek. She had failed the young girl, and this saddened her. The girl from the past staring back at her had a sweet naivety. She was full of hope and in love. Now, she was none of those things. She had been hardened to the disappointments in life. Realism had taken the place of hope, and love was something other people had. There had only been one true love in her life, but none of that mattered now. Suddenly, the reflection was gone and staring back at her was an almost unrecognisable, troubled figure. She closed her eyes and wondered how she had managed to get so lost, but didn't allow herself to dwell on this thought. There was no place for self-pity. This would show weakness. There would be time to reflect on her life choices, but right now, she needed to have a clear head devoid of sentiment and nostalgia. As she turned to continue her leisurely stroll, she caught sight of something out of the corner of her eye which stopped her in her tracks. Turning around sharply, gasping in anticipation as she did so, George saw nothing. She wasn't jumpy, but she was certainly cautious. She had been streetwise from a young age, and her experience in adulthood had only enhanced this. Throughout the years, her suspicion of others had intensified. Once able to offer trust readily, she was now wary of anybody new she came into contact with. She slowly made her way towards the card shop, which was situated in the far corner of the square. It wasn't a special occasion, but she had wanted to thank Toby and Beth for their hospitality and felt a card would be a pleasant touch without the risk of being over-familiar. She was mindful she didn't know Beth, and Toby was no longer the youthful teenager she had known in what seemed like another life. They had been kind and though they had not directly suggested such a thing, would welcome a household with just the two of them again. George was mindful of outstaying her welcome, but at this moment in time, she had nowhere else to go. In fact, she had made no future plans at all. Well, not really anyway. She hadn't spent long in the card shop; sentiment hadn't been her priority. As she exited, she glanced up at the sky and noticed it suddenly looked a little darker. The branches of the trees were starting to sway gently in the steady breeze. It sounded quite cathartic. Her bus stop was around a ten-minute walk away. She walked briskly to avoid the inevitable shower that was looming. As she moved out of the square and onto the road, George heard a sound behind her. She turned around quickly but was met with an eerie quietness. She picked up the pace, almost breaking into a jog. The road was desolate, and she didn't like that. There were buildings, which meant side alleys. There were plenty of places for somebody to hide and stay unseen if they wished to do so. She felt anxious and questioned the bout of paranoia which had overcome her. Suddenly she heard what sounded like a dustbin rattling. Cats, she thought. Hoped more like. She was fearful of turning around and opted to keep moving. She could find no logical explanation for why somebody would be following her. Her heart rate increased, and she now had no inclination to hang around. Glancing round, she thought she had caught sight of a shadow lurking in the background. She began to run. An old lady making her way slowly down the opposite side of the road brought a momentary sense of relief to her. She was grateful for the company. That relief was transient as she hurried past and found herself once again alone. The wind was picking up, and every sound of a shaking branch sounded like footsteps. Every shadow cast looked like a dark figure. The last time she had felt this vulnerable had been with *him*. The sound of screeching brakes in a passing car did nothing to ease her increasing levels of anxiety. What had begun as a slight unease was now transitioning into something more resembling a panic attack. George now faced a dilemma. She needed to calm herself down, but she was in flight mode, and the very thought of stopping filled her with more dread. Now convinced somebody was stalking her, George broke into a sprint, heart beating at a dangerous level, deep breaths failing her. She thought about calling Toby but decided against it. She wondered whether the bus stop would provide any reprieve, or whether she would simply become an easy target in an open space. She prayed there would be somebody, anybody, to prevent her from feeling so isolated, so vulnerable. Recognising she was now moving into a more populated area, she slowed down a little. As she battled to regain an element of composure, she saw a figure walking towards her, which she could just about deduce was a man. He was wearing dark clothing and a cap. A scarf covered his face. As he approached her, he slowed down and stared directly into her eyes. He then began to shake his head slowly and put his finger to his lips. He said nothing, but his message had been clear. He wanted her silence. Her heart rate spiked as she tried to process not what she had seen, but who. It couldn't be, could it? It had been over ten years since she had laid eyes on him. Not long enough, she thought. She had known one day she would come face to face with him again, hoped really, but on her terms and in her time. How had he found her? More importantly, what threat did he feel she posed to him? As she watched him fade into the background, still shaking, she pulled out her phone and stared at it for a moment before making the call. As she hung up, she sat down on the kerb, head in hands, wondering whether she had the strength to see this through. Though the street had become a little busier, Georgina Sampson had never felt so alone.

Toby had awoken that morning feeling under the weather. This was unusual for him as he rarely got sick, so when he wasn't up before her having his obligatory morning coffee, Beth knew something was wrong. It was now just after nine, and he had finally opened his eyes for long enough to hold a brief conversation with Beth, though he wasn't sure how much sense he had made. He felt like his head was on the verge of exploding and had little energy. Beth placed a hand on his forehead before offering him a sympathetic smile.

'You're burning up.'

'I'll be ok, I just need a hot shower to get me going.'

'Stoicism or stubbornness?' she teased.

Toby looked at her, but could only manage a faint smile. He realised there was a third option Beth had omitted, and that was stupidity. There was no justifiable reason for Toby to force himself out of bed. He groaned as he struggled to pull himself up.

'My muscles ache,' he winced.

'Perhaps a soak in the bath?'

Toby nodded as he made his way slowly over to the bathroom, Beth at his side. As he lay there, now in solitude, he thought about the last year of his life. He regretted meeting Olivia Stanton, but more so his decision to drive to her house that night. The problem, however, was that whilst he regretted it, he knew the regret was based solely on the outcome. If he had that decision again, in those set of circumstances, he would likely make the same choice. That was one of the main reasons he knew he could no longer practice psychotherapy. He hadn't simply lost his confidence in himself; he had also lost trust. It was no longer simply about Olivia. It was about George. It was about Eric. There were still missing parts of the jigsaw for Toby. Why had Eric tracked him down and felt the need to intimidate him? What did he fear Toby would uncover? Then there was George, the woman who, as a teenager, had been the love of his life. She had suddenly reappeared after over twenty years with no warning or proper explanation. Worryingly, Eric's and George's actions to a degree hadn't been too dissimilar. Both had made a concerted effort to track him down, both had caught him off guard, and both had left him feeling apprehensive, though for different reasons. He wondered whether his illness was a sign of everything catching up on him, but didn't have time to ruminate as his phone, which had been placed on the windowsill above his head, vibrated vigorously. He reached over the side of the bath and searched around for a towel to dry his hands on before picking it up. A message from an unknown number.

SHE'S NOT SAFE, HE WON'T STOP

Toby fell cold, and in an instant, he was reliving the last message that had induced this reaction. His thoughts weren't with the subject, but with the sender. He felt the colour drain from his cheeks as he recalled the traumatic experience of that fateful day when he had ended up at a grizzly crime scene. He could once again smell the blood that had come from Eric Stanton, an amount that wouldn't have looked out of place in an exsanguination process. He could almost taste the fear he had felt when faced with Olivia Stanton walking casually towards him, hand raised, carrying a large, blood-soaked knife. He could see the panic, hear the chaos. Rationalisation was suddenly out of reach. Though submerged in warm water, he felt his body shivering. He thought about calling out to Beth, remembering the promise he had made to her, but decided against it. He needed to get things clear in his own head first. Perhaps it was the wrong number? The message was succinct and didn't hold any meaning to him, so it was viable he wasn't the intended recipient. Toby knew deep down, however, that this explanation was one of hope rather than expectation. With George back in his life, coupled with a less-than-pleasant encounter with Eric Stanton, it would all be too coincidental. Something wasn't right. He again felt on the periphery, like there was a joke he wasn't in on. He lay there for a moment, eyes firmly planted on the message in front of him. If he was expecting any sort of revelation, he would be sadly disappointed. Against his better judgment, and fighting every rational thought he had, he submitted to his curiosity and replied to the message.

'And you have no idea who this could have come from?' Beth asked, pouring Toby a coffee as they sat at the breakfast bar.

Toby, now dressed, though still looking fatigued, didn't answer as he stared up at the ceiling.

'Toby?'

'Huh? Sorry I was just thinking,' he replied, feigning a smile, which he knew Beth would see right through.

'Call Mike?'

'I'm not so sure a vague text message is high on the police's agenda.'

'It feels quite specific to me.'

'Perhaps.'

'Why are you so reluctant to speak to the police about this?'

He looked up at her and stared, eyes wide and bulging.

'My only previous experience with the police was far from pleasant. Do you know what it's like to be viewed as a common criminal, a liar, a co-conspirator? Do you know how it feels to have every answer scrutinised, to have your words twisted so much that you begin to doubt your own truth? In therapy we call that gaslighting, but in the interview room, it's a technique.

I looked to Mike, Beth, I looked to him, and do you know what I saw?'

Beth shook her head.

'I saw an officer of the law. I saw the way he looked at me. I witnessed the way he allowed his colleague to cast doubt on my integrity, to hound me to breaking point. He just watched Beth. He just watched.'

'Oh Toby, I can't imagine how hard that must have been, but you better than most know about professional integrity. I'm sure it can't have been easy for him, and perhaps there was a reason he was there in the interview room with you.'

'What do you mean?'

'Toby, whether with strangers or people known to them, the police will have a process to follow. He has to be seen to be doing the right thing, but I wonder whether he ever doubted your innocence.'

'You think he was there to protect me?'

'I'm just saying he was more senior than the officer who led the investigation, yet he was still in the room with you. Why was that? Besides, you said he came to see you off the record to talk to you.'

Toby looked up at her and smiled. This time, the smile was genuine. Beth walked over and placed her arms around him, squeezing tightly.

'I still associate the police with the Olivia Stanton ordeal. I was on the wrong side of their questioning and treated like a perpetrator. I guess I'm struggling to trust that they would ever see me as a witness, or even a victim.'

'Victim?'

Toby looked away from her.

'Toby, why would you be a victim? What are you not telling me?'

There was an uncomfortable silence before Toby finally replied.

'It was just a figure of speech. My trust in them was greatly diminished that day, and I'm hesitant to reach out to them again.'

He took no pleasure in lying to Beth. He knew he was doing it to protect her, but he also knew how she would feel if she found out. The truth was, he didn't know what Eric Stanton wanted with him, and whilst he was trying to figure that out, it was best to keep Beth away from it.

'Toby?'

He was thinking about how he could quickly change the direction of the conversation. He didn't want to continue to lie to Beth. He needed to settle her intrigue and throw her off the scent.

'There are two key questions here. Firstly, who sent the message, and secondly, who's in danger?'

'There's a third,' Beth interrupted.

Toby looked up at her curiously.

'Why?'

'Why what?' he replied, feeling somewhat confused.

'Why you? Somehow, you're linked to both people.'

'Where would I even begin with that?'

'You're the therapist,' she replied with a warm smile.

'Was, and I don't see how that would help me anyway,' Toby replied with an air of frustration.

'People and behaviour, that's your area. What type of person sends cryptic messages?'

Toby looked down at the floor, deep in concentration. As his mouth slowly fell open, he raised his head and looked to each side of Beth before settling his eyes on her.

'One who wants to conceal their identity. One who enjoys watching people agonise over deciphering something cryptic. More importantly, one who likes to be in control.'

Beth's smile faded and Toby knew in that moment they were both thinking the same thing.

'Olivia Stanton?'

'On the one hand, it makes little sense, however, on the other, it makes perfect sense. But that still leaves us with the question of who's in danger?'

'And where do you fit into this?'

'That's the part I'm struggling with. Olivia and I have no mutual friends or acquaintances that I know of.'

'Well, if this is her work, clearly she knows something you don't,' Beth said with a hint of anger having made its way into her voice.

'There is another option we haven't considered.'

'What's that?'

'Olivia is a very manipulative and vengeful woman. When I called the police at the house, I brought her world crashing down around her. Maybe this is her way of showing she can still get at me. Maybe this is part of her revenge.'

'If you ignore this, and it isn't a game, what then?'

Before Toby could answer, his phone lit up on the kitchen unit as a call came through. Moving out of the room, he answered. Moments later, he returned hurriedly to the kitchen, where Beth was waiting anxiously.

'I think I've just figured out another part of this puzzle,' he said before collecting his car keys, kissing Beth on the cheek, and dashing out of the door.

Beth returned to the living room with coffees for the three of them. She placed one of them on the table at the side of George and put her hand on her shoulder affectionately. George looked up and smiled at her, but it was clear to Toby that the smile was a mask.

'And you didn't get a look at his face at all?' Toby asked tentatively.

'His face and head were covered. I could scarcely see his eyes.'

'Would you be able to describe him to the police?' Beth asked so quietly it was little more than a whisper.

'I think he'd been following me for a while, but I only saw him briefly. It all happened so fast.'

Toby exchanged a glance with Beth, who was now positioned in the doorway behind George. Beth was shaking her head slowly and Toby realised she was dissuading him from mentioning the message. As far as George was concerned, this could still be a random incident, or even a case of mistaken identity. Both he and Beth knew differently, but there was no need to make this any harder for George right now. She needed to feel safe and take some time to process her ordeal. That would be much more difficult if she thought she had been specifically targeted. Beth gestured to Toby, and he followed her out into the kitchen.

'She's not safe here Toby.'

'I know, but how do we tell her that without panicking her?'

Beth shrugged her shoulders and looked up at the ceiling. Toby grabbed her hand and looked directly into her eyes.

'There's something I don't think we've considered.'

'What's that?' she asked with a look which suggested she was afraid to hear the answer.

'If we are correct in our assumption that Olivia Stanton sent the message, and today is more than a mere coincidence, then there is some sort of connection between Olivia Stanton and George.'

Beth stood motionless. There was a moment's silence, broken only by George entering the kitchen. Toby knew the only way to get George to safety, the only way to make her realise the severity of the situation, was to tell her about the message.

'George, I'm not sure it's safe for you to be here at the moment.'

She looked at him, offended.

'Not safe?'

'I received a text message from an anonymous number and I believe it was about you.'

'I don't understand. A text message?'

Toby was trying to minimise what he shared with her. He had no reason to mention Olivia Stanton right now, as he didn't fully understand what was going on himself. He didn't want to panic her unnecessarily, but his concern was enough that he wanted to move her to a safe place. Olivia knew where he lived and somebody had tracked George. It wouldn't be long before that link was made if it hadn't been already. Beth, sensing George's resistance, interjected.

'George, Toby received a message today warning him that somebody was in danger. We have reason to believe that someone is you, and naturally, we want to keep you safe.'

'Why do you think it's me?'

'You just have to trust us right now,' Beth replied reassuringly.

'I have a friend who lives on a farm out of town. You'll be safe there until we can figure out who's behind this,' Toby added.

'Jack?' Beth asked cautiously.

Before Toby could answer, George interrupted with her own question.

'If you're that concerned I'm in danger, why are we not involving the police?'

Toby felt Beth looking at him with expectation. Investigative work wasn't his area of expertise; none of this was, yet something was holding him back from involving the police. He wanted to believe this was because of his previous experience with them, but deep down, he knew this was just a smokescreen. The real reason was he was convinced that Olivia Stanton was behind this. The difficulty he was having was finding the link between Olivia and George. There was also the possibility, of course, that George wasn't the intended target, and that had just been a coincidence. If not George, who though? He suddenly felt cold at the realisation that the only other person close to him was Beth. What if he had this wrong and George wasn't the one in danger? What if Olivia's revenge came in the form of hurting the person closest to him? Beth grabbed his hand and squeezed it.

'Would you excuse us for one moment, George?' she said, pulling Toby into the dining room and closing the door.

'It's a valid question, Toby. You need to call Mike,' Beth said calmly.

'I think the message came from Olivia.'

'And?' Beth replied, now in a much sharper tone.

Toby stared at her for a moment.

'Oh Toby, you're not?'

'I think I can reach her.'

'Do you not see the control that woman has over you? She did it as a client and now she's doing it as an inmate. Why do you have a blind spot when it comes to Olivia Stanton?'

Toby looked down at the floor and let out a long and exasperated breath. He looked back up and met Beth's eyes. He flashed her a forced tentative smile and took her by the hand.

'Olivia Stanton took more from me than you'll ever know, but the one thing she will never take from me is who I am as a person. I've worked with perpetrators before and I don't regret offering help to anybody. Whilst I can't disclose the intricacies of the case, Olivia, in her own right, is also a victim. Though I regret meeting her, I don't hate her for what she did. I feel saddened thinking about what she must have endured to be pushed to that moment.'

'You're excusing what she did?'

'I'm explaining it. There's a difference.'

'Toby, you have nothing to prove.'

'What do you mean?'

'This is about you proving you can figure out the encrypted messages and beat her at her own games.'

'It's not about that, Beth. Remember, the message was a warning, not a threat.'

He had lied. Beth was right. He was actively choosing not to involve the police because Olivia Stanton had previously beaten him, and he didn't want others to think he couldn't outsmart her.

'But it could simply be a game to show she is still in control. Maybe this is her way of feeling like she is needed, like she still has relevance.'

'Quite the psychotherapist, aren't you?' he smiled, breaking the tension.

Beth smiled at him and took his hand.

'Why Jack?'

'Why not Jack?'

She frowned at him.

'He has no link to George or Olivia. His farm is out of the way and he is more equipped to protect her than we are. His place is secure and Jack knows how to handle himself should trouble find him.'

'Toby, none of this feels right, but I trust you. However, if we haven't figured this out after you visit Olivia, I'm calling Mike, okay?'

Toby nodded. He knew once Beth had decided on something, persuasion was futile. He held out his arms, and they embraced one another. That's the way they stayed until George opened the door and interrupted them. Her eyes oscillated between Toby and Beth as a worried look spread across her face. Toby could see she was frightened and needed reassurance. It was the same frightened look he had seen in her all those years ago, and it still had the same effect on him. He paused momentarily as memories of their time together came flooding back. He had glimpsed that teenage girl and with it had been reminded just how much he had cared for her. He knew he had to protect her at all costs and could muster only an anxious smile as he wondered who and what he was protecting her from. He took a deep breath, let go of Beth's hand and placed his hands on George's shoulders, looking her firmly in the eye.

'We leave tonight.'

{ 11 }

'Jack, it's Toby.'

'Here was me thinking you'd lost my number. How've you been?'

'I'm sorry I haven't been in touch for a while. I've had a lot going on,' Toby replied, ignoring Jack's question. 'I need your help.'

'Anything for you, buddy.'

'You might want to reign in the enthusiasm until you hear what I'm asking of you.'

'I'm flattered Toby, but you're married and I have to say, I'm just not into you in that way,' Jack said, unable to hold his laughter. Humour was his mask and Toby knew he was anxious about where the conversation may be heading.

'Do you remember me telling you about Georgina Sampson, the girl I dated back when I was at college?'

'George?'

'That's the one. I think she may be in trouble.'

'What kind of trouble? Have you spoken to her?'

'She's at our house.'

'Holy shit Toby, does Beth know about your history with her?'

'Yes, I've never hidden anything from her. Listen, Jack, I believe she's in danger. I don't have time to explain right now, but I need to get her somewhere safe.'

'Toby, what the hell happened to your peaceful existence?' Jack said with a nervous laugh.

Jack wasn't stupid, and he wasn't naïve. He knew where the conversation was going, but for some reason was delaying it from getting there.

'Can she come and stay with you for a little while?'

'What makes you think she would be any safer here?'

'You're out of the way. You have good security, but most importantly, you have no link to Olivia Stanton or George.'

'Olivia Stanton? What's she got to do with this?'

'I don't have time to explain that either. I just need you to trust me.'

'You're asking a lot here.'

'I know, but you're one of the few people I trust these days.'

The line fell quiet.

'Jack?'

'Still here.'

Jack's hesitance concerned Toby, as he had never experienced this resistance from him before. Jack was dependable and had never failed Toby, but there was a very apparent reluctance here.

'Jack, what is it?'

Silence greeted Toby.

'Come on, talk to me. What's going on?'

After a few deep breaths, Jack replied.

Revenge in Mind

'A few years ago I was seeing a girl, Caitlin. I fell pretty hard pretty quickly, mainly because I thought I could save her. She'd fallen in with the wrong people, had wronged those people, and ultimately her enemies became my enemies.'

'I'm sorry, I had no idea.'

'I didn't tell anybody. I felt embarrassed.'

'Why would you feel embarrassed?'

'I couldn't protect her, Toby. These people came looking for her and I was outnumbered. They beat us both badly. When I woke up, she was gone, and I never heard from her again.'

Toby moved the phone away from his ear and dropped his head. Jack was a close friend, and he'd been unaware of just how much he had suffered. He felt an anger surging through his body but couldn't determine whether it was his own pain or Jack's he was feeling.

'I'm so sorry. I don't know what to say. Did you report her missing?'

'These aren't the type of people you go to the police about. I tried searching for her, asked around a little, but people don't wanna talk in those situations. I guess I convinced myself she'd gone back to that life and didn't want to be found, but...' HIs voice tailed off.

'But what?'

'A few weeks later, her body washed up a few miles down the river.'

'Jesus Jack, why didn't you tell me?'

'What could you have done?'

'I could have been there for you. It's what friends do, right?'

He was now sensing the anger rising, but he knew this stemmed from the pain he was feeling at knowing somebody close to him had been through an unthinkable ordeal, and he had been oblivious to it. Jack ignored his question.

'So, you see, the reason I'm hesitant is because the last person I took in to protect wound up dead. I can't go through that again.'

'Her death isn't on you. You need to let the guilt go.'

'You think it was on her? We all make poor choices. Remember Olivia Stanton? Nobody deserves to pay for their mistakes with their life.'

Toby recoiled, shocked at Jack's words. This was a side of his friend he'd never seen before. He had dealt Toby a low blow mentioning Olivia's name, but Toby knew the origin of his anger was a deeply entrenched pain, and the last thing he wanted to do was to add to that.

'I'm sorry Toby, I didn't mean that.'

'I can't believe you went through this on your own and held onto it for so long.'

'Don't feel guilty Tobes, you're a psychotherapist, not a psychic,' he laughed.

Toby couldn't help but snigger as the momentary tension was broken. But this still left him with a dilemma…George. They still needed a place for her to lie low, and if not Jack's, where?

'You're right, I need to let go of this guilt, and I can't turn my back on you.'

'Jack…'

'It's fine. Bring her here if you think she'll be safer.'

*This doesn't feel right, Jack. You have to know that if I'd have known...'

'You'd never have called. I know. That's what I love about you, always looking out for others. Now let somebody else return the favour. I'll be expecting you.'

As Jack hung up, Toby was left staring at the phone. Walking back into the dining room, he sensed an atmosphere and felt certain he'd interrupted something. There had been a palpable tension between Beth and George since her arrival, but he had hoped things would clear. He felt guilty at the thought that George's presence at Jack's would be beneficial on more than one level.

'What did Jack say?' She asked this calmly, but Toby felt like this had been a concerted effort to deflect any animosity in the room.

'More than I expected,' Toby muttered, hoping nobody had heard him.

Beth looked at him quizzically.

'Toby?'

'We need to leave,' he replied.

A few minutes later, George and he departed for Jack's. As he closed the door to the house, he wondered whether he had, in fact, just opened another door for George to come back into his life.

{ 12 }

The steady pace at which Toby drove didn't reflect his frenzied state of mind. Inside, he was panicked and way beyond his comfort zone. He wasn't a detective; he wasn't a fighter; he wasn't even a psychotherapist. Then he paused. What was he? When he'd ceased practising, he had felt like he'd lost a large part of his identity, something he was still struggling to come to terms with. He looked over at his companion, not just his companion, but his past. A past that had somehow made its way into his present. There was a time when merely being in Georgina Sampson's presence would have set his pulse racing. His pulse was racing now but for very different reasons. She was an old flame, but he still cared. He'd never stopped, really. She was no longer that vulnerable young girl, but Toby sensed there was still a vulnerability about her. He just didn't know how deep this ran.

'Toby, what's going on?' she asked tentatively.

Toby's face had given him away. He'd been unable to hide his fear.

'I don't know, but something just doesn't feel right, and it's safer if you're out of the way for now.'

'Who's Jack?'

Revenge in Mind

Toby smiled as he thought about the most appropriate way to describe Jack.

'Jack's one of my closest friends. I'd trust him with my life. His place is secure and out of the way.'

'How long have you known him?'

'Since we were young,' Toby answered, only just realising he had never mentioned Jack to George during their relationship.

'You never mentioned him.'

'I was just thinking that same thing.'

'I think that's really sweet.'

'What?'

'The fact you were so attentive towards me, you didn't feel the need to really talk about any other aspect of your life.' She smiled at him. 'Aside from your mum, of course,' she added.

Toby's smile waned as the thought of his mother entered his mind.

'How is she, by the way?'

'You didn't hear?'

George shook her head slowly.

'She died when I was at university.'

'Oh Toby, I'm so sorry. What...?' she stuttered.

'She took her own life,' he replied sullenly.

George placed her hand on his and squeezed it tightly.

'I thought about calling you.'

George looked up at him.

'The night I found out, I wanted to call you. You were the one person I desperately wanted to turn to. I needed you, but I just couldn't.'

'Why not?' she asked softly, still holding his hand.

'I was worried it would have made things awkward between us. We hadn't spoken in a while and I didn't know how you'd react.'

'I would have been there for you, Toby. I've always been there for you.'

She let go of his hand, but didn't drop her gaze. As Toby glanced across, he could see something in her eyes. It was hurt, but he believed there was resentment sitting underneath it. He had always maintained their break-up had been mutual, but there had been that niggling feeling that George hadn't wanted it. Her recent revelation about the pregnancy had rocked him but had confirmed his suspicions that she had pushed him away for a reason.

'I would have been there for you,' she repeated now in a softer voice.

Instead of responding, Toby simply smiled, as if trying to calm the situation before it could escalate. There was silence for the next few minutes, with only the quiet humming of the engine in the background.

'I loved your mum,' George finally managed.

'She thought the world of you, you know.'

'Really?'

'Really. She was upset when our relationship ended. She always thought we'd get married.'

'That makes two of us.'

As Toby looked across at the first person he had ever loved, he could see a genuine sadness in her eyes.

'George, my college days were some of the best days of my life. That was because of you. A relationship ending doesn't detract from what it was. I look back on that time with fondness, not regret.'

'I wish I could have been there for you.'

'I know, but I closed myself off from everybody, even my father ultimately.'

'You know, there were so many times I thought about contacting you.'

Toby briefly turned to face her, but with thoughts of his late mother at the forefront of his mind, struggled to raise a smile. He hadn't had much chance to contemplate how the conversation with George would unfold during the trip to Jack's. One thing he had known was that it would be inevitable that any pleasantries would be merely a precursor to a more profound conversation, which would almost certainly involve reminiscing about the past.

'Toby, I don't know what's happening, but I need you to know I would never willingly put you in danger.'

He looked over at her and grinned.

'Don't worry, you're no Olivia Stanton.'

George giggled, which seemed to break some of the tension that had been building since they had set off.

'I couldn't believe what I was seeing when you were in the news. I never doubted you,' she said with a compassion that he felt.

'Many of my clients did,' he replied succinctly and without emotion.

'How...' She stopped herself.

'It's okay, you can ask me. You want to know how it happened?'

George nodded her head slowly.

'It's a question I have been asking myself repeatedly, yet the answer continues to elude me. I could have withstood the media attention on my practice, I could have withstood the judgment from clients, neither of those was ultimately behind my decision to leave the profession. The prospect of continuously doubting my clients as well as myself was the reason I turned my back on psychotherapy.'

'Why would you ever doubt yourself?' she asked calmly.

'Therapy has to be built on trust. You have to believe your client and work with what's in the room. Suspicion and doubt have no place. If I am questioning whether a client has a hidden agenda, my ability to remain objective is compromised.'

'You must hate Olivia Stanton.'

'She isn't responsible for my situation.'

George looked at Toby wide-eyed, yet confused.

'How can you say that?'

'I have no doubt that clients will have been disingenuous with me in the past. Sometimes this will be to keep a truth from me, other times from themselves. Olivia Stanton was no different, though she went to greater lengths. But here's the thing, George. If I'd remained professional and left my personal values out of the equation, then no amount of manipulation from her would have made a difference. Psychotherapists aren't there to fix or save people. The moment I tried to save Olivia, I stopped being a psychotherapist and became something more emotionally invested. That decision, George, that decision, is what cost me my career. That's on me, not Olivia Stanton.'

George just shook her head and smiled.

Revenge in Mind

'I can only imagine how much of a loss you are to your clients.'

She placed a hand on Toby's knee. Toby looked down, feeling uncomfortable. George, noting this, removed her hand abruptly.

'It was easy to blame Olivia at first, but the truth is there were several warning signs I should have heeded. I knew something wasn't right. I had my doubts, Beth had her doubts, my clinical supervisor had his doubts, but...' he tailed off.

'But what?'

'Richard, that's my former supervisor, passed a comment which really stuck with me. You see, Olivia presented as somebody who was vulnerable. That's not unique by the way, most of my clients have a vulnerability about them. But she was different, and I really sympathised with her situation. That was the first mistake.'

'You're not supposed to be sympathetic?' George asked curiously.

'You're supposed to show empathy, not sympathy. When you allow sympathy to enter the fray, you are opening yourself up to the potential of becoming invested as a person rather than a therapist. Once this happens, you can find yourself colluding with the client and therapy becomes a distant memory.'

'So, you felt emotionally connected to her?'

'Not her, but her situation, because it reminded me of two significant occasions in my life where I was unable to make things better... my mother.' He paused and slowly turned his head to face her. 'And you.'

She gazed at him with a look of surprise.

'I don't understand.'

'I couldn't save my mother, and I was powerless to stop what was happening to you. I think I saw you both in Olivia, and that's why I was so drawn to her. It was never about her. It was about who she reminded me of.'

'I don't know what to say. I didn't need saving.'

'I see that, but that sixteen-year-old kid didn't,' he replied quietly.

The next few minutes passed with both Toby and George in quiet contemplation. They would soon enter the countryside and regardless of the weather, Toby found this route cathartic because of its beautiful scenery. As he drove, he thought about their past together and wondered how much of those teenagers were still inside them. He was still unsure what had brought her back into his life, doubting the vague reasoning she had provided him with. There was a missing part of the jigsaw he couldn't get his head around. They had a common acquaintance. There was a third person somewhere that linked them, but Toby was coming up short on answers. This felt like Olivia. She was cold, manipulative and could find out things. She also had a motive for revenge. Then he realised. George's ordeal. That had been real. Whoever had sent him the message had done so to warn him. There was a fourth person. Somebody else was involved in this, which added further complexity and created two thought-provoking questions for him. Who was his antagonist, and who was the guardian angel warning him of danger? He glanced at George. Clearly noticing the vacant look on his face, she broke the silence.

'Are you okay?'

Revenge in Mind

'Is it me or you?' he drawled, as though trying to work through the answer as he spoke.

'I'm not sure what you mean.'

'Your encounter earlier. I'm wondering whether they are targeting you or whether they are targeting me?'

'Why would they target you, and how would anybody deduce we know one another?'

'That's the bit I'm struggling with,' he replied before pausing for a moment, deep in thought. 'That's what I don't understand. The fact I received a warning the same day you were followed and approached cannot be a coincidence. However, this implies that we must now identify at least two individuals. None of this makes sense.'

Toby slowed down, pulled over into a layby, and lowered his head between his hands onto the steering wheel. He lacked the energy and felt somewhat resentful about being involved in this situation, whatever it may be, at a time he was attempting to rebuild his life. George undid her seatbelt and moved closer, placing her hand on his shoulders and rubbing them in a way which felt like it had more feeling than it should have. Toby turned to look at her. He felt confused, vulnerable, and out of his depth. It wasn't just about George; it was about Olivia Stanton; it was about Eric Stanton; it was about the loss of purpose since he had left the profession which he had invested so much into. As he sat and reflected, head still in hands, he thought about how much that one decision had cost him. A sudden anger overwhelmed him.

'George, I have to know something. Why now? Why, after all this time? This isn't about nostalgia or catching up with an old friend. We dated, we had fun, and it ended. It was sad, but we moved on. We both moved on. Now here you are, and I have to know why. You said you needed my help. Even so, I have no idea what it is you've got us into.'

Toby banged the steering wheel, which drew a gasp from George as she jumped back. Unable to meet his stare, she looked down at her feet.

'Got us into?' she replied slowly, but with a tone which made no attempt to hide her disdain for his comment.

'I didn't ask to be stalked, Toby. I didn't ask to be driven away to a stranger's house in the middle of nowhere, and I didn't ask you to get involved.'

Her voice was rising with every point she was making. Toby didn't reply.

'When I said I needed your help, I meant your professional help. I needed somebody to talk to, somebody to fix me and get me out of this hole I have been in for a long time. I needed your fucking mind Toby, nothing more.'

Toby took a deep breath, looked down at his shoes, and then slowly looked back up and turned his head towards her. George was gazing directly into his eyes.

'Did you know there is no single aspect of body language which implies somebody is lying? What experts do is really quite simple. They will ask you a series of questions both they and you know the answer to and will study your body language. At that point, they have a picture of how you respond when you're telling the truth. What they then do is look for deviations to find out when people are being disingenuous. It's simple, yet incredibly clever.'

'I'm not sure why you're telling me this,' George said tentatively.

'Working as a psychotherapist had its blessings and curses. One of the best things was developing an ability to read your client and understand what was really going on, what wasn't being said. But here's the thing…that can also be a burden because regardless of the situation you're in, you find yourself analysing every word, every non-verbal cue, every change in tone. But you know what the worst thing is about having that knowledge?'

It was rhetorical, but George shook her head slowly, nonetheless.

'Sometimes you see things you really don't want to see. So what I know is when you're giving me answers you genuinely believe to be true you look me in the eye and your hands remain either by your side or on your knees, depending on your position. What I also know is when you're searching for an answer, you look up to your left. But when you are not being truthful, you look away and bite your bottom lip right before you answer. You also squeeze your thumb and index finger together. That's what I do know. What I don't know is why you're lying to me.'

By now George was sitting with her mouth ajar, unable to look him in the eye. Toby felt surprisingly calm, considering how awkward the conversation was about to get.

'It worked out pretty well for you, didn't it? A university degree, private practice, a doting wife, a nice house and car, whilst I'm a mere afterthought.'

She was deflecting the question, but he knew if he let her speak for long enough, she would provide him with the answers he needed.

'When you left me, my world fell apart, but you just coasted through life and found everything you wanted. How dare you sit there and judge me when you don't know the struggles I've encountered in my life? You know nothing about me or what I've endured.'

Toby could see George visibly shaking with anger but felt certain there was a deep emotional pain sitting behind it. With a single strike, she made him feel a sudden sadness as he came to the realisation she was right. He knew very little about the person who had once been his entire world. He reached over to place his hand on hers, but she jerked back, rejecting his gesture.

'Do you want to know what really happened to me, Toby? Why I found you?'

Toby couldn't answer. His anger had dissipated, replaced with a genuine fear of what he may be about to hear. Suddenly he didn't want to know, but he was about to find out, regardless.

'When I was in my twenties, I got into a relationship with a guy and we moved in together. He seemed quite charming, but over time I saw something change. At first it felt subtle, of course, but looking back, I should have seen it for what it was. He was controlling and slowly I withdrew from my friends, gave up my job and thought he had my best interests at heart. But it was never about me, it was about him. It was about him controlling every aspect of my life and making me so dependent on him I didn't have the confidence or self-esteem to leave him. I felt worthless and unlovable.'

'I'm so sorry. I had no idea.'

This was like a dagger through the heart for Toby. Her revelation seemed to stir up feelings he had once held for her. He felt devastated, not just for her, but for himself too. Seemingly oblivious to his words, George continued.

'I stayed in the hope I would once again see the person I fell in love with so soon after meeting.'

Toby placed his hands on hers and offered her a sympathetic smile.

'One reason people don't leave abusive relationships is they struggle to believe that somebody who they love, somebody who is supposed to love them, could be that person. You showed tremendous courage and strength by taking that decision, George.'

Toby noticed George steady herself as though building towards something. She had detailed psychological and emotional abuse and had clearly been controlled throughout the relationship. What else was there? Suddenly, he felt cold. The last time he had felt like this was the night in his practice when Olivia Stanton had disclosed...He paused and stared right into the eyes of Georgina Sampson as he braced himself for where this was ultimately leading. She didn't need to tell him. He could see it in her eyes, but still...

'He raped me, Toby. That's why I left in the end. He tried to convince me it was consensual, but he knew what it was. Deep down, he knew what he'd done. When I left, I came close to calling you, but I didn't want to disrupt your life, and in all honesty, I wouldn't have known where to begin.'

'I'm so sorry, I truly am.'

She smiled at him, and for a fleeting moment, he saw that sixteen-year-old girl again. Whatever doubts he had had, this was genuine. Her ordeal had been real, and nothing else mattered.

'I would have been there, George. I promised you when we were kids I'd always be there, regardless.'

'I know. I remember the day you said that to me. We were sitting on the park bench. You were holding me tightly. I remember feeling so safe and secure.'

'It was the middle of winter and I was only wearing a tee-shirt. I was hugging you for warmth,' he replied, smiling.

Looking into each other's eyes reminiscing, they were suddenly transported back twenty-three years to a time when things were much simpler, a time when the only responsibility they had was making it to lesson before the teacher. Staring into George's eyes right now, Toby knew there was still a part of him that mourned the breakdown of their relationship. Beth was his world, but there was no denying the feelings he once had for George had never fully disappeared. As he slowly withdrew from her grasp, he adjusted his seat and started the engine. Little over thirty minutes later, they were making their way up the long track to Jack's farm. They had spoken little in the latter part of the journey with any exchanges superficial and brief, often coinciding with the adverts in between songs on the radio. Toby felt sad, almost numb at what George had told him. He had never been comfortable hearing about rape from clients, but hearing about it from somebody he had invested so much into emotionally felt like a blunt instrument striking him in the stomach with force. This alerted him to what he'd been trying so suppress from the moment she had entered his car at the prison. Part of him was still in love with her.

{ 13 }

'What's going on?'

'I'm sorry, Jack. I don't have that answer right now.'

'Is this to do with that Olivia Stanton?'

'I don't have that answer either.'

'What *do* you have the answer to, Toby? You're dropping your ex-girlfriend on me with no notice, expecting me to act as her security for God knows how long, and you're giving me nothing. I'm taking an enormous leap of faith here.'

Toby couldn't remember the last time he saw Jack animated like this. In fact, he couldn't remember a single occasion. It wasn't part of his persona. He approached life with an incredibly laid-back attitude and just took things in his stride. He could only remember one instance when Jack seemed uneasy, which was during their earlier conversation about his ex-girlfriend's death.

'I'm sorry. I know what I'm asking of you, and I'm mindful I'm not giving you much.'

'I get more from the cat buddy, and he's rarely around,' Jack said, grinning.

Toby returned the smile, but it hid a deeper concern. Jack was right. He had questions. He also had concerns, but what he lacked were any answers. He questioned whether this was an elaborate hoax to get at him, but Olivia's warning that he had put a target on his own back reverberated through this mind. There were too many coincidences here. George coming back into his life and he still not understanding fully why. The preordained encounter orchestrated by Eric, which was meant to serve as a warning to Toby. Then there was the warning message, which only made sense when it became clear George had been followed. He couldn't come to any other conclusion than he was being targeted, but still he had no idea what he was involved in. The obvious choice of who was behind this was Eric, but something told Toby that it would be naïve to eliminate Olivia from his suspicions. Both had lied to him and both had threatened him, though in different ways. Piecing this together, however, was proving difficult, and it all remained conjecture at this point. He felt bad but reasoned with himself that as he wasn't fully aware of the facts, he wasn't actually keeping anything from Jack. Besides, the less he knew, the better.

'She's vulnerable Jack. Look after her.'

'You can trust me.'

'With my life, that's why I came to you. There's nobody else I would have turned to in this situation.'

Jack smiled and patted Toby firmly on the shoulders.

'She doesn't know how lucky she is to have Toby Reynolds looking out for her,' he smiled.

This time Toby's laugh was genuine, and for a moment he allowed himself to be free of the suspicion and worry which had clouded him for so long.

'Can I ask you one thing, Tobes?'

Toby nodded, but wondered where this was going.

'Where does this end? What I mean is, what do you hope to achieve? You're not a fighter or a cop. You operate in circles where people fix heads, not crack them open. What are you hoping to get out of all this?'

Toby laughed.

'How many times have I told you psychotherapists don't fix anything?'

'Why haven't you called the police, by the way?' Jack replied, ignoring Toby's playful retort.

'Have you ever been arrested?'

'Not that I know of.'

'I can't describe what it felt like to be in that cell. It was empty, literally empty. Yet, sitting in the interview room, I yearned for that emptiness. I would have given anything to be sat in that void away from the questioning, the insinuations, the suspicion. It felt like gaslighting. I started to question things myself. It's like one attack after another. They don't stop, Jack. They're relentless.'

'Didn't you have a solicitor?'

'Naively, I assumed not having legal representation would highlight to them I had nothing to hide. I soon found out that wasn't the case. I don't think I ever told you, but one of the lead detectives was a friend of mine.'

'Was?'

'Is, maybe, I don't know. I thought I'd feel better knowing he was there, like I had an ally.'

'Surely he, along with anybody who actually knows you, would realise you weren't capable of attempted murder?'

Revenge in Mind

'He had to do his job. He remained mostly quiet, but there was this one point where he came back into the interview room on his own and switched off the recording.'

'Shit, what was that about?'

'He was warning me, to be honest. He told me some things about Olivia Stanton he probably shouldn't have.'

'So, he helped you?'

'Maybe, but that's the point, don't you see?'

'You lost me Toby.'

'I came close to being wrongfully convicted, and that's with somebody I considered a friend in the room. What would have happened had he not been there?'

'But this is different. You're the complainant, not the accused.'

Toby looked away and screwed up his face.

'What is it?'

Toby was aware of the need to choose his words carefully. He trusted Jack, but it wasn't Jack he was worried about. The more Jack knew, the more he had to keep from George. If his tongue were to slip, Toby was unsure how George would react, and he couldn't risk her unpredictability.

'It's nothing, really. I guess I'm still hoping this is just a highly elaborate prank and until I know otherwise, I don't want to bother the police with it.'

Jack looked at Toby with a serious look on his face. It was a look Toby wasn't used to seeing.

'If you thought it was a prank Toby, you wouldn't have brought her here. Listen, whatever this is, I have your back, but you don't need to lie to me. I can see you're nervous.'

Toby didn't speak. Instead, he put his arms around Jack and patted him several times on the back before pulling away and turning to pick up his car keys. In that very moment, he heard the shower upstairs being switched off. George would be down in a few minutes, but he had no intention of hanging around.

'I better go. Thanks again, Jack. I'll call you tomorrow.'

'Wait, aren't you going to say goodbye to George?'

'I think it's best if I go,' Toby responded, noticing Jack's puzzled expression.

As Toby exited out of the front door, he looked around his surroundings and wondered whether George would be safe here. He questioned whether she was the actual target or simply a pawn in a game of revenge against him. As he drove away, he thought about what he was asking of Jack and felt a sharp attack of guilt that when Jack had been at his most vulnerable, Toby hadn't been able to be there for him. Of course, that was Jack's choice, but he wondered why Jack hadn't felt comfortable enough to confide in him. Then there was Beth. He had put her through so much, and now here he was, once again, asking her to trust him. Then an icy shiver descended into the depth of his spine as a recent intrusive thought returned. What if George's ordeal wasn't aligned with other events? What if this wasn't actually about her? What if it was Beth? This would make more sense, as she was the closest person to Toby. Who would realistically know his link to George? It was Beth. It had to be. She was the one in danger. What had he done? How could he live with himself if anything happened to her? With the thought entrenched in his mind, he squeezed the accelerator as he raced down the track and onto the main road. The more he thought about it, the more it made sense, and the more sense it made, the more anxious he became. He looked down at the speedometer and noticed he was now in excess of 100mph. The adrenaline was flowing through him like a wild river, but the anxiety wasn't about the increased chance of losing control of the car. It was about what he would find when he returned home.

{ 14 }

Beth Reynolds hurried down the stairs to a knocking at the door. Although she wouldn't label it as impatience, it was clear the individual was eager, as they had also pressed the doorbell to ensure their presence was noticed. With few visitors, there was often a mixture of intrigue and excitement when somebody called round. She sighed as she thought to herself it was likely a delivery for something Toby had ordered and considered how she would mask the disappointment to preserve the feelings of the delivery driver. She laughed to herself and reached forward to open the door. Facing her was a man with short dark hair, well presented, with a smile on his face that she imagined had probably sent many hearts fluttering in its time.

'Hi,' she said tentatively, trying to place him, but failing.

'I'm really sorry to disturb you, but I was wondering if Toby was around?' the man replied.

Beth studied him for a moment. She knew Toby's friends, his acquaintances. She knew Richard, but this man didn't look familiar. She wondered if he was a former client.

'I'm sorry, Toby isn't in at the moment,' she responded politely.

Revenge in Mind

The man stared down at his feet briefly, looking disappointed.

'Is Toby expecting you?' Beth asked gently, noticing this.

'Toby saved my life. He was there when I needed help.'

She smiled. Whilst Toby was uneasy with compliments, she felt nothing but pride on the occasions a former client would send a thank-you card or a gift.

'He really is something else, your husband,' the man continued.

'I don't think he'll be long. I can call him if you like?'

The man looked anxious. Beth wondered whether he was a little shy or was worried Toby wouldn't want to see him in a personal capacity, having worked with him professionally.

'It's okay, I'm sorry to have troubled you,' the man said, turning to walk away.

Beth felt a sudden sympathy for him. It had clearly taken a lot of courage to come here. She wondered what Toby would do, but didn't have to ponder on that thought for too long. Toby wouldn't turn anybody away, but the man was a stranger to her, nonetheless. She wouldn't compromise her own safety. The sunshine was now breaking through the clouds and the temperature increasing on what was turning out to be a pleasant spring day. They had recently built a gazebo in the garden, which could be visible to a passer-by. It was a private location, yet not completely secluded. You could access it through the side gate, which meant you didn't need to go through the house.

'I don't think Toby will be too long. Would you like to wait?'

'Thank you. I'll sit in the car and catch up on the news.'

'Now that wouldn't make me much of a host,' she smiled.

She stepped out and gestured for the man to follow her.

'Take a seat,' she said politely.

'I don't want to intrude.'

'Coffee, tea or a soft drink?' Beth replied assertively, ignoring the man's response. 'Toby has a rather nice coffee machine, which I'm always looking for an excuse to use,' she added with a smile.

'That's really kind of you, if you're sure? A coffee without sugar would be lovely. I wouldn't want to deprive you of such an opportunity,' the man replied, winking.

Beth headed towards the gate, which would take her around the side of the house to the front door. It would have been quicker to walk down the garden and enter through the kitchen doors, however, she was still mindful of the man being known to Toby, and not her. Just as she reached the gate, she turned back to see her guest tapping away at his phone screen, with a broad smile spread across his face.

As the two sat talking, Beth noticed a scar on the palm of the man's hand. She hadn't wanted to seem rude and instantly averted her stare, but he had noticed and smiled warmly at her.

'Misspent youth,' he said, opening his hand up to her.

'I'm sorry,' she replied awkwardly.

'It's fine. Looking back, it's an amusing story. I was fifteen and up to no good with some friends. It was dark, and we had entered an old abandoned hospital to see what we could find. It seemed like a good idea at the time, but these things always do, right?'

Revenge in Mind

Beth nodded, but couldn't really identify with him. Her upbringing had been very different, having spent her teenage years mourning her parents rather than seeking mischief. It would have been easy for her to rebel and take a very different path, but at that age, she had not been a social butterfly. This was likely because the biggest influence she had had through her journey to maturity had been from her grandparents, who perhaps had different values to those of her parents.

'Anyway, we'd been in there for about ten minutes when we heard a noise. At that age, your instinct is to run, right? So we run towards the exit, except we don't actually know where the exit is. In a panic, I charge through this door, trip over something, and am sent sprawling face first towards the floor. Without thinking, I bring my hands down and instantly experience a sharp pain. When I was able to see my hand, there was a large piece of glass sticking out of it. So you see, this scar right here serves as a lifelong reminder of stupidity.'

'That must have been painful,' Beth said, grimacing.

'More than you can imagine.'

Beth looked away, feeling somewhat embarrassed she had been caught staring and had forced him into an explanation he may have preferred not to have given. Picking up on her awkwardness, the man spoke slowly and softly as his eyes perused the garden.

'I love what you've done here. It feels very...'

'Therapeutic?' Beth interrupted, smiling.

'I can see why you'd want to be out here, that's for sure.'

'Toby loves it out here. We both do. After his accident...'

She stopped herself, realising this man was a stranger to her and, from what she could gather, a former client of Toby's.

'I was really sorry to hear about that. How is he?'

'Rehabilitation has been tough, more so emotionally than physically.'

The man smiled as he picked up his cup.

'You must be really proud of the work he does.'

'Did. Toby doesn't practice anymore,' Beth said, looking rather regretful.

'I can imagine he will be an enormous loss to the profession. You can see why people would feel comfortable divulging their deepest, darkest secrets to him.'

Beth paused for a moment. That last sentence felt like somebody speculating rather than speaking from personal experience. Why would he need to make assumptions about Toby's demeanour if he had first-hand experience working with him? Suddenly Beth was alerted to the fact she had invited somebody onto her premises, whom she knew nothing about. Well, actually, there was one thing…Whoever he was, he wasn't a former client of her husband's.

The screeching sound of brakes announced Toby's arrival. He jumped out of the car and dashed towards the front door, hurriedly turning the key and charging through in a manner which befitted the panic he was feeling. During the journey home, with time to think, he had convinced himself that it was Beth, not George, who was at risk. The guilt he had felt had grown with every minute that had passed. A guilt which had begun with that seemingly tiny, yet incredibly significant question of whether he had prioritised George over Beth. But he'd not realised Beth was vulnerable. Everything had pointed towards George being the target. The last time he had hastily burst into a scene, he had been faced with a critically injured man. He didn't allow himself to harbour on this thought as he raced into the kitchen, the place where Beth would often spend time sat at the breakfast bar enjoying the tranquillity of an empty house. The kitchen was empty, though Toby noticed it looked unusually immaculate, something usually only seen when they had visitors. Nothing looked disturbed, but still he couldn't shake the feeling that something wasn't right. He ran into the lounge, but that too was empty.

'Beth? Beth?' he shouted, getting louder and more desperate. After checking the conservatory, he headed upstairs, now with a feeling of dread at what he may find. The door to the bedroom was slightly ajar. Suspicion enveloped him. The doors were usually always open. Beth was a firm believer in embracing daylight and liked to have the light flowing through the house. She had teased him that closed doors meant there was something to hide. Toby swallowed hard and placed his hand on the door handle. Taking a deep breath, he pushed the door open. His eyes were immediately drawn to the bed. The duvet was curled up in a corner on the floor, and the sheets and pillow slips were in a heap at the bottom of the bed. A sound which appeared to come from the garden startled him. It wasn't just any sound, it was something smashing. He raced down the stairs, through the kitchen, and flung the patio doors open. His heart pounded as he noticed Beth in the far corner of the garden under the gazebo, clutching a towel which was soaked with what he could only assume was her blood.

'Beth!'

Toby sprinted towards her.

'I appear to have had a minor accident,' she replied, smiling.

'What the hell happened? I've been worried, and when I couldn't find you in the house, I thought...'

'Thought what Toby? What's going on?'

'I was just worried, that's all. We need to get that cleaned up. How did it happen?'

'I was clearing up, and the handle smashed in my hand. It's just superficial, don't worry. Now maybe you can explain why you're acting so strangely.'

Toby was about to explain to Beth when something caught his eye. There were two cups. The floor was dry, so the broken one that lay in pieces must have been empty. He walked over to the other cup on the table and picked it up. The drink was cold. This wasn't a freshly brewed replacement. Somebody else had been here. He looked at Beth, but not with suspicion. He trusted her implicitly, but they rarely had guests, and events recently had heightened his awareness. Beth saw him studying the cup.

'You had a visitor,' she said hesitantly, noting the worried look on his face.

Toby's face stiffened.

'Did he give you a name?'

'What makes you think it was a man?'

'Lucky guess. Did he give a name?' he repeated.

'Strangely, no, but he said you'd helped him, so I assumed he was a client, except...'

'Except what?' Toby asked curtly.

'There was something he said which made me believe your relationship with him wasn't a professional one. I could be wrong, though.'

'What did he say? Can you describe him to me?'

'This feels like an interrogation.'

'This is important. What can you tell me about him?'

'Dark hair, well presented, quite charming really. Oh, and apparently he didn't like my coffee,' she added, looking over at the cup, where the untouched contents remained.

Toby froze, eyes glazed as he studied the cup on the table. This was his calling card. He had known Toby wouldn't be here and did enough to conceal his identity from Beth, but left subtle hints which he knew Toby would decipher. Seeing Toby at the house was never his intention. He had simply wanted to show him he could get to those whom Toby held closest. Beth, noticing the look of sudden panic on his face, reached out and squeezed his hand.

'Honey, what is it?'

Suddenly, he faced a dilemma. He had promised Beth he would never keep things from her again, that they would be a team and face everything together. She had a right to know. She needed to be vigilant for her own safety. But the truth had consequences and the thought of Beth living in fear, looking over her shoulder, was something he simply couldn't face. He looked up and smiled at her, taking her by the hand that wasn't bleeding.

'I think I know who it was and I'm sorry I missed him. I'll catch up with him later, but let's get that hand of yours sorted first.'

As they walked through the garden and into the kitchen, Toby's smile faded. The reality of the situation was becoming clearer. George and Beth weren't targets, they were merely pawns. He was the real target, but he needed proof. Though he had believed at the time he had done a good job of convincing Beth, he had an inkling she regarded him with suspicion. Beth was savvy and knew him better than anyone. He hated keeping things from her, but he hated more the fact that it was his actions which had put her in this position. As his eyes closed later that night, they did so with several things circling his mind, each one vying for attention. He needed to step out of his comfort zone and take back some control. He needed to show he wasn't prepared to be a victim, that he couldn't be intimidated. He needed to reaffirm this was about him and not about Beth or George. Against everything he stood for, he needed to seek out that confrontation and place himself in a situation which would almost certainly cause him a great deal of angst. At best he was treading water, at worst he was being carried by a rampant tide to a place where he would be soon out of his depth completely. Guilt consumed him with the thought that anything that happened to Beth or George was on him. It was his decisions that had put them in danger. Now he faced a stark choice. Everything was telling him he should back off, but the truth was he wasn't sure what he would be backing off from. The fact Eric Stanton was going to such lengths to silence him only served to make Toby more suspicious that whatever he was trying so desperately to cover up, it was something big. This did nothing to quell his nerves, yet he discovered a spark inside which frightened him. Toby, typically reserved, found himself unexpectedly driven to uncover whatever Eric was concealing. He wondered whether this was fuelled by a stubbornness he had developed during his time as a therapist. In session, he had been in control. He was the expert. He was comfortable. But there had been one exception. Olivia Stanton had played him beautifully and the feeling that she'd got the better of him had never left. The promise to himself to not allow anybody to be in control of him again was almost certainly responsible for his thought process now. As his breathing became deeper, he thought about how much the last few months had changed him. How his optimism had drained and been replaced with cynicism. Life-changing traumas often breed dramatic life changes, but this hadn't happened the way he had expected. He'd become suspicious and mistrusting, and questioned himself frequently. Instead of seeing a world enriched with kindness and altruism, he now viewed it through damaged eyes and saw something much darker. There was no mistaking Toby had been walking under a cloud of impending doom since his ordeal with Olivia Stanton. That was his final thought of the evening. The room fell quiet, with nothing more than the faint sounds of breathing disrupting the tranquillity of the night.

{ 15 }

Mist descended upon the chilly night air, and a gentle breeze blew through the trees, causing them to shake rhythmically. The street lights had only stretched so far up the track, leaving the building at the top cloaked in darkness. If it had desired a clandestine existence, it had surely achieved this, the secluded location probably a reflection of its occupant's insular life. A haven for anybody craving geographical isolation, the natural beauty of the surrounding area simply added to the appeal. The spring months still reflected that beauty, but winter time would present its challenges. Ice from a cold snap would make it difficult for anybody to get up or down the track, whilst any substantial snowfall would render it unusable for most vehicles. It felt like a place where one could immerse themselves in nature, a place where troubles were easily forgotten, a place that offered a ray of light on the darkest of days.

The serenity of the night was disrupted by the quiet footsteps of two men carrying flashlights. Their identity was concealed. Their reason for being there, less so. Though the track was secluded, the individuals were clearly taking no chances as they trudged slowly towards the house at the top of the track. Their stealth-like behaviour, as well as the fact it was

Revenge in Mind

after midnight, suggested they were not there by invitation. They had taken their van as far as they could without drawing attention to themselves. It wasn't ideal, but they would have to improvise once they'd got what they had come here for. As they drew closer to the large wooden gate, which would open out into the grounds, they stopped to survey what lay ahead. With no words exchanged, the smaller of the two men opened the black rucksack he had been carrying and pulled out a grey pouch. He picked up the gun it had been housing and studied it for a moment before placing it back in position. Then he closed the pouch, leaving a set of wire cutters, a pair of handcuffs, and a small crowbar meticulously placed. They weren't needed...for now. As they climbed over the gate, taking every caution not to make a sound, the taller man waved his hand in the air, motioning for them to stop. He reached into his jacket pocket, removed a pack of cigarettes, and pulled one out for each of them, placing the rucksack on the floor whilst he did so. Both men then removed their balaclavas and stood for a moment admiring the view, the burning ash the only light in the vicinity. Wearing expressions of unspoken nervousness, they stood silently. They had no agenda, simply an incentive, money. Little was known about the target other than it wasn't about harm, it was about leverage. This wasn't personal, it was solely about survival. Times were hard, and they needed to make a living in any way they could. They would argue they weren't unscrupulous; they had a code. Murder was out of the question, and they would never take on anything involving children. Criminals with morals, they would argue, but criminals all the same. As they silently approached the front door, cigarettes hanging out of their mouths, a bat flew past, startling the pair. The flashlight, which had now been dimmed, slipped from the grasp of its handler, but a quick reaction ensured it didn't hit the ground. The cigarettes weren't so lucky, tumbling to the ground, much to the frustration of the men. Sweat ran down the face of the smaller man as his nerves began to tell. As they looked up, they noted the bedroom windows were ajar. Realising they were likely occupied, they made a split decision to head around the back to see if there was another way in. Entering here with a crowbar would be too risky. They quietly made their way around to the rear of the large farmhouse, finding a smaller window above the backdoor. This would likely be the bathroom. It would be much safer to enter here. It didn't take them long. With one last look around the outside, pushing the door open just enough to allow the shape of their bodies to fit through, they were in.

George awoke with panic at the sound of footsteps below her. She tried to calm herself by rationalising it was likely Jack. His work throughout the day was demanding, and occasionally he would fall asleep on the sofa shortly after his evening meal. This, of course, meant by the early hours of the morning, he was wide awake and looking for something to occupy him. This thought quickly disappeared as she realised the sounds were coming from more than one place. She could feel the palpitations as her heart rate increased to an uncomfortable level, a similar level to the one it had reached recently when she had become aware she was being followed. Toby had been wrong, she thought. He had promised her she would be safe at Jack's.

Revenge in Mind

Any uncertainty about whether Toby had been overly cautious vanished, as she now believed without a doubt, she was the intended target. This wasn't one incident, it was a series of events aligning, meaning the scenario of it being a coincidence was now looking less likely. She closed her eyes as her lips quivered. They, whoever they were, knew where she was. She was no longer safe here. In fact, she was no longer safe anywhere. Her immediate reaction was to curl up and submit. Perhaps her ordeal would be swift, perhaps her pain would be bearable. It felt like a preferred option to her living the rest of her life in fear, looking over her shoulder, always wondering who was watching, who was lurking in the shadows. She sobbed silently in despair. She covered her mouth at the faint sound of creaking floorboards coming from the hallway. They were here. She was defenceless. She could scream for Jack, but that would only draw attention to herself. Sitting up in bed, she felt vulnerable. She desperately wanted to move, but was faced with a sudden paralysis. Down the hallway was Jack, the person she had been told would keep her secure, yet her sole longing was for Toby. This thought was fleeting, as she heard footsteps outside the room. They were getting closer. She clung tightly to the sheet as the door handle turned slowly. They were here. She was unable to look as the door creaked open and a dark figure, which she couldn't make out at first, entered the room. Squinting through her teary eyes, she was just about able to see the figure place his finger to his lips as if to warn her against making any noise. The man walked over to her bed slowly and knelt down next to her.

'Jack,' she exclaimed before throwing her arms around him in relief. 'What's going on?'

'We appear to have some uninvited guests, but don't worry, I'm not gonna let them hurt you,' Jack replied, trying his best to reassure her.

'They're here for me?'

'I didn't say that, but whoever or whatever they are looking for, they've made a mistake coming here.'

Jack said this with a confidence that reassured her. Toby had said little about him, only that he could handle trouble if it found him. Looking at his confident demeanour and his muscular build, she realised she saw a lot of her brother in him. Dylan had always looked out for her as a kid, and though they had lost touch for a while, that bond had remained. When she had reached out to him recently, it was as if they had never been estranged. She thought how good it would be to have him here now, but considered whether his approach would be quite as measured as Jack's. Dylan was a loose cannon; diplomacy was a stranger to him. A straight talker with a temper. Not a good combination, she thought.

'What are you going to do?'

'We have two options. We either sit it out in here and wait to see if they approach, or we take the fight to them. And when I say we, I actually mean me,' he qualified with a grin.

'Okay, I like the idea of staying here. I don't want to be left on my own,' George whispered nervously.

'There's a problem with that.'

'What's that?' she asked hesitantly.

'Well, if they are burglars, they may stay downstairs.'

Revenge in Mind

'And why is that a problem?'

'I don't like thieves.'

'Okay, so what if they aren't thieves?'

'Then my belongings are safe,' he grinned.

'How can you be so calm?'

'Do you know how many times somebody has broken into my property, George?'

She shook her head slowly.

'Three times. Before tonight, that is. And do you know how many times anybody has walked out with anything of mine?'

She shrugged her shoulders.

'Never. No burglar has ever left here with anything other than bruises. I'm amazed word hasn't spread, to be honest.'

George stared at him, unable to determine whether he was genuine or simply teasing her. Perhaps this was his way of providing her with some reassurance that the situation wasn't as grave in reality as it was in her head.

'Please don't leave me,' she whispered, grabbing his arm and pulling him in close enough to feel his warm breath on her neck. As she did this, there was a creak on the staircase which they both heard. He leaned over to her and whispered in her ear.

'I guess they're not here for the loot.'

How could he be so nonchalant? She felt angry at his laid-back manner when she was so frightened. She was the one at risk. It was she who they had come for. How could he dismiss the danger they were both staring at?

'Hey, it's gonna be okay, I promise,' he whispered.

He placed his hands on her shoulder and slowly turned her around, pointing towards a cupboard situated in the corner of the room. She opened her mouth to speak, but he placed his fingers over her lips and nodded at her. This time, there was a warm smile rather than a grin. She felt comforted. As she tiptoed quietly towards the cupboard, Jack stood up and crept towards the door, knowing precisely where to tread in order to avoid drawing attention. As she climbed into the cupboard and gently pulled the door to, the last thing she saw was Jack staring intently at the bedroom door, fists clenched. She felt helpless, but was counting on him being able to help himself. Georgina Sampson closed her eyes and thought about the last time she had felt so vulnerable. It had been with *him*, the time *he* had raped her. She had felt powerless then, and she felt powerless now, but she had to trust Jack. She had to trust that Toby knew what he was doing when he brought her here. She placed her fingers in her ears and screwed her eyes closed, the same way she had done as a child when trying to pretend something wasn't happening. For a moment, Georgina Sampson was eight again. She sat snuggled between her parents, engrossed in the cartoons on the television. The sun was shining, the holidays had arrived, and she felt happy. More importantly, she felt safe. There was no bipolar. Her mother didn't view the world with suspicion, and her only worry was picking out a dress at the beginning of each day. Education was still fun, and the only man in her life was her father. Troubles were something other people had, and the harsh reality of life was something she wouldn't learn for a few years. Then she was conscious in the moment again, wondering whether those days where she had lived without worry were the last time she was truly happy. Of course, her experience with Toby at college had been wonderful, but by this time she was battling her mental health, and at the tender age of sixteen, it had already taken its toll on her. Removing her fingers from her ears, George strained to hear, but was met only with silence. She wondered whether they had walked past her room, whether there was something else they were looking for. She questioned whether they were simply thieves who had succumbed to their own greed, or whether they had simply turned around and descended the stairs, satisfied with what they already had. As she received her answer, her heart started beating at an unhealthy pace.

The bedroom door handle turned slowly as Jack prepared to come face to face with the intruders. At best, they were common burglars. At worst, they were here not for something, but for someone. Either way, he would defend everything and everybody in his property the only way he knew how...with his physical prowess. The first of the men entered the room slowly, but he had little chance to take in the surroundings. Jack reached out and grabbed his arm, pulling him into the room. He then kicked the door shut firmly as he threw the man to the floor and moved towards him. The intruder tried to regain his feet but was met with a ferocious blow to the face. Jack, hearing a crack followed by a blood-curdling shriek, knew the man's nose was broken. If he needed further evidence, he only needed to look at the unhealthy amount of blood which was now staining the wooden floor. The man was stunned, bleeding heavily and trying to speak, but Jack was in no mood for conversation. He hated thieves and took it personally. He was geographically isolated, and that made him a target. People associated farmers with wealth and often thought there was value hiding out in a farmhouse or barn. Whether it was cattle, machinery or belongings, there would be a demand on the black market for whatever a burglar could lay their hands on here. Jack's attention turned to the sound of footsteps on the staircase, seemingly making no attempt to remain inconspicuous. He had given little thought to the accomplice, but soon he would meet Jack's acquaintance. This time there was no thought of a surreptitious entrance. There was no attempt to conceal an uninvited and unwanted presence. Just as the footsteps reached the top of the staircase, Jack heard a groan from behind him. In an instant, his attention was diverted from the intruder about to enter the room to the man climbing back to his feet. That momentary lapse was all that was needed, as the door burst open. Jack didn't see too much of the man, but he was bigger in stature than his partner, and looked more able to handle himself. Before he could regain his focus, the man had landed a blow on the side of his head, taking him by surprise. He was stunned but still standing. As the man swung at him again, Jack ducked, resulting in the fist merely grazing the top of his head. Had it connected with his face as was the intention, it would have surely broken his nose. The punch not landing had sent the man off balance, and this was the only invitation Jack needed. As he saw him losing his footing, Jack placed his hands on the man's back, grabbing a handful of his coat, and threw him against the wall with force. The room shook with a thud; the man trying desperately to scramble back to his feet. Jack would take no chances. The only way to ensure his and George's safety was to incapacitate the intruders. He grabbed the man around the neck and swung at him. He didn't miss, but his adversary wasn't giving up. He came back with a volley of blows, which took Jack by surprise. As the man launched himself, Jack ducked down and threw him over his shoulders. He hit the bedside table with force, breaking it into several pieces in the process. He tried to stumble to his feet, holding his back, but he was the least of Jack's problems. The other intruder, who had been nursing a broken nose throughout the commotion, picked up an object and crept up behind Jack. Upon turning, Jack was faced with the sight of a silver lamp coming towards him. Instinctively, he raised his hands in defence to cushion the blow, but this proved futile and he found himself tumbling towards the floor. Looking up with bleary eyes, he could just about make out the shadow of a man stood over him. He was joined by his accomplice and for a moment, all that could be heard was the heavy breathing of the three men, each trying to gather their thoughts and each clearly pained by injury. In a fair fight there weren't many tougher than Jack Newby, but this wasn't a fair fight and he'd been blindsided. He felt a sharp pain on the side of his head and noticed the blood oozing as he rubbed at it with his hand. Realising he had not been struck there, he figured it must have been from the fall. It took him a moment to gain perspective. He wondered why the two men had not continued with their attack and then realised they were also badly injured. He climbed to his feet, knowing maintaining his current position on the floor made him susceptible to another attack. He was still unsure of the motives of his assailants, but this wasn't his primary concern right now. He needed to keep both him and George safe. His head felt hazy, likely from the blow, but this didn't stop him from wondering why this had taken place upstairs. His car keys, along with his wallet, were in a bowl on the kitchen table. They wouldn't be difficult to locate and were the only thing of any value in the house, really. The real value was in his livestock and his machinery out in the barns. They had no need to move upstairs, and doing so felt personal. Whether these were amateurs who got greedy or professionals with an ulterior motive, Jack felt a burning anger beginning to rise from the pit of his stomach. The anger suppressed the pain and suddenly he charged at the men, aiming directly for the biggest one. As he connected, he lifted him off his feet and ran. The man grimaced with pain as he hit the angle of the wall, his back taking the full force. With the two men falling down in a less than pleasant embrace, Jack landed two blows to the man's face. As he swung his fist again, he felt a sharp pain in the middle of his back, which had come from a blunt instrument, possibly the antique candlestick which was usually housed on the bedside table. Jack slowly crawled away from the man lying on the floor, anticipating another attack and wondering how much more he had left to continue the fight. Surprisingly, the attack didn't come. Instead, the man went over to his co-conspirator and bent down to pick him up.

'We need to get out of here,' he said sharply, seemingly not in the mood for negotiation. The man on the floor rose to his feet, still holding his back.

'What do we do with him?' he asked, glancing over at Jack, who was still sitting on the floor. Before there was time to answer, a noise from the cupboard alerted the two men. Jack, realising they were about to uncover George's hiding place, quickly opened his bedside drawer and pulled out a large knife.

'We're done here,' he said sternly, gaining the men's attention.

Both men exchanged nervous glances and cautiously retreated from the door, raising their hands in a submissive gesture. Jack followed them slowly down the stairs, still wielding the knife. They moved down the staircase, eyes firmly planted on him. He could see the fear in their eyes and thrived on it. The pain would subside, the wounds would heal, but his pride would take a little longer to mend. He had the upper hand, but it had come at a cost. There was broken furniture and possibly broken bones as well. As the two men moved closer to the door they had recently broken in through, a grin spread across Jack's face.

'Those injuries are gonna serve as a reminder that you messed with the wrong person. Tonight, you get to walk away, but if I ever see you again, I promise you won't be so lucky.'

He made a motion with the knife, not with intent but to further highlight they had made a grave mistake coming here. The men scrambled quickly and at that they were out of the farmhouse, making a hasty retreat down the track. As Jack approached the door, he noticed something had fallen from the pocket of one of the intruders. It was the key to his truck. Bending down to pick it up, he heard a noise behind him. He turned around, startled, but it was just George making her way gingerly down the stairs. She saw the blood on his face and ran towards him.

'Jack!' she exclaimed in a panicked tone.

With the adrenaline now dissipating, Jack was visibly pained by his injuries. He mustered a smile, but she wondered whether this was simply for her benefit. He looked hurt.

'Who were they?' she asked.

'Burglars who targeted the wrong house.'

'How do you know they were just burglars?'

Jack held up his car key. He then walked over to the kitchen table and picked up his wallet. He held it out to George, turning it upside down.

'Empty.'

She hugged him with relief and then jumped back quickly as he grimaced with pain.

'I'm sorry. I felt so helpless, but I was certain they were here for me.'

'They were downstairs too long to be looking for somebody.'

'But they came upstairs.'

'They got greedy; it was a grave misjudgement.'

George looked on unconvinced.

'We need to call the police.'

'That's only going to get us some unwanted attention.'

'What do you mean?' she asked sheepishly.

'You're here because Toby believes you're in danger. The fewer people who know your location, the better. The only people who know you are here are Toby, Beth and myself. We don't want the police asking questions.'

'Jack, I'm frightened.'

He looked over at her and held out his arms. She felt comforted and safe in his embrace. He reminded her so much of Dylan.

'You know you can't tell anybody about what happened here tonight?'

'Toby?'

'Especially not Toby,' he said assertively.

'I don't follow. Isn't Toby the one person we can trust?'

'I'd trust him with my life, but he'll panic, and when Toby panics he makes poor decisions, and that could jeopardise us all.'

George stared down at her feet with a look of vulnerability. She was uncomfortable keeping things from Toby, especially as he had taken her in and worked tirelessly to protect her. She had no real insight into the situation, but the one thing she knew was that everything Toby had done recently had been for her.

'Jack...'

'He's been through enough. I'm not prepared to add to that,' Jack interrupted.

After a few minutes of quiet contemplation George rose out of her seat and placed her hand on Jack's shoulder before walking over to the sink. She glanced over at the clock on the oven and noticed it was just after two in the morning. Until now, she'd had no concept of time throughout the ordeal. She knew she had gone to bed just after ten, but everything after that was a blur. As they sat down, Jack nursing his injuries, she with her head in her hands, George began to cry. Jack placed his hands on her shoulders and rubbed them gently, as she slowly raised her head and looked him in the eye. The tears weren't just about tonight. They were about the rape, the teenage abortion, the breakdown of her relationship with Toby, having no place to call her home. They represented regret from the past, fear of the future, and every bad decision she had ever made. As she wiped her eyes, she realised she felt out of control and completely out of her depth.

'What now?'

'I'm gonna grab some overdue sleep, then tomorrow I'm heading out to bolster the security in this place.'

'Do you not think you should get yourself checked out? That cut on your head looks nasty.'

'I'm more pissed off than hurt,' Jack responded with a grin.

He rose out of his seat and headed towards the back door. George could hear banging, but didn't leave her chair. A few minutes later, Jack walked back into the kitchen area and took a seat opposite her.

'I've done a quick repair job on the door. I'll fix it properly tomorrow.'

George glanced at him across the table.

'I don't want to be alone tonight.'

Jack smiled at her but didn't reply. He simply stood up, reached for her hand, and led her upstairs, switching out the light on the chaos the night had brought.

{ 16 }

Toby felt his heart rapping at the walls of his chest. It wasn't a panic attack, but his body was certainly questioning his decision making in this moment. Necessity? Curiosity? Desperation? Perhaps a combination of the three, he thought. He stopped and considered whether to turn back. He questioned whether he was fuelled by expectation, or simply hope. He'd reasoned this was a calculated risk, but standing here, he now wondered whether he was merely stirring up the hornet's nest. Yet gripped by resilience, inspired in some misguided way by optimism, and consumed by anger, he was about to step into the bear cage.

The first thing he noticed was how well she looked. She still had that spark, which suggested she could get what she wanted with little effort. He'd be lying if he said he hadn't thought about her, but whatever that image of her had been in his mind, it wasn't this. Her hair had grown and was now jet black. As she approached him, he was unsure whether she was smiling or smirking. She paused and stood over him for a moment before taking her seat.

'Jesus Christ, I never thought I'd see *you* here again,' she said now with an unmistakable grin.

'Hello Olivia,' Toby replied, taking a deep breath in a futile attempt to calm his nerves. He felt angry, but more than anything, he was disappointed that simply being in her presence had this effect on him.

'What's he done now?'

'Sorry?'

'My husband. I'm assuming he's the reason you're here, as you and I have nothing else to discuss. So, what's he done?' She sounded cold.

Toby looked down at his hands on the table. There would be no small talk and no exchange of pleasantries. Olivia's sharp opening was enough to suggest there would be no easing into the conversation. He shuffled back in his chair and unzipped his coat.

'When I came here last, you shouted something to me, something which stayed with me, but only now appears to have significance.'

Olivia laughed.

'I wish I could say your visit was memorable enough for me to remember, but you're going to have to enlighten me.'

'Your asymmetrical facial expression says otherwise.'

Olivia looked shocked, yet was seemingly also actively trying to hide her admiration at how astute he was.

'The left side of your face is trying to smile, but it's the corner of your mouth on the right-hand side which gives you away. It's kind of like a smirk. There was one thing you were right about…I am good.'

'And yet you bought every lie I ever told you.'

Revenge in Mind

'My job as a psychotherapist was never to cast doubt on the validity of what my clients were disclosing. Whatever they presented to me in therapy was their thing, not mine. If clients sought to use therapy to be deceptive, they deceive only themselves.'

'Do you think I deceived myself?'

'The question is Olivia, do you?'

Olivia stared at Toby for a moment, but didn't answer his question.

'For you to come back here, he must have really rattled you.'

'Receiving veiled threats in the coffee shop was one thing, but having him turn up at my house knowing my wife was home alone was something which went significantly beyond unacceptable.'

Olivia recoiled in her chair. She looked genuinely surprised. Toby continued.

'Since the arrest, I have removed all traces of myself online and we have no mutual friends or acquaintances, so I'm left wondering how he was able to track me down.'

'You think I gave him the information?' she asked in a manner which Toby thought could be sarcasm or genuine hurt.

'The last thing you said to me was if he thought I suspected him, I wasn't safe. Then I have an unpleasant encounter with him in a public place where he tells me he's been to see you and that you took delight in taunting him with my suspicions of him. Coincidence?'

'He came to see me, and I'm not gonna lie, I did take great pleasure watching the bastard squirm. If he's threatening you, you have his attention. I have to be honest, I hadn't seen him scared like that in quite some time. You must have really got under his skin.'

Toby looked confused. This felt like they were having two separate conversations. Olivia, picking up on this, proceeded.

'The guy who has been asking after him beat up a couple of his pals. I'm assuming that's why you're here? Well, I'll tell you the same as I told him. It has nothing to do with me. She paused for a moment. 'Though I almost wish it did,' she added smugly.

Toby placed his hands on the back of his head and slowly guided them down his neck before looking up at the ceiling. This revelation by Olivia explained Eric's sudden obsession with him. Eric had come here believing Olivia was behind the threat, but had left convinced it was actually Toby. The first question was, had Olivia deliberately served up Toby as a sacrificial lamb? The second was, what was Eric Stanton capable of doing in order to protect himself?

'You look surprised,' Olivia said slowly.

'Why would Eric believe it was me who was behind this?'

She sat back and smirked, which gave him the answer to his question. Toby felt a sharp burst of anger, which he struggled to contain. The target wasn't just on his back; it was on the backs of people he cared about, and for what? A misguided notion that somehow his suffering would enhance her situation?

'You're angry,' she grinned.

'I sacrificed my career for you...'

'I never asked you to.'

'Everything I did that night was with the intention of helping you, saving you.'

'You weren't supposed to be there, Toby. Had you kept your nose out, I wouldn't be in this shithole and that fucking rapist wouldn't still be a danger to women.'

'I thought you were in trouble.'

'You were supposed to think that. I needed you to believe I was the poor abused wife. What you weren't supposed to do is turn up at my house.'

She was angry and her voice had risen to a level Toby didn't feel comfortable with. He was shaking, but desperately trying not to let it show. She would exploit any sign of weakness. He had to gain the upper hand for the sake of his family. Whether or not she was behind the threat to Eric, she still had the reach to pull his strings. She had the power to divert Eric from Toby's direction, but he suspected that her influence would diminish the longer this went on.

'What does he want with me?'

'Perhaps you should ask him that.'

Toby ignored her response. If she was as vindictive as he believed, she would get off on watching him lose his composure. She'd manipulated him before for her own gain. He wouldn't allow that to happen again.

'There are two key questions here. The first is what's in it for you...'

'And the second?' she interrupted, smirking.

'If somebody is looking for Eric, and neither of us is behind it, who is?'

'Why does that bother you? He's running scared and it couldn't happen to a nicer person. Sit back and enjoy the show,'

Olivia replied, displaying her delight at the very thought of somebody seeking revenge on her estranged husband.

'If Eric is being threatened, that's no concern of mine, but if he believes I'm behind those threats and comes after my family, then it becomes my concern. I have no idea what he's capable of and would prefer not to put that to the test.'

'There's one question you haven't answered. What's my involvement in all this?'

'You haven't asked that question.'

'I'm asking it now,' she replied seductively.

'Why did you imply to Eric that I was involved in whatever it is that's going on?'

'What makes you think I did?'

'He told me when he cornered me in the coffee shop.'

'And you believed him?'

'He lied to me three times during that conversation. That wasn't one of them.'

'You're advocating for him now?'

Toby felt she was baiting him, but he wouldn't give her the satisfaction of biting.

'It was simply about picking up on the things he wasn't saying.'

Olivia took a deep breath as the smile on her face faded. For a moment, she looked like the vulnerable woman he had first met. He thought about how a place like this could either harden or break you and deliberated which way Olivia had gone. She was portraying as somebody who enjoyed being in control, but Toby sensed there was something lurking behind this. He wondered whether she had allowed him and Eric, the two people she had most disdain for, to visit because she generated a perverse pleasure in the knowledge they needed her, or simply because she was lonely. She sat forward with her arms on the desk.

'I'm not evil, I'm just damaged, you know.'

Toby flinched in surprise. She was seeking validation.

'Trauma can have an overpowering impact on us.'

'What do you mean?'

'That good people can make bad choices.'

'You still think I'm a good person, Toby?'

'I believe there's good in everybody. You just have to look at bit harder for some people, but when you have to look deep enough, you will often uncover some deep-seated trauma.'

'Doesn't that just excuse malicious behaviour?' she asked with a genuine curiosity.

'Explanation isn't justification.'

'Do you see that same goodness in Eric?'

'I see a deeply flawed individual, but I suspect there is a vulnerability that sits behind this.'

'Your outlook on people is something to be admired Toby, but I'm afraid when it comes to my soon to be ex-husband, that good you speak of is well and truly absent.'

'You're divorcing him?'

'He's divorcing me. I received the papers last week. It turns out he didn't take too kindly to me trying to murder him after all. Who would have thought it?'

Olivia smiled, but Toby questioned whether there was a sadness underneath. Her contempt for Eric was indisputable, but this wasn't just about him. Her lifestyle, her home and her opportunity to be a mum were all ending along with her marriage.

She knew Eric could present himself as the victim to Tyler and would have no difficulty conveying her as violent and abusive. Tyler would grow up to believe whatever his father decided to tell him, and there was nothing she could do about this.

'He'll never let me see Tyler, you know.'

'I'm sorry. I know how much you love your son.'

Olivia smiled, and this time it seemed sincere to Toby.

'You know it was never anything personal against you, Toby. I need you to know that.'

'Why is it important to you I know that?'

'Because after all I've done to you, everything I've put you through, you're still sitting here seeking to understand my motives. Others have simply condemned me.'

Toby smiled cautiously. He couldn't be certain Olivia wasn't playing mind games with him, but he had an advantage. The element of surprise was no longer a factor. He knew which direction to look in and if he looked there for long enough, she would give her intentions away.

'You think Eric is targeting your family?'

Toby thought for a moment. He didn't want to give too much away. He wasn't worried about any loyalty she may have to Eric. That had disappeared the night she plunged a knife into him. His concern lay with her sheer contempt of him. She would love nothing more than to goad him and had already shown she would use anybody as a pawn if it allowed her to twist the knife. This made her unpredictable.

'He's been following you?' Olivia asked.

'What makes you say that?'

Revenge in Mind

'You mentioned he turned up at your house when you were out. I know Eric and that isn't something he would leave to chance. He likely charmed your wife, probably enough to get her to question your assessment of him. Am I right?'

Toby smiled.

'I haven't told Beth who he was. I didn't want to panic her.'

'Are you certain it was him?'

Toby nodded.

'He wanted me to know it was him. He left me just enough to figure it out.'

'Like what?'

'That doesn't matter. What matters is that your husband has gone after people I care about to get at me, and I need to know how to stop him.'

'People?' Olivia probed.

'I'm sorry?'

'You said people, which implies there is more than one person. I was just curious, that's all.'

Toby had slipped up. He'd given away more than he'd intended. Perhaps he had underestimated how astute Olivia was, or perhaps subconsciously a part of him wanted to open up to her about the situation. If he needed a sounding board with somebody of whom he had no emotional investment, Olivia would be an ideal candidate. The fact she found Eric repulsive was a bonus, but Toby still needed to tread carefully. The two occasions on which he had visited her had followed the same path. She had initially displayed hostility, gleefully taunting him, but had settled into something more approachable. This may not be about which of the two she liked the most, rather which of them she hated the least. Her opinion of him wasn't his concern though, he didn't need a friend. What he needed was her knowledge, her insight. Toby was counting on the fact that her desire to see Eric lose everything was enough to convince her to help him.

'You must really have him worried if he's going to these lengths to silence you.'

'The question is, what does he believe he needs to silence?'

'Eric and logic have never really been well acquainted. If he gets an idea in his head, even though it may be irrational, he'll run with it. If he's convinced himself you're behind the threat to him through the attack on his friends, he'll seek retribution. He's much more subtle than violence. He'll come for you in other ways.'

Toby frowned and looked down at his hands on the table, which were now trembling. He lowered his head into his hands and began massaging his forehead.

'Do you remember when I told you I tracked down one of the women whom Eric had raped before we had met, the ex-girlfriend?'

Toby nodded, unsure where this was leading.

'She was petrified of him. I mean, this woman was literally shaking at the very mention of his name. He had long since departed her life, but still he had a grip on her. This is what he does, Toby. This is what that son of a bitch does. Once he has hold of you, he never lets go.'

'What about you?' Toby asked calmly

'You think he's let go of me?'

'I don't believe he ever had hold of you.'

'You think I had hold of him?' she laughed somewhat demonically.

Toby stared at Olivia for a moment. He was trying to play to her ego, but knew it might antagonise her if she still saw herself as his victim. It was a risky move.

'I wonder whether you were the one person he couldn't break, the one person he couldn't control.'

'Oh, he broke me alright, when he fucked me against my wishes.'

Toby screwed his eyes. He was walking a tightrope here and knew at any moment the slightest of misjudgements would see him crash to the ground with a thud.

'I think you're perhaps stronger than you give yourself credit for, Olivia.'

'Because I stabbed the bastard?'

'Why did you stay?' Toby asked, ignoring her response.

'Because of Tyler. I tried so hard to provide him with a normal childhood. I didn't want him to be raised in a broken family.'

Toby smiled sympathetically.

'When did you stop having sex with Eric?'

Olivia recoiled, shocked. She looked deep in reflection as she searched for an appropriate way to answer Toby's question.

'Right after the bastard raped me,' she finally replied, looking defiant.

'That was when you took the control away from him. That was the point he realised you wouldn't simply comply. It would have angered him, but it would also have frightened him because at that point, you became unpredictable. Rape can feel like it's about degradation, but it's mainly control that sits behind it. Sadly, often within a relationship, rape is not the end product, it's simply a method that is used to lay the foundations for the dynamics of that relationship. It's a vicious way of communicating a message.'

Olivia managed a weak smile. Regardless of the criminality of her actions, her deceptive and manipulative behaviours, she was still human. Toby wondered how she would have turned out had she never met Eric Stanton. He wondered how much of the person he saw before him was down to personality traits, and how much was attributed to trauma damage. He felt sorry for her. After everything she had put him through, he felt a sadness at her plight. The difference was he no longer reproached himself for this.

'Can I ask you a question?' she asked tentatively.

Toby nodded.

'How do you do it? How do you stare into evil and draw out goodness?'

'I'm not sure I've ever stared into evil.'

'What do you see when you look into my eyes?' she continued.

'Why is that important to you?'

'The one thing you have a lot of in a place like this is time, and this means an awful lot of soul-searching and reflection. So far, I've found few answers. I guess I'm wanting a second opinion,' she grinned.

'If I held up a mirror to you, what would you see?' Toby replied, deflecting her original question.

'A pale reflection of who I used to be. A woman who saw her optimism ripped away from her and replaced with cynicism and mistrust. A woman once occupied by love, now overrun by anger and a thirst for revenge. I wasn't always like this, you know.'

'Nobody ever is.'

Olivia smiled at him, and Toby felt its sincerity.

'Earlier, you alluded to the fact Eric had targeted more than one person.'

For a split second, he looked away, unable to meet her gaze. One thing he had learned about Olivia Stanton was she was perceptive. He would struggle to lie to her without being discovered. He took a deep breath to buy himself some time to consider how to find the right balance between answering genuinely whilst also hiding George's identity.

'I believe he may have been behind a stalking incident recently.'

'What makes you think it was him?'

'It coincided with the time an old friend came to stay with us and happened soon after he cornered me in the coffee shop. It felt more than a coincidence.'

'Is she okay?'

Toby looked up at her, suspicion etched on his face.

'I didn't mention it was a she.'

Olivia looked surprised as she battled to keep her composure.

'Just an assumption,' she replied calmly.

She was lying. Her face had given it away, but if he antagonised her now, he risked losing the one person who may be able to help him stop Eric Stanton. He had avoided police detection to date and was now seen as a victim, which stacked the odds in his favour. Toby needed Olivia, but he now had suspicions about her own involvement in all of this. He now faced a dilemma. Did he go along with her lies and tread with extreme caution, or did he challenge her in the hope it would get him closer to the truth? She made the decision for him.

'You think I'm involved in this, don't you?'

'Are you?'

'Not in the way you think I am.'

Toby looked perplexed.

'Did you never wonder who sent you the message?'

'Message?'

Olivia raised her eyebrows and stared at him as though she was waiting for him to figure it out himself. Then it hit him. Toby sat back, mouth open. The message. His focus had been on George, on getting her to safety. How could he have overlooked the message? He'd been convinced of her involvement in this, but she wasn't his adversary. She was his guardian angel.

'It was you.'

Olivia didn't reply, instead she ran her hands through her hair and then removed a bobble from her pocket and tied it up.

'I'd like to ask why, but I feel there's a more urgent question here.'

'How?'

She had a platform, she had her audience, and she was suddenly relevant. She wanted to talk, and she had his attention.

'I can see the question you're dying to ask Toby; it's eating away further at you with every second that passes. You're desperately trying to make the link between myself, my husband and…'

She paused as though waiting for just the right moment to deliver the blow.

'...and Georgina Sampson,' she finished.

Toby froze. If he'd wanted to speak at this moment, he couldn't have. It felt like a heavy strike to the stomach. He'd hit the canvas and remained there dazed, confused, and with no idea of how to regain his feet.

'You looked shocked. I'm guessing you want to know my relationship with Georgina Sampson?'

Toby remained silent. She nodded, as though receiving non-verbal permission to proceed.

'As I've said to you before, my husband is a very dangerous man, but he's also charming and well connected. What that means is he can easily manipulate people into doing things for him. But Eric is the type of person who won't simply come after you. He'll come after the people you love to prove a point. He's the type of person who'll continue to hit you whilst you're on the floor. Eric will find your Achilles heel and put pressure on it until it snaps.'

'I'm still struggling to understand where Georgina fits into this,' Toby said, finally able to find his voice.

'He knew she was close to you and...'

'And what?' Toby snapped.

'You still haven't figured it out, have you?'

'I'm not sure what I'm supposed to be figuring out.'

'Do you remember asking how I knew about Eric's past? How I knew he was a rapist?'

'I remember.'

'And I told you I dug into his past and tracked down an ex-girlfriend of his.'

Toby nodded slowly.

'She was a sweet girl, a little older than me. Never struck me as his type, though I'm not sure I know exactly what his type is. She had left him whilst he'd been out, that much she was forthcoming with. I got little more from her aside from one detail.' She paused. 'Her name...Georgina Sampson.'

Toby felt sick as a shiver passed down his spine. Not George. Everything she had battled as a teenager, that sweet innocence and kind nature destroyed in an instant. He bowed his head. He wanted to be anywhere else but here listening to this, yet he needed to know. As much as it pained him, he needed to know.

'She was the ex-girlfriend?'

'I'm sorry.'

None of this made sense to Toby, but he wondered whether that was perhaps because he didn't want to accept the reality of the situation. He had so many questions, yet felt no inclination to hear any answers. He didn't want to know any detail. His dislike for Eric Stanton had now turned into a loathing. What he did to Olivia Stanton was sad, but she had been a client. George was somebody who he had cared for deeply. He still did. This was now personal, and he felt a sudden eruption of anger, one he hadn't recalled feeling for quite some time. But something about this troubled him. There were significant details which made no sense.

'How did you or Eric link George to me?'

'Is that your name for her? That's cute.'

Revenge in Mind

Olivia had changed again, like a switch being flicked. Toby suddenly became suspicious of her sincerity. She was oscillating between a scorned woman, determined to get her revenge, and something resembling a more genuine individual wishing to atone for her mistakes.

'You haven't answered my question.'

'I didn't make the link at first, but I have ways of finding out things. I didn't have to look too deep into her past to find you there.'

'It was you who told Eric. You gave him the link.'

'I had to make it clear to him he no longer had control over me and that I was no longer intimidated. His face. Oh, his face Toby as I told him his ex-girlfriend had gone to find the one person who could satisfy her.'

Olivia Stanton began cackling uncontrollably. She wasn't his guardian angel. She just despised her husband so much she would use anybody and anything to exact her revenge. She gazed up at Toby, now with a serious look on her face.

'Toby, you have only two options with Eric. Either walk away and accept what he's done...'

'Or?'

'Or go after him with everything you have, but make sure you nail him, because if you don't, he won't stop. I faced that very same choice, Toby, and I simply couldn't walk away and accept it. The question is, knowing he raped your college sweetheart, can you?'

Olivia's words shook Toby. He looked down at the desk, trying desperately to process what he was hearing. But something still concerned him.

'George and I hadn't been in contact for a very long time. You sent me a warning, which would only really make any sense if George was back in my life. How could you possibly have known she was at my house?'

Olivia stared at Toby. She looked serious, but Toby felt there was an element of smugness to it. She paused for a moment.

'Who do you think sent her there in the first place?'

The bell rang and Olivia Stanton rose to her feet. She backed away from the table slowly, a grin spreading across her face once more. Toby was stunned. As he watched her being escorted out of the visiting area, he felt sick. He had known George was hiding something, but could never imagine the depth of her deception. He wanted to believe this was just another of Olivia's games but had a strong inkling she was telling the truth. Toby lowered his head and exited the prison, slowly trying to process Olivia's revelation. She was clearly revelling in the cat-and-mouse game she had created, but for him, a part of his past had been destroyed. He questioned whether he had ever truly known George, and hated the thought of having to be guarded with what he said around her from now on. But her relationship with Olivia wasn't his chief concern, nor were her motives for seeking him out. His concern now was Eric Stanton. Toby was distraught at the thought of George falling victim to him. This had confirmed his fears that Eric was a serial rapist who thrived on fear and control. He had shown he would use any means necessary to silence Toby, including going after his loved ones. There was no mistaking he had to be stopped. It was now just a question of how far Toby would go to protect the one person who meant more to him in life than any other.

{ 17 }

'You look better than the last time I saw you.'

Toby replied with a polite nod, but felt a sudden unease as he experienced flashbacks of the last time he sat opposite Mike Thomas. He and Mike hadn't really spoken since the day of Toby's police interview. Mike had checked in with Beth from time to time, but Toby had wanted to keep a distance. The truth was, he didn't know how to feel about him. Toby believed he had been made to feel like a disingenuous criminal and blamed Mike for his role in this. Though he hadn't conducted the interview, Toby carried an element of resentment towards Mike for sitting idly by and allowing Nadia Williams to question his practice and his integrity. A conversation off the record briefly revealed the person Toby considered a friend, but now he could only see a contributing factor in an unimaginably traumatic situation. Yet here they both were, occupying the same table at the coffee shop in a meeting Toby himself had initiated.

'How have you been, Toby?'

'Are you here as an officer of the law or a friend?' Toby asked without cracking a smile.

'Are you really asking me that?'

'I'm sorry, that was uncalled for.'

'Good people make poor decisions, Toby. My job isn't to judge or speculate, it's to establish the facts. I pushed hard on the boundaries to try to protect you, but you were incredibly naïve. *That* I'm telling you as a friend.'

'When did you realise I wasn't guilty?'

'The moment we spoke outside of the crime scene. I've seen a hell of a lot of criminals in my time. I know when somebody is bullshitting me. As I said, I stretched the boundaries, but I'm an officer of the law and I have to follow due process.'

'There's something you should know, Toby.'

Mike paused before continuing.

'In an interview cell, there's a camera that is always recording.'

'Why are you telling me this?'

'Because our conversation, which appeared to be off the record, was still being recorded. Had somebody wanted to look through the footage, they would have seen the sequence of events. They would have observed an officer switching off the audio tape, alone in a room with a suspect. I'm sure you don't need me to tell you what sort of unwanted line of questioning that would have invited. I took a risk for you.'

Toby thought for a moment. Had Mike been in his corner the whole time? He'd attempted to suppress events of that day, albeit unsuccessfully. The one thing he continued to circle back to, however, was the feeling of isolation. Throughout the torment, he had felt so alone, unable to speak to the one person he needed above all others.

'What's troubling you, Toby?'

'What makes you think I'm troubled?'

Mike tilted his head and smiled.

'The last time I saw you was...'

'My arrest?' Toby interrupted, sensing the awkwardness.

'Yes, the arrest. This is early afternoon and neither of our wives are here, which rules out a social engagement. That then points to a more official reason and Toby, people don't reach out to the police unless something is wrong. Besides, your facial expression gives you away, so shoot.'

Toby smiled, and this time it was natural. He liked Mike's sense of humour and how straight-talking he was. It was a little different to Toby's approach, but then their respective professions saw them deal with very different people in very different environments.

'Perceptive and analytical, you could make a good therapist,' Toby teased.

'I don't have the patience. Besides, you know I don't like people.'

The ensuing laughter further eased the tension between the men, but Toby's smile quickly waned, giving way to a pained expression he knew Mike wouldn't overlook. This conversation wouldn't be an easy one. Olivia's revelation had rocked him. He thought of all the things he had worked with as a psychotherapist and felt a deep sense of guilt that none of it had affected him the way this had. This was different, though. The level of emotional investment in a professional setting is incomparable to a personal one. He liked his clients, but he loved George, always had. Naturally, that love came in a different form these days. Nevertheless, it was there.

'Toby'? Mike probed softly, noticing his smile had disappeared. Toby moved to speak, but stopped short of a verbal response. He sat back and contemplated the best way to approach. Something Mike had said had stuck with him. 'I'm an officer of the law'. He guessed he'd reached out to Mike as a friend, regardless of his ambivalence towards him, but now questioned whether he was ever off duty. Yet the very reason he had chosen Mike was because of his profession and his seniority within that profession. Olivia's words reverberated, and he knew a police visit wouldn't deter Eric. It would simply anger him further. Toby didn't have an audience. He could do little to affect Eric's reputation, but police presence would be damaging. Eric had slid under the radar and the media had conveyed him as a victim. If they looked into him now, it would tarnish that image. More importantly, if they stopped seeing him as a victim, they would almost certainly revisit the Olivia Stanton case. This was something Eric would be keen to avoid at all costs, and Toby was wary of setting off a chain reaction. Sitting opposite Mike now, he realised he really didn't know what he needed to get out of the conversation and wondered whether it would be wise to mention anything at all. He could simply lie, make something up, but Mike was astute. He had worked with many criminals and could surely identify whether or not Toby was lying. As Toby mulled over his dilemma, his concentration was disrupted.

'Tell me why I'm here, Toby. As nice as it is to catch up with you, this simply doesn't feel like a social gathering.'

Toby drew in a deep and stressed breath.

'I think somebody may be in trouble,' he managed.

'You think?'

'You sound like a therapist.'

'You mean I sound like you?'

'I'm not a therapist.'

'I don't believe you'll ever stop being a therapist. It's ingrained in you,' Mike replied kindly.

Toby smiled and nodded, not wishing to dismiss Mike's attempt at a compliment, but not wishing to labour on it either.

'I've been to see Olivia Stanton.'

'I'd heard.'

'Beth once said you know about things before they've even happened. I'm beginning to get the impression she may have been right,' Toby said with a more relaxed smile.

Mike grinned at him.

'I have my sources.'

'It's not the first time I've visited her.'

'That I also knew.'

'That source again?'

'Actually, your wife,' Mike replied. 'I rang to see how you were and she mentioned you'd gone to the prison,' he qualified.

Toby studied Mike, still contemplating where to begin. Much of this was circumstantial, but that may benefit him, he thought.

'I think a friend of mine may be in danger.'

'What kind of danger?'

'I'm not sure at the moment.'

'What makes you think they're in danger?'

'I can't really say.'

'Toby, you're not giving me much to go on here,' Mike replied in a frustrated tone.

Toby retreated into his chair and rubbed his hands up and down his face slowly. There was a reason he was here and a reason he had chosen Mike, but what was less clear was the manner in which he would approach this. He felt like he was walking a tightrope, and one false move would see him fall to the ground from a great height.

'After I left the prison that first time, I came face to face with a ghost, somebody who had once meant a great deal to me. I was suddenly staring twenty years into the past. She said she needed my help, but wouldn't go into detail.'

'And you think she's in danger?'

'Except I don't believe she's the actual target.'

'So, who is?'

Toby sat up and composed himself, but remained silent.

'Toby, who do you believe is the real target?' Mike repeated.

'I am.'

Mike looked shocked, but Toby felt surprisingly lighter. He knew, however, questions would inevitably follow and he couldn't remain cryptic. It wasn't a coincidence he had opened up to Mike. Now he simply had to trust he could find some clear guidance on how to proceed.

'You're not making any sense here. Why would you be a target?' he asked in disbelief.

'It's not what I've done, it's what somebody thinks I could do. Does that make sense?'

'So, somebody's in danger, but you don't know what type of danger?'

'Yes.'

'And you believe it is you and not them who is the real target?'

'Correct.'

'And it's not for something you've done, but something somebody believes you could do, right?'

'I know how this must sound.'

'I'm glad you said that, because I was beginning to think it was just me,' Mike grinned.

Toby looked away for a moment. He felt conflicted. Part of him wanted to trust he could unburden himself and get a fresh perspective on things, from somebody who would know better than most. Yet there was a reluctance to be completely open in fear of the repercussions. It wasn't about not trusting Mike, but Eric Stanton had eluded the authorities for a long time now. More than that, the encounters he had had with the police, he had done so as a victim. Changing the perception from victim to perpetrator would be no easy feat. Adding in a lack of evidence for good measure would make it nigh on impossible. Mike had spoken candidly with Toby before, however. He was professional, but had been known to sail close to the wind. He had already likely disclosed things to Toby he shouldn't have. Toby decided in that moment that to become unstuck, he would need to take a leap of faith. He steadied himself and leaned forward, arms resting on the table in front of him.

'Before I went to see Olivia Stanton, the first time, I went to the hospital to visit her husband.'

'Eric?'

Toby nodded.

'It turned out I'd met him before without realising. There was a specific moment where I gazed into his eyes and observed something that disturbed me.'

Toby paused and looked up. Mike was focused on him, his face expressionless. Toby had his attention.

'After Olivia was charged, I believed Eric was a victim, but...'

'You don't think he's the victim here?'

'His wife stabbed him in a premeditated attack. He's most certainly a victim, but that doesn't tell the whole story.'

'What are you saying?'

'Eric Stanton has masterfully directed your attention in one direction.'

Mike looked at Toby rather scornfully and Toby realised he had just inadvertently insulted those involved in the investigation.

'You think we missed something with this guy? All the evidence we compiled pointed to him being the victim, Toby. The evidence stacked up against Olivia Stanton.'

'It was supposed to. He made sure of that.'

Mike shuffled in his seat, sat back and breathed in loudly through his nostrils. He rubbed his hands together before resting them on his chin.

'I'm assuming you're coming to me with more than just a feeling you got from looking into this guy's eyes?'

'When I visited Olivia, she warned me about Eric.'

'Toby, Olivia Stanton tried to murder her husband in cold blood, and this wasn't the first time she had been acquainted with the police. She also tried to lie her way through her police interview and only confessed when presented with irrefutable evidence. She's not known for her trustworthiness.'

'She was telling the truth.'

'No disrespect Toby, but this woman lured you into her web of lies and deception, which ended with you being arrested on suspicion of attempted murder.'

'She wasn't lying.'

'She's lied to you before.'

Toby smiled. This felt very much like a character assassination, though he didn't believe that was the intent.

'This time I knew where to look. But more than that, she was right.'

'What exactly did she say?'

'That he was a serial rapist, and if he thought I suspected him, he would come after me.'

'Toby, what you're telling me is very serious, naturally I'm concerned. Do you have any evidence at all?'

'Not of the rape...'

'Okay?' Mike replied before pausing as though expecting Toby to elaborate.

'I had an unpleasant encounter with him in here, and I believe he visited the house.'

'I'm guessing the encounter you're referring to wasn't set up beforehand?'

'Not by me.'

Mike looked at him, puzzled, which encouraged Toby to continue.

'What I mean by that is it was staged to look like a chance meeting, but I strongly suspect it had been planned.'

Mike studied Toby, which made him nervous. He wondered if he believed him, and then debated whether it would actually be better if he didn't. He was still unsure what he needed, but the overarching feeling was one of trepidation as to what an investigation into Eric Stanton could mean for Toby and those close to him. Finally, Mike broke his stare and his silence.

'You still haven't told me why I'm here.'

Toby sighed and turned his head to look out of the adjacent window. The trees were shaking and passers-by were moving hurriedly to minimise their exposure to the biting wind and cruelly low temperature, considering they had exited winter. He felt grateful for being indoors, but the warmth of the coffee shop was in stark contrast to the cold shivers he was experiencing thinking about Eric Stanton being alone with his wife.

'Forgive me, Mike, but I'm a little wary about where this could lead.'

'Toby, so far your evidence consists of an unpleasant encounter in a coffee shop, a visit to your house when you weren't home, and hearsay from the very person who is currently serving a long sentence for trying to murder her husband. I don't wish to alarm you, but that's not exactly a slam dunk for the CPS.'

Mike grinned, which helped to relax Toby a little. This was the humour Toby had warmed to when he and Mike had first met. He couldn't help but smile.

'I can see how it looks, but Mike, Eric Stanton isn't the victim he's being portrayed as.'

'Toby, I want to believe you, but you have to give me something to go on. Tell me more about what happened in here. Give me something I can investigate.'

Toby pointed towards the corner of the room. 'I was seated at that table over there. Eric walked over and took a seat, uninvited. I determined at an early stage he was lying to me, but I was unsure what he actually wanted. When I got up to leave, he clasped my wrist tightly and forced me to sit back down. But the part where he called me a failed shrink and told me to be very careful about digging into the past is what really aroused my suspicions.'

'He threatened you?'

Toby laughed.

'It was more of a warning. Certainly not enough to excite the CPS,' he said with a grin.

'But it wasn't his words I found chilling,' Toby continued.

'Oh?'

'It was the look in his eyes as he uttered them. That same look I saw at the hospital. There was a defiance, and I wondered whether I was facing a psychopath. He looked me directly in the eye without breaking sweat and lied to me several times.'

'How did you know he was lying?'

'The best way to understand if somebody is lying to you is to study their body language when you know they are being honest with you. Then you look for deviations, but I don't need to tell you this, as I am sure you're much more experienced in this field than I am.'

'There are, of course, experts we can draw upon, but ordinarily in the interview room, we focus on the evidence we have at our disposal, along with any inconsistencies in accounts,' Mike replied politely.

The two men sat in silence for a moment. Mike was looking directly at Toby, but Toby had turned his head and was once more looking out of the window.

'You know you can ask two people the same question. They can give different answers, yet both can be right.'

Mike looked confused.

'This is a little cryptic for an informal chat over a coffee.'

Toby smiled.

'There's a point to this.'

Mike wore a look of intrigue as he sat back in his chair, seemingly in anticipation of Toby offering further clarity.

'If you asked Eric and Olivia Stanton who was at fault for the breakdown of their marriage, Eric will tell you Olivia is a manipulative, vengeful woman who, spurred on by anger, tried to murder him. Olivia will tell you Eric is a controlling rapist and a bully who will stop at nothing to get what he wants. Both are correct.'

'These are very serious accusations, but so far all I have to go on are your suspicions based on an unpleasant conversation, of which there were no witnesses, I'm assuming?'

Toby shook his head.

'What makes you believe Eric Stanton is a rapist?'

'A serial rapist,' Toby corrected, with an assertiveness that took him by surprise.

Mike Thomas cleared his throat.

'Okay, a serial rapist. I know you Toby, and idly tossing allegations around without substance isn't in your nature.'

Revenge in Mind

For the first time since his arrest, Toby looked at Mike and saw a family friend. As an individual, he had a reassuring aura about him, but he had been very different as a professional. Toby had struggled to see beyond Mike in his official capacity, but now he was getting a glimpse of the person he had shared many laughs with over the years. Then the irony hit him, the reason he was here. He needed Mike's knowledge and expertise. He could have had this conversation with other friends, but he had chosen Mike for a reason. Originally, he had thought it was about testing the water, but in reality, he had already dived in and submerged himself.

'Olivia Stanton...'

'Jesus Christ Toby,' Mike interrupted before leaning forward, elbows planted on the table, chin resting on his hands, which had now been made into fists.

'Again, just so I'm absolutely clear, your evidence is a conversation in a coffee shop and a scorned woman currently locked up for attempting to murder her husband...the same husband she is now accusing of rape? Toby, she's already shown she is manipulative and hell-bent on getting revenge on this guy. You're a smart fella. Are the alarm bells not ringing?'

'She wasn't lying.'

'She's lied to you before.' It was the second time he had affirmed this point and his voice was now rising.

'I wasn't looking for inconsistencies before.'

'Toby, she lied her way through her police interview. From what you've told me, she also lied her way through her therapy with you. What's your obsession with this woman? Hasn't she already cost you enough?'

Toby looked up at the ceiling. Mike's words had stung him, but he knew this wasn't about an obsession. He didn't want Olivia. He needed her. Once he knew Eric Stanton was no longer a threat to him, he would close the door on Olivia Stanton once and for all.

'My only obsession is with finding what passes for normality in my life these days. I want Eric Stanton out of my life, and if my suspicions are right, that means keeping Olivia Stanton in it for a while longer. You know there's a certain paradox here that the person who had a hand in the abrupt ending of my career, and my arrest, may just be the person who holds the key to releasing the shackles currently strangling me.'

'Knowing you, there's some logic in there somewhere, but I have to be honest and say I'm just not seeing it.'

Toby looked down at his hands on the table and noticed he had been clenching his fists. He didn't feel anxious, but wondered whether he was a little more uneasy with the conversation than he had first thought.

'Do you remember me mentioning the girl I was dating in college, George?'

Mike nodded his head slowly.

'The last time I saw Olivia Stanton, she told me that George had been one of Eric's victims. As much as I didn't want to believe her, I knew she was telling the truth.'

'Toby, I don't know what to say,' Mike said in a genuinely sympathetic tone.

'She doesn't know that I know. I mean, how do you even begin that conversation?'

'Perhaps the more important question Toby is whether that's a conversation you want to begin.'

Toby smiled, but there was a sadness behind it. Mike, of course, was right. Toby didn't want to have that conversation because that then made it real, and the last thing he wanted was for George's plight to be real.

'I guess you can't do anything without a complaining witness, anyway. This amounts to little more than hearsay.'

Mike rubbed his hands on his knees before taking a sip of his coffee and then relaxing back into his chair.

'You're half right Toby. This does amount to little more than hearsay at this stage, but we don't need a complaining witness to press charges against a perpetrator. However, we would need to collect sufficient evidence that points to probable cause, and that would require a thorough investigation.'

Toby smiled inwardly as he realised Mike had given him exactly what he needed. Toby had piqued his interest enough to put Eric Stanton on his radar, but had been scarce on detail so far. He would now change tact to ensure Mike didn't begin the immediate investigative work into the man who he now believed was going all out to silence him.

'Maybe you're right about Olivia.'

'Oh?'

'She has lied to me before and certainly has an agenda when it comes to her husband. Maybe this is further evidence of her lust for revenge.'

'On her husband?'

'On both of us,' Toby replied.

Mike looked at Toby curiously, but didn't question his comment.

'If you really think about it, I'm more responsible for her situation than her husband. The hatred she has for him is unquestionable, but it was my intervention that separated her from her son and took away her freedom, regardless of my intention.'

'You think she's pulling the strings and playing you off against one another?'

Toby thought for a moment, staring down into his now empty cup.

'Mike, I know there is more to Eric than meets the eye, but consider this for a moment. He believes I am looking into his past and am responsible for a couple of his friends getting roughed up. He believes this because his wife, the woman who tried to kill him, pointed him in my direction. The reason I am living in fear not for myself, but for my family, is because Olivia was able to convince me that Eric is a dangerous man and I'm in his sights.'

'So, Olivia Stanton is the common denominator here. She has you both playing a cat-and-mouse game whilst she sits back and enjoys the show.'

'That's what I'm beginning to think, but then there are inconsistencies within that narrative.'

'Inconsistencies?'

'She was the one who warned me that George was in trouble. It feels like she's battling with two different personas, each trying to suppress the other. I witnessed this when I first met her. It was like she could just flick a switch and morph into somebody else. At the time I put it down to trauma, but now I'm not so sure.'

'Look Toby, I'm not saying I don't believe you, but I wonder whether Olivia is your fundamental problem here, not Eric. Could this all boil down to somebody being pissed you're taking an interest in them and reacting angrily?'

'You mean Eric?'

'Yes. If I thought somebody was asking questions about me and had a couple of my friends beat up to prove a point, I think it would be enough to get my attention and prompt a reaction,' Mike responded.

'Maybe you're right. Perhaps this is Olivia's work.'

'Toby, as a friend, I want you to listen carefully to what I'm about to say. You don't need me to remind you how it ended for you the last time you took something on yourself and decided against involving those actually trained in that area. Don't play detective. If you want to make this formal, come and see me at the station, but my advice for now would be to remove Olivia and Eric Stanton from your life.'

Mike smiled as he finished the remaining dregs of his drink. He stood up and shook Toby's hand.

'I have to go now, but if you need anything, you know where I am.'

'Good to catch up, Mike.'

Toby watched as Mike walked down the street, hurriedly battling the strong winds. He'd done enough to plant the seeds, but questioned whether he had thrown Mike off the scent. His last comment had concerned Toby, but he hoped it had been said as a precaution rather than a suspicion. Though he had implied to Mike that he was now sceptical of what Olivia had told him, in reality he was more convinced than ever that everything Olivia had disclosed about Eric's past was true. The question now was what he would do about it. If he backed off, then maybe Eric would leave him and his family alone and he could resume a life without fear. This, of course, was what he desired more than anything, but it came at a cost. That cost was a rapist walking the streets, free to offend again. But he wasn't simply a rapist, he was George's rapist, and that revelation had hit Toby hard. Every instinct he possessed was screaming at him to walk away, but the thought of George being subjected to such a heinous act proved a compelling counter-argument. Whatever he did next would have consequences. It was now about choosing the path of least harm.

{ 18 }

Toby stopped, silently regretting his choice to go for a walk in the countryside on an overcast day. It had been a week since he'd met with Mike and, during that time he had kept a relatively low profile. Though he had been mostly inactive with any kind of physical action, his mind had been focussed on little else. The conversation with Mike had effectively told him two things. First, there didn't need to be a complaining witness for the police to take action, though they would need sufficient evidence to seek prosecution. Second, though he had tried to convince Mike to the contrary, he couldn't simply walk away from this. What had begun as an uncomfortable feeling had now developed into something with far more complexities. A fleeting suspicion had become a certainty of guilt. Originally, it had been about treading carefully, but this had now escalated into a genuine fear of what Eric Stanton was capable of. This had been compounded by the threat to George, the visit to Beth, and finally the knowledge that his first love had been one of Eric Stanton's victims. He had endeavour, and he had motive, but still Toby was unsure what he needed to, or indeed could, do. He marvelled at the picturesque surroundings, noticing the stillness of the trees. Solitude and tranquillity were the antithesis of his life, which appeared to descend into deeper chaos by the day. This wasn't simply a quiet place, it was complete isolation, just what he needed. Beth was visiting a friend for the weekend, so he had taken some long overdue respite and reacquainted himself with his love of nature. Naturally, this also gave him undisturbed time for quiet reflection, and right now there was a lot to reflect upon. The last year had been a difficult one. He had almost lost his life in a car crash, been arrested on suspicion of attempted murder, walked away from his career, and found out his childhood sweetheart had fallen victim to an unspeakable crime by somebody he was now linked with. Then a chilling thought entered his mind. This was the first time he had visited this part of the country since his accident. He hadn't thought about it on the drive, but now the images of that fateful day were vivid. His body shook as he visualised swerving off the road, remembering his last thought as he careered down the embankment. Of course, everything after that moment was a blur until he woke up in the hospital. Beth had filled in the gaps slowly over time, but hadn't wanted to add to his trauma. Toby got the impression that there were details from the accident Beth had never disclosed to him. His rehabilitation had been a slow process, but not the reparation of his physical injuries. It was the emotional impact with which he still battled, a trauma he had struggled to suppress or find any closure for. It still made little sense to him, but that was because making sense of it would likely lead him in a direction he was reluctant to head in. Olivia had manipulated him. Richard had seen this coming and had warned him beforehand, but Toby had felt he had the situation under control. Admitting this had never been the case had been hard for him because it had meant him accepting his own professional limitations. It was that realisation which had ultimately made his mind up to walk away from psychotherapy, his love, his livelihood. Things had been difficult since, but Toby had taken on occasional consultancy work, which had allowed him to continue his work within the field, though not seeing clients directly. Beth had been astute with the proceeds she had inherited from the estate of her parents, so they didn't worry about money, though Toby didn't like the idea of Beth having to draw on her savings because of the decisions he had made. Psychotherapy had afforded him a good living and allowed him to save over the years. They had now adapted their lifestyle accordingly, but were still some distance from the poverty line. The thought of Beth and the sacrifices she had made for him filled him with guilt. It was difficult for him to admit he had not prioritised her, but in truth, he hadn't. He had made her promises that deep down he had known he could not keep. She was his life, yet still he grappled with his conscience for putting Olivia Stanton before her. He was aware he was oversimplifying this. It hadn't been a simple choice between the two. Still, he felt like he had neglected her needs. He wondered whether he had been overcompensating out of guilt, a thought which saddened him. His love for Beth was genuine and above everything, which only exacerbated those feelings of guilt. He zipped up his coat as far as it would go and removed the pair of gloves from his pocket. Rearranging his scarf for extra warmth, Toby took a deep breath and continued his walk. The cold air was biting, but he smiled to himself as he absorbed the natural beauty, more importantly, the tranquillity of his surroundings.

He could just about make out two other people in the distance, but other than that, he was completely isolated, and on occasions like this, that was just how he liked it. Beth knew the significance of the time Toby spent on his own, and would only disrupt him in the case of an emergency. She had her friend and George had Jack, which meant Toby could focus his time on himself. He didn't feel guilty for doing this occasionally, instead recognising the importance of his own self-care. He had always reasoned the more emotionally healthy he was, the more equipped he felt to help others. But he did also acknowledge it was sometimes nice to do things for himself, things he enjoyed. This area of the countryside wasn't unfamiliar to Toby; he knew his way around it. This had been one of his favourite routes to walk in the past, though admittedly he hadn't undertaken it for quite some time. The distance was approximately twelve miles, which Toby expected would take him around five hours, accounting for lunch and the occasional break. With the wind now beginning to die down, the chill factor didn't feel as severe, meaning the pace Toby had begun with had now steadied. The sound of his phone ringing broke his concentration. His immediate reaction was one of panic. Beth. What if something had happened to her? What if she had been in an accident, or worse still, what if Eric Stanton had got to her? Then his mind shifted to George. Was she safe at Jack's? As he withdrew the phone from his pocket, he observed the number was withheld. It wasn't Beth or George, which prompted a feeling of relief, though hearing the voice on the other end meant that relief was short-lived.

'Hello Toby.'

Revenge in Mind

Toby felt sure his heart stopped momentarily as he removed the phone from his ear and looked around hastily. Had he been tracked? The timing seemed more than a coincidence, with Toby isolated and in a position of vulnerability. Consumed with an overwhelming panic, he frantically studied every aspect of his surroundings. His safe place, his respite, suddenly didn't feel safe. He was out in the open, yet geographically isolated and several miles from his car. He had no escape here. It would be the perfect ambush. He was defenceless and felt helpless. He questioned his naivety. How could he have allowed himself to get into this position? He leant back against the wall of an old ruin and moved the phone back into position. He didn't want to sound anxious, yet wondered how he could disguise the internal panic which had complete control over him. His voice would undoubtedly give him away. There was little else he could do. He had to take himself out of his comfort zone and somehow find a confidence and resilience he simply wasn't familiar with in social situations. Whatever he was feeling, he couldn't allow it to manifest. Desperately seeking composure, he inhaled slowly and deeply.

'How can I help you, Eric?' the only response Toby could muster.

'I dropped by your house. It was most disappointing not to see you.'

'Something tells me you didn't drop by to see me.'

There was a pause on the other end of the line. Toby had no doubt Eric was grinning sadistically, taking a moment to calculate his next move.

'Your wife was most accommodating; she makes a great coffee. Such a shame I'm a...'

'Tea drinker?' Toby interrupted.

'You remembered.'

'You were counting on me remembering. It was your way of letting me know you'd been in my home.'

'So, I got your attention?'

'Perhaps the more pressing question is why you would want it.'

Toby felt his pulse racing. He was in unfamiliar territory. He questioned whether the contrived confident persona he was displaying was bordering on arrogance. The last thing he wanted to do was further antagonise somebody who he now knew to be a dangerous man with a grudge and a purpose. He was deliberately provoking Eric, playing a dangerous game, but he couldn't reveal any vulnerability. He couldn't allow Eric to control him or the situation. He had no strategy and no idea of how and when this would end, but he needed to figure that out whilst somehow convincing Eric that he wouldn't be bullied. If he could plant any seeds of doubt in Eric's mind, it could buy him some time. He had options. He was just yet to determine which one had the most chance of success and the least chance of inflaming the situation.

'When I was a kid, I dreamed of being rich and would dream of the things I would have. I knew what my house would look like, the type of car I would drive, even the places I would visit. I didn't have an education or even a supportive family. My dad used to beat the shit out of my mum. My mum retaliated by fucking half of the village. I had nobody to encourage me, but do you know what I had?'

Toby, knowing Eric didn't need an invitation to continue, said nothing.

'Determination. When my friends were hanging out drinking and causing damage, I was planning how to make my fortune. Every night throughout my teenage years, I would think about ways to become rich. You see Toby, I had nothing as a kid. My dad was a waste of space and provided us with little aside from an occasional beating. My mother was too busy screwing around to really care. They were great role models in that respect. They showed me how not to do it. I made a promise to myself I would never be involved in the rat race they were. I had my motivation right there; they just didn't know it.'

'Why are you telling me this?' Toby asked inquisitively.

'I had the perfect life, Toby. You've seen my house, my car and the reach I have around here.'

That last bit. What did he mean by reach, and why did he assume Toby was familiar with it? Toby felt a sudden unease, like something was happening and he was on the periphery. Having wanted nothing more than to end the call, he now wanted to keep Eric talking. Eric liked to talk and Toby knew if handled in the right way, he would give him all he needed. Every impulse had told him not to provoke Eric Stanton, but here he was, about to do just that.

'I also saw you lying face down in a pool of your own blood, close to death, with a wound inflicted upon you by your very own wife.'

'What does that have to do with anything?'

'I'm wondering just how perfect that life you speak of was.'

There was a silence on the other end of the line, and Toby wondered whether Eric had hung up. He removed the phone from his ear, confirming his thoughts. The relative calmness of the countryside struck him, but that tranquillity which added to its appeal also provided an eeriness as he quickly recognised he was alone out here. His concentration was broken by his phone ringing, number withheld. He pressed to answer.

'Sorry about that, Toby. The signal out here isn't great, is it?' The words were said slowly, yet purposefully.

Filled with dread, Toby frantically looked around. Originally, he had worried about being completely isolated, yet now he wanted nothing more than to be alone. He wasn't, though. Eric Stanton was here. He was toying with Toby, sending him a message that he could easily get to him or his family. Toby thought about all the times in his life when he had felt helpless, but nothing compared. The night at Olivia Stanton's house didn't compare. Being laid in a ditch surrounded by flashing lights didn't compare. This was sheer terror. Eric could kill him and dispose of his body out here, and there would be no trace. Suddenly the thing which was most appealing about his walk was now the most terrifying. He was on his own and he needed to think fast.

'You've gone to a lot of trouble to make a point, yet I'm still unsure precisely what that point is,' Toby replied, deciding not to respond to Eric's comment.

'It's very simple, Toby. Stop playing detective and go back to your psychology.'

'Psychotherapy.'

'Yeah that.'

'I don't practice that either,' Toby replied flippantly.

There was a brief silence as Toby deliberated where this was going to end, and not just today.

'That bitch who still calls herself my wife warned me about you,' Eric said sharply.

'As she warned me of you. Does that not arouse your suspicion?'

'What do you mean?'

'She has a grudge against both of us, for different reasons, of course. She's incarcerated, so carries no physical threat, but she certainly has the opportunity and motive to inflict harm in other ways.'

'Everything she said about you was correct,' Eric snarled.

'Was it?'

'So, you're denying you've been looking into me?'

'I didn't begin looking into you on the back of anything Olivia said. It was *your* actions, not Olivia's words, which made me question whether you had something to hide. Cornering me in a coffee shop and visiting my wife to get my attention didn't exactly quell the flames.'

'If I'm backed into a corner, I'll come out swinging Toby.'

'Of that I am sure, but you're looking in the wrong direction.'

'I don't follow.'

'It isn't me backing you into the corner,' Toby explained calmly.

'Aside from the obvious, what would she have to gain from this?'

'You're looking at it wrong. It's not what she would have to gain, it's what you and I would have to lose.'

'And what's that?'

'Everything. Business, family, friendships.' Toby stopped. 'Even freedom,' he finished.

'Freedom?'

'If she thinks I'll find something incriminating.'

'How does that affect your freedom?'

'Living in fear and constantly watching over your shoulder is to live without freedom,' Toby clarified.

'You sound frightened Toby, and in your current position, you'd say just about anything right now.'

'You're here,' Toby said, unable to hide the panic in his voice.

It was met with silence.

'Tell me Toby, if a tree falls in the middle of the woods and there is nobody around to hear it, does it make a noise?'

Toby stiffened up. Did Eric plan to kill him out here? Was it all going to end with his death? Nobody would hear him scream. Eric was savvy. He would likely have covered his tracks already. He wouldn't be careless enough to leave any trace of his presence. He couldn't run. Eric would have him in sight. He wasn't a fighter, so confronting him wasn't an option either. His survival would hinge on him drawing on all of his experience.

'She felt threatened by you, you know?'

'What?'

'Olivia, she felt threatened by you. She was jealous of your relationship with Tyler.'

'Isn't that breaking some kind of confidentiality?' Eric asked in a sarcastic tone.

'Professional ethics aren't my primary concern right now.'

'Why are you telling me this?'

'I'm hoping your love for your son will outweigh your dislike for me.'

'Why would that even be a choice?'

'Because regardless of how meticulous you think you have been, you will already have made several mistakes which will ultimately tie you to whatever happens to me.'

'What mistakes do you think I've made, Toby?'

'My phone has a tracker on it. The signal is weak, but Beth knows exactly where I've been. You could say it was part of my promise to her after I ended up nearly dying in a ditch. Then there are the phone records. Whilst you've withheld your number, you've omitted to consider that phone companies can trace an underlying number if legally requested to do so. But do you know what your biggest mistake is?'

'What's that?'

'You underestimated me. You see, I have a good friend who is quite senior in the police force. I've already aired my suspicions to him, so if anything happens to me, you can be sure you'll be labelled as a person of interest. Of course, you could always go on the run, and you may even elude capture, for a while, but what sort of life would that be for Tyler, and what would he do with both parents in prison when you're inevitably caught? He would essentially become an orphan.'

Toby's heart was racing. He had been backed into a corner and was fighting for his survival. He hadn't been able to reason with Eric; he hadn't been able to successfully deflect onto Olivia Stanton. This was his last roll of the dice. He knew Eric loved his son and valued his freedom and his lifestyle. He had to show him what he risked losing. If Eric planned to kill him, he needed to plant the seeds of doubt around the aftermath, the consequences. Toby bit his lip firmly, not realising just how much so until he rubbed his finger over it and saw blood. He was in fight-or-flight mode, except flight wasn't an option. He waited anxiously for Eric to respond. He considered moving, but at least here he had a small building which offered an element of protection. However, Toby faced a disadvantage. He was almost certain Eric had him in sight, whereas he had no clue as to Eric's location. He was a sitting duck.

'That's a rather wild imagination you have there, Toby. You think I'm a killer?'

'You've tracked me to a desolate area where I'm completely isolated.'

'Perhaps I just enjoy the countryside like you.'

His tone was what Toby would describe as playful, yet sinister. He was enjoying this. Perhaps this was his intention. Perhaps this wasn't about killing him, but simply showing Toby how easily he could get to him.

'How's that girlfriend of yours?' he continued.

Toby froze to the spot and gritted his teeth. Was he talking about George? But how could he know about Toby's link to her? Had Beth let slip, but why would she? Then it became obvious. Olivia. She was having fun pulling the strings, creating a paranoia within Eric which was consequently creating a fear within Toby. She was playing this perfectly; they were mere subjects in her game. Toby swallowed hard, but didn't respond. He wanted Eric to play his hand; Toby would give him nothing.

Revenge in Mind

'I hear she's staying out of town. Who knows what she's getting up to with that farmer boy,' Eric continued in a sadistic tone.

Toby felt the anger rising inside, but knew he had to somehow suppress it. If he yielded now, he would show his weakness, something he was certain Eric would use to his full advantage. Eric clearly knew about Toby's link to George, but was he aware of how much Toby knew about his own relationship with her? About his brutal attack on her?

'What's the matter? Lost for words?' he goaded.

'Perhaps you could tell me what words you're looking for.'

Eric didn't have the opportunity to respond.

'Perhaps you could also tell me what your agenda is here because I'm still unsure. If you were going to harm me, you wouldn't have made the mistake of calling me first.'

'What makes you so sure?' Eric interjected.

'Because if you leave me alive, you leave a witness, but if you leave me for dead, you're the last person to call me. Either way, you'd be implicated. So, this then becomes about intimidating me, right? Flexing your muscles, showing you can get to me?'

'Your wife was very accommodating. It would be nice to get better acquainted with her.'

'You son of a bitch, leave her out of this.'

He desperately tried to retract the words as they tumbled out of his mouth. He'd allowed Eric to rile him, and Toby wasn't one for losing his temper. If Eric hadn't known what buttons to push before, he knew now.

'Maybe it's not your wife you should be worried about?'

Toby stood silent, heart pounding violently.

'I hear there was a break-in...at the farm. You can't be too careful these days, you don't know who's about.'

Toby was stunned. The tone of the conversation and Eric's demeanour told him he wasn't lying. George wasn't free of him. The sadistic bastard not content with raping her all those years ago was now putting her through another ordeal as part of his vendetta. Her only crime had been to leave his abusive ways, yet she now found herself a victim all over again. Both he and Eric had a past with George, but whilst to Toby she was somebody whom he still cared for deeply, to Eric she was simply collateral. There was a contrast with what George had meant to each of them, but as diametrically opposed as they had been in their respective relationships with her, ultimately, both had let her down. Those words sat with Toby for a moment. He couldn't let her down again. She was in this position not because of anything she had done, but because of Toby. Eric would have no nostalgia about their time together. He would have no hesitation in putting her through further anguish if it benefitted him. She meant nothing to him, probably never had, but she meant something to Toby, perhaps more than he had been prepared to admit to himself.

'What have you done?' Toby asked calmly, using everything he had to suppress the disdain he was feeling for his adversary.

'That sounded like an accusation.'

'It sounded more like a question to me.'

'I know a lot of people, Toby. Perhaps you should remember that.'

'That sounded like a threat.'

Revenge in Mind

'It sounded more like a statement to me,' Eric replied, mimicking Toby and clearly enjoying the control he now had.

'I have to admire you, though I don't envy your position,' he continued.

'My position?'

'Torn between two women. Here's a question for you. Knowing you can only be in one place at a time, which one would you choose to protect? Actually, let me rephrase that...which one would you sacrifice?'

If there had been any doubt remaining around Eric's capabilities, the type of person Toby was dealing with, it had now disappeared. His search to find any compassion or humility within Eric Stanton ended here. He would stop at nothing, but he was wrong about one thing. Toby didn't need to make a choice; George was in safe hands. He trusted Jack with his life and couldn't think of anybody more suited to protecting George. Were he not a farmer, Toby was convinced Jack would have been security or a bodyguard of some sort. He knew how to handle himself, and others, for that matter. He was streetwise and well respected. Those who knew him would never cross him, and those who crossed him, didn't know him. Jack wasn't the type of person to start a fight, he was the type of person to finish one should trouble find him. Even so, Eric's comment had unsettled Toby. He had a strong suspicion there was truth to what Eric had said. How else would he know George was staying out of town at Jack's farm? Then a more burning question entered his mind. Why hadn't either Jack or George told him? He had history with George. He was still close to Jack, yet he was in the dark. More than anything, it irked him that the words were coming from the mouth of a callous and vengeful individual. Eric was no doubt taking delight in twisting the knife further into Toby, allowing him a moment to catch his breath, before plunging it in further with another cruel blow. Toby tried to compose himself as he wondered whether keeping Eric on the phone longer aided or hampered his chances of survival.

'You still haven't told me what you want from me,' Toby finally managed.

'Walk away, forget you ever heard of me.'

'You cornered me in the coffee shop, visited my wife when you knew I wasn't home, and followed me here today. It doesn't sound like I'm the one who needs to walk away.'

There was a pause on the other end of the line. It was only a few seconds, but it felt like much longer to Toby.

'Listen carefully, Toby. You're talking to somebody who has surveillance on you, somebody who easily accessed your home and charmed your wife, and somebody who knows the location of that pretty little girlfriend of yours. To the police and the public, I'm the innocent victim of a brutal attack trying to piece my life back together. Being accused of attempted murder and getting arrested at a crime scene is something I've never encountered. I didn't have to give up my profession because people questioned my ethics. Tell me Toby, can you say the same?'

Toby felt wounded. Eric's words had cut through him. He felt vulnerable and out of his depth. Eric had shown with little effort he could get to the people Toby loved most. He desperately wanted to retaliate, yet everything was telling him to simply walk away and forget he had ever met Eric Stanton.

Revenge in Mind

A few weeks ago, this would have been a very simple choice, but a few weeks ago, he hadn't known George had been one of Eric's victims. He'd abandoned her once and couldn't do it again. George had spoken of needing his help when she had first walked back into his life. To this point, he still had no idea what she meant, but one thing was for certain; there was a lot more complexity to the situation now. He placed his hands on his head, deliberating how to respond. He needed to speak to Jack. He needed to know George was safe, but his priority was ensuring his own safety.

'How do I know you'll leave us alone?'

Silence.

'Eric?'

The phone line was dead. He looked around frantically, anticipating an ambush, but there was nobody in sight. In the eerie quietness of the now deserted countryside, Toby collapsed to the floor with his head in his hands, wondering if Eric had really been there at all.

{ 19 }

'You need to take a breath. What the hell's going on?'

'Where's George?'

'Why?'

'Is she safe?'

'Well, I'm not doing the cooking tonight, so yeah, she's safe.'

'Now isn't the time for your jokes, Jack. I need to know what's going on.'

'I appear to be as much in the dark as you. Perhaps you could enlighten me?'

'I just had a very unpleasant experience with a very unpleasant character. He took great pleasure in telling me there had been a break-in at what I can only assume is your place.'

'Who's the guy?'

'That doesn't matter.'

'If somebody is threatening my best friend, it matters.'

'The last thing I need is this situation escalating.'

'He wouldn't see it coming. It wouldn't take a lot to make it look like a random disagreement. There would be absolutely no connection to you at all. I just need his name.'

'I appreciate you looking out for me, but the only thing I need from you right now is to keep George safe.'

'She's fine, I promise.'

'Jack, is there anything you're not telling me?'

'Like what?'

'You're being deliberately evasive.'

Jack took a deep breath and hesitated for a moment. The pause made Toby uneasy, as he felt certain he wasn't going to like what Jack was going to say.

'This is important. What happened?'

'A couple of guys broke in, things got a little nasty, but I handled it.'

'Jesus Jack, why didn't you tell me?'

'It was just an attempted burglary. It's not the first time it's happened.'

'You said it got nasty. How?'

'They came upstairs and entered the bedroom.'

'Whose bedroom?'

Jack stayed silent.

'Whose bedroom did they enter?'

'George's.'

'Jesus fucking Christ, you're not describing a burglary. Burglars don't go upstairs. They don't chance hanging around entering bedrooms. They weren't looking for something, they were looking for someone. How could you be so naïve?'

Toby was angry, but this wasn't directed at Jack. It was perhaps this moment where Toby realised he could never simply just walk away from Eric Stanton. Olivia had once said she would never be free of him. Toby wondered if he was now experiencing those same feelings.

'They emptied my wallet and dropped the key to my truck as they made their retreat. I genuinely thought they were burglars who got greedy. I never believed George was a target. The reason I didn't tell you is that I knew you'd panic. You're a worrier, Toby, always have been, and you've been through enough without me adding to it,' Jack replied.

'Jack, I need you to tell me what happened to see if I can piece this together, but I'm almost certain I know who's behind it.'

'I heard noises coming from downstairs. Instinctively, I headed straight to George's room...'

'She must have felt terrified,' Toby interjected.

'She thought they'd come for her.'

'Who are they?'

'I was hoping you could tell me that.'

Toby pondered. He'd known this wouldn't be a straightforward conversation, and though he trusted Jack with his life, for now, he needed to keep his cards close to his chest. Jack's lack of diplomacy was well known. If he knew the truth behind the break-in, if he knew about Eric Stanton's threats to Toby, if he knew about George's rape, he would respond the only way he knew how... with his fists. Whilst Toby had no regard for Eric's well-being, he felt certain this would only add fuel to an already roaring fire, and he was looking to defuse, not amplify.

'You don't need to know any specifics at this time. All I need you to do is to keep George safe for me. Can you do that?'

'That would be easier if I knew what I was keeping her safe from. Who's targeting us?'

'They're not targeting you, Jack.'

Revenge in Mind

'What are you involved in, Toby? Is this linked to that Olivia woman you used to see?'

Toby smiled. Jack had a way with words. All the years they had known one another, and he still questioned whether Jack really knew anything about his profession. But it wasn't his mind or his intellect which made Jack such a good friend. He was loyal, dependent, and had never let Toby down. Toby had a few friends, but when he sought complete reliance and trust, his circle shrank. He had never had to rely on anybody, but on those rare occasions when he had needed somebody, there was only one person he would feel comfortable enough showing his vulnerability to aside from Beth, and that was Jack.

'You know I trust you, right?'

'I'd like to think so,' Jack replied.

'Well, right now, I need you to trust me. There will come a time when I will explain all of this, but that time isn't now. Can you trust me?'

'You know I have your back, Toby.'

'It's George's back I need you to have.'

'I'm out enhancing my security as we speak.'

'Where's George?'

'Back at the farm, watching what passes for daytime television these days.'

'Jesus Jack, she's there on her own?'

A question with an accusatory undertone. It had come from a place of fear. He couldn't protect George, but he had been counting on the fact that Jack could. He thought she would be safe, but suddenly she was a sitting target. Toby was convinced the break-in was staged as a burglary, but they were there for

George. What he didn't know was whether the plan was to kill her or to abduct her. Jack had been the barrier between the intruders and George, now that barrier had been removed. Toby's heart sank.

'Jack, listen very carefully to me. You need to drop whatever you're doing and get back to the farm immediately.'

'What's going on Toby? I didn't sign up for this.'

'How do you think they knew she was there? They have surveillance on her. They have surveillance on both of you. You need to reach her before they do. If they know you're out, they also know she is isolated.'

'Shit Toby, I'm sorry I didn't realise. I'll head back now. I'm about thirty minutes away.'

The sound of screeching brakes and a shriek from Jack preceded what Toby could clearly identify as the sound of a metal-on-metal collision. The breaking of glass was the last thing he heard before the line went dead. His heart sank as he shouted Jack's name several times, each one more heavily enveloped in desperation than the previous. Toby clutched his head in his hands feeling helpless. Jack's fate was out of his control, but he was under no illusion he was responsible for it. He realised he had put his best friend in danger and would now have to live with the consequences. He felt responsible for everything that had happened around him and regretted ever laying eyes on Olivia Stanton. Despite knowing it was safer to walk away, Eric had sparked a fire in Toby that made him determined to pursue him and bring him to justice...at any cost.

{ 20 }

Georgina Sampson sat comfortably in the chair closest to the fire. Spring was here in name only, as the temperature continued to drop. This made her ever more grateful for the wood burner just feet away. She looked around the room and took in its natural beauty. Wooden beams and brickwork on display gave it an authenticity and character she felt was lacking in more modern homes. She thought back to the house she had lived in with *him*. On the surface, it had appeared to be everything she had wanted, but upon reflection, she questioned whether she had ever truly settled there. Looks can deceive, she thought and then smiled to herself as she wondered whether this was directed at the house or the person she had lived with. She liked it here; she liked Jack. He made her feel safe. He also made her laugh, but she would describe him as unintentionally funny. It was his general demeanour. Romance wasn't on her mind, but she would be lying if she said she'd never looked at Jack in that way. Tall, muscular, combined with kind and sensitive. What was there not to like? Her smile waned as she realised she could never have this. Her aim was clear, and this didn't form part of it, at least not now. As she gazed at the flickering flames, mesmerised, she gripped her still hot cup of coffee tightly. Sitting back and closing her eyes, she sighed, wondering whether she could ever live a life that resembled normality. Thinking about her past was hard for her. Her journey through adolescence had begun so well, with her college days being some of the fondest memories she held. But when she and Toby separated, her life had taken a different path. A path stooped with lies, mistrust, desperation, and trauma. The thought of possessing any ill-feeling towards Toby had broken her heart, but she could no longer deny she harboured some resentment. Having seen his car, his house, she hadn't wanted to, but couldn't avoid feeling like Beth's life should have been hers. She wasn't jealous of Beth, but felt cheated out of the life she and Toby had planned together when they had fallen in love back in college. The question wasn't whether she had changed, this was beyond denial, but whether she could rediscover the fun-loving, optimistic girl she had once been before *he* had destroyed it. The thought of him sent a shiver down into the base of her spine. There was a time when she had hoped she would never lay eyes on him again, but this had changed. She now had knowledge there had been others. As she comprehended the depths of the abuse she had endured, she realised he wasn't done. George longed for the moment she would confront him, where the tables would turn and she would…

A sound outside abruptly interrupted her thought. She rose out of the chair and crept towards the window, peaking out cautiously from behind the curtain. In the distance she could see a black range rover parked just before the gate, which was now open. It wasn't Jack's truck, and the blackened-out windows did nothing to suppress her suspicion. She couldn't make out much in the distance, but she could see both the driver and passenger seat were empty. She realised the only reason a vehicle would be parked before the gate would be to avoid it being noticed. Though they had failed on this front, they had done enough to go undetected until they had entered the grounds. George was consumed by a panic and fear she had only ever experienced once before, the time when she had been faced with the inevitability of being raped. She moved away from the curtain, carefully making her way towards the staircase near the kitchen. Perched on the bottom step, she pulled out her phone and dialled Jack. The line was dead.

'Shit Jack, where are you when I need you?' she whispered.

She thought for a moment, tapping her fingers on her phone. After scrolling down her contact list, she paused and dialled again.

'George?'

'I think there's somebody here. I think they've come for me.'

'Where's here?'

'I'm staying with one of Toby's friends out of town. It's a small farm. I'll send you the address now.'

George removed the phone from her ear and typed out Jack's address in a message before hurriedly hitting send.

'Who are they?'

'I really don't know,' she replied, becoming more distressed.

'What are you involved in?'

'I can't answer that question, but I'm assuming this has something to do with the two guys who broke in recently, who Jack roughed up.'

'Who's this Jack guy?'

'Toby's friend. He's allowed me to lie low here for a while after Toby received a message saying I was in danger.'

'Where is he now?'

'Toby?'

'No, Jack,' he replied somewhat impatiently.

'I don't know. He went out a while back and I can't get hold of him. Jack said they were burglars, but what if they weren't? What if they were here for me? What if they've come back? I'm frightened.'

Dylan Sampson removed the phone from his ear momentarily and walked over to the bedside table of the cheap hotel room where he had been staying. He paid cash. They didn't ask questions or require any identification. He could disappear without a trace, without notice. He was simply a paying guest and seeing the same guests check in with different people regularly, told him the owner was interested in profit, not morals. This suited him just fine. He would fly under the radar with relative ease. He removed a pair of gloves, a knife, a screwdriver and a rope from the draw, placing them in his small bag. Walking into the bathroom, he removed a hand towel which had been delicately balancing on the radiator. Putting on his coat and a dark hat, he briskly exited the room.

'Listen closely. I want you to head upstairs and find a closet or something which can buy you time. Stay quiet, don't move and I'll be there soon.'

'Don't go, Dylan,' George pleaded with desperation.

'There's something I need to do first, and let's just say I'm gonna need both hands for it.'

Revenge in Mind

'Please don't do anything stupid. I can't lose you.'

Dylan could feel his body tensing. There was a rage burning away in the depths of his stomach, fuelled by the thought of somebody trying to harm his sister. They would pay, but his priority was to reach her, and fast. He jogged out into the car park and headed towards the handful of spaces at the back, which were surrounded by trees. The view of this area from the main road or the hotel was obscured. Just what he needed. He quickly glanced around to see if anybody was in sight. His eyes were drawn to a car in the corner, covered in leaves. It had likely not been moved in a while. It was inevitable the car would be reported stolen, but he wouldn't need long. Once he got to the farm, he would dump it, leaving no trace of himself. Taking one last look around to ensure privacy, he pulled the towel out of his bag and wrapped it several times around his hand. The breaking of glass was less than diplomatic, but it was necessary. He had taken a calculated risk the car wouldn't be alarmed. It was old and would hold little value. He was probably doing the owner a favour, he thought, as he placed the hand towel back into his bag and put on his gloves. As he climbed in through the passenger window, he manoeuvred over to the driver's seat, not a straightforward task for a man of his stature, his lack of suppleness exposed. He reached into his bag and pulled out the screwdriver. He placed it in the ignition and turned it. Nothing. He banged his hand gently on the screwdriver to push it down further and tried again. Still nothing. He was wasting valuable time. Every second was vital. The moments lost could be pivotal. Then something caught his eye on the back seat. A book. He reached over to pick it up and, in one movement, hammered at the top of the screwdriver before he became convinced it wouldn't go in any further. The screwdriver turned in the ignition, sparking the car into life. He reversed out of the space and headed towards the main road, stopping only briefly to input the address George had sent him into his phone. He was roughly twenty minutes away, yet faced a dilemma. Time was of the essence and he needed to cut that time down, but by doing so, he risked drawing attention to himself, something he categorically needed to avoid. George needed him, but she was smart and he felt sure she could avoid detection for long enough to allow him to reach her. He pressed his foot on the accelerator, watching the speedometer needle reach eighty. He wasn't familiar with the area, so finding a shortcut wasn't an option.

George crept slowly up the stairs, functioning solely on adrenaline. She tiptoed cautiously, mindful to avoid any creaking floorboards. The noises she had heard had been outside, but one glance out of the window had told her it was only a matter of time before they entered the house. They? She was assuming it was the same two intruders as before, but with no visual, she couldn't be certain of identity or numbers. She stopped at the top of the staircase and stared at the door to her bedroom. The cupboard she had hidden in during the previous break-in was deep and contained several large boxes which could conceal her presence. It also homed a set of golf clubs, which looked like they had been gathering dust over the years owing to their lack of use. They could prove handy should she be forced to defend herself.

'Time,' she said out loud to herself.

Revenge in Mind

This was all about time. She couldn't fight her way out. She was streetwise, but no match for attackers likely carrying weapons. This was about holding out long enough for Dylan to reach her. She turned and headed for Jack's room. It was at the far end of the corridor and would, therefore, be the last room they would check. She slowly pushed open the door and entered. In the far corner was an en-suite bathroom. Too obvious. If they were weaponised, an internal door would provide little resistance. Then she noticed the wardrobe. It didn't look roomy, but that could be advantageous to her, as it may not be a place they would assume a fully grown adult could fit. Though she was no contortionist, she was supple enough to squeeze in behind his clothes and climb to the back. They weren't inside yet, but it was only a matter of time. She pulled out her phone and tried Jack again. Still not connecting.

'Damn it Jack, where the hell are you?' she said with a hint of frustration. This was supposed to be a safe place. He was supposed to protect her, yet here she was alone and vulnerable. She was a sitting target, and he was nowhere to be found. Feeling exasperated, she dialled Dylan's number.

'Where are you?' she whispered.

'I had car problems.'

'You don't have a car.'

'That was the problem. Now it's solved,' he replied somewhat nonchalantly.

'Shit Dylan, do I want to know?'

'You have other things to worry about.'

'Are you close?'

'I'm about fifteen minutes out. Hang tight.'

'I'm scared Dylan,' George replied, now realising the adrenaline was subsiding giving way to panic.

'Are they in the house?'

'I don't think so.'

'Why didn't you call the police?'

'I don't want to become known to them. The last thing I need right now is having the spotlight shone on me. It's vital I stay under the radar.'

'You did the right thing.'

Just then, there was a loud noise, which sounded like a door being forced open. It startled her, and she hurriedly placed her hands over her mouth to muffle her involuntary scream.

'They're here Dylan, they've come for me,' she cried in a whisper, which was barely audible.

'Stay calm. Remember what I taught you. Be alert, not afraid,'

'What do they want with me?'

'Right now, it's about survival. Just hold on a little longer until I get there. I promise I won't let anything happen to you.'

Dylan Sampson squeezed the accelerator gently as he swerved in and out of traffic. This wasn't lying low. In fact, the erratic nature of his driving was as far from inconspicuous as you could get. But he had submitted to desperation. George was in danger. He didn't know to what extent and he didn't know why, but that wasn't important. He just needed to get to her, and fast. There was no fear, only anger. His thoughts turned to what he would do to the assailants once he had them in his sight, within reach. He wasn't an emotional person and didn't view problems in any other way than something which required a fix. He was practical and very much about the moment, which worked just fine for him. This, however, was different. Somebody was deliberately targeting the one person he truly cared for. He knew she was hurting; he knew she was afraid, and this stirred something up inside of him. His decision to leave home and join the Armed Forces had been a difficult one for his parents to accept. They understood his need, but an inevitable distance had grown between them. It wasn't that he didn't care, more he now lived his own life, and they weren't a part of it. George was different. He knew how much his decision had hurt her and they had been close growing up. He had wondered whether losing contact with her had arisen from the guilt of leaving her in the first place. He hadn't been there for her when she had truly needed him. He wouldn't allow that to happen again. Whoever was going after her had made a grave mistake. Soon enough, they would realise this.

'Listen, I don't want you to talk, so we need to communicate another way to allow me to understand what I'm walking into, okay? I want you to press any key on your phone twice if you are still there.'

Nothing.

'George.' His tone was now more hurried.

'Give me a sign you're still there.'

Among the sudden heavy breathing came the sound of the keypad. He closed his eyes for a brief second, feeling the relief. She was still alive.

'Okay, I'm going to ask you a series of questions. One press for yes and two presses for no. You got that?'

The phone beeped once.

'George, are you sure they're in the house?'

One beep.

'Do you have any idea who they may be? Are these people known to you?'

Among the sniffling, there was a pause.

'I thought they may have been upstairs, but I can hear a lot of noise from downstairs,' she whispered.

'What kind of noise?'

'Things are being smashed.'

'That's personal. They're proving a point. Destruction implies they're sending a message and want it to be known they were there. This benefits us. The longer they spend having their tantrum, the more time it buys. He must have roughed them up good. I'm beginning to like this guy.'

Dylan looked down at the speedometer, which now displayed 90mph. His eyes widened in amazement that an old car like this would reach such speeds, but it was certainly letting him know he could push no further. His GPS was telling him he was now less than ten minutes away, ten minutes, which would be crucial for George. He needed to keep her on the phone; he needed to keep her calm; he needed to keep her safe. George was tough. She'd had to be growing up with her bipolar diagnosis, but outnumbered and unarmed, the odds were stacked against her. She was vulnerable, and staying hidden long enough for him to get there was her only hope of survival.

'I never understood it, you know, growing up. I couldn't see how, without anything changing, your mood dropped the way it did, not at first. But I saw how much you suffered, and it hurt.

Revenge in Mind

I nearly didn't go, you know. I was desperate to get away, and I knew I needed to, but leaving you was hard. There were many times I regretted leaving you alone.'

'I understood. I knew how important it was for you. As much as I didn't want you to go, I got it,' she replied in a controlled whisper.

'I always feel like I abandoned you, but I promise I won't let that happen again.'

George fought back the tears. It wasn't because she had missed him and regretted the years they had drifted apart. It was because in this moment she was wondering if she would ever see him again. Her body was shaking. She was convinced her heavy breathing and racing heart would give away her location and ultimately seal her fate. She knew neither their identity nor their motive. If it were the same intruders, they were risking a lot by returning. Jack had shown he was not to be messed with, which would highlight there was somebody they were more afraid of than him. Last time they had left without what they had come for. George felt a sudden sinking sensation at the realisation they wouldn't make that mistake again. The noise had died down and Dylan couldn't have arrived yet. This meant only one thing. They were on their way upstairs. They were coming for her. The slow and pronounced creaking of the old floorboards confirmed her fears. Downstairs had been about anger; it had been about proving a point. To her it had felt unnecessary, but she also clung to the hope it had been a mistake. Dylan was right, the time they had spent downstairs causing as much damage as they could was time they weren't searching for her, time he was using to get ever closer to saving her. But that time was quickly running out. The clandestine manner within which they were making their way up the stairs suggested they were now moving towards the real reason they were here. Any slight doubt she may have had over their intentions had now disappeared. George felt a resignation as she strained her ears to see if there was anything which gave away their location or their numbers. She heard the faint sound of a door opening, but it was in the distance. It was her room. Jack's room was at the end of the corridor, and she now felt thankful she had opted for his wardrobe rather than the cupboard in her own room. She heard them rustling about, doors swinging open and closed with the occasional murmuring. She assumed their frustration was building at being kept waiting. The longer they were here, the more they risked detection. The thought of what her brother would do to them so soon after Jack left his mark made her smile. She didn't just want to survive this encounter; she wanted them to suffer for what they had put her through, and for what they had done to Jack's farm.

'I'm only a few minutes away, George. Are you okay?'

George was paralysed with fear and unable to respond. She simply pressed a button on her phone, feeling grateful she had turned off the keypad tones. She heard the door close and, as the intruders drew closer, could make out a brief exchange between them.

'The bitch has to be in here somewhere.'
'And with her boyfriend out of the picture, she's all alone.'
'You've had confirmation?'
'Made to look like an accident, I've been told.'

'Teach the bastard a lesson.'

Accident? Who were they talking about? She panicked.

'Toby,' she gasped without thinking, before quickly covering her mouth.

'George, what's going on? Is Toby there?'

She could no longer respond. Her mind raced as she was overcome with emotion. What had they done to him? It remained unclear to her if she had been drawn into Toby's situation or if he had been drawn into hers, but one thing was clear. This was now personal. She wanted to burst out of the wardrobe and hurt them, but this wasn't a realistic option. Unarmed and unequipped, she wasn't a fighter. She looked down at her watch. Surely Dylan must be close. She wouldn't have to hold on too much longer. The moment they heard his car, they would leave the room. If they were sensible, they would make a hasty retreat. If not, they would confront him, which would be a grave mistake on their part. Dylan on any day was tough, but spurred on by fury, he was unpredictable. The footsteps drew closer as they entered the room. She had no visibility and dare not move to change this. From the brief conversation and their footsteps, she had established there were two and remained convinced they had been acquainted previously. The door to Jack's ensuite bathroom creaked open. They would realise quickly it did not house a hideaway. The next noise she heard suggested they were down on their knees and looking under the bed. Someone slowly thudded on the floor and groaned as they lifted the bed to investigate what it may be hiding. They would again come up empty, but they were getting closer, and it was only a matter of time. She closed her eyes and prayed for the timely arrival of her brother to end her ordeal, but this was now in hope rather than expectation. He was still on the line. She'd left it open, but he had likely muted himself so as not to give away her position. George realised she was on her own and gasped as the handle on the wardrobe turned. As the door burst open, she was unable to hold in the scream, which she felt she had been storing forever. Suddenly, she was face to face with the intruders. George tried to run past them, but her efforts were futile. She screamed again as the phone fell out of her hand and hit the floor. Her hands were quickly bound behind her back with tape silencing any screams. She was helpless, and she was isolated, but her last thought as she was bundled down the staircase was of Toby. One intruder had picked up her phone and placed it to his ear. A grin spread across his face as he listened to the voice on the other end. Then she felt calm. The panic subsided, yielding to a stubbornness, a refusal to accept her fate. She jerked away from the man holding her and kicked out, connecting with his knee. He felt the blow and shouted out in pain. This was the last she remembered of the house as she was struck with a blunt object in the side of the head, collapsing in a heap on the floor.

'She can't talk right now.'

Dylan clenched his fists and banged the steering wheel with force in a rage he had never felt before. He was too late; they were already there. He ground his teeth together and took in a deep breath through his nose.

'When I find you, and I will find you, I will hurt you in ways you never thought imaginable. The pain you'll feel will be indescribable and relentless. By the time I've finished, you'll be begging me to end your miserable, meaningless life. The decision you've made today is a very bad one, and it's going to cost you. You've fucked with the wrong person.'

But the line was already dead. They had her.

{ 21 }

The car came to a halt, accompanied by the sound of the brakes being pumped harshly. Dylan hastily exited the vehicle and hurdled the farm gate, though it was ajar. Operating purely on adrenaline, he had no time to take in the surroundings as he headed straight for the front door, which was both open and damaged. He'd left his bag in the car, but had taken the knife and placed it in his pocket. Though he knew George and her kidnappers were gone, he was still vigilant as he entered the house cautiously. The fire of anger burned in his eyes. His job here was brief and simple. He would retrace George's steps and search for anything which may give a clue to her whereabouts or the identity of her attackers. His hopes were slim, but it was a necessary step. His training had emphasised the importance of being thorough. If there was anything of relevance here, he would find it. He stood in the doorway faced with a large kitchen and dining area, the staircase ahead of him. The first thing that caught his attention was the fact that the place had already been ransacked. Chairs were upturned, the oven doors had been damaged, the kettle was in the sink in pieces, and there was a mixture of broken glass and crockery on the floor. Unnecessary, he thought. This wasn't simply about a kidnapping. Whoever had done this had wanted to send a very clear message. This was personal, and he felt a momentary degree of sympathy for the owner. George had been hiding in the back of a wardrobe and he knew she had chosen the room furthest away from the staircase at the bottom of the corridor. He had his starting point. He made his way through the glass, past the table, which he noted had also fallen victim to the rage of whoever had been here. On first glance, it looked to him like there were markings of a hammer deeply embedded in the oak. He made his way tentatively up the stairs, not because he feared a confrontation, but because of the damage the handrail had sustained.

'Jesus, whoever this was, they've proved their point,' he whispered to himself. As he walked down the corridor, he pushed each door open just to ensure there were no surprises. Finally, he came face to face with the last bedroom in the house. The door was open, and the room looked like it had seen a struggle. This was where they had found her. This was where she had fought and screamed. He headed for the wardrobe. The door was open and whatever had been hiding her had tumbled out as they dragged her. He wasn't sure what he was looking for, but George was streetwise. She would have put up resistance. He grabbed the remaining clothes and threw them onto the floor behind him as he climbed in. He glanced around, but could see nothing.

'Come on George, I know you've left me something,' he said as he searched frantically. Suddenly, something written in the far corner caught his eye. The wardrobe was a darkish colour, but he could just about make out the scribble in front of him.

20S

Dylan made a note and wondered what '20S' could mean. He got little time to advance this thought as he felt a pair of hands grip the back of his neck. Dragged abruptly out of the wardrobe, he headed with speed towards the wall. Dylan hit it with a thud. With no time to gather his thoughts, he felt a blow on the side of his head, followed by another to his chin. As another fist swung his way, he grabbed it before it connected and, for the first time, could see the face of his attacker. He was tall, well-built and hit hard. There was a sudden movement and Dylan felt a sharp pain in his leg. As his knee buckled, he used his left arm to strike a blow into the man's midriff, which drew a groan as his attacker instinctively reached for his stomach. Without a pause, he picked up the man and ran with him towards the opposite end of the room. A pained look appeared as the man's back hit the wall, taking the full force. They fell to the ground and began wrestling, each trying desperately to gain the upper hand. Both men tried to land blows, but the proximity made it difficult for either to strike with any conviction. A pained expression followed a loud shriek as Dylan felt something pressing down on the bottom of his chest with force. Through his somewhat bleary vision, he could just about identify it as a barbell. The pain was intense, but he had been subjected to worse. He wriggled his arms free and got hold of each end of the bar. With everything he had, he pushed at it to ease the pressure from his chest, but it wasn't easy. His attacker was strong. In a swift movement, he used his body weight to twist and turn the man onto his back. He hadn't expected this. The one thing he knew was he was in a fight with a tough son of a bitch, and would need to use all of his training and experience to be able to walk away at the end of it. Where this left his attacker was no concern of his. He would do whatever it took, use whatever he had, and feel no remorse in doing so. Pushing down harder on the bar, he could see the face of the man on the floor turning a deeper shade of red, as he winced with pain.

'Where is she?' he snarled.

'Go fuck yourself.'

The man suddenly reached out behind him, picked up an object from the floor, and struck Dylan full in the face. The pain was excruciating, and the force had been enough to disorientate him. He stumbled to his feet and staggered towards the door, wondering what the hell had just hit him. He gathered his thoughts just in time to see a figure lurching towards him. The ferocity of the attack sent both men tumbling to the ground, rolling perilously towards the top of the staircase. They continued to grapple as they tumbled down the stairs, each step producing a painful shriek from its victims. Then there was quiet.

The two men lay motionless, the trail of blood and destruction telling only part of the story. Looking at the scene, it was difficult to see whether it was the house or its occupants that had sustained the most damage. At first glance, both men looked dead, at best critically injured. It looked like a classic crime scene, a far cry from the beautiful, inviting farmhouse it had been previously. The damage was significant but not beyond repair. The two men were another matter. The geographical isolation of the property meant any disturbance would go undetected. Nobody knew they were there; nobody was coming to their aid. The room was chilly, with an eerie quietness about it. The fire in the lounge would have now petered out, and perhaps the gradual extinguishing of the flames was symbolic of the scene in the kitchen. The only noise now was the unhinged door, occasionally swinging back and forth against its frame.

Dylan slowly opened his eyes and writhed with pain as he tried to move. He looked over at the man in the corner, who was now sitting up, holding his ribs. Neither of the men looked like they had the energy or inclination to continue the fight. It had been brutal, with no victor. Dylan focused on his assailant.

'Who are you and what have you done with my sister?' he snarled.

There was a look of confusion on the man's face, as though he hadn't understood the question.

'Perhaps the more important question is, what the hell are you doing in my house?'

'This is your place?'

'Yeah.'

'You're Jack?'

Jack nodded, still dazed from the fall.

'Shit. George, where is she?' he asked with impatience.

'That's what I'm trying to find out,' Dylan replied curtly.

'She was here when I left,' Jack qualified, trying to piece things together.

'When you left?'

Revenge in Mind

Dylan looked down at his knee, which was swollen from the attack. He felt pain, but he was fairly sure nothing was broken. He'd had worse.

'We've been wasting time here,' Dylan said with frustration.

'I thought you were involved. I thought you'd come for her.'

'I came for the bastards who broke in and took her.'

Jack rose gingerly to his feet and walked over to the drinks fridge. Though it was an old building, there were subtle touches of modernity. He pulled out two cans, handing one to Dylan.

'Something they didn't destroy,' he said with a smile.

'Your insurance company is gonna love you.'

Jack laughed before clutching at his ribs.

'You put up one hell of a fight there. Special forces?'

'Rough school,' Jack replied, grinning.

'I spent years in the forces and didn't come across many who could fight like you.'

'I grew up with a fight-or-flight attitude, and not exactly being athletic narrowed those options down for me.'

Dylan's smile disappeared as the reality of what was happening suddenly hit.

'Jack, what the hell's going on? Who has George?'

'I don't know, but I think Toby might.'

'Toby Reynolds?'

'You know him?'

'I know of him. George dated him back in college, but I never met him. I'd already left for the army. How's he involved in this?'

'George had been staying with him and Beth. That's his wife. Toby called me out of the blue, asking if she could stay here with me. Said he was concerned about her safety but wouldn't go into detail.'

'Do you trust him?' Dylan asked suspiciously.

'With my life. We go way back and they don't come more trustworthy than Toby. But there's something else.'

'What's that?'

'Toby's rarely wrong. He picks up on things most of us wouldn't even think to look for. If he was concerned about George, he would have had good reason.'

Dylan lowered his head, trying to absorb what he was hearing, before addressing Jack again.

'George was on the phone with me when she was taken. Before they got to her, she mentioned some intruders from a recent break-in.'

'We woke up to two men in the house. I had assumed they were burglars. They came upstairs, and we got into it. They jumped me, but I gave them something to think about and they left with their tails between their legs.'

'Where do you keep your car keys and wallet?'

'Downstairs on the kitchen table.'

'So why the hell would burglars come upstairs and risk detection if they can make off with your money and car with little effort?'

'Toby said the same thing.'

'Jesus, Jack, how could you be so stupid?'

'In their haste to escape a further beating, they dropped the keys to my truck. My wallet was also emptied. I assumed they came upstairs because they got greedy, or they were looking for something in particular.'

'Or *someone*,' Dylan emphasised.

Jack screwed up his eyes.

'Look around you. My home is completely trashed, and I've been pulled into something I would have preferred to stay out of. I've been jumped, burgled and have now become a target...and for what? I'm not a fucking babysitter, nor am I a bodyguard. I'm a farmer who had a quiet and simple life before your sister arrived on the scene. Where were you throughout all this? Why weren't you protecting her?'

Dylan felt the anger rising inside him. He got to his feet and moved over towards Jack, who was now standing. The two men faced each other down.

'We have a choice that's very simple. Either we waste our energies on each other, or we locate the individuals behind all of this and ensure they pay. I'd rather have you on side, but make no mistake, get in my way and I will go through you,' Dylan said, not breaking his stare.

Jack looked down at Dylan's hand, which he had extended. He pondered for a moment and then smiled, accepting the handshake. He then jerked at it, pulling Dylan close.

'Know this. I don't start trouble, but I will finish it, and I don't take too kindly to threats.'

There was a brief pause as the two men stood looking one another up and down. There was suspicion, but a mutual respect. If they were to find George, they would need to work together.

'Dylan Sampson.'

'Jack Newby.'

'You look a little sore there,' Dylan observed.

'Someone hit me in my truck earlier.'

'This isn't your day.'

Jack grinned.

'It would appear not.'

Dylan held his side as he sat back down on the stairs.

'Does 20S mean anything to you?'

'Should it?'

'It's written on the inside of your wardrobe,' Dylan qualified.

Jack's eyes widened in disbelief.

'Show me.'

As the two scaled the staircase gingerly, Dylan was reminded of how much easier it had been the previous time he had made this journey. They were both bruised, and the pain, once camouflaged by the adrenaline, was now beginning to show through. The two men carefully manoeuvring their way through the effects of the carnage, which had taken place moments earlier was a painful reminder of the damage they had done to one another. The wardrobe door was hanging from its hinges, but their fight hadn't caused this. It happened when they had taken George.

'That wasn't there previously,' Jack said, crouching down with his flashlight, studying the writing.

'How can you be certain?'

'Because I've had this from new, and it's only ever been in my room.'

Dylan looked troubled, unsure whether to feel pleased George had left them a clue, or disappointed that it now made her kidnapping more real. Jack backed out of the wardrobe, but before he could speak, he heard the sound of a car coming from outside. The two men drifted towards the top of the stairs.

'Any ideas?' Dylan asked.

Jack shook his head slowly.

As they heard what remained of the front door slam back against its frame, Jack and Dylan looked at one another and nodded. It was a look which said they were prepared for whatever may await them, a look which said they were in no mood to negotiate, a look which said whoever had come back to the house had made a very grave error in judgement. As they cautiously made their way down the stairs, they heard a rustling in the kitchen. In their current position, they could just make out the legs. A couple more steps and they would have more of a visual on the identity of the intruder. Dylan wasn't waiting any longer. Face incandescent with such rage that it could have lit up a dark night, he ran down the remaining stairs and jumped at the unsuspecting man who was studying something on the worktop. He grabbed him around the throat and lifted him off his feet, pushing him up against the wall.

'Dylan, no!' came a shout from behind him.

Dylan drew back his fist as the man covered his face and pleaded not to be hit. He was in no mood for negotiations though and swung at the man, whose feet were still several inches off the ground. During the commotion, Jack had positioned himself next to Dylan and was able to intercept his fist before it struck its target. Dylan turned to him in surprise as Jack stood between him and the intruder.

'What the hell is wrong with you?' he asked angrily.

'He's not involved, Dylan.'

'Then what the hell is he doing here?'

'Let him go. He's not the person you're looking for.'

'Then who is he?'

Dylan slowly relinquished his grip as the man, now breathing heavily, rubbed his throat. He looked distressed and frightened as his eyes moved between Jack and Dylan. Despite not looking like much of a fighter, Dylan was still cautious about underestimating anybody. The man composed himself, taking a few quick breaths, and held out his hand to Dylan.

'Toby Reynolds.'

The man who moments ago had Toby by the throat, bowed his head and extended his hand.

'Dylan Sampson, George's brother.'

Toby had only seen pictures of Dylan; he seemed much bigger in person. By the time he'd met George, her brother had already departed for the army, so any picture he had built up of him had been influenced solely by George's stories.

'What happened here?'

Jack and Dylan exchanged a look, perhaps each considering where to begin.

'Where's George?' Toby asked, now glancing round the room anxiously.

'They have her,' Dylan replied angrily.

'Who's they?'

'That's what we're trying to figure out,' Jack interjected.

'How could you leave her alone?' Toby asked angrily, turning towards Jack.

'I wasn't gone for long. She said she was going to relax with a bath whilst I was out.'

'You shouldn't have left her alone.'

'Where were you, Toby? I told you from the beginning I wasn't comfortable with any of this. Look around you. This hasn't happened because of me. George hasn't been taken because of anything I'm involved in. Believe it or not, I was content with my drama free life before all of this,' Jack replied defensively.

Toby stood shocked, not because this was out of character for Jack and they had never really argued in the time they had known one another, but because he was right. This was Toby's fault. *He* had antagonised Eric Stanton. *He* had allowed himself to be manipulated by Olivia. It had been his decision to send George to Jack's. The intention had been to keep her safe, but the reality was he had unintentionally isolated her, making it easier for the kidnappers to strike. He suddenly noticed Dylan's eyes were fixated on him, and not endearingly. As he met his stare, he caught a glimpse of what it must feel like to cross a man of his size and with his temper. He'd only been in his presence for minutes, but in that time had quickly realised he would much rather have him on side. He didn't appear to be the type of person you would cross, and Toby wondered how many who had taken that liberty had later regretted it.

'I think somebody needs to give me some answers here, and fast,' Dylan said impatiently. Jack gestured for them to head towards the living room.

'Perhaps that room's still intact,' he said with a hint of a smile.

Toby and Dylan made their way through the hallway, Jack following moments later, drinks in hand. The intruders had focused their attention on the kitchen area and the upstairs, leaving the lounge seemingly unscathed. As the three men sat quietly, it struck Toby how calm the scene was, which felt out of place considering the desperate situation they found themselves in. With his stare oscillating between Jack and Dylan, he was unsure whether he was witnessing quiet reflection or trepidation.

'Jack says you believed George was in danger. Why?' Dylan asked abruptly, directing his gaze towards Toby.

Toby, having been about to take a drink out of the can Jack had just passed him, placed it back down on the table in front of him, stunned by the directness of the question. It felt like one of those questions which was wrapped around suspicion and accusation. He was caught between exercising caution for self-preservation and speaking candidly in light of the situation. He was certain they all wanted the same thing, which was to find George, but questioned whether her brother had a hidden agenda of wanting to exact revenge on anybody who had had involvement in her disappearance. He wondered whether Dylan Sampson held him responsible.

'George had been staying with my wife and I,' he began.

'I understand this. The bit I'm interested in is why she ended up here,' Dylan replied sharply.

Toby felt cornered. This was the police interrogation all over again, and it didn't sit comfortably with him. That time, though, he felt reasonably assured of his personal safety. As he looked across at the man sitting opposite, he had no such reassurances. Dylan's body language told Toby he was a man with a temper, unpredictable at best. Adding emotion to the situation would only amplify this. He looked across at Jack and felt grateful to have him there. And then he noticed something. Both men were battle worn, both had cuts, both had been moving tentatively. The fact they were here together highlighted they had both been too late, which meant only one thing. They had fought each other. But why?

'I received a message saying she wasn't safe.'

'George?'

'At first I wasn't sure, but when she called me in a panic to say she had been followed through town, it seemed to suggest George was the one who the message was referring to,' Toby replied.

'Who sent the message?'

'It came through as an unknown number.'

'Toby, I spent years interrogating people. I know when somebody is withholding information, and you're withholding information. It's in your best interests to tell me what you know. I know your history with my sister and I believe you to be one of the good guys, but be certain of this. If you hold back anything that delays me finding her, I will bury you.'

He made a stride towards Toby. Jack leapt out of his seat and stood in between the two men. Toby wasn't a fighter, but Jack was, which offered him a little reassurance. Toby realised the potential harm each man could cause as they locked eyes. He stood up and positioned himself in between Dylan and Jack.

'Working under suspicion will not help us, or ultimately, George. We need to piece together what we know to ascertain what we don't know. We have to trust one another.'

'I've told both of you what I know,' Jack said, sitting back down.

'Do you believe those same people returned?' Toby asked.

'At first, everything told me they were burglars who chanced a greater reward. I didn't join the dots at the time. But now, with everything that's happened today, yes, I think it could be related. I'm sorry, I didn't for one moment think they were targeting George.'

'This isn't the time to feel sorry for yourself,' Dylan snapped sternly.

Toby could feel the temperature rising again. It was clear there was a mutual disliking between Jack and Dylan, but it was imperative they put that to one side. They were facing enough hurdles without adding more to the situation.

'How did you end up here, Dylan?'

'George called me in a panic. She'd heard voices outside and was convinced somebody had come for her. I told her to go upstairs and hide in the room furthest away. I rushed here as quick as I could, but was too late. One of the bastards picked up her phone. I heard his voice. The next time he hears mine will be the last time he hears anything.'

'So that's your car outside the gate?' Toby asked inquisitively.

'Something like that,' Dylan responded in a way that made Toby not want to question him any further on the matter.

'Where do you fit into this, Jack?'

Revenge in Mind

'I got back to a ransacked house and heard a noise upstairs. I thought somebody was still here so went to investigate. That's when I saw Dylan. I assumed him to be an intruder, and well… you can probably guess what happened next. Second time today I got roughed up a little.'

For a moment Toby tried to imagine what a fight between the two might have looked like, but the condition they were both in told its own story.

'What happened to your truck?'

'Somebody hit me and sped off. It's not drivable.'

'They sped off?' Toby asked suspiciously.

'Yeah, ran me off the road and took off.'

'So the moment George is alone, they eliminate the one person standing between them and their target. Coincidence?'

'What are you saying?'

'It was no accident. This place was being watched, and so were you. You were deliberately taken off the road to buy the kidnappers time. They did just enough to delay you, but not enough to cause serious injury, which would have drawn too much attention.'

'So, there are more people involved.' Dylan responded.

'I believe so.'

'Do we have any clues where they may have taken her?'

'If this is a kidnapping, there'll be a ransom. The longer we hear nothing, the more this will point to something else.'

'Like what?' Toby asked innocently.

Dylan paused for a moment, as though appearing to consider his words very carefully.

'If it's about money, they will keep her alive. If it's about revenge...'

Toby's heart sank. He closed his eyes for a moment. The thought of any harm coming to George was unbearable, but the knowledge that he was responsible was a burden he knew would remain with him for the rest of his life.

'Now isn't the time to feel sorry for yourself. Do you have any idea who may be behind this?' Dylan asked harshly.

Toby swallowed slowly. Dylan noticed his hesitation.

'Toby, if you know anything at all...'

'I'm starting to believe there is somebody who may be trying to get to me by targeting those close to me.'

'Who?' Dylan asked angrily.

'A man called Eric Stanton. I became suspicious of him and I'm now convinced he is trying to silence me through intimidation. I've had a couple of unpleasant encounters with him. Maybe he's behind this?'

Dylan's eyes widened with a rage Toby hadn't seen in anybody before. They looked wild and had an intent about them. He knew this wasn't the first time Dylan Sampson had heard Eric Stanton's name.

'You've heard of him,' Toby said, as more of a statement than a question.

'He's the reason I came here. I got acquainted with some of his goons recently. I've been looking for him ever since, but he's eluded me so far.'

'You were the one who had been asking questions about him,' Toby said, piecing things together.

Dylan looked at him blankly. Toby continued.

'He thought I was behind it. He was convinced I'd hired somebody to intimidate him. That's the reason he followed me out to the countryside and threatened me.'

'Wait, what?' Jack replied, conveying both concern for Toby and also a little offence at being left unaware.

Toby waved Jack's concerns away and walked across the room, deep in thought, fingers tapping on his lips.

'If Eric believes I am behind this, his focus is going to be on me, which means he won't be looking in your direction. He turned to face Dylan. Did George mention anything that could shed light on the kidnappers or the place they were taking her to?' Toby continued.

'She was hiding in the wardrobe. I don't think she saw anything until they had her. At that point, her phone hit the floor.'

'Where is her phone?' Toby asked.

'I searched, but they must have taken it.'

Jack, who had been little more than an observer to this point, turned towards Dylan.

'What about the scribble in the wardrobe?'

'What scribble?' Toby asked with haste.

'There is something written on the inside of the wardrobe, which I am almost certain wasn't there previously.'

'Show me,' Toby said, already leading the way towards the stairs.

As the three men reached the bedroom, Toby headed straight for the wardrobe, flashlight at the ready. He knelt down, moving the light around until he found what he was looking for.

'That's George's writing. Does 20S mean anything to either of you?' Toby asked, slowly manoeuvring his way back out.

Both men shook their heads.

'George is bright. This isn't random. She's leaving us a clue. She must have seen or heard something.'

'The clue was intended for one of us. We just need to figure out who,' Dylan added.

'Here's what we know. Eric Stanton is already known to both you and me, Dylan, but he only knows me. He suspects I know things about him, things he doesn't want to come out. He's made several threats to me, which have included a veiled threat by visiting my house when my wife was home alone. A matter of days ago Jack, you had intruders in the farm who you originally believed to be burglars, but we now strongly suspect were kidnappers, possibly the same two who returned today. Earlier, someone took you off the road in what would appear to be a deliberate ploy to keep you away from here, therefore isolating George. Dylan, your phone records will give us an accurate time of when the kidnapping took place.'

'So, what now?' Jack asked.

'As Dylan said, we need to figure out who George was leaving the message for. It's clearly meant to resonate with one of us.'

'And in the meantime?' Dylan asked impatiently.

'We begin our own search. Any abandoned buildings, warehouses, even farms within the vicinity.'

Toby and Dylan made their way outside before Jack fetched a plinth of wood to secure the front door, which was still hanging from its hinges.

'I just need to grab something from the car,' Dylan said, jogging towards the old vehicle, which looked like it had been abandoned.

Revenge in Mind

'I'm gathering from the broken passenger window that this isn't your car,' Jack smiled, pointing.

'It's not, and it's probably best it stays hidden,' Dylan replied as he closed the door, clutching the bag he had just retrieved from the passenger seat, which was still covered with broken glass.

As the three walked towards Toby's car, Jack stalled for a moment and glanced back over his shoulder. He wore a pained look, and this induced a deep regret within Toby. Jack was his closest friend, and yet his simple existence had been turned upside down through no fault of his own. He hadn't asked for any of this. In fact, he had been a reluctant passenger throughout. Weeks ago, Jack had a successful farm and not a care in the world. Now with a damaged house, no truck, and a stolen car on his property, he was entangled in uncertainty. His cosy and peaceful farm would forever be tarnished and now only represent the place where the kidnapping took place on his watch. On the precipice of criminal activity, whatever chaos awaited them would be unfamiliar to somebody who just rolled with life. Toby felt a profound sadness for his friend, but sentiment had no place right now. He placed his hands on Jack's shoulder and squeezed slowly.

'What now?' Jack asked, turning towards him.

Dylan stared at Toby as though awaiting instruction.

'I need to make a stop at home.'

'Then what?' Jack asked casually.

'Eric seems intent on discovering who's been looking for him. Perhaps it's about time we satisfy that curiosity.'

{ 22 }

The journey from the farm to Toby's house had been strangely subdued. Dylan had chosen to sit in the back seat, quietly contemplating throughout, offering only occasional conversation. His facial expression and general demeanour again reminded Toby this was a man you would much prefer fighting your corner. Jack had been slightly more talkative, but even his typical sarcasm was missing. Toby knew this was more of a reflection on the circumstances which had thrown the three of them together like this. He had called Beth before they had left, briefly apprising her of the situation. Naturally, she had been shocked and had urged Toby to contact the police. Toby had relayed his feeling that police involvement at this point could have dire consequences for George. It would also bring unwanted attention. Dylan had already been involved in a bar fight where he had done some damage, Jack had been involved in a crash and had left the scene, and Toby himself had continued to look into Eric Stanton against the strongly worded advice of a senior police officer. Add to this the fact they had just had to hide a stolen car, and it was perhaps understandable why Toby was reticent to involve the authorities. He knew he was asking a lot of Beth. This would undoubtedly bring up unwanted memories of the Olivia Stanton ordeal. He'd promised her this was over, but George's life was at stake and a rapist was still at large, free to prey on those vulnerable enough to fall for his superficial charm. But now it was different. His behaviour was escalating. Now, it was personal to Toby, not only because George had been identified as one of his victims, but also because he had come after Toby and involved his family. He could feel something within himself changing, and he didn't like it. In the past, he had worked with many challenging clients, some who held overtly opposing views to him, but there was something different about Eric Stanton. There was something deeply disturbing under the surface that Toby struggled to understand. He wondered how he would have felt had he met Eric in practice rather than under these circumstances. No doubt there was an expectation on him to formulate a plan to track down George, but the reality was he was frightened and felt out of his depth. His adrenaline had anger for company, but at the stop where anger would get off, vulnerability would take its place on the journey. That was how Toby felt right now, vulnerable. He inhaled slowly and closed his eyes. Turning the handle, he readied himself for what would inevitably be a tough conversation with Beth. As he did so, he could hear voices coming from the lounge. She wasn't alone.

'Toby, please don't be mad, but...'
'She did what you should have done, Toby. I warned you not to go playing detective.'
The stern words had come from Mike Thomas. Sitting opposite him was a female officer, but it wasn't Nadia Williams. She

was younger than Mike, perhaps a similar age to himself. Her hair was tied up, her makeup pristine. She smiled at Toby, but it looked a nervous smile. Beth looked uncomfortable, but then didn't they all?

'This is Dylan, Dylan Sampson,' he said, stepping aside. 'George's brother,' he qualified.

Beth smiled. It was a warm smile, the thing he loved most about her. She was always welcoming, but she was also protective, and that was why Mike Thomas was currently sitting in their living room. She stood up out of her seat and walked towards Toby, whispering in his ear as she embraced him.

'I'm sorry. I hope you understand.'

As she moved away, she walked past Dylan, placing her hand on his shoulder as she did so. She approached Jack and held out her arms.

'It's lovely to see you. It's been a while.'

She stepped back from the brief embrace as Jack winced with pain. Toby saw her glance at Jack and Dylan, noting their injuries, wearing a curious look as though trying to piece together what had happened. She turned to Toby, who gave a subtle shake of the head as if to warn her not to verbalise what she was thinking.

'It's nice to meet you, Dylan. I'm so sorry to hear about George's ordeal. I can't believe it.'

Dylan gave a slight smile but didn't respond. It was clear to Toby he wasn't a social creature, and this scenario would almost certainly make him feel uncomfortable.

Mike Thomas rose to his feet as the three men took a seat.

Revenge in Mind

'I don't need to tell any of you how serious this incident is. You may think you have this covered, but you would be wrong. Step aside and let us deal with it. I need you to walk me through everything that you know so far so we can begin the search immediately. As I'm sure you're aware, time is of the utmost importance here, and any little detail is essential.'

'Perhaps we should begin with some introductions,' Dylan said suspiciously.

'Well, assuming you're already acquainted with Toby and Jack, I'll introduce myself. I'm Detective Inspector Mike Thomas and this is PC Natasha Jenkins. Now the introductions are over, perhaps you could explain what your involvement is and why you look like you've been in a boxing match with Jack, who's looking rather sheepish.'

'As you say, time is of the essence, so perhaps you could explain how you plan to find my sister?' Dylan replied, avoiding Mike's question.

Toby, sensing the atmosphere, sat forward and addressed Mike.

'A few weeks back, George called me to say she believed she was being followed whilst she was out on her own. Around the same time, I received an anonymous message warning me she wasn't safe.'

'She being George?'

'That was the assumption I made. I reached out to Jack and asked if George could stay with him for a while, given his farm's secluded location outside of town. I felt certain she'd be safe there.'

'Why didn't you call us at that point, Toby?'

'I was sure Eric Stanton was behind it, that it was just a warning.'

Mike sighed, irritated, shaking his head

'Even if that's the case, what is it you thought you could do?'

'I don't know.'

Toby felt exasperated. This felt like another police interview, and he was mindful his palms were now sweating.

'Toby, you're a psychotherapist...'

'Former psychotherapist,' Toby interrupted.

'Regardless, you're not an officer of the law. I thought you'd have learnt from the last time.'

'Respectfully, my last experience of the police involved me being treated like a murderer and interrogated like a common criminal. You'll forgive me for not being overly enamoured at the prospect of repeating such an experience.'

Whilst Toby's eyes were facing the floor, he could feel the gaze of Mike upon him. Beth had invited him here as a familiar face, but Toby was again reminded Mike had a duty to uphold the law. As he lifted his head, he noticed Jack staring intently at Natasha Jenkins. There was something quite alluring about her. Jack had a thing for women in uniform, but Toby thought it was more specifically the image of a strong woman he was drawn to.

'Why don't you tell me about the break in?' Mike asked politely.

'Which one?' Jack sniggered before realising his humour had gone unappreciated.

Mike looked surprised.

'There's been more than one?'

Revenge in Mind

'Just over a week ago, George and I were awoken by the sound of intruders in the house. Two guys came upstairs, and we got into a scuffle. I assumed they were burglars who got carried away.'

'Burglars don't go upstairs unless they're looking for something specifically,' Mike replied.

'So I keep hearing.'

'Did you get a good look at them?'

'I had two guys trying to beat the shit out of me in the middle of the night. It was about survival. Besides, I'm a farmer, not a sketch artist.'

Toby had never seen this side to Jack. Sure, he had a sense of humour, but there was a frustrated undertone. While Jack wasn't typically passive aggressive, he was exhibiting those tendencies here.

'Is there anything at all you can give us? Facial hair, scars, tattoos?'

'As I said, it was dark, and I was more focused on keeping George safe than anything else,' Jack replied, now a little more cooperative.

'You said there were two break-ins?'

'The second one was today. I'm assuming that's why you're here.'

'What can you tell us about that?'

'I received a call from George. I was on the phone with her when the bastards took her,' Dylan snapped.

'Did she describe her captors to you?'

'I told her to go to the room at the back of the house and find a place to hide. She wouldn't have had a visual up to the moment they grabbed her.'

'What time was this?' Mike asked.

Dylan pulled out his phone, retrieved the call log and walked over to Mike to show him. Toby noticed Natasha Jenkins, who had said nothing up to this point, was taking notes in between sipping the coffee Beth had prepared for her. Her face gave little away about her thinking. He couldn't get a read, and this concerned him. With Nadia Williams, he had discovered quickly she was out to impress her superior, but with the officer sat next to Mike now, if this was her intent, she had a much more subtle way of going about it.

'What makes you think Eric Stanton is behind this, Toby?'

Dylan and Jack looked at Toby in a manner which suggested they didn't want him to answer the question.

Toby hesitated for a moment.

'I don't know. I guess it made sense earlier, but now I'm not so sure the dots join.'

'What do you mean?'

Toby breathed in deeply and prepared to lie, hoping the officers in front of him weren't as astute at identifying deception as he was.

'He's already made his point. This would feel like an unnecessary risk. Besides, the guys who broke into Jack's tried to take his truck as well as some other valuables. This has more of a monetary feel to it, and Eric Stanton doesn't need money.'

'A ransom?' Natasha asked softly, speaking for the first time, before her superior followed up.

Revenge in Mind

'Was there a note? Has there been any contact from the kidnappers? Is there anything you can give us at all?'

Toby looked at Mike, considering the question. He then turned towards Jack and Dylan. There were reasons they didn't want police involvement, but Toby suddenly realised what really sat behind this. It wasn't because of the misdemeanours; it was because this was personal. Neither of them wanted Eric dealt with by the law. They wanted to hand out their own justice, not only to him, but to anybody associated with him. Jack had experienced an invasion of privacy, extensive property damage, and a physical assault. A guilt that George had been taken on his watch when he was supposed to be protecting her would fuel him. He would likely be reminded of the last time a girl living with him had disappeared. For Dylan, it was much simpler. They had taken his sister. Of the three of them, it was he who had a level of emotional investment which Toby and Jack couldn't reach. Toby wasn't a fighter, but Jack and Dylan were. He wondered what they would do to Eric should they find him. Whilst he deplored violence, he found it difficult to have sympathy for this man. When Eric had involved Beth, he had surpassed what was acceptable. Toby still believed ultimately he would need to outsmart Eric, but having a couple of guys like Jack and Dylan in his corner wouldn't harm. He now knew what he needed to do. He needed to point the police in a different direction, whilst he continued the hunt for Eric, but that wouldn't be easy considering he had already raised his suspicions with the man sat opposite him previously.

'Toby, may I speak with you outside for a moment, please?' Mike gestured.

Toby felt his heart skip a beat, but declining Mike's request wouldn't look good on him. He moved over towards the door and held it open as both men exited the room.

'What's going on Toby?'
'Isn't that what we're all trying to figure out?'
'That's my concern.'
'I don't follow.'
'Let's cut the bullshit. Neither you nor your friends are being honest in there,' Mike said angrily, pointing towards the lounge.

Toby looked startled. Mike was frustrated, something Toby hadn't seen previously. He felt uncomfortable.

'Don't look offended, Toby, and don't paint me as the bad guy here. This is the second time you've name dropped Eric Stanton and we can now add kidnapping to the rape and intimidation allegations.'

'Why have you brought me out here?'
'Because we need to talk about Eric Stanton. I'm assuming that unit in there wouldn't take too kindly to discovering you're withholding information from him.'

'Like what?'
'Like the minor detail that the man you suspect has kidnapped his sister has also allegedly raped her.'
'What makes you think he doesn't already know?'
'When you mentioned his name, he didn't flinch. Either he's one cold son of a bitch or he doesn't have the complete story. Which one is it?'

Toby closed his eyes and looked down. He had tried to bluff Mike, but had underestimated him. In truth, he didn't know what George had told Dylan, but one thing he was certain of was that he didn't want to test Dylan's resolve.

'Shall I tell you why I'm suspicious here, Toby?'

Toby didn't respond.

'When we met in the coffee shop, you went all out to convince me of Eric Stanton's guilt, but do you know what really struck me about that conversation?'

A tight pain gripped Toby's chest as he shook his head slowly, unsure of where this was leading.

'The way you recanted. You tried so hard to convince me Eric Stanton was a criminal mastermind who had eluded the authorities by presenting as a victim. Then you suddenly backtracked, though I didn't see it at the time. It only became relevant when you did exactly the same in there a few minutes ago.'

Toby stared at Mike, realising his mouth had slipped open. He thought he'd done enough to throw Mike off the trail, and perhaps at the time he had. But now, that had been undone. He'd tripped up and needed to think on his feet. He didn't like the idea of lying to Mike, not just because he still considered him a friend, but because Mike was experienced, and good at his job. Toby knew there was every chance he would be found out, and that it would look worse on him when he was. In this moment, he hated what he was becoming. What he had perhaps already become. He worried he had gone so far down the track that it would be difficult to come back from this. A series of poor decisions plagued him, but he still believed his intentions had always come from a good place. Right now, there wasn't enough evidence against Eric. Olivia had warned Toby that Eric was a dangerous man and Toby needed to be certain should he decide to go after him. Police involvement at this stage would only antagonise him further, which would put Toby and Beth in further danger. The decision was a simple one. Mike's disappointment and frustration wasn't ideal for him, but it was a preferred option to what Eric may do if he saw Toby coming. Mike would have a role to play, but not right now.

'Your observation is correct, however, you're mistaken in viewing the two occasions as being intrinsically linked.'

Mike looked at Toby with suspicion. He would take some convincing.

'In the coffee shop, I was afraid of what Eric Stanton may do. In there, I'm afraid of what Dylan may do.'

'You're not making sense, Toby.'

'The game's changed, Mike. It began with mild intimidation, but now it's escalated. Am I afraid of what Eric will do to me if he believes I am responsible for the police looking into him? Yes. But now there are more players and added complexity. There's a rather large complication sat on my sofa in there and whilst I'm glad I'm not in his sights, I feel he's walking that line between tolerant and psychopathic. I don't want to be the one responsible for him deviating onto the wrong side of that line if you understand me.'

'How much do you know about Dylan Sampson?'

'Not a lot. When George and I dated back in college, he'd already left for the army. All I knew about him back then was what she told me. I met him for the first time just a couple of hours ago.'

'What's your first impression?'

Toby smiled.

Revenge in Mind

'You've seen the size of him, right?'

'Toby, contrary to what you might see in the movies, vigilante groups very rarely have success in these instances. I've already called this in and there are people out looking for George. Whatever you're thinking, I am urging you to reconsider. Leave this to the trained professionals. If you impede this investigation, I will have no choice but to reprimand you. I'm asking you as a friend, don't put me in that position.'

Toby nodded. He respected Mike. This wasn't the first time he had offered him a patience and leniency that likely wouldn't be afforded to others in the same situation.

'Nobody needs to know what we've been discussing in here,' Mike said calmly.

Toby nodded slowly in agreement, but hadn't taken in what Mike had said. A thought he had had worried him, but it wasn't something he wanted to explore now.

Toby and Mike re-entered the room to an awkward silence. It was perhaps down to the fact that out of the four, only Beth and Jack were acquainted, he thought. The very nature of the situation simply compounded the general mood. Mike didn't re-take his seat, instead he gestured to Natasha Jenkins to join him.

'I'll tell the rest of you what I've just told Toby. The best chance you have of Georgina's safe return is to keep us informed about anything which might be relevant, and let us do our jobs. I'm strongly advising you to work with us, not against us. You might think you're helping, but the likelihood is you'll be hampering our investigation. This is now a high priority, official police matter. If there is anything at all you feel might assist us, however small a detail, you can reach me personally on this number,' Mike said, retrieving several business cards from his pocket and handing them out around the room.

Toby hadn't been focused on him as he had been speaking. Seemingly, neither had Jack, who all the while had been staring at the female officer, but his look wasn't a lustful one. Toby wondered what he was missing, but didn't dwell on this thought. Instead, his attention had been diverted to understanding why Mike had suddenly referred to George by her full name. Mike turned to Beth and thanked her for her hospitality, but Toby wondered whether the gratitude was more for involving the police. He had tested her patience and her loyalty, and now knew she had reached her limit. He wasn't angry, but it meant until this was over, he had to be careful what he shared with her. It would pain him to keep things from her, but he had a strong feeling Eric Stanton would continue to elude police detection, which meant there was only one way this was going to end. As Detective Inspector Mike Thomas and PC Natasha Jenkins exited the house, Jack turned to Toby, looking confused.

'Jack?'

'I know her from somewhere. I can't place it, but that face is familiar.'

'Wishful thinking?' Toby teased with a smile.

Jack laughed as Dylan came out into the hallway to join them.

'Hate to break up the party, but we need to go.'

'Go where?' Jack asked.

Revenge in Mind

'If we go to the right places and speak the right language, we'll get what we're looking for.'

'You mean rough some people up?'

'You got a better idea?'

'I think we need to look at this logically. Remaining inconspicuous will be their sole focus. They won't have wanted to be in transit for long, and they will avert any risk of detection during the daytime. I think we take a five-mile radius from Jack's and look at any abandoned or remote buildings.'

Jack and Dylan studied one another for a moment. Both appeared close to boiling point and Toby realised he had a task to keep them calm. He had already identified Dylan as a loose cannon, but what concerned him more was the influence he was having on Jack. Usually a mild-mannered individual, Jack was portraying similar traits to Dylan, almost like he was trying to compete or impress. Toby couldn't decide which one. Finding George was their priority, but Toby realised he had another job, which was to keep Jack and Dylan focused. He went to his car and pulled out a map, a rare sighting these days, with satellite navigation technology as advanced as it was. He quickly pinpointed Jack's farm and drew a circle around it.

'Take my car and head to these areas. Look for any abandoned buildings or remote farms. Jack, you should have a pre-existing knowledge of this area. Ask around, but don't get heavy-handed. You heard Mike in there. He'll be watching and one call to the police will bring any investigation from us crashing down.'

He stopped for a moment and looked at Dylan.

'A man of your size isn't hard to describe. That description in association with the name of Eric Stanton leads right to you. I can only imagine how angry you are, but you need to use that to your advantage.'

He threw his car keys to Jack.

'What about you?' Jack asked curiously.

'I have something to do first, but I'll check in with you later.'

Though he was mindful he was acting secretively, Jack and Dylan didn't probe. Exchanging a glance, they nodded and walked out of the door, clutching the map. Toby wondered whether his words had resonated with them. He had been forthright on all but one point. The detail he had kept to himself was that a part of him believed this was now a recovery exercise, and they were, in fact, searching for a body. Closing his eyes, Toby allowed his mind to wander to the one place he had desperately wanted to avoid. That solitary thought, that George was already dead.

{ 23 }

'I have to be honest Toby, I always envisaged us being sat here again, though it's come a little sooner than I thought.'

'Thank you for agreeing to see me. I needed some perspective, and there's nobody who understands me better.'

'Beth may have something to say about that.'

'Beth tolerates me,' Toby laughed.

He felt uneasy about being here, but something didn't sit comfortably with him and there was nobody better than Richard to help him explore that.

'Am I on the clock?' Toby teased.

'I'm not here as your supervisor,' Richard replied matter-of-factly.

Toby admired his professionalism. Richard had been an excellent supervisor, but Toby had often thought there was more to their relationship. He was fond of Richard and respected just how good he was at his job, but he also liked him as a person. He was kind and sincere and, even in Toby's darkest moments, had never cast judgement. The main reason for Toby's trepidation was that Richard had warned him about his relationship with Olivia Stanton. Had Toby listened to his concerns, this would be a professional meeting, rather than Toby clinging to the hope that he had gained enough respect over the years to warrant a non-judgemental, off-the-record conversation.

'You look well.'

'Looks can be deceiving. Below the surface I'm a car crash,' Toby replied before noticing his choice of words hadn't gone unnoticed by Richard.

'Why don't you start by telling my why you're here.'

'I'm at breaking point, but that's not the actual issue.'

'Then what is?'

'I can feel myself changing as a person and I don't like it.'

'In what way do you feel you're changing?'

'I'm becoming angry, less tolerant, and being deceptive appears to come to me rather too easily these days.'

'Let's begin with the anger. You know where it comes from, right?'

'Fear, pain and frustration,' Toby said with a smile, wondering how many times he had explored this very concept with his clients in the past.

'When do you first recall feeling like this?'

Toby paused, wondering how much he should disclose. He needed to choose his words carefully, but Richard was observant. If Toby held back too much, he would notice.

'Recently, I discovered that somebody who had once been close to me had suffered a brutal and heinous attack. But being honest with you, I think this began with Olivia Stanton. She changed me.'

'Olivia Stanton didn't change you, Toby. She brought something out of you that was already there. I think you already knew that, and that's where your actual concern lies.'

Richard's words had struck a chord. He wasn't wrong, and that's what hurt.

'Toby, there is something hidden inside us all. Some of us will go our entire lives without it ever surfacing, but other times...'

'Something or someone brings it to the surface.'

Richard smiled, nodding slowly.

'Perhaps I should never have become a therapist,' Toby said, looking rather subdued.

'You were an excellent therapist, one of the best I've worked with, in fact. You made a bad decision, but I know you did it in good faith and with the best of intentions. Good people can make poor decisions. Don't forget that.'

'When I was a psychotherapist, even when working with perpetrators, I could empathise and identify a desire to change within them. Now I wish harm on somebody who has committed unspeakable acts.'

'Toby, I'm far too experienced to believe you've never sat opposite a client who contravened your own value system and not had that urge to challenge them.'

'I always remained professional.'

'That I don't dispute, and you have just proved my point.'

'What point's that?'

'That what we feel is innate and involuntary. It's something we have little to no control over. How we respond to those feelings, however...'

'That we do control,' Toby interrupted.

'Precisely.'

'So, the feelings of anger make you human. They are likely coming from the pain of seeing somebody you care for suffer. But I'm not so sure that's the primary cause.'

'Then what is?' Toby asked, hoping Richard could provide him with the answers he hadn't been able to find himself.

'I'm wondering whether there is a frustration bubbling because you can't resolve it. We can't control or change what's already passed. I've always admired how devoted you are to helping people, healing their pain, but that which made you such a good therapist also makes you vulnerable.'

Toby bowed his head, not out of shame, but out of the fact Richard had been right with everything he had said.

'How do I get back that part of me that's missing?'

'It never left you. It's just a part of you that had previously laid dormant found its voice.'

'I miss this,' Toby said with genuine sorrow.

'Forgive yourself Toby. The Olivia Stanton incident wasn't your fault. If you accept responsibility, you take away her accountability. You don't choose whether she puts that on you, but you choose whether you accept it. We can't change the world Toby, we just work one case at a time with those who want to change themselves.'

Toby rose out of his chair and shook Richard's hand with sincere appreciation.

'Thank you for seeing me. I won't take up any more of your time.'

'You take care of yourself Toby, my door's always open.'

Toby picked up his keys and headed out of the door. The conversation had been brief, but necessary. Nothing had changed within the situation, but Toby felt his headspace had cleared. He knew to see this through he would have to be emotionally capable. As Richard's house faded into the background, Toby reminisced about the number of times he had been here. For a moment, he felt overwhelmed, grieving his former life, but things were different now. He had people relying on him, just in a different way. As he squeezed the accelerator in Beth's car, he looked down at his phone, which had an incoming call from Jack. He deliberated whether to take the call, allowing his mind to play out the scenario he feared the most. A scenario he simply didn't have the emotional capacity to deal with. The phone continued to ring.

{ 24 }

Mike Thomas and Natasha Jenkins exchanged a look of mutual admiration for the approaching house and its grounds as they slowly made their way up the long drive. At first glance, it appeared perfect, seamlessly merging with its environment. It exuded an ostentatious, yet classy and simple vibe. Mike was reminded of the last time he was here, finding it difficult to believe that something so beautiful on the outside could hide such unspeakable acts of terror on the inside. The circumstances may have been different, but it still had an unpleasant feel to it, and this visit wouldn't be a comfortable one. Ordinarily this wouldn't have been a case Mike would have got involved in, but considering the fact Eric Stanton was now on his radar, he had decided this was a good excuse to get better acquainted with the man who had got under the skin of Toby. He climbed out of the car, closing the door slowly, and glanced at the house. It was difficult to determine whether this was with envy or suspicion. As he walked towards the front door, he noticed Natasha peering down the side of the house a few yards to his right. She joined Mike presently at the front door as they prepared to meet the owner.

'This is a rather large house for just two people to search,' Natasha said, taking a step back.

At that moment, there was the sound of a vehicle approaching. As the car came to a halt and the two officers got out, Mike smiled at Natasha.

'How's that for timing?'

Mike regarded the officers.

'As you all know, obtaining a warrant with a single source of intel is incredibly difficult. We're relying on Mr Stanton being cooperative. I hope you haven't had a wasted journey.'

He could hear movement in the house as he knocked on the door, yet nobody answered. He knocked a little louder, this time hearing the footsteps approaching. Eric Stanton opened the door with a smile. The first thing that struck Mike was how well dressed he was.

'How can I help you officers?' he asked, peering outside at the vehicles which looked more abandoned than carefully parked.

'Eric Stanton?'

'That's correct.'

'We've had an anonymous tip that you're distributing drugs from this house,' Mike said calmly with a smile.

The well-dressed owner of the house stared in disbelief for a moment before breaking out into laughter.

'This is a joke, right?'

'Perhaps we could come inside and take a quick look around?'

'Do you have a warrant?'

Mike Thomas shook his head nonchalantly.

'Then it looks like you've had a wasted trip. No warrant, no entry.'

'Where there is a genuine concern that the delay in obtaining a warrant may impede the investigation, we don't need one. In this case, it wouldn't be too difficult to convince a judge that because of the nature of the search, there was a genuine possibility that you would remove or destroy the evidence whilst we awaited a warrant. However, we would much rather clear this up amicably.' Mike replied.

Eric smiled, but it didn't seem genuine. Mike knew getting a warrant at this stage of an investigation was going to be a tall order, so if his bluff failed, any small lead they may have would dissipate quickly.

'Come on in, I have nothing to hide,' he said, stepping aside and waving the officers past him.

Mike noticed how much bigger the house looked from the inside. With its grandiose interior design, it was nicer than most hotels he'd stayed in. He signalled for the officers to gather around him, towards the bottom of the staircase.

'Natasha and I will take the upstairs. You concentrate on things down here, but I don't want him out of your sight. We can't take any risks. Be thorough, but be respectful.'

At that, he and Natasha made their way up the staircase. The house had five bedrooms, which seemed excessive for a man and a small child. Perhaps more of a statement than a necessity, Mike thought.

'Every room, every bit of furniture,' he said, turning to Natasha.

'With the amounts that were reported, if it's here, it shouldn't be too difficult to find,' she responded.

Revenge in Mind

They entered the first bedroom, the master bedroom. The décor was modern, yet the architecture had more of a traditional look to it. The wooden beams gave the feeling of being inside a period cottage, yet in many aspects, the two couldn't be more different. There was an en-suite bathroom in the corner of the bedroom, which was similar in size to most spare rooms. Mike shook his head and smiled as he glanced around the room.

'God knows how long I'd have to work to afford a place like this,' he said, walking over to the bedside table and opening it.

A picture of Eric, Olivia, and their son sat proudly on top. Mike picked it up and stared at it for a while. He turned to Natasha and handed her the photo frame.

'Help me understand something. A guy's wife tries to murder him in cold blood, accuses him of rape, and sets out to systematically dismantle his life and discredit him. Why would he still have a family photograph at the side of his bed?'

'A reminder of happier times?'

'The Olivia Stanton case wasn't about impulse. Things had been building for a long time. He'd filed a previous report for aggressive behaviour. He knew exactly what she was like.'

'I'm not sure what you're saying, sir.'

'I'm saying I don't subscribe to the family man persona he appears to be trying a little too hard to portray here.'

Natasha didn't reply. As they combed the room, Mike became increasingly more frustrated.

'Sir, what if we're wrong about him?'

'Here's the thing Natasha, I've known Toby a long time and you know what?'

Natasha Jenkins stayed quiet, but looked attentive.

'He's rarely wrong. Toby was incredibly good at what he did, one of the best. If he gets a feel for someone, you can be sure there's a reason for it.'

'He was wrong about Olivia Stanton, wasn't he?'

Mike stopped what he was doing and swung round to face the junior officer, who sensed she had spoken out of turn.

'Toby always had his suspicions of Olivia. Yes, he was naïve, but that naivety saved the life of the man downstairs. Don't you forget that,' he said harshly.

Natasha Jenkins, wearing the look of a scorned schoolgirl, resumed the search.

'Sir.'

Natasha was holding up a small bag she had retrieved from the back of the wardrobe. Mike walked over to where she was standing, took the bag from her, and peered inside it.

'What do you think?'

'There's a lot of money in there, but this isn't what we're here to search for.'

'But surely it's relevant?'

'It simply shows he has some money stashed away. Using banks isn't a legal requirement,' Mike replied.

Natasha sighed.

The search continued for several minutes, but nothing of relevance was discovered. The officers searched the next two rooms thoroughly, but came up empty-handed. There was a growing sense of frustration within Mike that he was missing something. The entire scene appeared a little too serene for him. His suspicions of Eric Stanton had grown significantly since the moment he greeted them at the front door. They had been reliant on this being a consensual search, but the moment Eric had invited them in, the chances of them finding anything decreased significantly. Mike had worked with a lot of perpetrators and knew the signs of guilt. Eric had shown nothing apparent, but there was something in his face that made Mike feel uncomfortable. He wondered whether it was that same look Toby had described seeing. He was sure Eric was hiding something, but the evidence so far wasn't supporting his hunch. As they made their way down the corridor, Mike was struck by the number of family pictures, which were placed neatly along the wall. Except out here, Olivia was notably absent. Still, the pictures weren't what drew Mike's attention as he walked towards the wall in the middle of the corridor. He knelt down and ran his fingers over the skirting board, turning to Natasha to show her his findings.

'Interesting.'

'I don't follow, sir,' she replied, somewhat confused.

'Someone put this up recently.'

He stood to his feet and moved down the corridor.

'All of these have been put up recently.'

'How can you tell?'

'Look around. The place is immaculate, to a disturbing extent. Why go to all the effort of keeping a place so clean and then leave bits of plaster and paint on the skirting boards and floor? It doesn't make sense.'

'You think he's hiding something?'

'Yes, but that's not what this is. This is somebody who is trying to impress upon us he is a family man.'

'Why do you think that is?'

'Olivia's picture serves as a reminder that he was almost fatally stabbed. Seeing the images of him and his son reinforces the fact that he is a father. It's an attempt to distract us from seeing what may be lurking behind all of this.'

'You got all that from a few bits of dust?' she asked with a smile.

'No, the dust actually raises another important question.'

'It does?'

Mike nodded his head slowly. There was a strange paradox that, as it became clearer, it also became more confusing.

'If, as I suspect, this was done for our benefit, how did he know?'

'Know what?'

'That we were coming.'

Natasha regarded him with concern.

'I'm almost certain we will not find anything of note here, certainly nothing related to drugs. This has a contrived feel about it, and that can only mean one thing,' he continued.

'What's that?'

'That he was pre-warned.'

He opened the door to another room, a child's room. 'Take a look in there. What do you see?'

'A child's bedroom?'

'When did you ever see a children's bedroom so tidy? The toys are concealed, clothes neatly folded or hung,' he said, opening the wardrobe door.

'So, it's been tidied for a reason?'

'No. The tidiness itself isn't the problem. It simply serves to highlight the problem.'

Revenge in Mind

'And what's that?'

Mike looked at her, and for a moment wished it was Nadia Williams standing beside him. He didn't know too much about the officer accompanying him. She was relatively new into the role and seemed to focus more on complying than impressing. Whilst he didn't appreciate insubordination, he liked people who showed ambition and thought outside the box. Nadia Williams had done just that and had grabbed her opportunity with both hands when it had presented itself. Her reward...a promotion. He took a deep breath and smiled warmly, as though he had suddenly located a reserve of patience he hadn't known existed.

'Everything about Eric Stanton screams organised and meticulous. The house, the car, his appearance, to the very last detail. But that out in the hallway, that's careless. It's rushed, like he had little time to prepare.'

'How could he have known we were coming?'

'That very question increases the complexity of the case as it raises concerns about an insider.'

'Who?'

'That's something I intend to find out, but for now we'll continue the search just to see if he got careless anywhere else in the house.'

'You really think he's done all the things Toby Reynolds accused him of?'

'I never doubted Toby, but as you know, accusation without evidence is simply speculation. Do I believe Toby? yes. Do I think there is enough in what he said to arouse my suspicion? Also, yes. But do I think there is sufficient evidence to substantiate his claims and open up an investigation into Eric Stanton at this moment in time? No. The CPS don't prosecute on hunches Natasha, they prosecute on evidence.'

'It must be tough to have a suspected rapist walking the streets due to a lack of evidence.'

'That there are numerous criminals freely roaming the streets supports my point and explains why I am hesitant. If we present a half-arsed case with tenuous evidence, a decent defence solicitor will tear it apart. Despite the frustration and time it takes, our job is to create an airtight case that will unquestionably lead to a conviction.'

He closed the bedroom door as they moved back into the hallway. He had no optimism of finding anything here and questioned whether this was more about somebody with a vendetta who simply wanted to make Eric Stanton squirm. Even so, something didn't sit right with him. He noticed Natasha stop and stare out of the circular window at the top of the staircase. As he walked back to join her, he was met with the view of a stunning back garden which appeared to stretch for miles. At the bottom was an outbuilding, the same outbuilding Natasha had noticed on the way in. His concentration was broken by his name being called by one of the officers who had been assisting with the search. Mike tapped Natasha on the shoulder and signalled for her to join him as he descended the stairs. As the four congregated at the bottom of the staircase, the officer, a slender yet tall individual, moved closer to Mike and whispered.

'We haven't found anything, sir.'

'Has he said much?' Mike asked, peering over the shoulder of the officer fixating on Eric Stanton, who was now standing at the front door typing on his phone.

'He's been neither accommodating nor obstructive.'

Mike sighed and took a deep breath.

'What are you thinking, sir?' Natasha Jenkins asked.

'You ever wonder how a guy who fixes printers affords all this?'

'Inheritance?'

'In isolation I might agree, but I suspect there may be more to Eric Stanton's story, connecting Toby's accusations of kidnapping, the tip-off, and Olivia Stanton's attempted murder of him,' Mike replied.

Eric Stanton looked up from his phone as the officers walked towards the front door where he had positioned himself. He opened it with a smile which, under any other circumstances, would have passed for sincere, but Mike sensed there was something more sinister sitting behind it.

'I'm sorry you've had a wasted trip, officers, and thank you for being respectful of my property. As you can no doubt tell, I like things in an ordered fashion,' he replied with a charm that Mike was under no illusion had likely fooled many people in its time.

Mike Thomas and the accompanying officers walked over the gravel towards their vehicles. As he reached the side of the house, he noted the outbuilding situated towards the bottom of the extensive garden at the rear. He turned to Eric Stanton, who was standing in the doorway, and pointed towards the building.

'You've noticed my workshop. I'd like to say it was a deliberate ploy to add some mystery to the place, but shamefully, I just got lazy and allowed it to become overgrown. The job gets bigger every time I look at it,' he said softly.

'Mind if we take a look in there?'

'Actually, I do. I've been more than accommodating, but this is now bordering on ridiculous,' Eric Stanton replied abruptly.

Mike stared at him for a moment.

'Thank you for your time. We're sorry to have troubled you,' he said, opening the car door. He sat for a moment as Eric Stanton disappeared back into the house, closing the door firmly. He glanced at the officer next to him and noted the look of disappointment on her face.

'Is this your first search?' Mike asked her.

'Yeah, I wasn't sure what to expect, but it feels like a loss.'

'What makes you say that?'

'Well, we didn't find anything,' she said, looking confused.

'We may not have discovered what we were looking for, but that doesn't mean we didn't discover anything,' he replied unintentionally cryptically.

'I don't follow.'

'What we learned in there is this guy clearly has something to hide. The house is immaculate, the grounds match it, and even his car looks recently washed. Eric Stanton clearly takes pride in his appearance, so why would he allow that one building to become unsightly? That's not unintentional lethargy. It's a deliberate attempt to conceal something. The question is, what?'

The young officer shook her head slowly.

Revenge in Mind

'He seemed to get riled when we asked to look around that outbuilding.'

'Either he believed he had experienced enough inconvenience, or he had something to hide. He put on a show in there, but what he doesn't realise is that doing so only further aroused suspicion. As careful as he may have thought he had been, he gave enough away.'

'So, what's next, sir?'

Mike Thomas started the engine and headed down the long drive, ignoring the question. He was distracted. He'd undertaken many searches in his time and even those who were innocent displayed some degree of nerves at the prospect of having their homes picked apart by the police. Eric Stanton had been ice cool. He'd shown little interest in proceedings. That wasn't the sign of somebody who felt they had nothing to hide, it was the sign of somebody who knew what they were hiding had no chance of being found. Then his mind settled on what was perhaps the most disturbing aspect of all of this, the quandary Mike had been wrestling with since the moment he had seen the plaster on the upstairs carpet. There were only a handful of people who knew about the search. One of those had tipped Eric Stanton off, which posed an alarming question. Who, from the inside, was on Eric Stanton's payroll?

{ 25 }

'It's another dead-end Toby.'

Toby dropped his head in frustration. This had been their best lead. The geographical isolation, the distance from Jack's farm, it made sense, yet like several other places they had discovered, it lacked one key element...George.

'Toby, are you there?'

'Yeah, just thinking, wondering what we're missing.'

'I'm concerned about Dylan.'

'Concerned?'

'His behaviour is becoming more erratic. It's like he sees everyone as a suspect.'

'He's anxious. His anger is being driven by his pain, and if he's not finding his answers, you can add frustration to that,' Toby replied calmly.

'He's a loose cannon.'

'Jack, you're the most relaxed person I've ever encountered, making everyone else seem unpredictable by comparison,' Toby joked.

Jack laughed out loud, but Toby detected a nervousness.

'There's a quiet country pub Beth and I have visited. It's about five minutes from where you are. I'm sending you the address now. I'll be there in twenty minutes.'

'How do you know where we are?'

'The car has a tracker.'

'Beth's way of keeping tabs on you?' Jack laughed.

'My way of keeping tabs on you, buddy. Thanks for juicing her up, by the way.'

'What makes you think we haven't just pulled over for a snack?'

'The tank didn't have enough fuel for the places you've explored. Coupled with your extremely cautious approach to spending, and the fact that it's the least expensive petrol station in the area, I'm theorising with a fair degree of certainty that you've refuelled my car,' Toby nonchalantly replied.

'Sometimes you're too bright for your own good.'

'I'm gonna take that as a compliment. See you soon.'

Toby hung up the phone. The banter with Jack was the thing he had always valued about their friendship, but it felt somehow out of place in their current situation. It was approximately six hours since George had been kidnapped. The police had made her case a priority and Mike Thomas had promised significant resources. The worrying thing for Toby, and something he hadn't voiced in front of Dylan, was there had been no contact. Everything pointed to this being a preordained attack, not something simply left to chance. The whole thing felt very detailed. Therefore, a clear aim was a certainty in Toby's mind. There were only two explanations he could think of. Either this was about extortion, or it was personal. He wasn't a detective, but he knew people and, in the field of behaviour, had a greater understanding than most. Some would say this was a gift, but Toby had carried it for years as a burden. There were times when he didn't want to be right, didn't want to see things others didn't. This was one of those times. If this was about money, there would have been contact by now. It was this thought process that led Toby directly to Eric Stanton. He had wealth, money wasn't an issue for him. This meant it was personal, and if it was personal, there would be no leverage, no bargaining. It would be vindictive and motivated by revenge, not financial gain. But this presented another question. If this was indeed about revenge, who was the target? George was linked to all three of them. Jack had housed her and had already beaten up the men who had raided his house. Dylan was her brother and had made enemies in the short time he had been in town. Toby was her old flame and in the last few weeks, had been her protector, by all accounts. But then another thought entered his mind. George had a history with Eric Stanton and had suddenly appeared on the scene after years of being estranged from him. Toby had heard it, but she had lived it. George knew him better than most, and with Olivia Stanton stoking the fire, could inflict more damage on him than anybody else. He had been too fixated on the theory that George was a mere piece in a game of revenge, overlooking the possibility that she was the one they were really after.

Jack and Dylan had stationed themselves at the far end of the car park. In trying to remain inconspicuous, they had probably drawn attention to themselves as the only car in that area.

Revenge in Mind

The skies were blue and the sun was shining, yet there was a cool breeze. George had been missing for several hours and with the sun looking to set shortly, they were up against time. The best hours were behind them, and the thought of George being held against her will, frightened and confused as the darkness descended, was unbearable. Toby stretched out his arms and got out of Beth's car, walking towards his own. Jack was sitting in the driver's seat with the window down. Dylan stood outside the car, looking cautiously around the parameters. Toby was fairly sure underneath the calm persona he was projecting burned a rage which would only be extinguished when it tasted revenge. He wasn't, nor had he ever been, violent, but the thought of what Dylan would do to Eric Stanton once he caught up with him intrigued Toby. If he was honest, it ran deeper than mere intrigue. Nobody, not even Olivia, had got to him in the way Eric Stanton had. The threats against Toby were a problem, but when he invaded their home and dragged Beth into it, a boundary was crossed, which quite simply couldn't be undone. It was at *that* moment the lines had been drawn, *that* moment where Toby had realised there was no going back, *that* moment where he had decided against the better judgement of all the voices in his head, that he would fight back. He walked around the side of the car and stood next to Dylan. Jack opened the door and climbed out to join them. Toby smiled as the thought of two large framed men crammed into his less than spacious sports car passed through his mind.

'What's the plan, Tobes?' Jack asked, patting him on the shoulder.

Toby unfolded the map he had taken from Beth's car and placed it on the bonnet. The two men gathered round as he pointed to the red circle he had drawn.

'This is the area I think we should focus on. Jack, nobody knows the countryside better than you. Talk me through where you've already checked.'

Toby stepped aside as Jack stood over the map.

'There's the old farm at Mill End,' he said, pointing.

'Okay.'

'We tried a couple of houses out at Hambleden Moor.'

'That was like stepping back in time,' Dylan added.

'Then we drove out here to Coppice Hill as I know there are a couple of abandoned barns out there, but nothing.'

Jack sounded defeated. Toby took hold of the map.

'What about over here?' he said, pointing at an area that at first glance appeared to be all woodland.

'A remote area, probably no more than twenty minutes from your farm. To avoid detection, they will have wanted to spend as little time on the road as possible. Geographically, it makes sense,' Toby continued.

'It's worth a try, but what if...' Jack began before halting abruptly.

'Jack?'

'Say your theory is right, and they wanted to avoid detection. What if they move her tonight to somewhere further afield?' Jack responded, crestfallen.

'They would be less inconspicuous travelling at night than during the daytime. I don't think they'd risk it.'

'What if you're wrong?' Dylan hollered.

'Then time becomes even more precious.'

'Perhaps we should split up, cover more area,' Jack suggested.

Toby nodded in agreement, but knowing the most logical option was to pair himself with Dylan filled him with anxiety. Dylan was angry and unpredictable. If he blamed Toby for George's situation, it could be an uncomfortable journey. Toby reminded himself this was about George and not him as he circled a small area on the map with his finger.

'Jack, you head out there and see if there are any old farmhouses, dilapidated buildings, anything at all which would be appealing to somebody wanting to go incognito. Dylan and I will drive around this area here and see what we can find,' Toby said, pressing down hard on the map with the tip of his finger.

Toby and Dylan got into Beth's car. As they did so, Jack, who had positioned himself behind the wheel of Toby's car, suddenly switched off the engine and began walking at pace back towards them.

'Toby that officer,' he began.

'Mike Thomas?'

'No, the other one, Natasha Jenkins.'

'She appeared to have your attention,' Toby teased.

Jack looked uneasy.

'Her face looked familiar, but I was struggling to place it at the time. I've just figured out where I know her from.'

'Why are you telling me this, Jack?'

'I think it could be important.'

Toby stared at his friend with intensity, yet remained silent. Dylan also stopped what he was doing to focus on the conversation taking place next to him.

'A few years ago, I took up boxing, you know, to keep in shape and have something other than the farm to focus on. There were about seven of us in the group, all men except for one.'

'Natasha Jenkins?' Toby asked.

'Except back then she wasn't known as Natasha Jenkins.'

Jack paused and swallowed hard before continuing.

'She was known as Natasha Stanton.'

'Shit,' Toby exclaimed. 'If she's related to Eric, she knows enough about the case to be an asset to him,' he continued.

'You still think this is Eric?' Dylan asked.

'It all points to him, but I've been wrong before, so I'm remaining cautious. I need to call Mike.'

'Why are you involving the police?' Dylan snapped.

'The police are already involved, but if Natasha Jenkins is a relative of Eric's and he is involved, there's a conflict of interest that Mike needs to be aware of. If she's dirty, he can remain one step ahead of the investigation.'

Dylan shook his head slowly. Toby was worried his frustration would boil over, and the last thing he needed was Dylan being out of control. They needed to work on logic, not emotion.

He placed his hand on Dylan's shoulder tentatively, unsure of whether or not it was a good idea.

'Dylan, we all want the same thing here. The police too. We can help them with their investigation and still undertake our own,' he said gently.

Dylan gave a slight nod of the head, agreeing reluctantly. As Jack walked back to his car, Toby pulled out his phone.

'Toby, to what do I owe this pleasure?'

'How much do you know about Natasha Jenkins?'

'She's relatively new to the force. I've never worked with her directly before. Why?'

'Jack recognised her, but had struggled to place her until now. He knew her a few years ago.'

'Okay, so your friend knew Natasha Jenkins in a past life?'

'That's the thing, Mike.' Toby composed himself. 'He didn't know Natasha Jenkins...he knew Natasha Stanton.'

There was a pause on the line.

'Naturally we can't be certain she's related, but the age would fit the narrative.'

'Shit. Now it makes sense.'

Mike sounded angry. Toby rarely heard him swear, but was interested to see where this was going.

'Mike?'

'We had a tip off to search Eric Stanton's house. For a guy who was just about to have his home turned upside down, he was incredibly relaxed to the point of arrogance. Either he had nothing to hide...'

'Or he knew you were coming,' Toby interrupted.

'The entire scene made little sense. It felt too contrived, but he'd been a little careless, things that didn't fit.'

'Like what?' Toby asked curiously.

'Toby, I can't go into detail about ongoing investigation.'

'Perhaps I can help?'

'In what way?'

'Apparently, I understand how people work,' Toby smiled.

'If a guy is tidy to the point of obsession, and you find something out of place, what does it suggest to you?'

'It could point to several things. I would need more context.'

'The house is immaculate, Toby. I mean pristine. But it's not just the house, it's the whole grounds, but there's this one outbuilding that's completely overgrown. It won't be much longer until it's fully camouflaged.'

'Perhaps that's the intention.'

'That was my thought, but strangely, it was something much smaller than that, something which could have easily gone unnoticed, that aroused my suspicion.'

'You found something inside?'

'Not what we were looking for, but enough to tell me that something didn't seem quite right.'

'Oh?'

'There was a family photo on the bedside table. Why would you keep a photograph of somebody who tried to murder you?'

'Is that rhetorical?'

'Do you have a theory?'

'Regardless of how a relationship ends, it's not uncommon to see somebody cling to memories of better times. That picture may remind him of a happy moment, a version of Olivia that he desperately wants to hold on to. Whatever I feel about this guy, it's important to remember he's still trying to acclimatise to a world where his wife tried to kill him. That can't be easy.'

'Sounds like you're looking to excuse his actions.'

'I'm looking to understand them. There's a discernible difference,' Toby replied, offended at the insinuation.

'There was something else. The walls on the upstairs landing were full of pictures of him and his son.'

'You see that as suspicious?'

Revenge in Mind

'It was too crowded and unnecessary. It felt like he was pushing this image of a victim, a family man, and if this is what we saw on the surface...'

'You wouldn't look underneath.'

'But that's where all of this really gets fucked up, Toby. Underneath some pictures were bits of plaster and dust. On its own, this wouldn't have even registered with me, but it didn't fit with what we were seeing. If everything in the house is in perfect order, why are specific areas of the carpet left uncleaned?'

'The pictures were for your benefit. That small sign of disarray suggests he was pressed for time, showing he had knowledge of your arrival, but perhaps not long enough to adequately prepare. How many knew you were executing a search on Eric Stanton's property?'

Toby heard Mike take in a deep breath and thought about how difficult this must be for him. He was facing the prospect of a very uncomfortable conversation with a fellow officer. Toby didn't know the intricacies within the police, but suspected if Natasha Jenkins was guilty of deliberately impeding a police investigation, it would constitute gross misconduct and probably end her fleeting career.

'There was the officer who took the initial tip off, myself and Natasha Jenkins.'

'How well do you know her, Mike?'

'Barely at all, but she's about to get to know me. If there's one thing I can't stand, it's officers who have a duty to uphold the law, abusing their powers. I'm glad you brought this to me, Toby. I already had my suspicions something wasn't quite right, but this was the piece of the jigsaw that had been missing.'

There was a momentary silence on the line.

'Only now am I realising the signs were there with Natasha. I just wasn't looking for them at the time.'

'What did you see?'

'It wasn't what I saw, it's what I heard. She made a comment about Eric being an alleged rapist. We weren't there on suspicion of rape. I'd never mentioned it, so why would she make such a comment?'

'Unwittingly, I believe she has just given away more than she realised.'

'How?'

'There was never a complaint made, which means there isn't, and has never been, a police investigation. So, this now presents us with two possibilities. Either she's seen something, or she's heard something,' Toby clarified.

'Eric Stanton?'

'Possibly. If he's wary about any accusations, it would give him the opportunity to control the narrative.'

'What about George?'

'The way Olivia Stanton tells it, she had to track her down and use a lot of persuasion to get her to open up. I don't see George volunteering that information to the sister of her attacker.'

'Then it has to be Olivia Stanton,' Mike replied, sounding exasperated.

'Where her husband or anybody associated with him is involved, Olivia is without remorse. She would seem the obvious candidate.'

Mike inhaled slowly. Toby realised there was a lot for him to take in here and wondered how it must feel to be in his shoes right now. He didn't want to fuel the flames anymore, so changed direction.

'Have you had any leads on George?'

'Toby, I have all my best officers on this. I know this is personal for you, but please take my advice. Sit this one out and let us do our job.'

Toby wasn't sure how to respond.

'Your silence doesn't reassure me, Toby. I'm going to speak off the record and candidly, so I know there is no room for misinterpretation. Natasha Jenkins is about to find out just how much the police frown on people who deliberately manipulate an investigation. If I were you, I'd do everything I could to avoid putting myself in that same situation.'

'I hear you, Mike.'

Toby *had* heard Mike, but though his words had sent a very clear warning, Toby's agenda hadn't changed. He couldn't simply sit tight and hope the police found George. She meant too much to him. However long it would take, whatever challenges it would present, he, Jack and Dylan would continue their search. Mike's words had raised the stakes, and despite sharing the same goal, Toby understood they must evade detection, and not just from the abductors.

{ 26 }

The room had no windows, or perhaps someone had simply covered them to darken it. Time was a mere concept; she had no idea how long she had been here. Her body ached and her eyes were red, both from the trauma she had been subjected to. The room smelled damp, suggesting that the old building was likely exposed to the elements, as evidenced by the dripping she could hear coming from the corner of the room. Her hands had been tied, but her blindfold had now been removed. Small mercies, she thought. Her captors had spoken only once to her, their words succinct yet chilling. This wasn't part of her plan, their plan. This wasn't how things were meant to unfold. She questioned her decisions, not only over the last few weeks, but over the last few years. Her ordeal had been brutal, but she had harboured thoughts of revenge for a long time, and when the opportunity had presented itself, she had grasped it with both hands. However, the decision to dismantle his life piece by piece may now prove to be a bad one. She had walked away from him once and wondered whether she should have simply kept on walking. But despite leading a simpler life, she couldn't escape the dark cloud of trauma he had inflicted upon her. It had followed her around for years and she had made an active choice to cease feeling like a victim. Instead of living, she had been merely surviving, and now she needed to seize control of her path. There was a deathly silence surrounding her, which elicited mixed feelings. There was a feeling of relief knowing that she was safe whilst ever she was in the room alone, but contrasting this was a feeling of loneliness. She didn't know what she was facing and longed for Jack. Jack? Why was she longing for Jack she wondered? It had always been Toby. Even in her adult years, he was still the one who'd got away. She'd imagined their reunion a thousand times in her darkest days, yet the moment she met Beth, she had realised they belonged together. She would always care for Toby and he still meant a great deal to her, but Jack had made her feel safe. She had grown fond of his laid-back demeanour and loved how he made her laugh, often unintentionally. He didn't take life too seriously, but clearly cared for those close to him, a trait she couldn't help but admire. He was an innocent party who had found himself at the centre of her chaos, his only crime being he had tried to do a good deed. She felt a tinge of sadness as she thought of his house, damaged. He had suffered physical harm, but she wondered whether the emotional torture he would undoubtedly experience now paled this into insignificance. In Jack's mind, his sole responsibility had been to protect her, yet in doing so, he had left her vulnerable and she had been taken. She began to cry, the salty taste of her tears the first time her lips had experienced any sort of hydration since her capture. Her adult life had contained complexities she wouldn't have been able to imagine as a teenager. She often felt herself regressing back to her college days, the place where she was most happy. Her dream had been of adventure, romance and Toby. Her reality had been solitude, abuse, and Eric. She strained to hear a sound, any sound, but she was alone. She had heard no noises above, yet had heard nobody leave, which left her feeling both curious and anxious. She yearned for interaction, but above all else, she yearned for a familiar voice to reassure her that everything was going to be okay. She longed to hear the voice of Jack, Toby, or Dylan, men whom she trusted. She craved love and security. She pined for the feeling of being held tightly and cared for. There was only one other moment in her life that Georgina Sampson had felt as vulnerable as she did now. Then she heard a noise. Her heart rate surged as she realised the noise she was hearing was the sound of approaching footsteps. She braced herself as she heard the handle turn. The door creaked as it slowly opened. George squinted her eyes to try to make out the figure walking slowly down the stairs, approaching her. Part of her, however, didn't want to see. She was bound and defenceless. For a brief second, she allowed her mind to wander back to her darkest moment, the moment when Eric Stanton had taken something from her which he had no right to take. That one action had taken her control, her self-esteem, her identity. She had spent years in the depths of despair, allowing life to pass her by. She had resolved to never be in that position again, yet here she was, exposed. She had no control and was a mere passenger in whatever this was. In a game of chess, she was the last piece, awaiting the inevitable onslaught by the relatively unscathed opponent. The man walked over to the corner of the room and flicked the switch of a lamp, which was sitting dormant in its own company. The bulb was dull and only scarcely illuminated the room as he began pacing slowly in her direction. As the image became clearer, she recognised the figure as one of the men who had forcefully removed her from Jack's house. He walked over to a chair positioned in the corner of the room, picked it up and placed it down facing her. As he straddled the chair backwards, he rested his arms on its spine. His gaze travelled up and down her body, his face bearing no hints about his thoughts or plans. When he spoke, he did so in a low and husky tone. It was the first time she had heard his voice, and it was anything other than reassuring.

'This won't take too long,' he said, grinning.

George stared at him wide eyed, with a panic her face simply couldn't conceal.

'What do you want with me?'

The man shuffled back in his chair, smirking. He sat motionless, staring at her breasts. His whole demeanour made her skin crawl, this time his face having no difficulty betraying what he was thinking. She squirmed, but with her hands bound, she knew she was powerless and at his mercy, or worse, at their mercy. Two men had brought her here, but she had no idea how many there were now. After they had taken her out of the house, she had been blindfolded. George wondered whether this had been to avoid the risk of her identifying the vehicle or the location within which they were taking her, or whether it was simply a display of control, designed to strike fear into her. In a sea of uncertainty, there was one thing she was absolutely sure of. She would never willingly comply. She would fight with everything she had to inflict as much damage on them as possible.

'This will all be over soon, don't worry,' the man repeated, still wearing the same perverse grin.

'What do you want with me?' she asked again.

'That depends what's on offer.'

'Fuck you.'

She spat firmly in his face as she uttered the words. It had been involuntary. It was fight or flight, and she had no desire to simply submit. She had promised herself no longer would she be a victim. Even in a fair fight, her chances would be limited, but the fact she was bound handed him the clear advantage. As he slowly wiped his face, she wondered whether antagonising him in such a manner had been wise. The man's grin had disappeared. He was now incandescent with rage and lurched across the chair as his hand connected with her face with such ferocity it rocked her.

'Bitch.'

Fear consumed her, the bravery and resolve she had somehow found crumbling at an alarming rate.

'Who's paying you?' she asked, struggling to hide the pain as her face throbbed.

'What makes you think anybody is paying us?' the man replied with an arrogance that induced a nauseating feeling in the pit of her stomach.

'You're not bright enough to be the brainchild of an operation like this.'

'If I were you, I'd be a little nicer.'

'If I were you, I'd be looking over my shoulder.'

'Oh?'

'There are people looking for me.'

'The police?' the man asked sarcastically.

George shook her head slowly.

'No, the police looking for you would be your best hope.'

The man addressed her with intrigue.

'You see, the person who owns the house you broke into; you know the one who gave you and your friend upstairs those bruises you're trying so desperately to hide? Well, he's not somebody you want to anger, trust me. Then there's the small matter of my brother.' George paused as she broke into laughter. It's hard not to laugh when I say "small" because he's actually well over six feet tall, and military trained. He also has a temper on him. But what makes it worse for you is that he is incredibly protective of me. You have yet to be acquainted with Dylan, but you will be. My brother doesn't just hurt people casually, he derives pleasure from causing harm.'

'You seem pretty confident he's going to find you.'

'They,' she corrected.

The man regarded her with a look of disdain. She could see the desperation in his efforts to maintain control, but she had planted the seeds of doubt. He and his accomplice would be no match for Jack and Dylan. Their only hope was to avoid detection, but where did this leave her?

As Toby approached the table, drinks in hand, he could see Dylan and Jack deep in conversation. Dylan was gesticulating, but there were no raised voices. Toby sensed they walked a tight line. There was a mutual respect between the two, but it wouldn't take much to spark an unpleasant confrontation. It was more than a simple tolerance of one another, yet some distance from anything resembling a friendship. As Toby approached, the two men noticed him and halted their conversation. Toby felt anxious, but as he observed their body language, he questioned if it was something he'd rather remain oblivious to.

'Where is she Toby?' Dylan asked, clearly agitated.

Toby shook his head slowly, but didn't want to appear downtrodden. They were looking for him to fix this and telling them he didn't know how wasn't a conversation he particularly relished. But that was the problem. They were looking to him, yet he was neither a criminal investigator nor a criminal mastermind. He was just an ordinary guy, an ordinary guy whose poor decision had led to all of this. It was his error in judgement which had sparked this entire situation. He was the reason they were here. Whilst Jack knew this, Dylan didn't, and he preferred to keep it that way. He looked out of the window, quietly contemplating. Dylan and Jack kept their gaze fixed on him, as though awaiting further direction. He turned back to face the two men.

'We're missing something.'

'We've searched all farms and any dilapidated buildings within the area we identified, but we've come up short,' Jack replied.

'It was inevitable a search would be initiated. They would have known this, which means they would want to get to their destination as quickly as possible, and then stay hidden.'

'Toby's right,' Dylan agreed, taking Toby by surprise.

'We are missing something. The three people closest to George are sitting around this table. There is nobody else. Since none of us has been contacted, and the police haven't informed us about a ransom, we can safely say that this isn't about money.'

'Then what?' Jack asked, somewhat naively.

'It's personal'

'The question is, which one of us around the table has pissed somebody off?' Dylan added, turning toward Toby.

Toby looked down into his lap before bolting upright, eyes glazed open.

'George told us who did it.'

The two men regarded Toby with a look of confusion.

'The clue she left. She told us who did it. Her writing tailed off. She knew they were coming and she let us know who did it.'

'Twenty S?' Jack asked.

'Not twenty S, but two OS,' Toby replied.

'OS?' This time it was Dylan's turn to sound like there was an in-joke he wasn't part of.

'Olivia Stanton.'

'All this time we have been looking in Eric's direction, when we should have been looking at his wife.'

Jack's expression suggested he was desperately trying to connect the dots.

'But what does the two mean?'

'She told us only what she heard or saw. I assume the two refers to the number of captors we're looking for.'

'One thing doesn't make sense here. We are saying she was hidden in a wardrobe and scribbled something in haste. How would she know Olivia Stanton was behind her kidnapping?' Dylan asked suspiciously.

'Perhaps she heard them talking. It's the only logical explanation,' Toby replied, feeling somewhat mystified himself.

He stared out of the window. Dusk would soon be upon them, and that would present a whole new set of challenges.

'Okay, I'm gonna ask the question. Why would Olivia Stanton want to kidnap George?' Jack asked hesitantly.

'Perhaps we should ask the person who knows Olivia best,' Dylan replied in an accusatory tone Toby didn't like.

'Olivia was the one who warned me that George wasn't safe. She was right, but it wasn't Eric who was the threat. It was her all along.'

'She got you to believe that you were moving her to a safe place, but all you were doing was isolating her,' Dylan responded.

'How would Olivia know George was staying with me, though?' Jack asked.

Toby lowered his head.

'She's a very clever woman, but that's accompanied by a vengeful streak. That makes her dangerous,' he said sullenly.

Olivia Stanton had ways of finding out things, so it wasn't beyond the realm of possibility that she had deduced George's location under her own volition. However, there was a nagging feeling that perhaps Toby himself had disclosed something which had given his intentions away. The feeling that he was directly responsible intensified, but he fought with every fibre in his body to keep this from Dylan. As he sat there hoping his face wouldn't betray his thoughts, his attention turned to Jack.

'You know this area better than most. Could you have missed anything?'

Jack shook his head.

'Not within the area you highlighted.'

Toby thought for a moment.

'What if we expanded the search?'

Jack looked up to the ceiling deep in concentration and then pulled the map from his pocket, placing it down on the table.

'Right here, there's an old farmhouse. I used to know the guy who owned it. He was a nice old chap, but wasn't suited to the farm life, well not at his age, anyway. I once went up to fix a fence for him. The place looked like it was about to crumble. Then one day I was passing and decided to drop in, only to find the place was empty. He'd just packed his things and disappeared. He had no family, so I'm guessing it's just sitting there empty. It's one of those places that you wouldn't know was there unless you knew it was there, if you catch my drift?'

Toby smiled as he nodded at Jack.

'But that place is over twenty miles from my farm.'

'This has been planned. They've had two attempts, so it hasn't been done on a whim. They will have had somewhere in mind and they will have made sure it was clandestine.'

'They'll move her,' Dylan said abruptly.

Toby closed his eyes. He knew Dylan was right. It was the same thought he'd had moments earlier when he noticed the sun setting in the distance.

'We've already determined this isn't about money. It's a power play. They'll keep hold of her until they get whatever it is they want,' he added.

'What's that?'

'That's the part I'm not so clear on,' Toby interjected.

He continued.

'This made much more sense to me when I believed it was Eric Stanton behind it. He has a link to George...'

Dylan banged his fists down hard on the table, startling Toby and drawing attention from other patrons in the process. He knew. His body language gave him away. His pained look told Toby he knew Eric Stanton had raped his sister. But did Jack? As Toby and Dylan stared at one another, Jack glanced between them both with curiosity, looking like there was a silent conversation happening that he wasn't a part of. This made things awkward. Toby swallowed hard.

'Jack, Eric is known to George. They were in a relationship for a while.'

'He fucking raped her. That vile bastard raped my sister. He may not be behind her kidnapping, but let me be very clear about one thing. As soon as I have George, I'm going for him, and I won't make the same mistake Olivia Stanton did,' Dylan retorted angrily.

Toby went to speak, but thought better of it. He shared Dylan's hurt, even his anger, but they needed to channel their energies into ensuring George's safe return. As much as he despised Eric Stanton, revenge wasn't on his mind. He would leave that to Dylan and feel no remorse for whatever punishment he dished up. Toby himself just wanted to walk away from all of this and return to his life with Beth, whatever that would look like now. The traumatic experience caused by Olivia and Eric Stanton would always be etched in his mind, but he hoped time would gradually erase those memories.

Revenge in Mind

'We've been looking at this all wrong. If they're going to move her, they don't want the roads to be quiet as this draws attention to them. They want to blend in,' Toby said, as though having just had an epiphany.

'I'd opt for rush hour. Simply another vehicle trying to get home,' Dylan added.

Toby looked down at his watch.

'We're running out of time. I'll call Mike. They may get there quicker,' Toby said, reaching for his pocket.

'No!'

Dylan had grabbed Toby's wrist. Toby peered at his hand, surrounded by Dylan's grasp. He felt anxious because of the sheer size of the man, and he reminded himself again that it was best to keep him on side.

'We all know how this works. They'll plead out, rat out whoever they're working for, and be back on the streets before you know it. That's not how this is gonna go down. These bastards have crossed a line you simply don't cross, and for that, they will pay the price. You can introduce them to your police buddy, but not before they have a chance to meet me.'

He spoke harshly, leaving no room to misinterpret his message. Toby had failed in his bid to keep him focused and in control of his emotions. This left him in a predicament. He couldn't have Dylan working against them, but he also wanted to protect him from himself. The primary goal was finding George, and to do that, he needed to pacify Dylan. He nodded, and Dylan relinquished his grip on his hand. Jack had been observing carefully, and that was another reason Toby had relented. He knew Jack would protect him and had already witnessed the damage these two had inflicted upon one another. Working together they would be formidable, but should the threads holding their relationship together, snap, it would be explosive and highly damaging to all of them, including George. He returned the phone to its resting place in his pocket and reached for his car key. Without a word said between them, the three men left the café and climbed into Toby's car. The screeching of tyres signalled their departure. The car was filled with silence; the atmosphere reflecting the urgency. Toby felt a tear roll down his face as he wondered what state they would find George in. She was at their mercy, and it was his fault. He looked over at Dylan, who was looking remarkably calm with a wry smile on his face. He was clearly immersed in the thought of revenge and whilst Toby was wary, Dylan was seemingly relishing the prospect of coming face to face with George's captors. As the car sped through the countryside, he felt reasonably confident that prison would be a better option than meeting an angry Dylan Sampson. Soon enough, those involved in George's kidnapping would come to realise the same thing.

George coiled back in her chair as her captor moved closer. She could smell the stale stench of his breath as he leaned forward, pressing his nose against the nape of her neck, inhaling loudly through his nostrils as he did so. As he slowly withdrew, she noted his savage grin, which did nothing to ease her concerns around his intentions. She studied him closely as she was suddenly thrown into the past. That look in his eye was the same look she had seen the night Eric had raped her. She hadn't been bound by him, but she may as well have been. He had exercised complete control over her and induced the same feelings of helplessness she was experiencing now. She closed her eyes, but not out of fear. She was desperately searching for some resilience. She still held out hope of being found, but wondered in what condition. Time was of critical importance. Her only hope now was to stall them for as long as possible. Antagonising them wouldn't help her. She was a sitting target, free for them to use her as a plaything if they wished.

'I'm thirsty, please can I have some water?' she asked timidly.

The man stared at her as though trying to process her request.

'You think this is a hotel?' he replied sarcastically.

She closed her eyes as her head dropped. At this, the man stood up from his chair, and ascended the stairs towards the door of which he had entered through a short while ago. She could hear voices above, but despite her best efforts, could not make sense of the conversation. Instinctively, she looked down at her wrist before realising her watch had come off in the struggle, and was likely somewhere on Jack's bedroom floor. George estimated she had been there a couple of hours, but with no concept of time, couldn't be sure. The voices upstairs were getting louder, and though she was still unable to decipher any words, there was no mistaking the sounds of an argument having broken out. Then there was a moment of silence, which was disrupted by the groaning pipes. Based on her current surroundings, she doubted if the place had running water, though she hadn't seen the upstairs. It had an old, unloved feeling to it. As she sat deep in thought, the door creaked open and a shadow slowly descended the staircase. Her hands instinctively reached for her chest as she felt her heart rate spike. The figure walked slowly yet deliberately. She had quickly identified the man as the second assailant. He was taller, yet thinner than his accomplice, his shabby appearance in keeping with the surroundings. She considered whether he or his clothes had seen a wash recently. As he grinned at her, she noticed he had a tooth missing and wondered whether this had been at the hands of Jack. The memory of their grave error in judgement, breaking into his farm and finding him there, made her smile inwardly. The twisted truth was that the one thing keeping her going right now was the thought of retribution. Her motivation to survive this was her burning desire to watch Dylan exact revenge on her kidnappers. If retribution was her destination, rage was her driver.

'Drink this,' he said, pushing the glass towards her gently.

She looked down at her hands, bound.

'If I loosen those, am I gonna get any trouble from you?'

Georgina Sampson shook her head slowly. She felt tired, emotional, and lacked the energy to put up a fight right now. She held up her hands as the man tugged at the knots. George picked up the glass of water and studied it for a moment. It looked cloudy, but judging by the sound of the pipes, she thought it remarkable the taps had produced anything even remotely resembling water. She went to take a sip and then stopped, noticing the man watching her, eagle eyed.

'What do you want with me?' she asked calmly.

'I want nothing from you.'

'Who's your boss?'

'I don't have a boss, sweetheart. I answer to no-one.'

'I don't know you, and you don't know me. That suggests you answer to somebody else.'

She paused allowing time for a grin to spread across her face. 'Sweetheart.'

His smile disappeared in an instant. George had dug down and unearthed a hidden reserve of fortitude. Imbued by anger, she had no intention of giving up the fight. She had been so focused on Dylan finding her she hadn't allowed herself to consider the alternative, that she was on her own. She couldn't outfight them. Her only way out was to outwit them. The heated argument between the two suggested tensions were high. She could exploit this. She took a sip of her water and smiled softly.

'You're not like your friend up there.'

'He's not my friend.'

'I just assumed,' she began before tailing off.

She looked down at her feet before taking another drink. The water had a repugnant taste to it, but the magnitude of her thirst allowed her no opportunity to be selective.

'If you need money...'

'This isn't about money,' he interrupted.

He'd confirmed it was personal. This added a whole new complexity to the situation. There would be no negotiating her release, no exchange. Her chest tightened at the realisation her situation had just became graver.

'If it's not about money, then what is it about?' she asked, already knowing the answer, but trying desperately to buy herself some thinking time.

'Look, we don't ask questions, and it's perhaps best you don't either.'

George closed her eyes for a moment, feeling a little uneasy.

'Why are you afraid to talk to me?' she asked finally.

'What makes you think I'm afraid?' the man responded.

'You're avoiding my questions and won't look me directly in the eye. What are you afraid of?'

'I'm not afraid of anything, but if you keep asking questions, you may find out something that keeps you awake at night.'

'Oh?' she asked nervously.

'We're not going to be here much longer.'

'What do you mean?'

'You don't think this is your final destination, do you?'

'I don't understand,' she said, feeling a panic rising within her.

'Look, I've already said more than I should. Do yourself a favour and don't ask questions you may not like the answer to.'

'Where are you taking me?' she asked apprehensively.

'I don't have the answer to that question, but rest assured, soon enough you'll be out of our hair.'

George leaned back and regarded the man sat in front of her. She couldn't get a read of him, and this frustrated her. He seemed to fluctuate between amiable and gleeful, yet he still seemed different to his partner. She wondered whether that had been the reason behind their argument. Suddenly she felt tired, but it wasn't physical or emotional fatigue. Her eyesight blurred as she began rocking involuntarily. She looked at him wide eyed and noticed a grin slowly spread across his face.

'Don't fight it,' he said gently.

'I thought you were different from him,' she said, feeling more out of control with every moment that passed.

'You were supposed to.'

'The argument I heard...'

'All for your benefit. We had to be sure you drank the water.'

She looked down at the glass, now only loosely within her grasp, as she drifted in and out of consciousness. His sinister grin was the last thing she saw as the glass spilled out of her hand, smashing into tiny pieces.

Jack pressed the accelerator as they raced through the countryside. If there were any alternate routes or shortcuts that would make their journey faster, Jack would know them. Toby closed his eyes, not daring to verbalise what they were all probably thinking. This was the last roll of the dice for them. There was no plan B. If they were wrong here, they were out of options and George's life was solely in the hands of the police. Mike had warned him to stay on the side-lines and to keep control of Dylan Sampson. He could do neither.

'Jack?'

'We're almost there,' Jack answered, expecting Toby to ask the same question he had asked multiple times during their journey.

Dylan had been silent during the journey, which concerned Toby. When you had somebody who contained the rage he did, quiet contemplation wasn't a good thing. Toby held no uncertainty about what this meant. His focus wasn't on George right now, it was on retribution. As Toby became more restless, he cast his mind back to the very first conversation he had had with George outside the prison gates. She had been very evasive around her reason for returning, something he was still no clearer on. Her reappearance had been unspectacular, yet significant. Toby felt himself consumed with guilt once again that another woman had taken priority over Beth. He knew that this wasn't about giving priority, but questioned if Beth had the same perspective. He hadn't asked for this, any of this, but struggled to absolve himself of any blame. Though the Olivia Stanton and Georgina Sampson situations were very different, it was difficult to overlook what bound them together. Both had presented as vulnerable women, and though the intent may have differed, both could draw Toby into an unfamiliar world he didn't even know existed in reality. The abrupt braking removed him from his thoughts as he jolted forward, perilously close to hitting his head on Jack's seat.

'Sorry folks, the drawback of driving through the countryside,' he said, smiling and pointing to several sheep who were seemingly oblivious to the dangers of loitering on the road. Dylan turned to him and snarled. Jack went to speak and then thought better of it. He had likely seen the face of Dylan and realised it perhaps wasn't wise to anger him at this point. As Toby studied Dylan's body language for a moment, he realised he was now beyond reasoning. He was running completely on emotion and any rationality had long since departed. Whilst he would do everything within his power to protect Dylan from himself, he held little hope of achieving this.

'It's right up ahead,' Jack said, pointing towards a track scarcely visible to those unfamiliar with its presence.

'Is there any other way in?' Dylan asked, suddenly appearing lucid.

Jack looked at him blankly.

'I'm assuming this track is gonna lead us straight to the front door, right? If she's here, we don't want to announce ourselves and panic them into doing anything rash.'

'What do you think?' Jack asked.

'I think out of the three of us, I'm the least qualified to answer that question,' Toby replied, noting the disappointment on Jack's face.

Jack stopped the car at the bottom of the track, dimmed the lights, and turned to face Dylan. Toby leaned forward.

'Maybe we should phone the police and let them take it from here,' he said tentatively.

'There are two reasons that's not a good idea. First, time is of critical importance. Calling them now when we are outside adds a further delay we simply cannot risk. Second, Toby's friend at the house was very explicit in warning us not to conduct our own investigation. If we call them and George isn't here, we leave ourselves open to police attention. Considering some of the things I have been involved in over the last few days, the last thing I need is police attention,' Dylan replied.

'Toby?'

Toby thought for a moment.

'What are you thinking, Dylan?'

'Leave the car here, make our way up on foot. Stick to the tree line to avoid any detection.'

'Then what? We just burst in through the door, rough them up a little, force them to tell us who's behind this and just walk out with her?'

Dylan smiled.

'Exactly that.'

'I'm in,' Jack added.

Toby glanced at them both, recognising that under different circumstances, he may have considered them to be unstable. The longer he observed their interaction, however, the more he accepted their similarities. Jack made a move to get out of the car. Toby gently grabbed his wrist.

'There's something we haven't considered,' he said hesitantly.

'What's that?' Dylan asked.

'We've invested everything into George being in there, right?'

Jack nodded.

'And of course there is the chance that she isn't in there and the building has simply been abandoned, right?'

'Where's this going, Toby?' Dylan asked impatiently.

'There's a third option.'

'We're wasting time,' Dylan shouted, making a move to exit the car.

'What if it's not a ruin? What if somebody lives there?' Toby replied hastily.

Dylan let go of the door handle and turned to face him.

'Then we explain politely our reason for calling and apologise for inconveniencing them. Look Toby, my only concern is finding George and if that means inconveniencing some fucking farmer, then so be it.'

'It wasn't the inconvenience I was worried about. Three men turn up at a house in the early evening, a house you don't just end up at. What's the first thing they're going to do?'

'Call the police,' Jack added.

'With the greatest of respect, you're hardly inconspicuous,' he said, gesticulating in Dylan's direction.

Revenge in Mind

'So, what do you suggest?' Dylan responded.

'We'll walk up together and keep close to the treeline. Once we get within viewing distance of the house, I'll proceed on my own.'

'How will you know who you're speaking to?' Dylan asked casually.

'I guess I'm going to have to rely on my judgement.'

Dylan grabbed Toby's arm tightly, looking him directly in the eye.

'George is gonna be relying on that judgement.'

Toby recoiled as Dylan let go of his arm. Jack had been a passive observer up to now, but he wasn't stupid. Toby knew he recognised the veiled threat from Dylan. As the awkward silence abated, the three men got out of the car and began trudging up the track. After a couple of minutes, they had a visual on the house. As they stood looking at the house, they realised one option had now been removed.

The two men circled her like a pack of wild dogs circling helpless prey, preparing for the inevitable attack. There would be little resistance; they had made sure of that. She had taken enough to be sedated, but not quite enough to render her unconscious. She was alert but not responsive. There was no mistaking they had complete control over her. She wasn't permissive, and about as far away from lucid as you could get, but that was part of the game for them.

'This wasn't part of the plan. Are you sure this isn't gonna come back on us?'

'I'll leave the room if you're a little shy.'

'That's not what I meant.'

'Relax, the bitch isn't gonna remember any of this and the only other people who'll know what happened are you and me. I'm not gonna say anything. Are you?'

The man shook his head, but it didn't appear convincing. He wouldn't be a willing participant in whatever was about to happen, but it wasn't clear if it was the act itself or the consequences that made him reticent. He took a step back, contemplating.

'Shall we untie her?' he asked.

'Why would we want to do that?'

'I don't know,' the man replied, looking rather sheepish.

'Listen, those hands could easily become weapons if she panics. Do you want your DNA under her fingernails?'

'Of course not. Look, she's been through enough and this wasn't part of the job.'

'You chickening out on me?'

'Fuck you,' the man said aggressively.

As tensions intensified between the two men, the woman in the chair let out a sudden and elongated groan.

George tried to focus her eyes, but her efforts were futile. She could scarcely make out two figures in front of her, but anything more than that was a blur. Her head was sore and her eyes were heavy. With no insight into her location or her company, she began to struggle. As one of the figures drew closer, she could see he looked dishevelled. She didn't recognise him, but right now she wasn't sure she'd even recognise her own reflection. She desperately tried to piece her situation together, becoming more frantic with every passing thought. George had no recollection of how she had got here, nor why her hands were bound. What she knew only too well was she wasn't a guest here and hadn't come under her own volition. She could hear a noise, likely the two men conversing, but she couldn't make out anything coherent.

'Here, have a drink,' the man said, offering her a glass with what she could only assume contained water. Her lips were dry, but something told her this wasn't a kind gesture on their part. She shook her head slowly, but this didn't feel like an option. A pair of hands reached out and took hold of her chin, forcing her mouth open. She tried to resist, but whatever had happened to her had sapped all of her energy. With her hands tied, the two men would easily overcome any resistance she attempted. She choked as some of the water made its way down her throat, the rest spilling onto the floor as she tried desperately not to swallow. The room began to spin and the two figures in front of her appeared to morph into one. As she sat there helplessly, George felt a tugging at her clothes. Then there was a brief pause as the two men exchanged words before one of them disappeared. She was alert just enough to realise what was about to happen. As he stroked her face with the back of his hand, his grin widened. He took a step back and unzipped his jeans.

Toby knocked on the door a little louder, having received no reply the first time. The lights were on, but he couldn't hear movement. Peering through the window panel, he could now see a shadow approaching. As the door opened, Toby's heart sank. In front of him was a well-dressed woman, perhaps in her forties. She smiled tentatively.

'Can I help you?'

'I'm sorry to disturb you,' Toby began before stopping, wondering how he could begin to explain the reason for his calling.

'I'm looking for my friend,' he mumbled.

'We don't get many visitors up here, I'm afraid.'

'We?' Toby asked politely.

'My husband and I. It's just the two of us, and the dogs, of course.'

'It's a beautiful place. How long have you been here?'

'I wouldn't call it beautiful, but it's out of the way.'

'Was that the appeal?'

The woman looked at him.

'I'm not a people person, so this works for me.'

Toby smiled at her.

'I haven't seen anybody up here, but feel free to have a look around the grounds, she added.'

'I appreciate the kind offer. It was more in hope than expectation.'

'When did you last see her?'

'A few days back. We didn't leave things on good terms and I feel bad for that,' Toby replied.

An awkward silence ensued, with the woman clearly struggling to understand how to respond. She looked uncomfortable.

'I should be going. My husband will be home soon.'

Toby studied her for a moment before taking a step back.

'Thank you for your time. I'm sorry to have encroached on your evening,' he replied politely.

'I hope you find your friend.'

'Thank you for your time.'

As Toby made his way down the drive, he glanced back over his shoulder, but the woman had disappeared. As he walked slowly, deep in thought, Dylan and Jack leapt out of the shadows, startling him. They looked at him expectantly.

'I'm almost certain she's in there,' Toby managed slowly.

'What makes you so sure?' Jack asked cautiously.

'Sometimes what's not being said tells more of a story than the words actually spoken.'

'So, she told you what you needed to know by not speaking?'

'Actually, with her, it was both. I knew almost immediately she was lying to me, but then something she said told me exactly what she was hiding.'

'What was that?'

'That's not important. What's important is she's hiding something.' Toby replied sternly.

'Or someone,' Dylan interjected.

'What now?' Jack asked.

Toby turned to face Dylan.

'This is where I bow out. I've ventured way outside of my comfort zone already. Whatever's about to happen in there, I cannot be a part of. I hope you understand.'

'What you gonna do?' Jack asked.

'I'll be the one who calls Mike Thomas once you have her.'

'He's gonna be pissed you found her,' Dylan said with a gleeful smile.

'It won't be me who finds her. He warned me, not you,' Toby smiled.

Jack patted Toby on the shoulder affectionately. He then turned to face Dylan, and after the two exchanged a nod, they disappeared. As Toby moved in the opposite direction, he tried desperately to drown out the intrusive thoughts which were attempting to provide him with a graphic view of what was about to happen inside, but it wasn't Jack and Dylan he feared for.

{ 27 }

With the two imposing men nearing the house, Dylan grabbed Jack's arm.

'Whoever she is, we can assume she's not gonna open the door a second time.'

'I don't see us getting an invitation,' Jack grinned.

'On three?'

'On three.'

The door flung open with a force which couldn't possibly disguise their mood or their intentions. A woman came rushing out of the kitchen ahead of them to see what the commotion was. As she saw Jack and Dylan, she turned to run away, but was no match for Dylan's athleticism, strangely out of place for a man of his size. With one swift action, he seized her arm to pull her closer, before grabbing her around the throat and pushing her up against the wall. Feet several inches off the floor, she began to choke. He squeezed harder.

'Where is she?' he shouted angrily.

The woman, unable to speak, simply pointed to the floor.

Dylan didn't need to ask where the door to the basement was, as it swung open with a dishevelled figure appearing.

'Who the fuck are you?' he shouted, looking Dylan up and down.

'The last person you're ever gonna see.'

Jack, who had sprinted into another room off the hallway, reappeared as Dylan took a step forward towards the man. In an instant, he recognised him as one of the individuals who had unlawfully entered his premises. Jack was also fairly certain the man facing him had been the one responsible for striking him over the head during that eventful night. He felt a wave of anger swell inside of him as memories of the break-in surfaced.

The woman who had been trying to catch her breath after her attack ran screaming through the hallway, past the men and out of the front door. Suddenly, there was a noise from downstairs, which sounded like muffled screaming. Without delay, Dylan effortlessly lifted the man and sent him crashing down the staircase. As they pursued, a sight met them that stopped both men in their tracks. In the far corner of the room, George was bound to a chair, semi-conscious and semi-naked.

'George!' Dylan shouted, running over towards her.

Before he could reach her, he caught sight of someone rushing towards him with a metal bar. The subsequent blow to the chest was sudden and drew an ear-splitting shriek from its recipient. The pain was sharp, but wouldn't deter him. The man swung the bar again, this time striking him in the leg. Dylan grimaced with pain. As he looked up, he noticed Jack engaging in his own battle with the other assailant, who was wielding a knife. The momentary lapse in concentration allowed his attacker to land another blow, this time to his shoulder. His intentions were clear, he was trying to incapacitate Dylan to allow for their escape. The man swung his weapon again, but this time Dylan was ready for it, ducking and striking a hard blow to the man's rib cage all in one movement. The bar fell to the floor and for a moment Dylan considered retrieving it, but instead opted to kick it away.

'I'm gonna show you how real men fight,' he said, grinning widely.

His opponent wasn't small, but had this been a boxing match, there would have been more than one weight division between them. Dylan reached out and picked up the man who had been on his knees, holding his ribs. As he pulled him to his feet, he hit him square in the face with force. The man's screams were heard throughout the room as his nose haemorrhaged blood at an alarming rate. But Dylan was only just getting started.

As the two men circled one another, Jack didn't take his eyes off the knife being waved in front of him. Despite lacking training in armed combat, he was tough.

'I hope you know how to use that thing.'

The man stared blankly at Jack before a smugness spread across his face.

'You're only gonna get one shot at this, so make it count,' Jack added.

The truth was, he was nervous, but adrenaline currently camouflaged those nerves. This wasn't about revenge now; it was about survival. The man thrust the knife forward, more to drive Jack back than anything else. Jack wondered whether this was a sign of aggression or just desperation. Did he want to hurt Jack or just get him out of the way? Clearly, this hadn't been part of the plan, and Jack wondered whether he was regretting the decision he had made.

'I guarantee that whatever you've been paid for this, it's not enough.'

The man ignored Jack and jabbed the knife towards him again, this time with very clear intentions. Jack noticed blood seeping through his t-shirt as he glanced down at his side, feeling a sharp pain. Instinctively, he reached for the wound and as he did so, he felt the man push past him in an attempt to no doubt secure his escape. Jack swung round and grabbed the man's leg with just enough force to cause him to stumble to the ground. Kicking the knife out of reach, Jack grabbed the man by the hair and pulled him to his feet, taking delight in the high-pitched scream which emanated from his attacker's mouth as he did so. With a gaping wound on his left side, Jack was no doubt at a disadvantage. He'd been given a way out. The man had tried to escape, but Jack's actions had given him a simple message. Now it was about revenge. Rage consumed him, fuelling his relentless assault on the man's face. A groan from the corner of the room broke his concentration, enough to allow the man to kick him hard. The force of the kick buckled his knee and sent him to the floor. The man, now smiling through a bloody mouth, landed a punch to the side of Jack's face before another connected with his mouth. As he swung again, Jack was able to grab his fist. He squeezed mercilessly, which drew a pained scream. With a swift action, Jack twisted the man's wrist and snapped it backwards. A high-pitched wail echoing around the room followed the unmistakable sound of breaking bone. Spurred on by fury, Jack swung again and caught the man directly in his left eye. The force lifted him off his feet and sent him crashing against the wall head first. As he lay there motionless, an eerie silence presented itself.

As his adversary cupped his hands around his nose, Dylan casually walked over to the iron bar's resting place and picked it up. He walked up behind the man and, placing one arm around each side of his neck, pulled the bar tight to his throat. The man struggled, kicking wildly to force his release, but Dylan was too strong for him. The struggle took on a frantic tone with the man seemingly realising his situation was grave. Dylan was relentless as the life sapped out of the body of his attacker. This was nothing more than a burning desire to inflict pain on those who had inflicted trauma on his sister. It had gone way beyond survival and even revenge. This was about proving a point, sending a message, but there was no denying he was enjoying it. He relinquished his grip and dragged the barely conscious man over to where George was seated. He untied her hands and hugged her tightly, feeling the pain as he did so. He dragged the man and placed him carefully; the wall supporting his limp body. The man regarded him, but there was no fight in his eyes. The room fell silent, Jack standing over a motionless figure in one corner, Dylan stationary in another, his gaze oscillating between the captor on the floor and George, who was now standing. Jack made his way tentatively over to George, offering her a warm smile as he drew closer. As the two embraced, George whispered into Jack's ear. He squeezed her, closing his eyes as though losing himself in the moment. In the brief period they had known each other, Jack had noticed George seemed to bring out a newfound sensitivity in him, something he wasn't known for.

'I hate to break up the reunion, but what do we do with these two?' Dylan asked, pointing to the two men crumpled on the floor in different areas of the large basement.

'I think we've done enough. Let the police have them,' Jack replied.

'That's not what I was asking.'

Jack froze, suddenly feeling uncomfortable. George turned towards her brother, but said nothing. As the two exchanged a look, Dylan turned towards the attacker he had only moments ago nearly choked the life out of.

'Neither of you need to see this,' he said, walking over to the man and effortlessly carrying him and placing him on the chair where George had been seated.

'Wait, what the hell does that mean?' Jack asked, now looking beyond uncomfortable.

'This can end here for you both, but it's not where it ends for me,' Dylan replied calmly.

Jack turned towards George.

'Say something,' he urged.

George smiled and placed a hand on his shoulder.

'Perhaps you should go Jack, you may not want to see this.'

There was no emotion in her voice and Jack's hope she would be the voice of reason had disappeared in an instant.

'Jesus George, what the hell is wrong with you? These guys are going to prison. They're not gonna see the outside of a cell for quite some time. This can end now and we all get our lives back,' he said, now sounding desperate.

Revenge in Mind

'Don't you see Jack? I'll never get my life back. I've been raped, stalked, beaten and kidnapped. You can go back to your farm, your tranquil existence, but what do I have? No possessions, no friends, not even a home. My only dependable family is present in this room.'

'You have your freedom. I'm no lawyer, but I'd say this is the point where the self-defence plea ends. Think about this George. You have Toby, you have me, you can still walk away from this. *We* can walk away from this.'

George shook her head and smiled at Jack.

'Dylan?'

'It's best you don't see this, Jack,' Dylan said coldly.

As Jack made his way up the staircase, Dylan felt a fleeting regret for his involvement. Jack hadn't asked for any of this, yet had put his livelihood, his body, hell, even his life on the line for George. He respected that and admired his prowess when it came to fighting. Though he would never openly admit it, Dylan felt Jack was a tough son of a bitch and was glad he had ultimately had his back. As Dylan tied up the man's hands, George picked up the glass, which still had a little water left in it, and threw it directly into his face, leaning in close to him as she did so.

'You're about to experience indescribable pain, you worthless piece of shit. Every time you squeal, I want you to look into my remorseless eyes and be reminded of what you did to me. Someone may have paid you to kidnap and torture me, but my brother here does this for fun. He's done things to people which go way beyond anything you could imagine,' George goaded.

She took a step back and glanced at Dylan. There was still silence from the other side of the room. Perhaps the man was unconscious, perhaps he was dead. Dylan didn't care either way. He meant nothing to him, but his co-conspirator, currently tied to the chair, did. The actions he took were more than just a kidnapping, which meant a code had been violated in Dylan's world. When you were assigned a job, you didn't deviate by inserting your own agenda.

'You okay?' he asked, turning towards her.

George nodded her head slowly, but with no genuine conviction. She was resilient, but this wasn't her world. A moment of clarity appeared in the chaotic scene surrounding them. He heard a groan from the chair and instinctively swung round, striking the man in the side of his face. The groan escalated to a wail as the already seriously injured man cried out in pain, before silence filled the room once more. The only sound now was the quick, shallow breaths of George and Dylan. He turned back to George, whose demeanour appeared to have quickly transformed from vengeful to vulnerable.

'How far do you want me to go?'

'I don't know,' George replied, looking very much like the adrenaline responsible for her anger had now dissipated.

'My objectives for today were simple: find you and make those bastards pay.'

He seized the unconscious man's head and raised him by his hair.

'I can make it look like self-defence. Just say the word,' he continued.

Suddenly, a door slammed open.

Revenge in Mind

'Dylan, no!'

'Toby, what the hell are you doing here?'

'I brought him. I hoped he'd be able to stop you from doing something stupid,' Jack replied, following Toby down the staircase.

'Right now, you've defended yourself against two attackers who kidnapped your sister, Dylan. But look at him, he's bound to a chair. Anything from here goes beyond reasonable force. Best case you go on the run and elude capture, worst case you're behind bars. Either way, the person who needs you most, the person who you risked all this for, is left without you once again.'

'I'm doing this for her.'

'George needs her brother, not revenge. I know you're angry and I know that's because you're hurting, but this is the one decision right now you have complete control over. The moment you make that choice to place vengeance in higher esteem than love, you lose that control. You lose everything.'

Dylan began to shake with emotion, clearly torn. He pulled back his fist, preparing to deliver what he was certain would be a fatal blow. Nothing else mattered now. He loved his sister, but taking a vile piece of shit like this off the earth would keep others safe. He had skills, and he had contacts. He could disappear and still keep watch over George from a distance. He'd never really been a present big brother, so it wasn't like George would be losing anything she'd become accustomed to over the years. Mind made up, he swung his arm forward, but his fist didn't connect with the man's face. Instead, it was intercepted by Jack's hand, which was no easy feat, given its size. George reached out and grabbed Dylan's shoulder. Looking into his eyes, she embraced him with a hug, squeezing him tightly. After a moment, she withdrew.

'If I lose you again, they've won,' she said calmly.

Jack, who had now let go of Dylan's hand, smiled as he gestured for Dylan to move towards the stairs.

'What do we do about him?' Jack said, pointing towards the man he had left unconscious on the floor.

'We'll take him upstairs. I'm sure there will be something up there we can use to tie him up.' He stopped, before a smile made its way onto his face. 'Once we're clear, Toby can call this in.'

Jack picked the man up and threw him over his shoulder. The relative ease with which he did this impressed Dylan. As they made their way up the stairs and through the house into the living room, Dylan spotted an old curtain tie. The man began to come to as his hands were thrust behind his back. He was tied to the radiator at the far end of the room under the window, with little regard for his welfare. Without warning, Dylan struck the man on the side of his face, causing his head to jolt backwards.

'You fucked with the wrong person,' he said calmly as he turned to follow the others out of the house.

George grabbed Toby's arm.

'It wasn't supposed to happen like this.'

Toby halted. They had already fallen behind Jack and Dylan, who were now a good way down the long stretch of drive which would ultimately lead them to Toby's car, parked at the entrance.

'What do you mean, it wasn't supposed to happen like this?'

Toby could see she was now weeping. Her troubled expression gave him the sense there was more to her anguish than simply what had happened today.

'I've done something bad. Please don't hate me,' she managed between sobs.

Toby stepped back, nerves jangling in anticipation of what he was about to hear.

'George?'

'I never intended for this to happen.'

A stunned silence surrounded them.

'You have to believe me, it wasn't supposed to go down like this,' she continued. 'He found out, and he got to them.'

'Who found out, George? You're not making any sense.'

'I was just meant to disappear for a day or so.'

'You staged this?' Toby asked, lurching backwards with disbelief.

George screwed up her eyes and nodded slowly.

'Why?'

'Eric.'

'Eric Stanton?'

'That bastard took everything from me. I'm damaged, and it's because of him. I've spent years as a victim. I needed to take back control, and the only way I could do that was to ruin his life like he ruined mine.'

'That's the real reason you came back, isn't it?' Toby said, dropping his head. 'It was about getting close to him, but you couldn't have done this on your own.'

He placed his head in his hands and tapped softly with his index finger. His perception of her had changed in a heartbeat. The George he knew and had fallen in love with all those years ago had gone. In front of him was somebody he didn't know, somebody he wasn't sure he wanted to know. He questioned why he had devoted so much of his time and made so many sacrifices for two women who spoke the language of deception so freely. Yet the one person who had always remained loyal to him, the one person who had never let him down, was the person he had let down the most throughout all of this. His mind settled on Beth as he contrasted her with the woman stood in front of him now.

'Toby, I need you to understand...'

'Olivia Stanton,' he said slowly, raising his head.

George looked down at her feet before reaching out for Toby's hand. He pushed it away and stepped back, unable to hide his hurt.

'You can't understand the experience of living in fear with constant paranoia, afraid of your own shadow. You don't know what it's like to sleep with a knife under your bed. A knife which has the sole purpose of defence, but not against intruders, against the person who curls up next to you in bed every night. You don't have to sleep with one eye open.'

She sounded angry.

'I nearly lost my life. My wife came close to walking out on me and I was almost sent to prison for a crime I didn't commit.'

'You've led a fucking privileged life, Toby. Parents who loved you and a nice house. You've never had to worry about money or whether there's gonna be food on the table when you get home.

Revenge in Mind

You only needed one shot at love and found somebody who adores you. You've only ever seen one side of life. Do you want to compare?' George shouted, becoming increasingly animated. 'My mother had a mental illness and struggled to hold down a job. My dad spent most of his time out of the house because he had no idea how to handle it. My brother abandoned me for the army because he couldn't stand being at home. I've lurched from one disastrous relationship to another, been raped, abused and kidnapped. You can also add to that the sexual assault I've just suffered at the hands of one of those vile bastards in there,' she screamed, pointing to the house, tears now flowing down her cheeks.

Toby stood, mouth ajar.

'That's right Toby, he did things to me as I lay barely conscious, naked from the waist down. It was only Dylan and Jack's appearance that stopped me from being raped for the second time in my life. Don't stand there and judge me. You have no right.'

Toby pondered his emotions for a moment, unsure what he was feeling - anger at her disregard for his own struggles, sadness at what she had been subjected to, and regret that he had let her down. He became overwhelmed with conflicting emotions, leading to an unfamiliar discomfort as he fought to maintain control.

'I don't judge you,' he managed, finally. 'But I also don't understand you. I don't understand any of this.'

'I despise Eric Stanton and all he stands for, but I found somebody whose hatred for him runs deeper than mine.'

'Olivia.'

'Our paths had already crossed previously, before she ended up in prison. I went to her for answers, but left with a blueprint for revenge.'

'But something went wrong,' Toby observed.

'All I can think of is Olivia underestimated Eric's reach. Whether it was through fear or misguided loyalty, they switched their allegiance pretty sharply.'

'How did you know it was Eric?'

'As soon as they arrived at Jack's, I overheard them talking outside. That's when I knew I was in trouble. That's when I realised I'd made a mistake, but it was too late. I was already at their mercy. That's why I ran upstairs and hid in the wardrobe.'

Toby took a deep breath. There was no hiding the confusion he was feeling.

'The last time I saw Olivia, she said she had sent you to stay with me. Is that true?'

'Toby.'

'Is that true?'

His voice was now much more assertive.

'She said she'd found a way to draw Eric in.'

'You haven't answered my question.'

'I have Toby. Just not in the way you wanted me to.'

Toby lowered his head. His hurt had no place to hide. After a moment of silence, he raised his head and looked up at her.

'There's something I don't understand. If you and Olivia planned this to frame Eric, why did you lead us directly to Olivia?'

George looked up to the sky.

'George?'

*'*She put you through hell, Toby. I wanted her to suffer. I did this for you.'

'I don't follow. You wanted to frame Olivia all along?' Toby asked, trying desperately to make sense of a situation that made no sense to him.

'No, originally it was all about Eric. But the final time I visited her, as I was about to leave the prison, she said something to me and I genuinely believed I was staring right into the eyes of the devil. It was chilling.'

Toby felt a shiver run down his spine as he recalled having a similar thought about Olivia himself.

'What about Eric?'

'It was no longer about framing him.'

'Then what?'

'I'm not sure you want to hear that.'

Toby stepped back, glazed eyes fixated on her.

'No.'

She said nothing.

He shook his head in disbelief, now more convinced than ever that the woman standing in front of him had completely transformed from the sweet girl he once knew.

'I'm sorry Toby.'

He had no words with which to respond; she had rendered him speechless.

As George made her way down the drive, Toby stood looking sullen, trying to process what he'd just heard. He didn't recall ever feeling so conflicted. Not for the first time, he wondered how he'd become immersed in a world so different from the one he was used to. There was an important call to make, but he had no idea what he was going to say. As he removed his phone from his pocket, he turned back to look at the house. He knew what they were leaving behind, but had no foresight into what they were walking into. Whilst they had saved George from the kidnappers, a new struggle was emerging which could prove even more difficult - saving her from herself.

{ 28 }

Toby stared at his phone, in the vain hope it would provide him with an answer. It didn't. As he tried to unpack the events, not only of that day, but of the last few months, he felt completely alone. The only person he wanted to be around right now was Beth, but he wasn't certain she would reciprocate. This wasn't the life she had signed up for. Neither of them had. The life-changing drama that had preceded was undeniable. He looked up towards the now darkened sky and yearned for the tranquil life he'd once led. He didn't feel the need to be angry, since he knew he'd acted with good intentions. Right now, a sense of sadness flooded him. Sadness at how much George had suffered, sadness that in a desperate attempt to reclaim her life, she had resorted to such extreme measures, putting herself at risk in the process. But it was more than sadness. What she had said had hit him hard. As the cool wind ran through the trees, he thought about how different their lives had been. He had been fortunate, but his life hadn't been without tragedy. He'd lost his mum to a silent killer just as he was entering adulthood. His graduation, his wedding - she had missed key moments of his life, moments he had wanted nothing more than to share with her. He hadn't experienced some of the challenges George had, but it was wrong to claim he hadn't encountered adversity. *She* was wrong. He felt a bout of anger swelling up inside him. He'd suffered. Not in the same way she had, but he'd suffered, nonetheless. As he stared down at his phone, he realised he could delay no longer. Jack, Dylan and George were on their way back to Jack's farm, regardless of Jack being wounded. Beth was on her way, which gave him, he estimated, around twenty minutes alone with his thoughts. He wasn't entirely sure this was a good thing, but it was the preferred option to being around any further drama.

'Toby, what can I do for you?' came the voice on the other end of the line, sounding friendly yet professional.

'She's safe, Mike,' Toby replied quietly. 'George. We've found her.'

'Toby, I warned you not to go running around playing detective,' came the stern reply. 'Where are you? Where Is Georgina Sampson?'

'Georgina is on her way back to Jack's farm. I'm not entirely sure where I am.'

'What's going on?'

'I'm not so sure even I know. It's been a long day.'

'I can trace your phone signal and get your location. Are you safe?'

'What are you asking me that for?'

'You just informed me you're all alone and have no idea where. Naturally, that sets off alarm bells.'

'I'm fine, a little emotional, but fine.'

'Don't move, I'm on my way,' Mike said, hanging up the phone abruptly.

Revenge in Mind

Toby didn't know why he'd just lied. Mike would arrive, find Beth there and know Toby had been disingenuous regarding not knowing his location. He hadn't done anything illegal, but he had acted against the advice of a senior police officer, which meant inevitably an uncomfortable conversation would take place at some point. Then a thought struck him that momentarily sent him into a panic. He was a witness. He had been at the house and had seen the kidnappers. It was highly probable that he would face official questioning, leading to a return to the police station - a place he associated with a harrowing experience. He felt cold, but this had nothing to do with the drop in temperature. He rested against the fir trees, looking back at the house, which was now in the distance. He wondered how desperate George must have felt to feign her own kidnapping in order to break the emotional shackles Eric Stanton had attached to her. He questioned all the events which had involved George recently, events which had involved them all. How much had she known about? How much had she intentionally orchestrated herself? Toby realised this line of thinking was taking him to a place he'd rather not visit. His opinion of her was already tarnished. There was no benefit in torturing himself with questions he may not like the answers to. The further he dug, the more he might uncover, a scenario he was keen to avoid. He needed this day to be over. Hoping in vain, he closed his eyes, yearning to find himself back home in Beth's embrace. Only the sweet aroma of the trees and the countryside skyline greeted him when he opened them again. He smiled to himself, thinking how useful it would be if he could freely disassociate. He wondered where all of this would end and questioned whether his life would ever get back to normal, or whether it had changed forever. As the reality of what had happened that day hit, Toby felt overwhelmed. He sat down, placed his head in his hands and didn't fight the outpouring of emotion which followed. Not knowing how long he had been in that position, a touch on his shoulder brought him back to the present. He looked up to see Beth's reassuring smile, which did nothing to stem the flow of tears. Now he could be vulnerable. He looked up at her and smiled.

'I just realised I have your car,' Toby said apologetically

'You owe me for the taxi,' she smiled.

'I guess I owe you an explanation.'

'You seem to be making a habit of this.'

Her grin implied she was teasing, but her eyes showed something very different. They revealed hurt, exhaustion, exasperation, and he was to blame. Although the situations with Olivia Stanton and Georgina Sampson were very different in nature, they shared similarities. He had been off grid for the last few hours, and this would have undoubtedly impacted her.

'I'm sorry,' he managed.

'I'm not so sure you even know what you're sorry for, Toby.'

Beth had an ability to be angry and loving simultaneously, something he'd always admired in her. This was one of those times.

'You look tired. We should get you home.'

'I can't leave yet. Mike's on his way.'

'Jesus Toby, what did you do?' she said, looking up the long drive towards the scantily lit building. 'Toby?'

'Mike warned me not to get involved…'

Revenge in Mind

'Somebody else you pay little regard to,' she snapped.

'That's not fair.'

'Shall we talk about fair Toby?' she retorted angrily. 'Was it fair when you nearly went to prison for a client? When I was sleeping in a chair next to your hospital bed, was that fair? Was it fair when I had to come and collect you from a police cell, having not heard from you for hours, not knowing what the hell had happened to you? Was it fair I ended up with your ex-girlfriend living in my home, somebody who quickly became more important to you than your own wife? Is it fair that yet again I've come running and have no idea what the hell I'm running towards? Don't talk to me about what's fair.'

He reached out to pull her close for an embrace, but she pushed him away. He'd never seen her this angry before. She was right, none of this had been fair to her. She deserved better, better than him. As Toby looked at his wife, he suddenly realised, for the first time, she looked her age. Her face was tired, her eyes lacking that sparkle he had grown to love. There was no mistaking this was on him.

'You deserve better.'

'I can't keep doing this, Toby,' she replied, looking dejected. 'This person you've become is unrecognisable to me.'

'I haven't changed.'

'The Toby I fell in love with would never have shut me out.'

'I did it to protect you.'

'You did it to protect yourself.'

She wasn't even angry now, and that frightened Toby.

'Beth, what are you saying?'

'The one thing you've said that holds any truth is that I deserve better.'

'Please don't do this,' he pleaded.

As the tension between the two grew, flashing lights lit up the sky and two police cars pulled up at the bottom of the drive, close to where Toby and Beth were standing. Mike Thomas got out of one of them and hurried towards them. As he drew nearer, he stopped, clearly detecting the atmosphere.

'I feel like I'm interrupting something here.'

Beth glared at Toby, who was now doing everything he could to avoid her gaze.

'Beth, why don't you wait in my car. I need to have a chat with Toby.'

Beth didn't speak, but walked towards the car where another police officer was holding the door open for her. She climbed in without looking back at Toby.

'It looks like you've pissed more than one person off today,' he said, looking back towards the car.

Toby didn't reply. Suddenly, nothing mattered to him. If he lost Beth, he lost everything. He feared he'd hurt her beyond repair and wondered whether this was the moment she'd surpassed her limit. She had shown him nothing but honesty and loyalty, something which he hadn't reciprocated over the last few months. He wondered whether there was a tragic irony in George walking back into his life as Beth left it. As he looked up, he saw Mike studying the house in the distance.

'Toby, if I walk into that house up there, what am I likely to find?' Mike asked, pointing.

Toby looked up at Mike, but couldn't manage an answer.

'We need to speak to Georgina Sampson. Where is she?'

'Jack's, I assume.'

He didn't want to antagonise Mike, but he really didn't know where to begin. He'd had little involvement in anything other than locating George, but questioned whether Mike would see it this way. He had been a reluctant participant this time, acting out of necessity rather than anything else. Toby contemplated what Dylan was capable of and how far he would have gone had he not re-entered the house. He hadn't wished to be involved in any of this, yet strangely, he didn't regret it. George was now safe, and he was free to resume his life, whatever that would look like now. Beth's reaction was unfamiliar to him, and despite her forgiving nature, he feared he had pushed her to her limit.

'Toby?'

'The two men who grabbed George are currently tied up in there.'

Mike gestured to the two police officers in the second car, who had up to now been patiently awaiting instruction.

'There are two suspects in the house. Tread carefully. You may also want to radio through for the paramedics. I've seen the size of Georgina Sampson's brother. Toby and I are going to stay out here and have a little chat.'

Mike offered a reassuring smile, but it did nothing to elevate his mood.

'I need you to walk me through the events of the last few hours.'

'Is this official?'

'Would you like it to be?'

Toby didn't respond, but his demeanour betrayed his thoughts on the prospect of another line of official police questioning.

'I thought not,' Mike replied, clearly noting Toby's body language. 'How about we begin with why the hell you got involved in a police investigation I'd specifically told you to stay out of?'

'We didn't get involved.'

'So, you're expecting me to believe you boys were out for a leisurely drive and just happened across this place?' he said, pointing to the house. 'Don't bullshit me, Toby.'

'Jack mentioned this place. He knew the previous owner a little. We believed the place could provide enough seclusion for someone seeking to evade detection and stay hidden temporarily.'

'What happened when you arrived?'

'I knocked on the door and a woman answered.'

'Go on.'

'She seemed genuine, but her lies gave her away.'

'How did you know she was lying?'

'I listened.'

Mike gave Toby a puzzled look.

'I purposely withheld any details about George, but right before I left, she alluded to the fact the person I was looking for was female.'

'That could have been a lucky guess, surely? I mean, she had a fifty-fifty chance of being right.'

'In isolation, I would have agreed, but in a very brief conversation, there were several signs which suggested she was lying.'

'You'd be great on the right side of a police interview desk,' he teased.

Revenge in Mind

Toby smiled faintly.

'I think you're forgetting the fact that it was your fellow officers who detected the lies from Olivia Stanton that I was deceived by.'

'Don't be so hard on yourself. I'm told she was very convincing, but ultimately the evidence didn't support her story.'

Toby shrugged his shoulders. He noticed Beth engaged in a conversation with the officer inside Mike's car and deliberated the content of their discussion. It was a strange feeling that considering they had found George, he felt dejected, not relieved. As Mike studied his phone, Toby thought about George, Jack and Dylan. He felt an apathy he couldn't explain. Beth was his only concern, the only thing which mattered. This was over for him now. He wanted out. Mike's phone rang, bringing Toby back into the moment. He stared at it keenly before moving away to take the call. Toby studied his face, which appeared to change from curiosity to bewilderment in an instant. His demeanour was different now. Toby watched as he held the phone down to his chest for a moment before placing it back to his ear, continuing the call. He'd been looking around the tranquil surroundings, but fixated on Toby as he finished the conversation and slowly placed the phone back into the pocket of his jacket. He gestured to the officer in the car to step out and quickly entered what looked like a deep conversation with him. The officer picked up his radio and began speaking. Mike observed, stony faced. Toby noticed Beth staring out of the window, but she wasn't looking in his direction. He tried to catch her gaze as the commotion continued. Although they were not within hearing distance, it was clear to him that something had occurred. Mike looked troubled. Finally, he walked back in Toby's direction.

'I have to go. Naturally, I can't leave you here. We'll drop you at the station on the way. Don't leave town.'

Though Toby was sure that Mike had said the last part tongue in cheek, his face had given nothing away.

'Mike, what's going on?'

Toby wondered whether he was being overfamiliar. He wasn't sure whether or not Mike Thomas was here in official capacity. Was the apprehending of two kidnappers something he would ordinarily get involved in? He cast his mind back to the formal interview where Mike had spoken off the record with him and wondered whether this was another one of those occasions. Like Beth, his patience would surely be exhausted at some point if Toby continued to ignore those around him. Mike looked away before resting his eyes back on Toby.

'There's been an incident at the prison. I can't go into details, but it sounds serious and I have to go.'

'I'm sorry,' Toby responded sympathetically.

Mike studied him for a moment. His expression made it look like there were things he wanted to say, but couldn't.

A car screeched to a sudden halt.

'Sir?'

The voice belonged to the younger of the two officers who had just pulled up in another patrol car.

'PC's Andrews and Moran are up at the house. I don't believe the suspects are in much of a state to put up any fight, but let's not take any chances,' Mike Thomas said in an officious voice.

Revenge in Mind

The two officers ran quickly up the drive as Mike turned to face Toby.

'I can imagine it's been a rough day for you. Why don't you go and get into the car?' Mike said politely but assertively.

Opting not to argue, Toby approached the open door cautiously. As he got into the back seat, he experienced an unfamiliar awkwardness around his wife. It was unlike anything he'd experienced before. As the car set off, they looked more like strangers than the loving couple they had once been.

Beth headed straight into the kitchen. They had barely spoken on any part of the journey home. Following her hesitantly, Toby pulled out his phone. There were several messages from Jack and a missed call from George, but he ignored them. He knew with Jack and Dylan, George was safe, for now anyway. There were still things about the whole situation that made little sense to him, but any motivation to find answers had left him. As his marriage lay in tatters, he'd never felt so alone. Beth had been his constant, the one thing he could always depend on. Losing everything seemed bearable when Beth was there, but losing her would create a seismic void in his life that he could never fill. He walked up behind her and placed his hands around her waist tentatively. She didn't respond.

'Coffee?'

'Beth I'm sorry.'

'We've been here before.'

'I should have called.'

'It's more than that. You can't seem to avoid putting yourself in dangerous scenarios. But worse still, you've now involved me because that psychopath knows where we live and has shown he has no qualms about turning up uninvited. Where does this end, Toby? You've already been arrested. You've lost your career. You nearly lost your life. How much more until you realise you're not a detective?'

She was angry, but Toby could handle anger. What he struggled with was silence. He couldn't remember a time when Beth's rumination hadn't resulted in things escalating significantly past his level of comfort.

'It's over now. I'm tired and I just want my life back.'

'Until the next time she has a problem.'

Toby lowered his head, perhaps in shame, perhaps in embarrassment.

'You were such a good psychotherapist, but your naivety was your downfall.'

'What do you mean?' he asked, feeling hurt.

'It only took one conversation for me to realise that there was more to Georgina Sampson than she was portraying.'

'Why didn't you say anything?'

'Because I knew what she meant to you and I didn't want to be the one who destroyed your perception of her.' Beth moved closer and took his hand. 'Somewhere you became too emotionally invested in what was happening around you. You lost sight of what made you such a good therapist. I don't know if Olivia Stanton was responsible for this, or whether she simply brought something to the surface that had always been inside you.'

'What's happening to me?'

'You've lost yourself, your identity. You've been desperate to fill the void left by psychotherapy. But Toby, putting your life on the line and playing detective, isn't the answer.'

'I didn't see it with Olivia, and I made the same mistake with George.'

Beth stepped back.

'Mistake?'

It became clear to Toby that in order to rebuild Beth's trust, he couldn't hide anything more from her. It was time she knew the truth about George.

'When we realised George was in there, I made it clear my part was complete. I couldn't afford to be involved any further. Jack was pissed off, Dylan resembling something like a caged animal. I knew exactly what was going to go down, and I wanted no part of it.'

'Something changed your mind?'

'Someone. Jack came running down the drive shouting frantically. He was worried they were about to do something which was irreversible.'

'They?' Beth asked with a shocked look on her face.

Toby nodded.

'As Jack tells it, she encouraged it, but I'm certain she was speaking through her emotional pain.'

She stepped closer and embraced him.

'There's more,' Toby said reluctantly.

Beth smiled and gestured for him to take a seat at the breakfast bar, pulling up a chair alongside him.

'When George and I were leaving the house, she took me to one side. I could see there was something on her mind. She was saying things that didn't make sense.'

'Like what?'

'She said she was sorry and that it wasn't supposed to happen the way it did.'

'What did she mean by that?'

Toby gazed into Beth's eyes.

'The kidnapping was planned. Well, part of it was.'

'Part of it? Toby, what are you saying?'

'Her and Olivia planned the whole thing to frame Eric. But George's plan changed.'

Beth stared at Toby, bewildered.

'I don't understand. If this was all planned, why did it turn so violent?'

'That's what she meant when she said it wasn't supposed to happen like that. The kidnappers tipped Eric off and clearly he wasn't in a forgiving mood. George overheard them talking outside Jack's, and that's when she realised she was in over her head.'

'I don't know what to say,' she said calmly, reaching for his hands.

Just then, Toby's phone, now sitting on the breakfast bar, rang. They both glanced downwards, then locked eyes with each other simultaneously. There was a brief hesitation before Toby ultimately took the decision to answer the call.

'Mike?'

There was a crackle on the other end of the line. The signal was dropping in and out and, judging by the background noise and the distance of Mike's voice, Toby concluded he was driving.

'Mike, the line isn't clear.'

'Hold on, I'll call you back.'

The line went dead.

Toby and Beth stared at one another for a moment.

'What do you think that was all about?' she asked.

Toby gave her a worried look.

'Something's bothering you. What is it?'

'Look at the time. Mike wouldn't call at this hour unless it was serious.'

'Considering what's happened today, I imagine he has some questions for you,' Beth replied reassuringly.

'He received a call when we were at the farmhouse earlier. There had been an incident at the prison. He looked concerned, and I knew he was holding something back.'

'He's a detective, Toby. I would imagine there are a lot of things he keeps from the public.'

Toby screwed up his face. He was finding it difficult to really illustrate to Beth what he meant. He was almost certain Mike's call had nothing to do with the kidnapping.

His phone rang again.

'Toby?'

'You sound clearer.'

'I've pulled in at a petrol station and found a signal.'

'You know you're not supposed to use your phone in those places?'

'Appreciate your diligence, but you'll be pleased to know I'm parked up with a coffee,' Mike replied.

Beth was standing close to Toby. He wasn't sure whether this was through intrigue or concern.

'Toby, this isn't an official call.'

'It's off the record?'

'Very much so, but I'm cautious to avoid a chain reaction so wanted to speak to you directly.'

Toby gulped hard, heartbeat increasing in anticipation of what was to come next.

'It was already a media circus once I got there, so this is going to be public knowledge soon enough, but I wanted to control the narrative with you.'

Toby remained silent. Beth fixated on him, now standing closer.

'There's been a riot at the prison. It appeared to escalate quickly. A fire tore through one of the wings.'

'That's awful, but why are you telling me this?'

The line went silent and for a moment Toby wondered if he had lost Mike again.

'The fire was aggressive. Some women were still in their cells. Tragically, not everybody was able to make it to safety. There are two confirmed fatalities.'

Mike paused.

'One of them is Olivia Stanton.'

Toby's heart stopped momentarily. Beth stared at him, wide eyed. He wasn't sure how he was supposed to feel, but a tension in the pit of his stomach quickly quashed any sense of relief. Olivia had been responsible for so many of the things that had gone wrong in his life over the last year, but had he wanted to see her dead? He wondered if she had suffered, whether she'd been asleep or had simply watched on with panic, helpless as the flames surrounded her.

'Toby?'

'I'm not sure what I'm expected to say.'

'You don't need to say anything. I just wanted to give you a heads up before you hear it elsewhere.'

'Thank you.'

'There's one more thing.'

'What's that?'

'The guys we arrested at the abandoned farmhouse had been roughed up pretty good. Both are currently undergoing medical treatment, so we haven't had a chance to interview them yet.'

'You know I'm not a fighter.'

'That's the only reason you're at home now and not at the station. Naturally, we will need to speak to you, though. But George and your other friends are a different matter. I'll be speaking to them shortly.'

Toby nodded, before realising Mike was unaware of his acknowledgement.

'Don't leave town, Toby.'

Beth reached out for his hands. The two stood in a silence, but not looking in one another's direction. Finally, Beth reached for his cheeks and turned his head towards her own.

'I can imagine this is difficult for you, Toby. I know you, and I know you see the good in everybody.'

'A young boy has just been consigned to growing up without his maternal mother. There's more than one victim here.'

'I know, but you can't save the world, Toby. It's incredibly sad, but he isn't your responsibility.'

'His father is Eric Stanton. The poor kid doesn't stand a chance. Do you know how many Tyler Stanton's I have worked with over the years in their twenties, thirties and beyond?'

'Nothing I can say will make you feel better, but perhaps we can begin to move on now. We can finally put this ordeal behind us.'

Toby stepped back.

'This isn't over, Beth. Olivia was manipulative, but she wasn't the principal threat. Eric Stanton is dangerous and has already shown just how vengeful he is. As long as he's alive, this will never be over.'

A worried look spread over Beth's face as she contemplated Toby's words. Saying the words out loud suddenly made them real. He'd avoided thinking about it in any detail up to now, but as he stood facing his wife in the kitchen, the moment of clarity suddenly presented itself. Olivia had shown it was still possible to have influence from behind bars. Prison wouldn't be enough. The only way for Toby's ordeal to be over with any certainty, was if Eric Stanton was dead.

{ 29 }

With the fire roaring on a crisp but clear afternoon, Jack Newby positioned himself close enough to hear the aggressive crackling of the flames. It had been almost a month since his tranquil life was disrupted, the sanctuary of his home violated. Despite restoring the aesthetics and replacing the damaged contents, he still felt a lingering anger. The security of his home had been compromised, and that wasn't something he took kindly to. As he sipped his freshly poured coffee, he thought about how his life had changed so significantly over the last few weeks. He'd gone from a solitary existence without complications to having his home invaded on two occasions. His days, formerly taken up by farming, had more recently been about restoration and solicitor visits. Toby was his best friend, somebody he would do anything for, but in his more honest moments he was able to admit part of his anger was directed towards him. He'd never wanted to get involved in any of this, but trying to do right by his friend had cost him dearly. His home had been blemished, his reputation tarnished, and he was facing police charges. He'd suffered a great deal of physical trauma, but it was the psychological impact which would take the longest to recover from. Though equipped to handle himself, he now kept a bat at the side of his bed and would wake at any slight noise. It had felt to him like he had been sleeping with one eye open since the break-in. Most of his physical scars had healed, but there were still moments when he was reminded of the ordeal his body had endured. Fighting the two assailants had been straightforward compared to his battle with Dylan Sampson. Jack regarded him as a freak of nature and was glad they ended up united rather than divided. Dylan's physical stature was like nothing Jack had seen before, but it was his psychological state that frightened him. He'd seemed like a guy with nothing to lose and when you coupled that with his physical attributes, it created something formidable. When he'd looked into Dylan's eyes back in the abandoned house, he'd seen something which had turned him cold. He saw a man taking pleasure from inflicting pain, and was under no illusion that had he not pleaded with Toby to intervene, Dylan would have killed both of George's captors. More concerning, he'd have shown no remorse in doing so. Dylan was a loose cannon, hell bent on avenging the kidnapping of his sister, but Jack felt there was more beneath the surface and kind of understood his rage. George though, she had taken him by surprise. They had grown close prior to her kidnapping, but out of respect for Toby, had kept their feelings beneath the surface. While she had returned to the farm, the relationship had stalled, mainly because of his reticence. But this time, it wasn't about Toby. The image of George's face when she had suggested he leave her and Dylan with the captors had stayed with him, impossible to erase. At first, he'd thought it had been a manifestation of all the abuse she had suffered. A momentary release as she battled to exit her role as victim, a role she had been all too familiar with for too long. Yet something bothered him. A series of questions had been echoing in his head. What if that look in her eye hadn't been about the moment? What if she was more similar to her brother than she would care to admit? What if Toby hadn't got there in time? He was fond of her, but there were too many similarities with Caitlin, which had caused him to back off. They hadn't had a specific conversation, but there was a mutual understanding between the two that things should remain platonic, at least for now, though it was clear they both wanted more. When he thought about how she had changed, he realised he too had gone through a transition. The confrontation with the assailants and the subsequent clash with Dylan Sampson had initially felt like a matter of survival, but the altercation at the abandoned house had a distinctively different feel to it. He had felt vengeful, and whilst he hadn't been prepared to go to the same extremes as Dylan, it went beyond simply incapacitating his adversary. As he sat quietly contemplating, he heard the door close. Rising from his chair, he walked over to the window just in time to see George beginning the long walk down the track. Recently, this had become more of a regular occurrence, and he had felt powerless to make things better for her. She was becoming more distant, more disconnected. The kidnapping hadn't been the beginning or the end of her ordeal. She had been a prisoner for a long time, on more than one level. He felt a sadness as he thought about her pain, which he could never truly comprehend. The sadness was fleeting though, as a raw anger began to surge through his body at the thought of the individual responsible for stealing her innocence. He turned his head away from the window and gazed into mesmerising flames now flickering in all their glory. He remained that way for some time as the same thought ran repeatedly through his head. As long as Eric Stanton was alive, George would never have her closure.

Dylan Sampson took a seat at the foot of his bed. Hotel life suited him, for now. Naturally, he had moved across town to another budget hotel after the incident involving the stolen car at his previous place of temporary residence. Eventually, the police had located the abandoned car, but without substantial evidence, it turned into one of those cases where the victim prioritised insurance money over justice. He'd been very careful to remove any traces which could link him to the scene, which meant he'd effectively walked away without consequence. The incident at the abandoned house, however, had produced a very different outcome. Though he wasn't privy to any details, he understood that in an attempt to avoid a harsher punishment, the two men had been quick to name Olivia Stanton as the architect. What mattered most to him was that the man he had beaten had injuries that were inconsistent with self-defence, and exceeded reasonable force. This had left him facing assault charges, something which had done nothing to quell the anger which had been burning inside of him since that initial phone call with George. They had spoken, but had avoided talking about *that* day. She had seemed disconnected, and he had wondered about the extent of her struggle. In his mind, killing the men would have sent a very clear message to their employer, but ultimately circumstances had conspired against him, meaning they walked away. He had no faith in the justice system and chose to dispense justice using his own methods. It wouldn't be long before they were free to continue their bottom feeding on whatever scraps their boss threw them. But that wasn't his concern, *they* weren't his concern. Dylan had his sights firmly set on one person. There had been many contributors to George's pain over the years, but Eric Stanton topped the list. He had raped her and reduced her to a submissive and unrecognisable individual, an identity she had carried around for years. When she had finally discovered a courage to fight back, he had sought to exert his control over her once again, orchestrating a brutal kidnapping which included sexual assault. His palms felt clammy as the anger swelled around inside him. He peered around the room, wondering how his life had got to this. Once a respected officer in the armed forces, he now spent his time in cheap hotels, with nowhere to call home. Estranged from his parents after his dishonourable discharge, George was the only meaningful thing in his life. Though they had grown apart over the years, she had never judged nor given up on him. He had regrets; he realised this now, but each regret was simply a small piece of the jigsaw that made him who he was. She had been his main regret. Though he couldn't change the past, he could still shape the future after losing their once close bond. He'd vowed always to be there for her and never to let her down, a promise he intended to honour until his dying breath. The assault he was facing charges for had been vicious. He had beaten a man within an inch of his life, yet his sole regret was putting himself in a situation whereby he may not be around to protect George. He wasn't concerned about prison, given that very few would dare challenge someone of his physical prowess. The idea of George being isolated and exposed to another attack from Eric Stanton though, stirred up an uncontrollable fury within him. She had Jack, but Dylan had already seen he lacked that vital instinct to operate without limits when necessary. She had Toby, but intelligence could only get you so far on the streets. He slowly rose to his feet, walked over to the window, and peered out at the desolate car park. The trees were still, and the weather was calm, a stark contrast to the internal storm he was experiencing right now. Rubbing his hands up and down his face slowly, a sudden moment of clarity appeared from nowhere. Threats or persuasion wouldn't work on a guy like Eric Stanton. His ego wouldn't allow it. Regardless of whether he was in a hospital or prison bed, Dylan had learned he had reach and he had influence. The clock was ticking against him, but there was one way to halt Eric and restore all of his victims' peace. It was the only way he could truly protect George. He had to put Eric Stanton in a morgue before he himself was put behind bars. He walked over to his black bag, positioned next to the bed. Peering inside, he contemplated for a moment. He pulled out his knife and smiled, briefly marvelling at its glory before returning it to its rightful place. He pulled on a dark jacket before placing the bag over his left shoulder and moving towards the door. While turning off the light, he cast a lingering gaze around the hotel room, as if imprinting the image in his mind in the event this was the last time he would set eyes on it.

Georgina Sampson cut a solitary figure as she made her way through the countryside. Jack's land was vast and just at the edge of the woodlands, there was a small stream which had become her sanctuary. It was far enough away from the farmhouse to allow her the desired peacefulness, but close enough that she felt safe. Jack had invested in extra security around the parameters, which had allayed her anxiety in part, but still she found herself hyper vigilant and would startle at the slightest of noises. As she approached the stream, carefully stepping around a cluster of rocks, she took a seat on the large uprooted tree, which rested just a few feet from the water. Recently, she had found herself spending more time down here, something which provoked contrasting emotions. On the one hand, she felt comforted in the fact she had a safe place to explore, somewhere where she could be at peace with herself and not have to operate under a pretence. This, however, came at a cost because the more time she spent alone, the more alone time she wanted. She was withdrawing from Jack, and this upset her. He'd been the only person aside from Toby she had truly trusted. In any other scenario, they would have been great together, but their brief relationship had never really had a chance, not when they had been thrust together in these circumstances. She had never really valued herself, but then she had never really known her own identity. The one thing she did know was that Jack deserved better than her. She was bitter, damaged, and consumed by hatred. She had changed, though she was unsure from what. The effects of prolonged victimisation were noticeable, but she had confronted a stark decision - give up or stand up. She had refused to yield. Though the temperature was cool, she removed her shoes and walked over towards the stream to dip her toes. A shiver ran through her as she felt the water lap over her feet. As she looked at the cloudless sky, she wondered how such a bright day could provide such little warmth. Spring, though only in its infancy, had been disappointing. Nature was a comfort to her, and being close to it now made her realise just how easy it would be for her to live as a recluse. Her lack of trust in people had resulted in her preferring her own company. If she didn't place herself in that position, no one could let her down. She hated herself for feeling like this, but this had started with Toby. Everything had started with Toby. It was difficult to overlook the different paths their lives had taken. She was happy for him. She loved him too much to be anything other, but there were still moments when she thought about what could have been had they stayed together. It was unfair to apportion all blame to him, but there was no getting away from the fact his decision to go to university had placed a strain on their relationship at such a young age. He had experienced a different way of life, and though he had never openly admitted it, she had noted the changes in him and had questioned whether their eventual break-up was really mutual at all. But in this play, Toby had only a minor part. The lead villain, the person responsible for her rape, her kidnapping, her emotional abuse, was Eric Stanton. There was no mistaking others had played their role, Olivia Stanton, for one, but he was the reason she had lived as a victim for so many years. He had exerted an authority, a control over her, which had reduced her to a submissive figure, unrecognisable from the confident and outgoing girl she had once been. But she wasn't the only one who had been affected. Jack, Toby, Dylan, and even Beth had all become involved in something they had never asked for. Each had had their lives upturned in different ways. Each had

Revenge in Mind

become acquainted with a man who would stop at nothing to get what he wanted. She fixated on a large, yet unspectacular tree in front of her. It stood apart from the others, but seemed contented in its solitary position. Among felled trees, it stood tall and proud, almost like it was the victor, outlasting its brethren. She smiled to herself as she recognised the symbolic comparison to her own situation. In a moment of clarity, she knew her purpose. Georgina Sampson suddenly realised with no further doubt what needed to be done. In her battle, she needed to be the last one standing. As she looked down at the fallen tree she had been recently perched on, she saw Eric's face. She saw his limp body, defeated, as the life slowly drained out of it. He was the felled tree, and she was standing over him smirking. Georgina Sampson put her shoes on, buttoned up her coat and prepared to begin her journey, but unlike the other occasions, this time, she wasn't heading back to the farmhouse. The smirk never left her face.

Toby sat in the conservatory alone, with only his thoughts as company. By the time he realised he'd been staring at the same patch of grass for several minutes, his coffee had gone cold. Normally, Beth would toss a cushion at him to snap him back to reality from whatever world he had entered, but Beth wasn't here, and hadn't been for over a week. The news of Olivia's death had shocked them both, but the hopes she harboured of it providing some closure for Toby had been quickly dashed. Olivia had been the catalyst for his life spiralling out of control, but he had formed a therapeutic bond with her he hadn't formed with any other client. Though their relationship had always remained platonic, it had entered a very dangerous territory that no therapeutic relationship should enter. Still, he was no closer to understanding who the real Olivia Stanton was, and this bothered him. She had manipulated him, goaded him and had been solely responsible for her husband setting his sights on Toby, but still the thought of her dead induced emotions which not only surprised, but also worried him. They concerned Beth too, and ultimately, his subdued reaction to the news had proven too much for her. There hadn't been a heated argument, more a series of conversations which had ended the same way. As understanding as Beth was, she hadn't been able to see why the death of somebody who had caused so much destruction in their lives was being mourned. He had found it difficult to articulate his emotions since he didn't have a complete understanding of them himself. They had both decided it would be good for Beth to take some time out and visit Lara, though admittedly, it appeared they'd had different ideas of the time frame involved. Toby had suggested a long weekend, however, that time had come and gone, and Beth was still no closer to returning home. His loneliness intensified as he imagined a future without her. She was his best friend, and it had always been just the two of them. But that had changed. A once insular existence had now been opened up to people who intended to cause as much damage as possible, and who refused to leave quietly. As the sun began to set, he reflected on his career and marriage, and thought about how one moment had potentially cost him both. He didn't blame Beth. How could he? Everything that had happened had done so because of decisions *he* had made, actions *he* had taken. Yet still he felt angry at the situation he found himself in. He was a good person, but he knew good people weren't immune from making errors in judgement. He felt the tension increase as his thoughts shifted from Olivia to her husband. Hate wasn't something Toby was familiar with, but his feelings towards Eric Stanton were as close to anything resembling hatred as he'd ever experienced. Remembering their unexpected encounter at the country pub, the moment he first saw him, he struggled to accept that the Eric Stanton from *that* day and this Eric Stanton were the same person. He had appeared charming, friendly and outgoing, something Toby now knew masked his real identity. The more he learned of him, the more Toby believed it was entirely possible that he was dealing with a psychopath. His charm and ability to manipulate had been the very reason he had evaded detection for so long. Had he threatened people into silence, or simply been persuasive? Whatever his methods, the most effective thing he had done was to convince people he was a victim. He was now reacting angrily, but Toby believed this was out of panic. He'd been used to being on the front foot, but now the net was closing in. Dylan Sampson was an angry man who wouldn't think twice about killing someone, and not always out of necessity. Jack's life, ordinarily without drama, had changed significantly. His laid-back persona was a thing of the past, with anger and resentment more commonplace these days. Toby didn't place Jack in the same category as Dylan, but he could cause some damage to the wrong person, and right now, he was hurting. George had suffered indescribably both physically and emotionally. She had lived for years in fear, and Toby couldn't even begin to imagine how deep her scars ran. But something inside her had snapped, and this made her dangerous. She had been prepared to go to great lengths to get her revenge, including staging her own kidnapping, but this had ultimately failed, leading to her being subjected to further trauma. There was little doubt in Toby's mind that George was no longer the sweet girl he once knew, but just how far she would go to be free of the shackles she had been wearing for years, he didn't know. Then there was him. His life was in pieces, but this time he didn't know how to put them back together again. His career was over, his marriage not far behind it. His only real friend was Jack, but he was locked in his own emotional battle right now. As he looked around the empty house, he realised how it reflected his own life. He had nobody, and little left to lose. Eric Stanton had enemies, and he knew it. The police had, until now, protected him, but their suspicions of him were growing. Toby turned away from the window and made his way slowly to the hallway. He opened the closet and removed his coat from the hook. He reached for his keys and exited the house, gently closing the door as he did so. As he climbed into his car, he switched on the engine and sat back, staring through the windscreen at nothing in particular. He paused, but was now being led entirely by his unconscious. The plan was somewhere in there, but he was no longer certain of its details. As he sat ruminating, various thoughts ran through his mind, yet there was one which appeared to outstay its welcome. Eric Stanton was going to be taken off the streets, whether in a pair of handcuffs or a coffin.

Revenge in Mind

Mike Thomas pulled up at the bottom of the long drive and cut the engine. He studied the house in the distance and thought about the last time he had been here. The tip off had been tenuous, enough to pique his interest, he supposed, but it had been inside where his suspicions had been raised. Certain things hadn't appeared to add up, and his training had taught him to look for inconsistencies. Ultimately, they discovered that a relative of the suspect, who also happened to be an officer at the scene, had warned him beforehand. Somewhat predictably, this had resulted in her dismissal amid ongoing investigations. The thought of a young officer's career ending before it had really had the chance to begin, disappointed Mike. Yet her actions had further heightened his suspicions, though he wasn't entirely sure what those suspicions were. The suspect had been accused of distributing drugs, assault, rape, and threatening behaviour. During a recent conversation, Toby had added accusations of kidnapping to the mix. This had further intensified Mike's feeling that this man's public persona wasn't an accurate reflection of who he really was. His business here tonight wasn't official and it wouldn't be on record. As he had started to build up a picture of Eric Stanton, he had quickly realised he was an unsavoury character masquerading as a gentleman. In public, he was the type of person who would charm your grandparents, but behind closed doors, he was somebody very different. He had no concrete proof, but he trusted Toby and he trusted his instinct. Both were telling him there was something very sinister sitting behind those charming eyes. Looking up at the clear sky, ablaze with stars, he thought about the complexities surrounding Eric Stanton. Toby firmly believed that Eric was behind the kidnapping, but nobody else had confirmed this. The kidnappers had named no other accomplices, Georgina Sampson hadn't given them anything, Jack Newby and Dylan Sampson had also offered little. He questioned why nobody had identified Eric Stanton. It almost felt like they were protecting him, but why? Toby, on the other hand, had been adamant they should be looking in Eric's direction. It wasn't that Mike didn't believe Toby, but the lack of credible evidence made it difficult to act. Currently, anything he had was opinion or circumstantial, neither of which would satisfy the CPS. The sirens of an ambulance racing past disrupted the tranquillity of the evening. Suddenly, he was transported back to the first time he had attended this scene. He wasn't watching it through his own eyes, though. He had assumed the role of a bystander, silently observing his own interaction with Toby while also monitoring the ambulance crew's life-saving battle with a bloodied Eric Stanton. He saw the look on Olivia Stanton's face as she was being spoken to at the scene by officers eager to understand why a man was bleeding out just a matter of yards away from them. In a scene of chaos, he noticed how composed he looked, perhaps through experience, perhaps through being desensitised. And then he saw it. He hadn't made a conscious note at the time, but it had been stored somewhere in the depths of his unconscious, and now it was presenting it to him from the perspective of an observer who didn't exist. He studied the scene, everything within the chaos. He has Toby's physical presence, but his mind is elsewhere. Toby is looking over Mike's shoulder with concern. It looks like he's staring at the ambulance which is preparing to leave for the hospital with Eric Stanton, but

Revenge in Mind

his concern isn't with the stab victim, it's with the woman who pre-meditated the attack. He's fixated on Olivia Stanton. Mike closely observes Toby's face. He's unsure what he sees, but it isn't shock. There's something in that look he doesn't like... And just like that, the observer has vanished, leaving Mike present in the moment, unsure what he's just experienced. As he drew in a deep breath to compose himself, he peered up the long drive towards the house. The lights had now gone out, yet it was still early and nobody had passed him since he'd been parked up. Curiosity, however, wasn't probable cause, and he had no legal justification for being here. Regardless, Mike Thomas decided to take a stroll along the treeline, up the drive. As he neared the top, the sound of a door closing stopped him in his tracks. The drive was poorly lit, so concealing his presence wasn't a problem. The lights. Despite being present all along the drive, none of the lamps were illuminated. It felt deliberate, and the feeling in the pit of his stomach was telling him something was very wrong here. He heard footsteps, which prompted him to step further into the fir trees in an attempt to remain hidden. As the individual stepped out of the house, they were caught off guard when the outside light switched on, prompting them to shield their eyes momentarily. The woman had a familiar look, but if they had been previously acquainted, he couldn't place her. She dressed youthfully, yet her face looked weary. It was difficult to determine her actual age, but Mike believed she was perhaps in her early forties. She looked troubled and hurriedly moved away from the security light, as though anxious of someone watching from the shadows. He had seen enough to recognise she had been crying. Her eyes looked red, her makeup clearly smudged. She walked over the gavel, taking a seat on the grass. It was dark, but Mike could still make out the solitary figure sat with her head resting on her knees. He could hear the faint sound of sobbing. As he deliberated whether or not to approach, the security light flicked on once again sending a cold shiver through his body as his eyes began to make sense of the scene facing him. His heart pounded as he anxiously awaited his mind to confirm what his eyes had seen. Despite his lack of spirituality and belief in ghosts, he was confronted by a figure that would test his understanding of what was real. The dead don't walk. Yet despite the impossibility of an appearance from beyond the grave, Olivia Stanton casually exited the house without a scratch. Mike let out a gasp, but wasn't close enough to be heard. Of all the things he had experienced over the years, he'd never seen anybody return from the dead. Yet that was the image he was faced with as he felt the colour drain out of his face. He'd stayed hidden up to now through intrigue rather than fear. As he reached for his gun and prepared to make his move, he already knew Eric Stanton was dead. He doubted whether many who knew the real person behind the mask would mourn the loss, but as he made a desperate attempt to piece things together, this wasn't his concern. He wondered how he could explain his presence at a scene where a crime hadn't even been reported. As he saw the two women talking intently, he suddenly realised the identity of the first woman. He hadn't been involved in her interview, but he'd seen her picture. It was Georgina Sampson. He stood, hastily trying to understand the depth of the relationship between the two women. They of course, had a common enemy, having both been brutalised by the same man, but was there more to their relationship than this? As his heart rate began to slow, and visibility reduced, he squinted to see the two figures, now mere silhouettes merging into the night. His eyes widened as he realised why nobody wanted to give up Eric Stanton. In prison he was inaccessible, but on the streets, he was exposed. They didn't want him locked up. They wanted him dead.

Mike Thomas took a deep breath, stepped out of the shadows, and began to walk quietly towards the women. The security light startled them both and for the first time he was able to get a real glimpse of their faces. Whether they were co-conspirators or the guilt fell on only one of them, Mike was fairly certain what he was going to find when he eventually entered the house. Though still building a picture, he now believed Eric Stanton's past had come back to haunt him. His actions had antagonised several people, enough for at least one of them to want him dead. Whichever direction Mike looked in, he could see motive, but the question remained, who had taken the ultimate retribution, and how deep did this run?